PRAISE FOR BILL FITZHUGH AND
HEART SEIZURE

"A wickedly outrageous satire that takes on the federal government, the media, and today's health-care system with precise and scathing wit." —*Sunday Oklahoman*

"Funny. . . . One of the premier writers of comic mysteries. . . . Bill Fitzhugh leaps into that elite bunch of crime writers such as Carl Hiaasen and Donald Westlake. . . . *Heart Seizure* doesn't follow a predictable path, as Fitzhugh bends the rules with his deliciously odd sense of humor."
—*Sun-Sentinel* (Fort Lauderdale)

"A sick, funny book . . . for a sick, funny world."
—Kinky Friedman, author of
Kill Two Birds and Get Stoned

"Fast, funny, deft action. . . . Fitzhugh writes with comic flair. . . . This isn't a book you can describe—you have to experience it, hanging on tight and keeping those pages turning."
—*New Orleans Times-Picayune*

Janine M. Smith

About the Author

BILL FITZHUGH is the author of seven novels. He still has all of his original organs and plans to keep it that way until the very end, at which point he is willing to let the doctors divvy them up among anyone (with the exception of politicians) who might need them. However, he makes no promises about the quality of his liver. He lives in Los Angeles with his wife and all her organs.

HEART

SEIZURE

HEART

SEIZURE

BILL FITZHUGH

HARPER

NEW YORK · LONDON · TORONTO · SYDNEY

HARPER

A hardcover edition of this book was published in 2003 by William Morrow, an imprint of HarperCollins Publishers.

HarperCollins books may be purchased for educational, business, or sales promotional use. For information please write: Special Markets Department, HarperCollins Publishers, 10 East 53rd Street, New York, NY 10022.

First Harper paperback published 2006.

The Library of Congress has catalogued the hardcover edition as follows:

Fitzhugh, Bill.
Heart seizure / Bill Fitzhugh.—1st ed.
  p. cm.
ISBN 0-380-97758-3
  1. Donation of organs, tissues, etc.—Fiction. I. Title.
 PS3556.I8552 H43 2003
 813'.54—dc21   2002026420

ISBN-10: 0-06-081525-6 (pbk.)
ISBN-13: 978-0-06-081525-7 (pbk.)

11 12 13 14 15 ❖/RRD 10 9 8 7 6 5 4 3 2

For Kendall,
who seized
my heart

When the politicians complain that TV turns the proceedings into a circus, it should be made clear that the circus was already there, and that TV has merely demonstrated that not all the performers are well trained.

—Edward R. Murrow

It's not the world that's got so much worse but the news coverage that's got so much better.

—G. K. Chesterton

Acknowledgments

The most difficult aspect of writing a satire about our political system is trying to be funnier than the folks in Washington. Most of the actions taken by political characters in this story are based on documented behavior by actual government officials. I have the newspaper articles to prove it.

In addition to the inadvertent assistance I received from politicians on a daily basis, I owe a debt of gratitude to the following for their invaluable help: Dr. Bobby Robbins, Dr. Cris Glick, and Polly Richardson, RN—the best medical staff a writer could ask for; Debbie Robbins for being the hero; Sinclair Browning for letting me borrow from her book *Feathers Brush My*

Heart; Stew Hunsacker for help with the Utah Highway Patrol; Lewis Napper for permission to quote from his "The Bill of No Rights"; D. Victor Hawkins and Janine Smith for notes; Matthew Scott Hansen for his work on the original story and characters; Tom Dupree for editorial guidance; Yung Kim for able assistance; Maureen O'Brien and Katie Hellmuth for coming on board; and Jimmy Vines for representing.

In putting a few southern expressions into the mouth of one of my characters, I referred to Roy Wilder Jr.'s book *You All Spoken Here* (Brown Thrasher Books/ The University of Georgia Press). I also referred to this resource in the writing of my previous book, *Fender Benders*, but somehow the acknowledgment for so doing got lost in the shuffle. It is a fine collection of regionalisms and is highly recommended.

Finally, I wanted to give credit where it was due in regard to the name of a fictional medication referred to in this book. However, an exhaustive search of the Internet leads to the conclusion that the name was created simultaneously by many people, none of whom claim to have been the originator. If it was you, sorry.

HEART

SEIZURE

1

Unchain My Heart

Pete was hauling ass. He was driving a bloodred Dodge Viper with a 450-horsepower V-10. In his rearview Pete could see LAPD chasing as if he'd killed a cop.

It was daybreak. The sun warmed the particulates in the air above Los Angeles. Another tequila sunrise. They were in the hills of Encino. The roads were narrow and winding like a snake, but the Viper hung tight. After a series of daring turns, Pete assumed the confident look of a man who believed he had gotten away. He started to laugh until he fishtailed around a corner and saw ten police cars blocking the road.

There was only one way out, and it was a long shot. The sort of thing to make even a stunt driver hesitate.

But Pete accelerated. There was a splinter of space between one end of the police barricade and a house on the corner lot. At the last second, with police firing like an antiaircraft battery, Pete cut the wheels. He slipped the Viper through the tiny space in a blister of sparks, shearing off both side mirrors. Pete saw a flash of Looney Tunes as he raced past a big-screen television in the living room. He crashed out the bay window on the other side and went airborne. When Pete landed, he lost control. His seat belt tore loose as the Viper rolled violently down the hill. It finally slammed to a stop against a huge metal light pole and burst into flames.

Almost immediately a dozen men and women with chemical extinguishers were putting out the fire. A woman raced over, dropping to her hands and knees. She leaned into the overturned car. She saw that the roll cage had buckled. "Hey! Mardell! You okay?" There was no reply.

His real name was Mardell Coleman. Pete was just a character in another over-budget action movie. Mardell was a stunt driver—"was" being the operative word. His helmet had cracked like a three-minute egg, and he was slipping into a coma. "Get an ambulance!" the woman yelled.

As they dragged Mardell from the car, a Shotmaker camera truck pulled up. From his elevated seat the film's director looked down at the carnage, deeply saddened. He considered the trouble of finding a new driver, then turned to his director of photography. "I think that's a keeper, don't you?"

Spence Tailor didn't really have a suit personality. There were only three occasions for which he would wear one: funerals, court appearances, weddings. Now that he was thirty-nine, the majority of his friends were already married, so he rarely got invited to weddings anymore. Like most people, Spence did his best to stay out of court, but he was a litigator, so it was hard to avoid altogether. When he was standing in the halls of the courthouse with his shaggy blond hair and his coat buttoned against his trim build, Spence could have been an older surfer going to trial for holding a little weed. He had a compassionate bearing and soothing brown eyes, but they weren't looking at a courtroom today.

Spence stood at the back of the crowd with hands folded as they lowered Alan Caplan's casket into the ground. Respectful and unobtrusive. He wasn't family, and he'd met the deceased only a couple of times, briefly. Still, he couldn't help but cry. The boy was just fifteen, a real sweet kid. Never even got his driver's license. *How crappy is that?* Spence thought.

It happened like this. Alan's father came to Spence for help late one afternoon, just walked in and sat down, unannounced. In his work Spence saw a lot of people in hard circumstances. Mr. Caplan looked exhausted and overwhelmed, unsure where to start. After a moment he got the words out. "Do you know how painful bone cancer is, Mr. Tailor?"

Spence looked at the weary older man and shook his head. "No, sir, I don't."

Mr. Caplan told the sort of story Spence had heard too many times. Fifteen-year-old with bone cancer in his femur and his scapula. Osteosarcoma. Unremitting pain. Expensive treatment the HMO deemed inappropriate and refused to pay for, knowing the patient would die long before a lawsuit might force them to change policy. Good way to keep costs down. "You can see how much he hurts." The words came hard. "It's awful being so close, standing right there, not being able to help your own child."

"How long did the doctors say he had, Mr. Caplan?"

"Long enough to suffer more than anyone should have to." He couldn't seem to look Spence in the eye. Too ashamed he couldn't do more. "I spent all I had for some treatments, but they weren't enough." Mr. Caplan put a hand over his eyes. "All he wants now is to die, with some dignity, you know?"

"Yes, sir. I understand." Spence knew he'd take the case. Man's institutional inhumanity to his fellowman was the sort of thing that triggered a switch inside. Spence lived to fight for causes. But it wouldn't be easy. A lot of things working against them. He wished he could give Mr. Caplan assurances, but he knew the truth was better. "I assume you know that, uh, euthanasia is illegal in California?"

Mr. Caplan wiped his eyes and looked at Spence. "What I know is, it's his life, and nobody—not me, not the government, not some church group—nobody gets to decide what he can and can't do with it at this point. Not now. He's going to die soon. He just wants to take control of the process instead of having it control him. He wants to make the last decision of his life, you know?"

Spence nodded respectfully. "Have you contacted any organizations—"

Mr. Caplan reached into his coat and pulled out a document. "Yes, sir. I went online to get information, you know? I found a site that seemed real good, like they supported a person's right to choose. Like they'd help. I gave them all the details of the prognosis, the hospital where my son is, problem with the HMO, all that. Next thing I know, I got this." He held up the document. "Turns out that site was run by the Church of the Consecrated Few. They filed suit against the hospital to keep them from interfering with my son's . . . how'd they say it?"—Mr. Caplan read from the document—" 'glorious opportunity to suffer unto death as did our Savior.' " He handed the document to Spence.

The lawsuit attempted to enjoin the hospital from giving any pain medication or any other sort of treatment to the boy, since the Church of the Consecrated Few didn't believe in medical intervention in the case of illness or disease. They said "quality of life" was an unchristian concept. Suffering was saintly.

"Well, first of all," Spence said, "these people don't have any standing in the case. This lawsuit is moot on its face."

"That may be," Mr. Caplan said, "but it's got the hospital running scared. They're refusing to give anything stronger than Tylenol 3." He shook his head. "Hell, that doesn't work for a toothache, Mr. Tailor. It's like trying to kill a bear with a paper clip. Alan's being brave, trying to make it easier for me, but if we can't do something fast, I swear I'll go in there and put a pillow over his face. I don't care what happens to me. I can't let him suffer like this."

"Yes, sir, I understand."

Until Mr. Caplan had walked into his office, it had been a typical day for Spence. He'd spent a few hours working on briefs, made a few dozen phone calls, and attended a preliminary hearing. His clients included an abused-women's shelter that was being harassed by the city's zoning board, some sweatshop workers who were owed several thousand dollars by a multibillion-dollar clothes manufacturer, and the family of a poor black kid, an honor student at Kennedy High, on whom a couple of LAPD officers had planted a gun to justify shooting him five times.

"I can't pay you, Mr. Tailor, and I know this is a terrible thing to ask, but will you do it?"

Spence couldn't hide his surprise. He was willing to do a lot for his clients, and for very little in return, but this was . . . well, he didn't think he could do this. "You want me to . . . do it? You mean, like, pull the plug? I don't—"

Mr. Caplan waved him off. "No, sir, I don't mean that. I want you to help me stop his suffering. Help me get him to some state where it's not illegal. Get these damn

Christians—and I use that term loosely—get them off his back, help me get him some morphine, something. Anything." He was crying now, drying his eyes on his sleeve.

Spence glanced out the window at the towers of Century City, where he had worked for a year as a high-priced litigator. That was all it took. One year had convinced the young lawyer he was destined to fight for the toiler as against the main squeeze, or whatever that quotation was. So he rented an office on the second floor of a shabby building on Santa Monica Boulevard and hung out his shingle. It wasn't exactly the Southern Poverty Law Center, but it served his purpose. He charged clients on a sliding scale, depending on ability to pay. Ten years later Spence was still doing more pro bono work than a well-planned financial future called for. He reached out and shook Mr. Caplan's hand. "All right. Let's see what we can do."

Spence set a meeting with the hospital's lawyers. He showed up with the anchorman from one of the network news shows, a fan of Spence's work. The anchorman looked at the lawyers and said, "We can play this one of two ways. You're bad guys and cowards at that, intentionally causing this kid to suffer. Or you're righteous and heroic and unwilling to cave in to the awful tactics of this alleged church." He smiled his big TV smile. "It's your call."

After a brief huddle the lawyers opted for righteousness.

Two weeks later Alan died. He hadn't suffered much, thanks to the morphine. Thanks to Spence. As the cancer grew worse and they had to increase the dosage to the point where he was almost incoherent, Alan asked a sympathetic nurse for help. The autopsy indicated overdose, but Spence convinced the hospital to let it go. No point in having the word "compassion" on hospital letterhead if they didn't mean it.

When the funeral was over and the mourners were drifting back to their cars, a man came over and tapped Spence on the shoulder, his hand held out not too subtly below. Funeral director. Spence reached into his coat pocket and pulled out a personal check. He didn't have to, couldn't really afford to, but at the same time it struck him as the only right thing to do.

Spence was glad to have a date that night. Something more life-affirming than funerals and the parade of human callousness that was his workweek. He went back to his office and changed out of his suit and into his typical office attire, jeans and a T-shirt. He had a couple of hours to kill before he picked Suzanne up for their date. He was taking her to meet his family. A casual dinner at Boyd's with Connie, the kids, Aunt Daisy, and, most important, Mom. Spence hoped that Suzanne—a Hollywood wardrobe designer—wouldn't be put off by such a provincial gathering, but his mother wasn't well. Spence wanted to see her as often as possible in what were likely her last days. His having just attended Alan Caplan's funeral drove that point home. And who could tell about things? If it worked out with Suzanne, he'd want them to have met before his mom was gone.

Spence was reviewing a deposition in the LAPD case when the door opened and Suzanne stepped into the office. She was wearing gauzy black Armani pants and a less-is-more halter top of her own design. Raised to more than six feet by a pair of T-strap Manolo Blahniks with four-inch heels, she looked like the goddess Visionaire. Spence gawked, as surprised at seeing one of Suzanne's perfect nipples as he was to see her standing in his office. "I thought I was picking you up," he said, glancing at his watch, genuinely confused.

"Spence, I'm sorry," she said, "change of plans."

"Uhhh, okay. You're driving?"

A handsome black man in a Prada suit and a James Coviello hat stepped into the office behind Suzanne. He tipped his hat and smiled but didn't speak. "I don't think we should see each other anymore," Suzanne said. "We've sort of run our course. I just wanted to tell you in person, okay? No hard feelings?"

"Well, I . . ." Spence stammered as Suzanne turned and disappeared into the hallway. "I take it that's a rhetorical question, then." The guy in the suit flashed a peace sign and left, closing the door behind him. Spence stared at the door as the discouraging sense of being dumped pressed down on him. "You're overdressed anyway," he called out. "I said casual!"

Spence tried to look at the bright side; at least he'd been humiliated in the comfort of his own office. So much more convenient than having to go out for it. He beat himself up briefly for not seeing this coming and even took a few moments to feel sorry for himself, wondering if he'd ever find the perfect woman. Not perfect in the flawless sense, of course, but perfect for him. Was that too much to ask? Probably. Just be glad you don't have bone cancer, and stop whining.

Spence had two choices. He could obsess on his crappy love life or get lost in his work. He opted for the latter, dumping his hostility and humiliation into the strongly worded draft of a complaint. When he finally looked up, it was nearly seven. He was going to be late. He tossed the dust covers over the computer, killed the lights, and raced out the door.

Spence's brother lived in West Los Angeles with his wife and their two children. Boyd and Connie were in pursuit of perfection. Their organizing principles were planning, tight schedules, and low-risk behavior. Their kids were smart and, for the most part, respectful. The house and lawn looked like items ordered from a Pottery Barn catalog.

Only forty, Boyd was already doughy in the middle, exercise being the sort of thing he felt was best left to those with fewer responsibilities. He had the soft face of a man who had never been hit there. One of fifty vice presidents for First Santa Monica National Bank, Boyd dressed and behaved as if auditioning for a part in the old boys' network. His hair was sculpted into a short visor over his forehead, in a style that seemed a cartoonish homage to either a bygone era or Trent Lott, or perhaps both.

Connie was a compact brunette with bright eyes and a vibrant smile. Optimistic and extravagantly organized, Connie's life was a juggle of schedules, calendars, and timetables. The kids were involved in a dozen extracurricular activities. Boyd liked to entertain, so there were frequent dinner parties. Connie kept up the household, chauffeured the kids around, and somehow managed to find time for volunteer work.

She had an array of causes. Unable to support them equally, Connie had developed a three-tiered priority system. She gave her time for the cause she held most dear, her kids' education. She gave money to causes for which she lacked time, including a local faith-based charity group that fed the homeless. And she gave her vote to causes for which she had neither time nor money, like Second Amendment issues.

Now Connie came from the kitchen with a large roast on a serving platter. She placed it in front of Boyd at the head of the dining room table. Boyd closed his eyes and waved the aroma toward his face. "Smells wonderful, honey," he said. "You've done it again."

"I hope it's okay," she said as she took her seat. "It may be slightly overcooked."

Elsewhere on the table were serving bowls loaded with new potatoes and peas and a gravy boat filled with a quivering brown substance. To Boyd's left were his children, Boyd Jr., a curious nine-year-old, and Erica, his eleven-year-old sister. Sitting on Boyd's right was his mother, Rose. Frail and in her sixties, Rose was the sweet-natured matriarch of the clan. But she wasn't well, as evidenced by the vast array of amber-colored prescription bottles lined up by her silverware.

Sitting beside Rose was her sister, Daisy. Despite the fact that she and Rose were twins, Daisy looked ten years older. Her gristly face said she had played hard all her life, and whatever beauty she might once have possessed was long ago spent. She applied makeup with a heavy hand, and her honest-to-God blue hair suggested she needed either a new beautician or an eye exam.

As they waited for Spence, Connie made a polite inquiry about Rose's failing health, Erica complained about the sorry state of fourth-grade male-female relationships, and Boyd Jr. told a knock-knock joke involving boogers. Daisy remained uncharacteristically quiet, sitting there like a bourbon-sipping vulture, watching her sister with a covetous eye, a patient thief waiting for the perfect moment to steal something.

At seven-twenty, hungry and out of patience, Boyd calmly laid his hands on the table and said, "I think we've waited long enough. Let's just start without them." He took Rose's hand and bowed his head. "Heavenly Father—"

A sudden commotion in the foyer brought the blessing to a halt. The front door slammed, and a moment later Spence rushed in to the dining room. He kissed Rose and Daisy, took his seat between his niece and nephew, and assumed the position. Boyd resumed where he'd left off. "We thank You for this wondrous bounty, and we ask You to watch over Your humble servant, Rose Tailor, who is in need of a new heart."

Rose nodded slightly at this while Daisy, finding more salvation in alcohol than in prayer, picked up her bourbon and took another gulp.

Boyd continued in earnest. "We also pray that You will hasten delivery of this precious gift. In Your name we humbly ask these things. Amen."

Rose gave Boyd's hand a pat. "That was lovely, dear."

"Thank you, Mother." Boyd picked up the carving set and gestured at his brother. "And, on a personal note, I'd like to thank Spence for dressing as if he were attending a lesbian folk-music festival."

Connie tensed the way she sometimes did where there was company. "Boyd! Honestly, I don't believe we need to use the L word in front of the children." The sentence squeezed out between perfect, clenched teeth.

Boyd poked at the roast with his carving knife. "Oh, right," he said. "Sorry."

Spence glanced at his Lilith Fair T-shirt, then at Boyd. "You said casual."

Connie smiled like a saint and said, "You look fine." Then she planted an elbow on the table and pointed at Spence. "But you look so nice in a suit. I wish you dressed up more often, that's all." She wished Boyd had stayed in shape like Spence.

"All righty, then," Boyd said as he began carving the roast. "Who wants theirs rare?"

The kids grabbed the serving bowls and piled potatoes

and peas onto their plates. Connie started the dinner rolls around the table. Daisy finished her bourbon and reached for the wine while Rose began to fumble pills out of the amber vials. "Spencer, dear," Rose said, "where's Suzanne? We were so looking forward to meeting her."

"Oh, uhhhhh." Spence took his time selecting a roll. "Oh, she had a last-minute thing come up with work. Called from the airport, on her way to New York, said she was sorry. Asked for a rain check."

"That's a shame," Rose said.

"Yeah, well," Spence said without much conviction. "Tell you the truth, I'm not sure things were working out between us, so it's no big deal." He took the peas from Erica in exchange for the rolls.

Connie was looking at him sweetly, thinking, *Poor Spence, disheveled and disorganized. Out there flailing around, putting all his energy into his crusades instead of into a committed relationship. It's such a shame.*

Boyd Jr. turned to Spence. "Dad says you never bring a date 'cause you're a cake boy."

Connie nearly dropped a serving spoon. "A what? What did you say?"

Boyd rolled his eyes. "I was kidding!" He turned to his son. "I told you not to repeat that."

Connie made corrosive eye contact with her husband, then drank half a glass of wine. She always seemed edgiest when entertaining, even if it was just family.

Spence smiled and said, "I'm just waiting for the right girl."

"The right girl?" Boyd dealt a slab of meat onto a plate. "From what I can see, you're looking for some sort of Nobel Prize–winning supermodel. And good luck finding her, by the way. But let me tell you, with standards like that, you'll spend the rest of your life alone." He gestured at Connie with the carving knife.

Connie looked up from topping off her wine. "Excuse me?"

Daisy stretched a leathery hand toward Connie. "Pass me that gravy, would ya?"

Boyd scooped some peas onto his plate, then looked at Spence. "Where do you go to meet girls these days anyway? The gym? Bars? Court? What's your strategy?"

"My strategy?" Spence ground some pepper over his potatoes. "I wasn't approaching it like war."

"There's your problem," Boyd said. "You need a plan. Make a plan and stick to it, you'll find the right girl. It's the same as everything else. Be organized, be prepared, have a plan."

"I've seen your plan," Spence said. "It prohibits spontaneity. You'll never have a surprise in your life. How much fun is that?"

"I hate surprises," Boyd said. "There's no planning for them."

The conversation stopped as all eyes turned to Boyd Jr. He looked back, feeling accused. "What'd I do?"

Boyd smiled weakly. "Nothing, son. We love you."

Aunt Daisy smeared some gravy onto her meat and passed the gravy boat to Rose. Daisy then produced a pack of cigarettes, tapped one out, stuck it between her puckered lips, and lit it up.

Connie was so astounded all she could say was "Boyd?"

Boyd shook his head. "Aunt Daisy? Please put that out," he said.

Daisy took a deep draw before letting the thick blue smoke pour out of her withering nostrils. "Hey, speaking of plans, I got one, too." She held up the cigarette. "I plan to finish this."

Rose ladled a generous portion of gravy onto her plate.

Spence gently touched his mother's cold arm. "Uh, Mom?"

"It's okay," Boyd said proudly, "that's my low-fat gravy."

Spence stuck his finger into the brown muck, then tasted it. "Maybe, but how about the sodium? It tastes like a salt lick."

The kids giggled.

Boyd tensed at the accusation. "What?" He dipped his own finger into the gravy and tasted it. "It's fine," he said. "Go ahead, Mom, help yourself."

"It's fine if you're a horse," Spence said. "Mom, that's enough." Rose reluctantly put the ladle down.

"Hey, I don't insult your cooking," Boyd said.

"I don't cook."

"Let her enjoy," Daisy said. "A little gravy's not going to kill her. Load it up, sis."

Spence passed the gravy boat to Connie. "The doctor said low-sodium diet."

Rose dabbed *her* finger into the gravy and tasted it. She made little clucking sounds with her tongue against the roof of her mouth. "The gravy *is* a little salty, dear."

Spence raised his eyebrows. "A little?"

"A lot!" Boyd Jr. said, smiling at his uncle for approval.

Spence winked at his nephew. "Admit it," he said, turning to Boyd. "Your famous low-fat gravy tastes like salty floor wax."

Erica and Boyd Jr. giggled again. They'd been eating the same floor wax for years but were never able to say anything about it.

"Get off her back," Daisy said. "It's a free country."

"Oh, that reminds me," Connie said, hoping to steer the conversation away from the sodium debate. "I was listening to Winston Archer today when he read this very clever piece called 'The Bill of "No" Rights' by Lewis Napper, I think he said was his name. It was a takeoff on the Bill of Rights, but it was a list of things to which no one has an inalienable right."

"Like what?" Erica asked.

"Well, let's see if I can remember." Connie tilted her head and squinted. "Oh, yeah. You do not have the right to be free from harm. If you stick a screwdriver in your eye, learn to be more careful, don't expect the tool company to make you independently wealthy. Uh, you do not have the right to free health care. That would be nice, but from the looks of public housing, we're just not interested in public health care. Stuff like that. It was very clever."

"That's great," Spence said. "Except for the forty million Americans who can't afford insurance."

"Yeah," Daisy interrupted. "And what's all this crap about prescription drug prices going up again?"

"Aunt Daisy?" Connie wanted to stab her with a fork, but instead she sort of whispered in a singsongy way, "Language."

"Can we please not talk about politics?" Boyd said.

"Hey, I didn't bring it up." Daisy took a final drag off her cigarette before plunging it into the pool of beef blood that had collected near her potatoes. *Sssssssss.* "All I'm sayin' is, life's too short for skipping gravy."

Boyd Jr. turned to Rose and spoke politely. "Gramma, can I get your heart in a jar when you get a new one? Like my appendix?"

Rose had a big heart. Metaphorically that's fine. Literally it's not. Rose suffered from advanced dilated cardiomyopathy. Her heart muscle was distended to nearly twice its normal size. With heart muscle, bigger isn't better. The same amount of myocardium stretched over a wider area diminishes the muscle's ability to contract. Depending on conditions, Rose's heart functioned at somewhere between 45 and 60 percent of its capacity. Her hands and feet were often cold, as her heart wasn't strong enough to pump blood to her extremities.

"We'll see, sweetie," Rose said, "but we don't discuss our internal organs at the dinner table, all right?"

"Well, not so fast there, Rosie." Daisy seized the moment with a wave of her fork. "You know we're praying for you and all, but I went to my doctor last week, and he says my nephrons are shot to hell." Daisy washed down the roast beef with a gulp of wine. "Upshot is, I'll be on dialysis this time next year if I don't . . . well, what I'm getting at is, I mean, God forbid things don't pan out for you, sis, but I was reading about what they call a 'directed donation,' and it got me thinking about . . . well, about what you'll be doing with your, uh, kidneys . . ."

Connie's reflex action was too strong to control, and before she could get a hand to her mouth, she spewed white zinfandel across the table in a pale pink mist, with just a hint of peach. The kids, naturally, flew into hysterics. Erica reached into a serving bowl and grabbed a new potato. She reared back to throw it when Boyd shot to his feet, knocking his chair to the ground behind him. He pointed at Erica. "Young lady! I will harvest your organs with my spoon!"

A tense moment passed before Erica quietly lowered the potato to her plate, and all eyes came to rest on Daisy. "What?" she said. "Can't hurt to ask."

Boyd Jr. shifted in his seat. "Uncle Spence, what's a cake boy?"

Erica turned to him and said, "I think it's like a guy who's a lesbian."

After dinner Spence and Boyd walked Daisy to her car. "You okay to drive?" Spence asked.

"Don't worry 'bout me, kid," she said. "Ten Manhattans and I could still win the goddamn Indy 500." They reached Daisy's 1985 Cadillac. Spence opened the door, and Daisy got in, disappearing behind the wheel. "I still don't see why you people got so bent out of shape about the kidney thing. It's not like she's going to need 'em. I mean if, well . . . oh, the hell with it." Daisy cranked the engine and threw it into reverse without so much as a backward glance. Spence and Boyd jumped out of the way as she sent garbage cans flying. "Shit." Daisy threw it into drive, and the Cadillac lurched forward into the night.

Spence cupped his hands together and yelled, "Headlights!" They came on halfway down the street, and a moment later the Cadillac vanished around a turn.

"You sure you want to be on the road at the same time she's out there?"

"I'll give her a head start," Spence said.

"Give me a hand with my car cover." The brothers turned and walked back up the driveway, passing Spence's battered old Chevy pickup. They came to Boyd's pristine 1965 poppy red Mustang coupe with the Wimbledon white roof. Mint condition, with only a few aftermarket modifications. Boyd's pride and joy. After covering it, they walked back to Spence's truck.

Boyd patted Spence on the back. "Dress up next time."

"Learn how to cook."

They both smiled as Spence got into the truck. Boyd leaned against the door. A moment passed before Boyd said, "Mom's not looking too good."

"Yeah, I can see the difference since last week."

"Too bad she's second in line." Boyd brushed something from his sleeve. "At least if she was first, I might be able to hold out some hope."

"Well, at least we can cling to the notion that the guy at the head of the line is in worse shape than she is."

Boyd thought about that, then nodded. "Tacky but Darwinian."

"That about sums it up," Spence said.

Rose had been waiting six months for a new heart. According to the people at UNOS—the United Network for Organ Sharing—she was a "Status 2" candidate, meaning she was sick enough to need a new heart but still healthy enough to wait outside the hospital for it. Thanks to her rare blood type, AB negative, there was only one person ahead of Rose to receive the next appropriate heart. So there was hope.

"Thanks for dinner." Spence keyed the ignition of his old truck, but all he got was a loud, metallic clicking noise.

Boyd laughed scornfully. "Thing needs an engine transplant."

"I got an idea," Spence said. "Let's harvest the Mustang's." He tried the engine again. *Clickclickclickclick clickclickclickclickclickclick.*

"Here's a better idea," Boyd said. "Stop dicking around with all that pro bono crap and use your law degree the way God intended. Then you can buy a whole new car."

Spence turned the key again, and the engine roared to life. "There, I get to keep my soul one more day." He smiled, put the truck in reverse, and was set to pull out when he felt Boyd's hand on his arm.

"The truth," Boyd said. "There was no business trip, right? Suzanne just dumped you?"

Chagrined, Spence nodded. "Big time."

"The solvency of Social Security is a top priority for this administration," the campaign manager said. "You can't oversell that one, sir."

President Webster was bent over, stretching his reluctant hamstrings. "Top priority," he repeated. "Are you sure this is a good idea?"

Martin Brooks, White House chief of staff, nodded. "We got the okay from Bethesda, sir. Dr. Nichols signed off on it personally."

The campaign manager removed his glasses and tapped the earpiece against his front teeth before continuing. "You also need to sell your commitment to finding bipartisan solutions to the problem of rising health-care costs that working families face, as well as the problem of prescription medication costs for our seniors. In fact . . ." The man wrote something on his legal pad. "Why don't we announce the formation of a panel to make formal recommendations on that very issue?"

"Good," Mr. Brooks said. "But not just a panel. A *blue-ribbon* panel."

"Of course, blue ribbon," the campaign manager said, scribbling a note. "This administration wouldn't think of convening a panel of any other sort."

President Webster, his face like a beet, looked up from a vantage point between his legs. "Blue ribbon," he said as he lowered himself to the floor and began stretching his rigid groin. "It's all part of the Patients' Bill of Rights that I have long championed and for which I will continue to fight. Remember, we are the health-care administration."

"Excellent, sir." The campaign manager beamed down at the president. "I think that's all we need for now."

"Sounds good," the president said, turning to his chief of staff. "Pretty much the same thing we said four years ago, isn't it?"

"Yes, sir," Brooks replied. "You know what they say: If it ain't broke . . ."

"Yeah, yeah." The president struggled to his feet and tugged at the neck of his sweatshirt. "Why can't I just go play some golf?"

"Well, Mr. President, golf doesn't imply vigor."

"No?"

"No, sir." Brooks shook his head. "Our studies show people associate it more strongly with retirement, and that's not the image we want to associate with you at this point of the campaign."

"What about Tiger Woods? You can't tell me people associate him with retirement."

"Well, sir, with all due respect, if you were a handsome, young, skilled black athlete and winner of four Masters, this whole exercise would be unnecessary."

"Yeah," President Webster said. "And in more ways than one."

"Latest polls have you down by two points, sir. We're just doing an image tweak to correct that."

The election was four months away, and the folks in the White House marketing department were a little nervous. Of course they didn't actually call it the marketing department, but that's what it was. The polls bore out the conventional wisdom that, given two candidates making roughly the same promises their parties had always made but on which they'd never delivered, the American people tended to vote for whoever presented the better image.

President Webster was six foot two and tanned as animal hide. He'd been in politics for thirty-five of his fifty-eight years. He had a muscular head of hair and a smile you could read by. He was smart, personable, and telegenic. And, thanks to a genetic quirk, he remained remarkably trim despite hideously flawed eating and drinking habits. Because there were no visible signs, the public was unaware of his blood pressure and cholesterol problems and his bleeding ulcers. In fact, if he hadn't had open-heart surgery eight months earlier, he wouldn't have been bothering with the stunt at hand. But the fact remained that they'd cracked open the man's chest, and the public needed to see he was back in the pink. Plus, he was down the two points.

"Sir, our campaign is all about vigor." The campaign manager pumped a fist in the air. "We need to show you're the man with the energy to run this great nation. We need the public to believe you're the man with the strength and stamina to face a contrary Congress and make things happen. That sort of thing."

"I understand all that," President Webster said, "but couldn't we—I don't know—find someone who looks like me to do this? Like in that movie *Dave* with Calvin Klein?"

"Uh, that was Kevin Kline, sir, and I'm afraid we can't do that."

They ushered President Webster out of the changing room, down a hall, then outside to a waiting limo. Twenty minutes later eleven men were trudging in a pack along the Mall near the Reflecting Pool, moving slowly toward the Lincoln Memorial. Ten fit Secret Service agents surrounding one reluctant politician. After ten minutes, with the visage of Lincoln coming into focus, the president began to pray silently for an assassin's bullet or anything that might end his suffering. He was willing to do a lot of unpleasant things to remain in power, but this exercise routine was too damn much.

Then, as if the gods had been eavesdropping on his thoughts and had decided to grant his wish, President Webster clutched at his chest, made an *ack* sound, and collapsed like he'd been shot by Booth himself. It happened so fast the Secret Service men jogging behind the president couldn't stop in time. One of them stepped on the president's head. A blink later two others rolled him onto his back and began to administer CPR. "POTUS is down!" one of them yelled into a hidden wire. "I repeat, POTUS is down!"

2

This Old Heart of Mine

Bright as a star of unblemished white marble, the
U.S. Capitol Building was as imposing as it was
exhilarating. Poised atop the building's grand iron dome,
the statue *Armed Freedom* stood for democracy and
against tyranny. For sheer inspiration, the exterior of the
Capitol was unsurpassed. It was an architectural manifestation of liberty, honor, and integrity.

The inner workings of the Capitol were no less
admirable. The halls were busy with highly educated,
highly principled people working hard to serve the
republic. In fact, given that so many smart people had
been working so hard for so long to solve the problems of
the nation, it was a wonder there were any problems left

to solve. Yet somehow problems persisted, and so the honorable work of service to country continued.

Some of that work was going on in the office of Senator Peggy Check of Virginia. After serving three terms, Senator Check had become the darling of her party and the best candidate it had for the nation's top office. Her polls showed a high national level of candidate awareness and an impressive lack-of-disapproval rating. Party leadership acknowledged Senator Check's keen grasp of the issues, and up on the Hill she was considered an able consensus builder. Most important she was the best fund-raiser to come down the pike in decades. The head of the party's national committee had recently said of Peggy Check that for a fifty-dollar donation she'd throw an altar boy under a priest.

Of course it didn't hurt that Senator Check had been born into a prominent banking family in Arlington, Virginia, whose roots in political fund-raising were deeper than the Marianas Trench. These considerations, along with the fact that the party's first-choice candidate—a flamboyant fifth-term congressman with wide blue-collar appeal—had been convicted recently of ten felony counts of bribery, racketeering, and tax evasion, made Senator Peggy Check the obvious alternative.

So the political consultants and campaign strategists received the go-ahead, and after extensive focus-group testing they agreed they could build an effective ad campaign around the notion that a woman in the White House might not be the worst thing that could happen.

Senator Check was several years younger than Presi-

dent Webster but every bit as polished. Brilliantly cos-
tumed in designer labels, she conveyed a welcoming self-
assurance and a steely-eyed competence. Combined with
her terrific cheekbones, the result was a fabulous,
telegenic package, both authoritative and sensual, rather
like a dominatrix. Depending on her patrons' needs, the
senator employed either disarming southern charm or
reptilian cunning.

Among her many other duties, Senator Check was the
newly appointed chair of the appropriations subcommittee with jurisdiction over the Department of Health and
Human Services. Senator Check was also an influential
member of the Senate committee overseeing the Health
Care Financing Administration. Currently between committee meetings, she was taking time to meet with a
group of constituents who were keen on exercising what
they construed as their First Amendment right. The old
cash-is-free-speech argument.

The senator's office was appointed with supple
leather, dark wood, brass, and heavy curtains. It made for
a comfortable setting for the representatives from the
Pharmaceutical Research and Manufacturers of America
and its public-relations face, Citizens for Better
Medicare, to express their concerns about some upcom-
ing legislation that actually threatened to make Medicare
better.

They were almost through their meeting when the
news shot through the halls that the president had suffered some sort of medical emergency. Hopefully, they
turned to CNN to find out what they could. "The entire

incident was caught on video by a passing tourist," the news anchor said as they aired the footage of the president's collapse. "President Webster was said to be fully recovered from his heart surgery of eight months ago, and the jog had been approved by his medical team at Bethesda." After about fifteen minutes the news cycle began again. "A White House spokesman told CNN that President Webster's fainting spell . . ."

Senator Check hit the "off" button and shook her head. "Faintin' spell my foot," she said in her soft southern accent. "I have it on good authority that martini-drinkin' son of a buck's got more plaque in his arteries than my dog has on his teeth." The Citizens for Better Medicare chuckled at that. Senator Check continued, "In fact, I'd bet good money his poor little heart just blew out like a Firestone Wilderness AT." She smiled. "You saw how he grabbed at his chest before he fell?" She looked down, furtively reading from an index card. "I guarantee that poor man is standin' on the drop edge of yonder."

The lobbyists snickered and made a few HMO jokes at the president's expense before returning to the issue at hand. Senator Check assured the Citizens for Better Medicare that she was on board with their legislative agenda. They thanked her for her time, assured her of their organization's continued support, then went on their way to the next senator's office.

A moment later Senator Check's chief aide, Britton Belk, came into the office. Britton had recently earned a political-science degree from the University of Virginia, and she was an ardent supporter of America's current form of representative democracy. As such she was mercifully unburdened by any sort of traditional ethical code and had been told on more than one occasion that she had a future in politics. "Senator," she said, "you have a meeting with the American Insurance Policy Institute in ten minutes."

Senator Check held up the index card. "Standin' on the drop edge of yonder?" She nodded approval. "I like that one. Where do you get these?"

"A book of southern expressions. I'll put that one in the keeper file."

Given the gender hurdle facing any female presidential candidate, Senator Check's campaign consultants felt she needed to accentuate her southern roots if she had any hopes of winning Florida and Texas, states critical for the electoral votes needed in November. While she had never lost the ability to lapse into an authentic accent, Peggy Check had never been an authentic southerner despite her Virginia upbringing. She'd been sent off to Connecticut for boarding school, after which she was sent to California. She earned an undergrad degree at Stanford before going to Berkeley for her law degree. She practiced in San Francisco until about eighteen years ago, when she moved "home" to run for an open Senate seat at the urging, and with the backing, of the Center for American Financial Integrity, one of the banking industry's many voices.

Like all good politicians, Senator Check could feign great offense at charges she was controlled by corporate interests, that she was a mere wind instrument for the nation's financial institutions. With great indignation she would swear that her only interest was in serving her home state and, ultimately, her country. And people seemed to believe her.

Britton glanced at her notepad. "Let's see, a Mrs. Lynn Shirley wanted to meet with you to discuss some problem she's having back home."

"A contributor?"

"No, just a constituent."

A nostalgic smile flashed across the senator's lips before she waved dismissively. "The numbers come in yet?"

Britton looked at her notepad again. "Yes, ma'am. We're down one point."

"Damn. All right, what else?"

"Well, you need to be unavailable for the vote by the House Committee on Standards of Official Conduct."

"Senator Hansen's matter?"

"Yes, ma'am. We're trying to put that one to bed once and for all."

"It was a witch-hunt to begin with." She gave it a moment's thought. "All right, let's kill two birds here. Get me a meeting with what's-his-name over at CIA, and be sure it conflicts with the ethics vote."

"We'll say it has to do with your role on the Select Committee on Intelligence."

"Exactly, some aspect of national security. And as long as I'm there, I'll see what they can tell me about the president's situation."

Spence had been mulling death. It started at Alan Caplan's funeral, all his young friends staring with dull incomprehension as the casket was lowered into the earth. *Aren't we too young to die?* they seemed to wonder. It continued at dinner when Spence saw how weak Rose had become, how she would die without a new heart. These events in turn had Spence focused on one terrible thought. He'd been reduced to hoping for the deaths of two complete strangers. One so Rose could reach the top of the waiting list and another so there would be a heart available when she got there. And they had to die in that order.

Spence smiled wryly as he conjured a distant memory. He was sitting in a chair staring at the lifeless body of Mr. Fuzzy, his hamster, cupped in his hands. Spence was crying. He could hear his mother, so much younger then, trying to explain the inherent unfairness of life to an eight-year-old sad beyond repair. All Spence could do was sniff back the snot running down his tender nose and ask why. And though his mother's explanation didn't connect with Spence's mind, he was still comforted. That was one of her gifts, he thought, her ability to reach beyond what made sense and convince him. "Everything will be all right," she would say as she pulled him close and held him.

That was her way. Patient and kind and caring. Never tried to bully life's truths down your throat. She trusted you would come to understand on your own. It saddened him to imagine her gone.

The ringing phone snapped Spence out of his meditation. He hit the speakerphone. "Spence Tailor," he said.

"Uh, yes, Mr. Tailor, this is Dudley Chalmers. I'm with COPA." The man on the other end had an odd manner of speaking, Spence thought, almost funereal. Or was he simply projecting his own mood?

"COPA?" Spence figured it was some nonprofit organization in need of legal help. He turned to a clean page and started making notes. "Sorry," Spence said, "what is COPA?"

"California Organ Procurement Association," said the man. "I have some news."

Sixty-year-old Martin Brooks had the face of a man whose sense of humor had been surgically removed at birth. His eyes were the color of gunpowder and disapproval. While his staff liked to tell him he looked a lot like the actor Brian Dennehy with his no-nonsense chin and nimbus of startling white hair, in truth he resembled the Slavic tyrant Slobodan Milosevic more than anyone, except perhaps Newt Gingrich.

Mr. Brooks was in his office on a secure phone line. As the former deputy director of the FBI, Martin Brooks knew whom to call when he needed certain things done. Now, as White House chief of staff, whose immediate job was getting his dying president reelected, Brooks was in such need.

The FBI had ten official assistant directors, known informally as the Ten A-Dics. Brooks knew them all. He also knew there was an eleventh, unofficial, assistant

director who ran what was called the Special Affairs
Division, or SAD. Brooks knew that the SAD A-Dic was a
party loyalist named Howard Phillips. Brooks knew he
could count on Howard, because Brooks had promoted
him to his current position.

"My guy at NIH said they located a matching organ,"
Howard said.

"You have eyes on it?"

"No need. Guy's PVS in a hospital."

Brooks was silent as he tried to figure out what that
meant.

"Persistent vegetative state," Howard said.

"Where?"

"L.A."

Brooks chuckled darkly. "Couldn't have been on the
East Coast, could it? No, it's never easy like that, is it?"

"If things were easy, they wouldn't need us."

"Amen," Brooks said. "So how's this going to work?"

"First we have to make sure the donor meets harvesting protocol on our timetable. Best approach is to involve
someone at the hospital. That way, if anything blows up,
we've got an insider to help cover up. Worst case, if the
death triggers an investigation, the insider can always
commit suicide, taking the blame with him."

"Well, let's hope it doesn't come to that."

"Right. Then we'll put a bird on the roof and a guy in
the OR to escort the organ to the nearest air force
base."

"Which is what? The Sixty-first Air Base Group? L.A.
AFB?"

"Yeah, but that's no good. They don't fly. They don't even have a runway."

Brooks paused a moment. "They're the damn air force, what do they do if they don't fly?"

"They're the product center for Air Force Material Command at Wright Patterson."

"In Ohio? How much sense does that make?"

"Pork has to be spread around."

"I suppose. Okay, what's closer, Vandenberg or Edwards?"

"Actually, March Air Reserve Base in Moreno Valley, out toward the Riverside, San Bernardino area."

"Fine, the bird takes the organ to March, where we put it on something fast, like . . . I don't know, an F-15 or -16, whatever's got the range."

"SR-75 Aurora is faster."

"Yeah, but it doesn't exist."

"Still, it's faster. Damn thing'll go like Mach 10. Get you from L.A. to D.C. in twenty minutes."

Brooks gave it a moment's thought. Revealing the existence of an aircraft that they had previously denied might distract the media for a little while. But after the science and technology reporters finished oohing and ahing about the plane's specs and the costs, the political reporters would start asking why it was flown to D.C. of all places and did it have anything to do with President Webster's health—and who needed that headache? "Just go with a fighter jet," he said.

"Fine," Howard said. "Does UNOS know about this?"

"Screw UNOS, this is national security. Have your

man wave a federal seizure order at anybody who balks. If that doesn't work, have him wave something that shoots."

Sitting in a room at Mulholland Memorial Hospital, Mardell Coleman's mother had resigned herself to the truth, and the truth was that her son was gone forever. She'd been at his bedside holding his hand, sometimes whispering to him, sometimes praying in silence. She was an educated woman struggling with the steps of denial, anger, and depression on the road to acceptance. There was only one stage missing. And when the door to Mardell's room opened and the mousy little man eased inside, she knew the bargaining phase was about to begin.

He wore tan corduroy slacks and a brown cardigan over a blue shirt, making him look like an overly sensitive high school guidance counselor circa 1976. He avoided eye contact and spoke softly. "Mrs. Coleman? I'm Dudley Chalmers? With the hospital's Life Continuance Program?" Dudley kept his distance, his hands folded in front of him, his eyes on the floor. "I know this is a difficult period and that you've been here for quite a long time." He looked up the slightest bit and gestured at the door, trying to sound as if he'd just had an idea. "Would you like to go somewhere more comfortable, where we could talk? Maybe have some coffee?"

She shook her head. "No, I'd rather stay with my son."

Dudley nodded slowly, sadly. "I understand." He hated when people wanted to stay with their loved one.

He could empathize, but he didn't like it. His job was hard enough. Why did people do this to him? Having the body in such proximity undermined the metaphoric language Dudley had been trained to use. Still, he couldn't force the woman down the hall to the specially designed room with the soothing lights and sofas and expect her to be in a giving mood, so he forged ahead. "I was told you'd been apprised of my . . . uh, function."

"Yes, I have." She reached over and stroked Mardell's forehead, whispering, "Jesus is with you, baby." Mrs. Coleman stood and walked over to where Dudley was loitering. She was a tall, striking black woman wearing a conservative business suit. "You want me to sign a consent form."

"Yes, ma'am. The law requires us to do that before we can . . . proceed." He paused. "Are you sure you wouldn't like to go down the hall?"

Mrs. Coleman shook her head, then gestured at her son. "My boy Mardell, he's strong."

Dudley shrugged noncommittally. "Of course he is. But as I'm sure the doctors explained, he's in a persistent vegetative state."

Her loving eyes remained on her son. "But there's always a chance," she said.

Dudley knew Mardell had a better chance of winning a hockey scholarship than of emerging from his coma, but he couldn't say that. He had to remain nonconfrontational. He also had to get a move on. There were others in persistent vegetative states, and Dudley had to get consent forms from all their next of kin. And there were so many others at the brink of death—at *end-stage organ failure*—who were counting on him to get those consents and the organs they rode in on. Since time was of the essence, Dudley resorted to one of his old scripts. "You know, Mrs. Coleman, I remember seeing a young boy on a bicycle one day." Dudley used his hands as puppets in his illustrative drama. "He was riding down the street when all of a sudden he jumped off the bike." His right hand soared gracefully away from his left. "And you know that bike just kept on going? Wheels spinning, pedals going 'round and 'round?" Dudley began to nod his head, inviting Mrs. Coleman to share in the understanding. But she just stared at him, not buying it. So Dudley continued, "Well, Mardell's body is like that bicycle," he said. "It's still going down the street . . . but Mardell jumped off a while ago." She still wasn't buying it. "He's gone now." Dudley tilted his head slightly and almost looked at Mrs. Coleman. "Do you know what I mean?" He pulled the consent form from his pocket and weakly proffered it.

Mrs. Coleman looked at the document but didn't reach for it. "That's all fine and well, Mr. Chalmers, but I have to tell you, what I'm concerned about is how much that bicycle is gonna cost." She went to her purse and pulled out a document of her own. It was a statement from Mulholland Memorial for $37,432.

Dudley looked at the bill, then at Mrs. Coleman. "Didn't your son have insurance?"

"What he had was a policy that leaves me holding the bag for thirty-seven thousand dollars."

Dudley looked at the statement, then at the consent

form. He knew it was against the law to buy human organs, no matter what form the transaction took. Still, the hospital tended to look the other way if the organ-procurement guys had to do a bit of haggling, even if it meant forgiving outstanding balances. The cost-benefit analysis showed it was the right thing to do. "I suppose I could talk to someone in Accounts Receivable," Dudley said. "Maybe they could . . . help you out a little."

"How little?" Mrs. Coleman's voice had taken on a harsh tone.

"Uh, well, I'm not sure," Dudley hedged, "maybe ten percent?" He scratched at the back of his neck. "That's what, nearly four thousand dollars?"

Mrs. Coleman stiffened. "Kinda fool you think you dealin' with?"

"Uh . . ."

"Mr. Chalmers, I got news for you. I am the assistant director for the county's public-health administration."

"Oh?"

"Oh, yes. And I know this routine you're doing."

Dudley tried to look confused. "I don't follow you." His transparency made him feel cheap.

"That's right," Mrs. Coleman said. "You actin' from a script, and not very well, I might add. This hospital will gross half a million dollars, depending on how many of my boy's organs you actually transplant here. You know the net on that, Mr. Chalmers? I bet you do. And I tell you what else—you wanna part my boy out like a old Cheva-lay, you gonna have to pay for it."

Two days after it happened, Spence was still thinking about his chat with Dudley Chalmers, the man who called to say they were going to save his mother's life. Since then Spence had replayed the conversation in his mind many times.

"I have some news," Dudley had said. "Your mother is officially at the top of the waiting list. We also have a donor very close to meeting legislatively mandated surgical protocol requirements."

In other words, one person had died and another was on his way.

"Really?" There was disbelief in Spence's voice. "Are you certain?"

"Absolutely," Dudley said, "and given how . . . close the donor is, I suggest you get your mother admitted to the hospital as soon as possible."

"All right," Spence said. "If you're sure." The problem was, this had happened before. A year earlier Spence had received a similar call from the head of the local organ-procurement organization. He said Rose was at the top of the list and a donor heart was imminent. Naturally the family's hopes soared. But the donor lingered, and before he met protocol, the Department of Health and Human Services implemented a new organ-allocation system. Seemingly overnight Rose went from first to sixth on her list. The heart she would have received under the previous system was eventually flown to another state, and

Rose was sent home, where she slipped into a mild depression.

A month later the U.S. House Commerce Committee and the Senate Labor and Human Resources Committee held a joint hearing on HHS's new allocation system. Testimony revealed that new HHS regulations required that organs be allocated in order of decreasing medical urgency and that waiting time be used as a "tie-breaker" among patients in the same urgency category. But the most important change in the system was in regard to geographic distribution.

In testimony the president of the United Network for Organ Sharing said, "We must object to any implication that policy will be directed by the government rather than developed through consensus by physicians, patients, and donor families."

After additional testimony from the heads of Organ Procurement and Transplantation Network (OPTN) and the Scientific Registry of Transplantation, the new allocation system was rejected and replaced by the original system.

Now, a year later, Spence was taking his mother to her room at Mulholland Memorial Hospital, where she would again wait for a donor to meet protocol. Spence just hoped the federal government wouldn't do anything to screw it up this time.

"It was the only way to get her to sign the consent form," Dudley said. He held the phone away from his ear as the woman from the hospital's Accounts Receivable department told him things he already knew. "Well, yeah, and in a perfect world we'd get both," he said. "But in my imperfect little corner of the universe, I sometimes have to make trades like this." Dudley didn't understand why people seemed to go out of their way to make things so difficult. He was just trying to save some lives and make a living. So what if he cut a few corners? It was deemed necessary. Sure, he was working in an ethically and legally murky area, but if you looked at it from, say, the organ recipient's perspective, there were far more winners than losers. And wasn't there some popular school of thought about the Greater Good? Wasn't that what really counted?

The new girl from Accounts Receivable asked Dudley another question. "I don't know how you're supposed to book it," he said. "I'm in organ procurement, not accounting. All I know is, I got the full set, and that means we save some lives, give the gift of sight, and come out in the black. Ask Beverly how you do it. She's done it before." Dudley wondered why they put it on the books at all. That was one of the things that worried him. Evidence. He had nightmares about getting caught. He would try to shield his face from the TV cameras, but everyone would see him anyway. His superiors would hang him out to dry. *We had no idea,* they would say.

Dudley's heart leaped when he swiveled around in his chair. There was a man lurking outside his office. Perhaps he was someone's next of kin. "Listen, I gotta go," Dudley said. He hung up, then took a moment to switch to his procurement persona. "Sir," he said gently, "did you want to see me about something?"

The man slipped into Dudley's office and silently closed the door. He looked to be in his fifties. He had small teeth, gray at the root, and a fist for a nose. He wore a simple dark suit. The man threw the dead bolt and closed the blinds so no one could see in.

Dudley didn't know what to make of that. "Uhhh, can I help you?"

"Yeah, well, you more or less have to," the man said in a vaguely threatening manner.

The locked door began to worry Dudley. "Uh, who were you looking for?"

The man sat on the corner of the desk, stuck a cigarette in his mouth, and lit it.

"I'm sorry," Dudley said. "You can't smoke in here."

The man launched a smoke ring at Dudley's face. "I'm Agent Berger," he said. "I'm with the government." He flashed his badge, then slipped it back inside his coat. "I can do all sorts of things."

Dudley swallowed. *The government? What does that mean? FDA? NIH? IRS?* He hadn't gotten a clean look at the man's ID. "I'm sorry," Dudley said. "You went too fast." He gestured weakly at the man's coat. "Can I see your ID again?"

"Trust me," the man said. "I'm with FIB-SAD."

"Fibsad?"

"Federal Bureau of Investigation, Special Affairs Division."

A sickness sprouted in Dudley's stomach. *Oh, Christ,* he thought. *They know what we've been doing.* "What are you investigating?" His voice wavered.

Agent Berger stared at Dudley for a moment before pulling a gun from inside his jacket.

Dudley pushed back from his desk as if he'd just seen a snake. "How did you get in here with a gun?"

"What, this?" Agent Berger racked a cartridge into the chamber. "It's made from a new carbon-ceramic composite material. No metal, no metal-detector problems. Only certain federal agencies are allowed to carry them, though you see 'em at gun shows now and then. Oh, check this out." Agent Berger turned on the gun's laser sight, aiming it at the pen set on Dudley's desk. The light from the laser caught Dudley's attention. Like a house cat mesmerized by a flashlight beam, he followed the red dot as it crossed the desk to his phone, then his Rolodex. Then it climbed up his arm and stopped on his chest. "Now, here's the deal," Agent Berger said. "You don't get to ask any more questions. Okay?"

Dudley stared down at the tiny red dot hovering over his heart. He began to pray he would be offered a deal in exchange for testimony implicating someone higher in the organ-procurement organization, or the hospital, or anywhere.

Agent Berger flashed the beam of red light across Dudley's eyes. "I said, okay?"

Dudley nodded like a jittery squirrel.

"Good." Agent Berger slipped the gun back into its holster. "See, I'm here on a matter of national security. You have a Mardell Coleman admitted, yes?"

"Yes," Dudley said. "And we haven't touched him. He's still in one piece. It's not like we make backroom deals every time somebody slips into a coma. Please don't kill me."

"We'll see. Now, this is pretty simple. We need Mr. Coleman on the table first thing tomorrow morning."

Dudley shook his head automatically. "Can't harvest until a patient's brain dead," he said. "That's the law. But you probably know that."

Agent Berger shrugged. "Either he'll be brain dead or you will. Choice is yours." Agent Berger leaned forward and raised his eyebrows. "You *have* signed your organ-donor card, haven't you?" He pulled a small leather kit from his coat pocket. He unzipped the kit and tilted it so Dudley could see the contents. Three hypodermics," Berger said. "The one on your left, that yellowish stuff? That's phentolamine mesylate, brand name Regitine. The one in the middle is heparin." He handed the kit to Dudley.

"What?"

"Heparin. It's a heterogeneous group of straight-chain anionic mucopolysaccharides called glycosamino-glycans having anticoagulant properties."

"I know *that*," Dudley said. "But—"

"Now, that third one? That's interesting. That's a little something our lab rats came up with. Called it BD5. BD for 'brain death,' I suspect. Flattens the EEG and metab-olizes into thin air or blood or whatever. Can't find residue or anything. Necropsy shows nada."

"That's impossible."

"I know. It's amazing what they can do with a test tube and a Bunsen burner."

"Why the hell are you giving this to me?"

Agent Berger fixed Dudley with a disappointed look. He stood and walked to the door. "Like I said"—he dropped his cigarette and crushed it into the carpet—"the choice is yours."

It was four-thirty in the morning, and Joe was near the end of his shift. Ancient, stooped, and tired, Joe had only to empty the trash cans down in the morgue. The basement halls of Mulholland Memorial Hospital were dark, weirdly industrial, and creepy in a postapocalyptic sort of way. Joe pushed his cart down the hall under the bundles of wires and pipes that hummed and groaned and crackled. When he reached the morgue, he stopped his cart outside the door. He'd been in there a hundred times, but he didn't like it any more now than the first time. Dead bodies, even if they were covered in sheets, gave Joe the willies.

Most of the stiffs were in the refrigerator, where Joe wouldn't have to see them. But there were always more bodies than drawers, and the leftovers were lying on gurneys out in the open. This morning there were only three, but that was three more than Joe was comfortable with. They were lined up side by side with their heads to the wall, as if in the starting blocks for a race to the other side of life. On your mark. Get set. Joe emptied the first trash can, then looked around for the second one. "Oh, hell," he muttered. It was against the wall, under the gurneys. He'd have to move one of them.

Joe took a breath, grabbed the stainless-steel bar

nearest the cold feet of one of the corpses, and rolled it away from the wall with all due respect. He stepped into the space between the gurneys, bent over, and grabbed the trash can. As Joe stood up, he whacked his shoulder hard against the gurney on his left. The body on the gurney jerked to life with a shriek. Joe jumped back, then fainted as the corpse's arms flailed, tearing the sheet away from its head, revealing eyes wide in confusion. "What?" she cried.

Her blond hair looked as if it had been done by the Three Stooges. She sat up, rubbing her face, trying to get her bearings. When she finally figured out what had happened, she climbed off the gurney and went to Joe's side. She propped him up and shook him gently. "Joe? You all right? Can you hear me?"

Joe's eyes opened and focused. He blinked. "Dr. Robbins?"

After four years of medical school and three years as a surgical resident, Dr. Debbie Robbins still had two years of residency before heading into a three-year cardiovascular fellowship followed by another two years of research before she'd be board eligible for the American Board of Thoracic Surgeons. Debbie sometimes wondered if it would ever end.

The hours were brutal; she was starting her second thirty-six-hour shift in four days. The training was unforgiving. Either you made it or you were tossed on the heap and forgotten. They didn't care. They couldn't afford to. Being a heart surgeon was serious business, and Debbie was going to be one of them, no matter the costs—which were legion. No sleep, no love life, and plenty of mental abuse. Some of the surgeons who provided the training thought nothing of humiliating and belittling residents on a regular basis. Some did it to weed out the frail, others did it because it had happened to them, still others did it because they enjoyed being cruel. The fact that some residents responded to the method didn't help matters.

Debbie tolerated the behavior because the options weren't good. Becoming a transplant surgeon was something she had to do. There was something about the job. She needed it, and she wasn't going to let a few tyrants prevent her from getting whatever it was. Besides, not all of them were so petty. Some of the surgeons were quirky and kind, and a few of them were so smart and had such an intuitive way of teaching that they inspired with their genius and quick wit and gentle touch. Debbie aspired to being one of them. One of the good guys. In the meanwhile she aspired to get some sleep. *Maybe when I'm older,* she thought. *Or dead.* "Hi, Joe," she said, smiling. "Didn't mean to scare you." She stood and helped Joe to his feet. "You gonna be all right? You hit your head pretty good."

Joe nodded. "You shouldn't do that. Go home and sleep."

"I get more if I stay here." She tried to get her hair to lie down. "Let me look at that bump." Joe presented his head for examination. He liked the way her hands felt, warm and capable against his bald scalp. "You'll be fine," Debbie said, giving his head a little kiss.

"I'll be fine, long as no more corpses jump up on me," Joe said. "You know, you don't look much better than some of them." He gestured at the dead.

"But I have a brighter future." Debbie turned and headed off to start another day. Whatever day it might be. At this stage of her training the days and months blurred together, and until she had her morning coffee, Debbie couldn't say if it was Tuesday, July, or next spring. She walked down the basement hallway trying to shake the cobwebs from her head. A feeling nagged at her, like there was something she was supposed to do today. Attend a lecture? Pay bills? Change her oil? Maybe it would come to her after she had her coffee.

Debbie reached the elevator and pushed the button. Standing there, she studied her reflection in the stainless-steel doors. *Joe must be blind,* she thought. *I don't look half as good as the dead.* She smoothed her short white doctor's coat, slung her stethoscope around her neck, and, when her reflection disappeared, boarded the elevator.

Passing the fifth-floor nurses' station, Debbie waved at the duty nurse on her way to the coffeemaker. She frowned as she poured a cup. It was the color of tea. She hated weak coffee. "Who made this?"

The duty nurse looked up in no mood. "Who does your hair?"

Debbie let it go as she wandered over to the visitors' waiting room. A man was asleep in one of the chairs, his jacket thrown on the floor. She moved her coffee cup in his direction. "Who's this one belong to?"

The duty nurse looked at a chart. "That would be the son of Rose Tailor in 518."

"Advanced dilated cardiomyopathy."

"Doo-dah," the nurse said.

Debbie picked up the coat and laid it over Spence like a blanket. "That's so sweet." She sat a couple of seats away and sipped her coffee. "We could use more like him."

"Yeah, loyal as a hound. But don't get too attached. He snores bad."

Ever since Agent Berger had put the red dot on his heart, Dudley Chalmers had been considering anew the blurry line between life and death. Death, he knew, had many definitions—lawyers had one, theologians had another, doctors had several. And then there was the social definition, which argued that humans should be declared dead once they lost the ability to interact meaningfully with others. However, since anyone sitting in front of a television could be declared dead by that standard, the medical and legal communities had decided to come up with something more exact.

About thirty years ago, the Harvard Medical school published its criterion for determining when life ceased, which has been considered the Cadillac of measuring death ever since. The doctors in Cambridge said you were dead if you suffered irreversible and complete loss of brain function. In 1981 the President's Commission for the Study of Ethical Problems in Medicine and Biomedical and Behavioral Research turned it into an either/or proposition, expanding the criterion to include irreversible cessation of circulatory and respiratory functions *or* irreversible cessation of all functions of the entire brain, including the brain stem.

Now, as any doctor will tell you, there's dead and then there's dead. One definition sent you past "Go" without collecting two hundred dollars and led straight to a hole in the ground, while the other, more subtle definition landed you on the operating table as an organ donor. It was now incumbent upon Dudley Chalmers to get Mardell Coleman into the second category.

The plan was simple. Get in, do the deed, get out. Fast. Not wanting to be identified on hospital security tapes, Dudley was in a stall in the men's room pulling full surgical scrubs over his street clothes. He tied on the surgical mask and snapped the paper shower-cap thing over his head.

He slipped out of the bathroom and down the hallway, his paper booties crunching lightly beneath him. He eased into the room where a respirator was helping Mardell maintain the illusion of life. Dudley pulled out the leather kit and unzipped it. He'd start with the BD5, which, according to Berger, would stop all brain function without leaving any evidence in its wake. Then he'd inject Mardell with heparin, which prevented blood clotting and would help keep the organs viable until they could be harvested. Then came the Regitine, which vasodilated the patient to the point where there would be no detectable blood pressure, causing the heart to slow to the point where there would be no detectable neck pulse. As the grim ferryman approached, Mardell's body would automatically release adrenaline in a noble attempt to stave off his bony fingers. This was where the Regitine again came in handy. As an alpha-adrenergic blocker, it prevented the adrenal gland from poking its nose into the matter and delaying the inevitable. Depending on the velocity of the BD5, Mardell would meet all necessary definitions of clinical death in the very near future, and the harvest could begin.

Dudley made quick work of it. He tapped into an injection port on Mardell's IV line and loaded him with the BD5, then the heparin and the Regitine. He glanced at the monitors and saw the heart rate slowing. So far so good. He didn't have the time or expertise to run an EEG, so all he could do was hope that brain activity was grinding to a halt. Knowing that the room was about to turn into a goat circus, with nurses, interns, residents, and orderlies climbing over one another to get a look and offer an opinion, Dudley zipped the syringes back into the kit and beat a hasty retreat.

3

Nothing but Heartaches

The federal budget for the United States is nearly $2 *trillion*. That's trillion, with a *T*. Like tyrannosaurus. The U.S. Senate Appropriations Committee has jurisdiction over what is known as "discretionary spending," which amounts to roughly one-third of the federal budget. This part of the hog trough is filled with approximately $567 *billion*. That's with a B, of your tax money. This $567 *billion* gets spread among thousands of programs controlled through annual congressional appropriations acts. Among these are expenditures for matters of national security.

Buried somewhere in a subparagraph of a subsection of a section of the most recently passed Congressional Budget Act were several billion dollars to fund something called MSP. It was nothing new. MSP, which stood for Military Special Projects, had been funded this way since its inception, although you'd never find it in an audit because it would show up in most government organizational charts as SAS, or Special Activities Staff.

Like the National Security Agency, MSP had a secret charter and virtually no oversight. The key word being "virtually." While the members of our government were willing to fund all sorts of bad ideas on an ongoing basis, they did like to keep in touch with those to whom they gave the money. They didn't do this in case they needed a favor or anything, as such things never crossed the minds of the honorable people who sacrificed their lives to public service. They did it because . . . well, on account of you just never know.

Budget oversight for this sort of thing was typically handled by a congressional committee, the Office of Management and Budget, or the General Accounting Office, the auditing arm of congress. But the SAS (aka the MSP) wasn't typical. The only person with any oversight power was a member of the Select Committee on Intelligence, a legislative body that oversaw and made continuing studies of the intelligence activities and programs of the U.S. government. It was also responsible for preparing proposals for legislation and reports concerning said activities and programs. The ranking member of the Select Committee on Intelligence, having no use for this usually insignificant job, assigned it to one of his committee's junior members, Senator Peggy Check.

Intrigued by the possibilities, the senator did her

homework. Soon she knew all there was to know about the Special Activities Staff. It was one of the least-known covert units operating on behalf of the federal government. SAS kept a stable of talent from which branches of the government could draw trained personnel for . . . well, for "special activities." Working in small teams, SAS members were trained in everything from counterterrorist and hostage-rescue ops to taking down any sort of vehicle or building. They also executed paramilitary operations including, but not limited to, sabotage and friendly personnel and material recovery. Officially, when an SAS team was formed, it became known as a Special Operations Group, or SOG. SOG teams ranged in size from two to twelve men, all graduates of Force Recon, Combat Applications Group, Navy Special Warfare, Delta Force, and the other elite military training regiments.

With this in mind, and while pondering her presidential aspirations, Senator Check had an idea. An idea she took straight to the top. She arranged a meeting with the CIA's deputy director for operations during which she intimated that the Select Committee on Intelligence was having quiet discussions about a possible decrease in the MSP budget. "Of course, I'm dead set against such cuts," Senator Check said. "But I need something I can take to the committee. Something that justifies your budget."

The CIA DDO thought about it for a moment. "How about the mining of the Nicaraguan harbors? That's been declassified."

Senator Check shook her head. "No, that was twenty years ago," she said. "Not that you didn't do a fine job of it, but I think in order to keep your budget at current levels, we need a more . . . contemporary example."

"I'm sorry, Senator, I'm not at liberty to discuss any current activities," the CIA DDO said. "And I don't have any wiggle room there."

"Well, I have a few thoughts on that," the senator said. So she explained her idea.

When she finished, the CIA DDO seemed skeptical. "You're saying a simple material-recovery op will be enough to keep my budget out of harm's way?"

"I guarantee it." And that's how Senator Peggy Check came to control her own two-man SAS-SOG, which consisted of Agent Rodgers and Agent Hart. Two men whose fortunes in the world of espionage were on the wane. Rodgers and Hart weren't exactly the bottom of the barrel, but they had an excellent view of it.

Leech-faced and sinewy, Agent Rodgers was a hookworm of a man. He was white and in his late forties, a milky-eyed ex–Delta Force goon. Having graduated first in his class in vehicle dynamics and evasive maneuvers, he was driving a black Chevrolet sedan with a 450-horsepower Beck racing engine under the hood. "Can you believe this shit?" He threw a punch at the radio. "Idiot traffic reporter said the 405 was smooth sailing. It's five in the morning, for Christ's sake."

They were on their way to Mulholland Memorial

Hospital, but they were late, owing to the rush hour in Los Angeles, which seemed to start earlier with each passing day. The sun wasn't up, yet five lanes in both directions were going nowhere.

Riding shotgun, Agent Hart was a load of black intensity. He was handsome and dark as the barrel of a gun. He had the whole Miles Davis thing going, with the scowling eyes and a face that just dared you. He looked at the traffic, nodding philosophically, as if composing his thoughts. "Cars, fuming and still. Stretched far as the eye can see. There goes the ozone."

Rodgers turned and looked at his partner. "The hell is that?"

"Haiku, motherfucker."

"I prefer the limerick, personally. There once was a redheaded wussy."

Agent Hart glared at his partner. "I will kill you if you finish that." Agent Hart considered himself the poet laureate of the intelligence community. He'd been published in *The Encryption Quarterly,* the CIA's in-house literary magazine.

"Poetry's a losing game," Rodgers said. "You wanna write something"—he wagged a finger back and forth between them—"me and you ought to write a damn screenplay, all the shit we know. We'd make a fortune."

"I suppose if you can't sell your soul directly to Satan—" Hart's cell phone rang, interrupting his sermon. He flipped it open and answered, "SOG Two." He listened for a second. "Uh-huh. Okay. Close, but traffic's a bitch. We're on it." He flipped the phone shut. "The senator's aide says things are in motion. Said FIB SAD's already moved on the target. Got a brick agent on site and a chopper on the way."

"They know the FIB asset?"

"Berger."

Rodgers snorted derisively. "That fat dog-ape?" He shook his head like he couldn't believe the quality of people they hired at the FBI. "So whadda we do?"

"We make sure the heart misses the flight or we bring their bird down."

"We got any Stingers?" Like they were groceries.

"One in the trunk. Course, we actually have to be in the vicinity of the hospital to use it."

"What? The traffic's my fault?"

Hart shrugged.

"You just work on your little haikus," Rodgers said. "We'll get there." He pulled the Chevrolet to the shoulder of the highway and floored the huge racing engine. "And when we're done?" Rodgers said. "If we still have the Stinger, I just might use it to shoot down that damn traffic copter that steered us wrong."

Agent Hart glanced coolly out his window. "I'll look the other way."

The code alarm sounded at the nurses' station. The duty nurse spun in her chair, tensing for action. When she saw that the code was Mardell's, she relaxed. She pushed a button, silencing the alarm, then picked up a phone and punched an extension. "Houston, we have an eggplant," she said. "Yeah, beep the harvest teams." She paused. "No, I got Dr. Robbins here. She can call it."

Debbie stood at the counter finishing her coffee. "Whadda we got?"

"Organ donor just crossed the finish line down in 219. You wanna go call it?"

"Sure." Debbie started to go, but the nurse touched her arm.

"Do me a favor?" She pointed to Spence, still asleep in the chair. "Wake him up and tell him his mom's heart is on the way."

Debbie went back to the sitting area and stood by the chair where Spence was sleeping. "Sir?" she whispered. But he didn't respond. Debbie nudged his shoulder and spoke up. "Excuse me?" Still nothing. Debbie then thumped his ear with her middle finger, startling him awake.

"Hey!" He bolted upright, grabbing his ear. "Damn. That hurt." He looked up and saw Debbie smiling down on him. He noticed her hair standing up in a funny way. "Who are you?"

"I'm the heart fairy." Debbie pointed at the nurses' station. "Go see the nurse. She has some news for you. Now, if you'll excuse me." Debbie turned and disappeared down the hall.

As she headed for Mardell's room, Debbie's brain engaged, automatically calling up the information necessary to the task at hand. Exclude hypotension, hypovolemia, intoxication from cerebral depressants; get EEG;

confirm absence of cerebral blood flow; and on and on. There was so much to remember. It seemed certain that patients at Mulholland Memorial would have been dismayed to know Debbie was also thinking the following words: "Oh, orally consume virgin pussy." But she was. It was one of the many obscene mnemonic devices medical students used. In this case it helped Debbie remember the names of nerves used to test critical brain function: oculocephalic, oropharyngeal, corneal, vestibuoocular, pupillary—OOCVP, "Oh, orally consume virgin pussy." It wasn't pretty, but it worked, and that's all that mattered.

But there was one thing for which she apparently didn't have a mnemonic. Either that or she'd forgotten it. Great. Now she needed a mnemonic to help her remember another mnemonic. Ever since she woke up, Debbie had been trying to remember what it was about today she was supposed to remember. Maybe it would come to her later. Did she have a date? Yeah, right. What the hell was it? Had she left the stove on? Was it a doctor's appointment? She tended to forget those. When she arrived at Mardell's room, Debbie dropped it and got the lab tests started immediately—serum electrolytes, sodium, potassium, anything potentially correctable.

A moment later Dr. Gibson, the neurologist and resident EEG specialist, arrived. "I'm here looking for signs of life on Mars," he said as he wheeled his machine to the bedside and began connecting the electrodes to Mardell's head.

A few seconds later two orderlies wandered in just for the entertainment value. They were followed by several interns and a few nurses. Everyone crowded in asking questions, making suggestions, or just talking among themselves. There wasn't much else going on this early in the day, so a code tended to draw a crowd. Surrounded by this morbid little audience, Debbie went through the drill she'd done dozens of times. After assessing apnea, she took a strand of cotton and touched Mardell's eye. "No corneal reflex," she said as she wrote the words on the chart. She pulled a rubber reflex hammer from her pocket and abruptly struck Mardell on the chin.

One of the orderlies jerked, hitting his head against the wall, as if his own reflexes had been tested. "Why'd you do that?"

Debbie kept her eyes on Mardell's mouth. "That's the snoot test," she said. "If Mr. Coleman here had any brain activity, his lips would have pooched out like this when I hit him." Dr. Robbins stuck her lips out like a grouper. "Here, watch." She hit him again.

The orderlies craned their necks to look at Mardell. "What'd he do?" one of them asked.

"Nothing," Debbie said.

"What's that mean?"

Dr. Gibson spoke from behind the EEG. "Means the poor man has no more worries."

Debbie turned to Dr. Gibson. "Brain dead?"

He cocked his head to an angle and held one finger in the air. "Brain dead, you ask? Why, this man could be president."

Debbie looked at Mardell for a moment. "Except that he's black."

"Word up," said one of the orderlies.

"True," the other agreed.

An intern piped up. "But he could be secretary of state."

"Except that he's brain dead," Dr. Gibson said. "So we're back to where we started."

As Debbie listened to the comedy stylings of Dr. Gibson and the orderlies, she wondered what had led the first person to try hitting someone on the chin with a rubber hammer to determine if he was dead. And what else had that person tried? *What weird business,* she thought. Debbie returned her attention to the potential organ donor. "Seriously. Is this man legally dead?"

The neurologist went Munchkin on her. "He's not only merely dead, he's really most sincerely dead." He held up the EEG printout as evidence. He signed his paperwork and left, followed by the orderlies and the interns. The show was over.

Debbie was double-checking the four-vessel cerebral arteriogram, just to make sure they weren't jumping the gun, so she didn't notice when Spence appeared in the doorway. "Excuse me," he said.

Debbie glanced up but didn't recognize him. "You're not supposed to be in here," she said. She looked back to Mardell. This was the standard comment hospital personnel made to any civilian they encountered outside of visiting hours.

"Oh, sorry. I'm Spence Tailor." He gestured back toward where he'd been sleeping, as if to remind her. "Rose Tailor's son."

Debbie stayed focused on whatever she was writing. "You can stay if you're family." Then she glanced at him again. "Are you related?"

Spence thought for a second. "I will be. Sort of."

"The reason I ask is, you don't look like family." Debbie folded her arms as if to challenge him. "I think it's the complexion."

Spence was already anxious about his mom's surgery. Debbie's confrontational attitude left him stammering. "I'm the, uh . . . well, it's my—" He didn't know what to say. "You're the, uh, heart fairy" was the best he could do.

Debbie remembered. "Ohhh!" She pointed at the side of Spence's head. "Out there. Right. In the waiting room. Sorry about your ear." She turned and pointed at Mardell. "Your mother, his heart, 'sort of related.' I get it. Still, you're not supposed to be in here."

"Yeah, sorry, but the nurse told me what was going on, and I was on my way to my mom's room, and I saw you again so I . . . I stopped." Spence held out his hand. "I'm Spence Tailor."

"So you said." Debbie shook his hand perfunctorily. "I'm Dr. Robbins." She wanted to end this little tête-à-tête as quickly as possible, before the guy started to form an attachment. It happened all the time: The worried relative would engage a doctor and try to form a lifelong bond. She understood why it happened, but she'd been trained to keep things on a professional basis. "It's been nice talking to you, Mr. Tailor, but I need to go scrub in."

"You're not the transplant surgeon, are you?" Spence quickly waved his hand as if to erase the tone of his question. "I don't mean that like you couldn't do it, I just thought . . . I mean, it's my mom and I was—"

"No, I'm a surgical resident. I watch and assist. Dr. Squires will be performing your mother's transplant."

"How long before they start?"

Debbie looked at her watch. "Pretty soon. You should go see your mom if you want to talk to her. They should be prepping her now."

"Is Dr. Squires pretty good?" Spence's face looked like it might twist off with worry.

Debbie smiled, unable to maintain the robot persona. "Relax," she said. "Dr. Squires is terrific. The best there is." She put her hand on Spence's arm, reassuring. "Everything's going to be fine." Just like his mom used to say.

Spence had a distant look in his eyes. After a moment he nodded at Mardell. "Is that, I mean, is he . . . the one?" Debbie nodded.

"Ohhhh, nooo," a plaintive voice came from behind. Spence and Debbie turned to see Dudley Chalmers standing in the doorway, all but wringing his hands. "Mr. Coleman's . . . gone?" He pursed his lips as if to stanch a flood of emotions. "It's so . . . sad, you know?" He tilted his head like a curious dog. "But at the same time it's a relief, isn't it?" He nodded while looking to Spence and Debbie to see if they were in fellowship with him. They stared at him silently for a moment before Dudley spoke again. "Dr. Robbins, have you called it?"

Debbie nodded. "Teams are on their way."

Dudley was relieved. No one seemed to suspect a

thing. He allowed himself to wonder about the feasibility of doing this more often, strictly in the interest of those waiting for organs, of course, then just as quickly returned to his task. "Well." He clapped his hands together. "Must get started on the paperwork." He did a pirouette and left.

Debbie checked her watch again and started to leave. "I have to get ready," she said, pausing at the door. "Trust me, your mom will be fine."

After she was gone, Spence stood there looking at Mardell. He felt guilty being in the same room with the person whose death he had been hoping for. He thought about Alan Caplan's funeral. He knew Mardell was heading that way, too. Spence thought maybe he should say something to the man who was about to save his mother's life, even if it was just symbolic. But what? Ashes to ashes and all that goes with that? What if the man were Muslim or Buddhist or agnostic? He didn't want to say anything that might offend, sending the poor guy off to the afterlife in a bad mood. Spence was out of his element on this, but he refused to let that stop him. He stepped over to the bedside and gently placed his hand on Mardell's forehead. He knew whatever he said had to come from the heart. He looked down and said, "Thank you."

Debbie put on her surgical cap and mask, then stepped up to the sinks just as the nurses and circulators were heading into the OR to prep the room and tables for Mardell's harvest. Debbie liked to start scrubbing before the rest of the surgical team, as she found their typical scrub-in gabfest a tedious exercise, and pointless to boot. She preferred to spend the time visualizing the procedure in which she was about to engage. Something she picked up from a sports-psychology class she took as an undergrad.

Getting sterile wasn't simply a matter of washing one's hands. It was a highly specialized ritual drilled into medical students during their third year. Debbie enjoyed the process, being the sort who took comfort in ceremony, warm water, and clean fingernails. She squirted the antimicrobial soap onto her hands and began rubbing it into a brown foam. She was working up her forearms when the door behind her opened. Assuming it was Dr. Squires, Debbie turned to say hello. She was surprised to see a middle-aged man in a dark suit. "You're not supposed to be in here." Her reflex comment.

"Yeah," the man said. "I get that all the time." He tapped a Marlboro out of a pack and clamped it between teeth stained as brown as Debbie's hands.

Debbie couldn't believe it. She turned to face the man. "And you're certainly not allowed to smoke."

He shrugged. "Who're you, the surgeon general?" He pulled out a gleaming Zippo.

With the exception of her mnemonic devices, Debbie wasn't prone to foul language, but having grown fond of the respect and fear with which most people treated surgeons, this impertinence led her to say, "I'm Dr. Robbins. Who the hell are you?"

The man stopped short of lighting his cigarette. He

reached into his coat, then flashed his badge. "Agent Berger. FBI." With the snap of a finger he fired the Zippo and lit his cigarette.

Debbie jerked her head toward a sign on the wall. "There's oxygen in the next room, you moron." Agent Berger seemed unimpressed by this detail, so Debbie grabbed the green squeeze bottle of betadine and aimed it at him. "Put out the coffin nail and get out of here before I call security."

Berger smirked, then took a deep lungful from the cigarette before flipping the butt into the scrub sink. *Sssssssss.* "Look, Dr. Schweitzer, I'm with FIB SAD, and I have a federal seizure order." He pulled a document from his coat. "Your security doesn't mean dick."

"A seizure order? Which means what? You're seizing me? 'Cause I've been waiting for a man to come into my life and do just that, but, honestly, you are *not* what I had in mind." She moved toward the phone on the wall.

Berger exhaled a blue cloud toward Debbie. "The heart you're about to harvest is now official U.S. property."

"What?" Debbie put the phone down and grabbed the document. "You can't do that."

"You know, people keep telling me that but"—he shrugged again—"here I am." He snatched the document back. "Sorry, you don't get a copy."

Aside from a load of legalese and citations of what she assumed was federal law, the only thing in the document Debbie could make sense of were the words "Bethesda Naval Hospital." "Well, I'm sorry, too, Mr.

Hoover, but that heart's going into a little old lady who's been on a waiting list for a long time."

"Negative," Agent Berger snapped. "There will be a chopper on the roof"—he glanced at his watch—"in nineteen minutes. The heart will be on that bird. I'm here to escort it."

"Look," Debbie said, "I don't know, maybe you've read too much Tom Clancy, but you can't just waltz in here with a piece of paper and start procuring organs. You want a heart? Get in line with the rest of the world. You don't like the process? Write your congressman."

Agent Berger pulled his gun. "Here's the deal, Dr. Doolittle: You get the heart out of Mr. Coleman, I get it to the roof. That's the process. You don't like it? Not my problem. I've got the gun."

When one is about to be set upon by a man intent on cutting one's heart out with a knife, absence of fear is not an option. Extreme anxiety is inescapable. It is innate, stemming from the function of an almond-shaped mass rooted deep in the brain. Like a sponge squeezed by fear, the amygdala weeps a substance into the limbic system, triggering the physiological response that helped move *Homo sapiens* up the food chain. Flight or fight. It is fixed in the genes, out of one's control. A downhill racer without brakes or steering. This amygdalic secretion triggers the adrenal glands to discharge glucocorticoids, compromising the immune system and escalating blood pressure. Heart and breathing rates rise, blood thickens, increasing the likelihood of stroke or heart attack, none of which is conducive to being put under general anesthesia, which is, of course, preferred when one is about to be set upon by a man intent on cutting one's heart out with a knife before replacing it with another.

The adverse consequences of this reptilian response are compounded by activity that transpires in the folds of one's cerebrum. Thought. Will the surgery be successful? Will the doctor slip? Will I fall prey to infection? Will my body reject the new heart? Will I live or die? Will they say nice things at the funeral? The uncertainty of the answers to these questions provokes more fear, thus intensifying the cycle.

It was for these reasons that Rose Tailor was currently high as a kite, smiling and giggling dreamily as Spence stood nearby. "You're going to feel a little pinch," the nurse had said as she gave Rose a shot of anxiety management. "Someone will be here to get you in about ten minutes, honey. You just relax." Not that Rose had a choice. Benzodiazepam ruled.

Twenty minutes later Spence was the one with an anxiety-management problem. "Where the hell are they?" He stuck his head into the hallway for the sixth time, looking for someone to accost. "The nurse said ten minutes half an hour ago," he said loudly enough to be heard down the hall. He ducked back into the room, fearing the worst. *Something's screwed up,* he thought. But what? Had they resuscitated the donor? Had the government somehow enacted new organ donation laws in the past half hour? Had the insurance company notified the hos-

pital that the transplant was elective surgery? Spence
took Rose's hand. "Mom, how are you feeling? Is that
sedative starting to wear off?"

Rose smiled like a happy chimp and shook her head.
"Ooohhh, no, issssss fine."

"Can you wait while I go see somebody? Will you be
all right?"

"Fffffine." She liked the way the Fs felt between her
teeth and lower lip. In fact, Rose had never been happier.
"Relasssh," she slurred. "They'llllll be here, boy . . . here,
boy, come on, that's a good boy." Her lazy fingers snapped
in a feeble attempt to call a long-dead dog. She giggled.

"I'll take that as a yes," Spence said. "I'll be right
back."

Debbie was in her office, seething into the phone.
The president of Mulholland Memorial was on the other
end. "Look," Debbie said, "it's hard enough practicing
medicine when the federal government hog-ties us with
stupid rules and regulations, but when they start sending
armed agents—"

"Dr. Robbins, you're out of line. Now, do you really
want to try to find another cardiac program at this stage
in your education?" *Click.*

"Thank you for clearing that up, sir," she said to the
dial tone. Debbie slammed the phone down and looked
at her brown hands for a moment, wondering how much
it cost to buy the head of a hospital. A peek into Debbie's
permanent record would show no entries indicating dis-
respect for authority. She tended to toe the line. But she

never cowered to a threat, and she wouldn't tolerate an abuse of power. Something her mother taught her. Debbie figured if she queered the deal on some billionaire trying to buy a new ticker—which is what she assumed was going on—and got canned in the process, she'd be exonerated when the facts came out. Until then she fully intended to keep asking questions. She pulled out her personal address book, found a number, and punched it in. After two rings a man answered. "Dr. Conner."

"You stole my heart," Debbie said.

Dr. Tim Conner hesitated only a moment. "As I recall, it was the other way around. Fact, I've still got the 'Dear John' letter to prove it."

"Well, that's pathetic."

"I know. Welcome to my life." Debbie and Tim had dated during their third year in med school, while doing their clinical work in pediatrics. A torrid six-week affair. When Tim started to make wedding plans, Debbie starting writing the "Dear John" letter. She knew they weren't meant for each other in any long-term way, but she appreciated the sexual distraction and let him down as easily as she could. "How are you, Deb?" Tim asked.

"I don't know if I'm more confused or pissed off."

"Been there."

"We're about to do a harvest, right? So I'm at the sinks when this FBI goon—at least that's who he claims he's with—marches into the scrub room, smoking a cigarette, no less, and waiving a document he says trumps the UNOS position on the heart. Now, that's weird enough, but what's weirder is, Bethesda is listed as the destination."

"Hey, we need hearts, too."

Debbie paused before saying, "Tim, what's the ischemic time for a heart?"

"Well, you really ought to know this by now, Deb. Are you taking a test or something? Because that would be considered cheating where I went to doctor school."

"Six hours, dipshit. You can't get a heart from here to Maryland and into a chest in that time. It's wasted meat after that. So what the hell's going on? We got a lady out here who fully expects—"

"I can't tell you, Deb. They made that clear."

"Who made what clear?"

"Look, I owe about a hundred fifty thousand in student loans. And they said anyone divulging—"

"Tim, I don't have time. If some rich yahoo is buying his way to the front of the line, I want to know about it. And if you don't tell me what you know, I will hang up and call a friend at the *L.A. Times*, and I will use your name as my source."

"That would be ill advised."

"Who is it?"

"Deb, it's not what you think. That guy really is FBI."

"And you know that how? Just give me a clue."

Dr. Conner took a breath. "Hang on a second." Debbie heard his door shut, and then he came back on the line. "I didn't tell you this."

"I never even talked to you," Debbie said.

"Yeah, stick with that." He paused. "Okay. Deal is, your AB-negative pump is going to somebody *really special*." He said the words like he was telling a fairy tale to a six-year-old.

"Tim, would you like to tell my patient's son that your patient is more special than his mother?"

"Deb, let me put it this way. The president didn't faint the other day. Do you follow?" It took a moment, but the next thing Tim heard was a very small sound.

"Oh." There was a long pause as Debbie tried to get her brain around the implications of Tim's statement. "Jeeeeze. Us."

"I can't explain the time discrepancy," Tim said. "Maybe they're meeting in Denver to do the transplant. I suspect they listed Bethesda since our illustrious Dr. Nichols is the president's heart man." It crossed Tim's mind that there might be some reward for endangering his career by giving Debbie this rare bit of information. "Listen, I'm going to be out your way in a couple of weeks for a seminar. I was just thinking maybe we could get together for a quick . . . rekindling, you know? No strings or anything, just . . . well, you know, sex."

"Tim. Honest to God. You're telling me it's for the president?"

"No, the sex would be for me. The president's on his own."

"Whoa, whoa, whoa. Wait a second." Spence narrowed his eyes and held up a finger to focus the duty nurse's attention. "When you say 'a change of plans,' do you mean, like, a different surgeon is going to do the operation?"

Appraising Spence in his rumpled clothes, the nurse slowly stepped backward, out of his reach. "Well, not exactly." She pointed to the alcove. "If you'd just go take a seat over there, someone will be along to explain in a little while."

"Well, nooooo, because in a little while my mother is supposed to be receiving a heart transplant. At least that's what we were told thirty minutes ago. So—"

"I'm sorry, Mr. Tailor, I got a call from my boss, who got a call from her boss, and . . . I'm sure they'll send someone to explain what happened if you'll just have a seat."

A couple of red flags raced up the pole in Spence's mind. The nurse's body language and tone of voice were way off. "What are you saying?" Spence bore in on her. "Who's your supervisor? I want to talk with her right now!"

"I'm not saying anything, sir, except you can go ahead and take your mother home 'cause we need her room." The nurse picked up the phone, punched two numbers, then hung up.

"Take her home? Nooo, no. You people are going to transplant that heart into my mother, or I'll sue this hospital back to the damn Stone Age! We went through this once before, and we're not doing it again!"

"Please lower your voice, Mr. Tailor." The nurse looked around as if expecting someone to show up at any second. "And there's no need for that kind of language.

I'm sure there's a perfectly reasonable explanation." She pointed again toward the waiting room. "And if you'll just wait over there, someone will be here any second to take care of . . . your situation."

At that moment Debbie erupted through the double swinging doors, having to pass the nurses' station on her way back to the OR. She saw Spence too late to avoid a confrontation.

"Dr. Robbins!" Spence grabbed for Debbie, but she sidestepped him and kept moving forward. "What the hell's going on?" He pointed at the nurse. "Nurse Ratched here says there's been some kind of mix-up and I'm supposed to take my mom home."

Debbie spoke over her shoulder as she kept walking. "I can't talk right now." She picked up her pace, hoping to get through the doors marked AUTHORIZED PERSONNEL ONLY before Spence could catch her. "I've got to get back to OR."

Spence caught Debbie just before she reached the doors. He grabbed her arm and spun her around. "You better tell me you're putting that heart into my mother."

"Mr. Tailor, I am very sorry, but it's out of my hands." She gestured toward the ceiling. "There's a damn helicopter on its way, and, well . . . I'm sorry. I'll try to explain later." She pulled her arm free and made it through the doors. Spence was so stunned by the sudden turn of events that it took him a second to start after her. He took one step and jerked backward like a dog reaching the end of his chain. Spence yanked his collar free and turned around to find himself facing a security guard the size of New Hampshire. "You're not allowed in there," he said.

Sensing an array of options that ranged from being humiliated to getting his ass kicked, Spence turned and walked away. He pulled out his cell phone and punched a stored number. A second later a groggy voice answered. "Hey, it's me," Spence said. "Get your ass down to the hospital—now!"

After Spence called, Connie couldn't get back to sleep. It was still dark outside, but she got up anyway. She could use the extra time. The kids had a school bake sale coming up. Connie decided to go ahead and make a couple of Bundt cakes. She was pouring the batter into the molds when Boyd passed through, heading for the back door. "I'll call you when I find out what's going on," he said. "I'll go straight to work from the hospital." He left without kissing her good-bye, a slight she no longer gave much thought.

Connie put the cakes in the oven and sat down with some coffee to consider the rest of her day. Mostly routine: cook breakfast for kids, get them to school, pick up dry cleaning, go to post office and grocery store, back to school to pick up kids, take one to soccer and one to swim team, pick up gardening supplies, take them home, go back to get kids, take them home. The one thing on her agenda that would require more than driving skills and a credit card was tonight's school board and parents' association meeting.

That would require plotting and deceit. She'd already

figured out the plot and started on the deceit, but there was more to do. There were a dozen issues scheduled for debate. A few were inconsequential and would be passed as a matter of routine, but there was going to be trouble with a couple other issues, and Connie needed to find a way to use the conflict to her advantage. Her goal was simply to maintain the current funding level for art and music classes, which, by her count of the votes, was severely threatened by a group of parents who didn't understand the difference between training and education.

The first big controversy would involve a crusade by a group of parents who wanted to remove *Huckleberry Finn* from the library because of objectionable language and racist terms and content. When the spokesman for the group brought this up at the last meeting, someone pointed out that his kids heard far worse on the rap CDs they listened to. "Exactly," the man countered. "So they don't need to be exposed to more of that kind of crap in school." He received a round of applause from half the association.

The other screaming match of the night would stem from a different group of parents, who wanted the school to distribute condoms to sixth-graders. As one of Connie's friends had said, "They want to give them condoms based on a study showing they eventually have sex anyway? Why not give them cigarettes, the clap, and divorce papers?"

After some informal head counts, Connie figured she

was a few votes shy of keeping Mark Twain in the library, condoms out of the sixth grade, and art funding at current levels. But she'd been forced to lie to parents in both groups, telling them she could deliver more votes for their cause than she really could if they would vote for hers. The question was in what order would the issues be voted? If either the Twain or the condom vote came up before the arts vote, Connie would be screwed. Thus she needed to find some parliamentary procedure that would allow her to bring her motion to a vote first so she wouldn't be found out until it was too late.

If she couldn't pull that off, her alternative strategy was to vote for the ban on *Huck Finn*, in exchange for votes on the other two issues. Her thinking being that there was nothing more likely to get kids to the public library to check out a book than a group of parents saying they shouldn't read it. And quite frankly she felt it was just plain stupid to give sixth-graders condoms.

It irked Connie that she had to spend so much time fighting so many parochial minds, but until someone anointed her queen, she didn't see any alternatives. She looked at her watch. Cakes were baking. She was ahead of schedule. Good. It was still too early to start making calls on the school-board issues, so she started breakfast instead.

Like a black falcon on the wing, Agent Hart scanned the landscape around the sprawling medical complex in search of their prey. His muscles twitched whenever something caught his eye. "Hey! Over there!" He pointed across a low grassy knoll. "Take a right up ahead and get over there quick. I think I see one."

Despite having successfully completed the world's most advanced training programs in all things automotive—from evasive high-speed emergency driving to the use of the car as a weapon to the Fort Hawkins barricade confrontations practical—Senator Check's two-man SAS-SOG couldn't find their way into any of the parking lots at Mulholland Memorial. They'd been circling the area for fifteen minutes searching for a place to park.

Following his partner's instructions, Rodgers sped the sedan like a laser-guided missile into the gaping spot and threw it into park with a self-satisfied "Ha!" They were only half a block from what they assumed was the main entrance to the hospital, which consisted of eight different buildings spread over an enormous plot of land.

As Rodgers popped his seat-belt latch, Hart reached over and grabbed his arm. "Wait a second." He craned his neck to look up at a pole with four signs attached to it. At the top, in red letters, was a sign reading NO PARKING SUN., TUE., FRI. 8 A.M.–6 P.M., AND MON., WED., THUR. 10 A.M.–8 P.M. Below that, in green letters: 2-HOUR PARKING THUR., SAT., MON. 9 P.M.–MID., AND SUN., WED., FRI. 6 A.M.–NOON. Below that, in blue letters: PARKING BY PERMIT ONLY—NO OVERNIGHT PARKING, PERMITS B, F, H ONLY. Below that, in black letters: LOADING ZONE EXCEPT WED., FRI., SUN 8 A.M.–2 P.M., 6 P.M.–1 A.M. Agent Hart squinted up at the signs. "I'm not sure we can park here."

"We're parked already," Rodgers said. "What's the worst that can happen?" As if on cue, a tow-truck rounded the corner behind them, heading their way. The driver slowed, eyeing the dark sedan. Rodgers thought he saw the tow-truck driver lick his lips. "Shit," he muttered.

Agent Hart threw his door open and stood up on the sill to scout their options. He pointed past a concrete traffic island. "Over there, I think you can turn on that transfer ramp and get into that lot."

Rodgers showed his middle finger to the tow-truck driver, then gassed the sedan up the street to the ramp and made the turn. He saw the driveway and was about to take it when he spotted the directional tire spikes. He jammed his brakes. "Goddamn it!" He hit the steering wheel, then looked around. "Wait a second." He pointed at a low hedge past a sidewalk right next to the hospital. "What about that lot? It's almost empty. How do you get in there?"

Hart stood on the doorsill again and looked for an entrance. "Looks like there's only one driveway, but it disappears behind that building over by where we just came from." He got back into the car and looked at his partner. "I don't remember a driveway over there, do you?"

Rodgers looked utterly mystified as he shook his head.

"Who designed this damn place, M. C. Escher? It's impossible to get in anywhere, yet there are cars in there. I can see them."

Rodgers heard something roaring overhead. He stuck his leech face out the window. "Great," he said, gesturing at the black helicopter passing overhead. "That's the FIB bird." The chopper landed on the roof of the main building.

Hart's face assumed a dim urgency. "All right, enough of this bullshit." He pointed ahead at the landscaped berm separating the street from a lot next to the hospital. "Let's grab some air."

4

Can't You Hear My Heartbeat?

Agent Berger was nowhere to be seen when Debbie returned to the sinks. She wondered if he'd gone to the roof to lay down flares for the approaching helicopter or something equally dramatic. Okay, she realized that was a bit much, but, by God, this was exciting. Debbie had gone from being furious about the breach of organ-allocation protocol to being thrilled by the news that she was about to assist in the harvesting of a heart for the president of the United States. Before she knew it, she was humming the "Star-Spangled Banner" and thinking of U.S. athletes on the medal stand at the Olympics with the flag being hoisted in the background, a sight that always brought a swelling patriotism she embraced.

Debbie focused on her scrubbing technique; being

the cause of an infection under normal circumstances might be considered malpractice, but doing so today might be seen as attempted assassination. As she brushed diligently under her fingernails, Debbie imagined herself as an invited guest to the White House. She couldn't help but think she might one day be at least a footnote in history. She thought about some of the photos she'd seen in *Time* and *Newsweek*. The surgical staff at a news conference surrounding the chief surgeon after an important procedure on a celebrity or a major political figure. She decided she'd wear her surgical cap for the photo, given the way her hair had been acting this morning.

Debbie turned from the sink and slipped into the sterile gown held up by a nurse. She twirled around, and the nurse tied the strings and rolled up the sleeves, since Debbie's arms were shorter than the gown's designer had in mind.

Dr. Squires, the chief surgeon, was already in gown and gloves. "Dr. Robbins," he said from behind his mask, "you know what's going on here today?"

She nodded. "Yes, doctor."

"Fine. Let's do good work. I voted for the man." Hands raised, Dr. Squires backed into the OR and waltzed over to the table where Mardell Coleman lay. He looked around the room at his staff. "Are we ready to dance?"

"Ready, sir."

He looked down at Mardell. "Name? Occupation?"

"Mardell Coleman," Debbie said. "Stuntman, I think."

"Ooooh, dangerous business." Dr. Squires patted Mardell on the chest. "Well, Mardell, better luck in the next life." He held out his hand. "Sternal saw."

"You put on a suit." Spence yanked Boyd's tie, skewing the knot. "Unbelievable."

"Why wouldn't I?" Boyd brushed away his brother's hand. "I'm going straight to work from here."

Spence muttered, "Don't be so sure." They were standing in the vast lobby of Mulholland Memorial Hospital. The place was starting to show signs of life. Relatives arriving to start their day in the waiting room while loved ones underwent early surgeries. Volunteers drifting in with coffee and pastries to staff the information desk.

Boyd found his reflection in a window. He straightened his tie. "What do you mean, 'Don't be so sure'? What's that about? You think the banking industry should grind to a halt because some situation's got you in a dither?"

"You think the banking industry's going to grind to a halt because you're not issuing credit cards at twenty percent APR to people who can't afford them?"

Half bored, half annoyed, Boyd threw his hands in the air in mock panic. "The sky is falling, the sky is falling. Jesus. Whatever it is, we'll deal with it like adults, and then I'll go to work."

Spence bristled at the Chicken Little reference.

"Goddamn it, Boyd, I call you at five in the morning, tell you we have an emergency, and what do you do? You put on a suit so you can be sure to get to work on time."

Boyd shrugged. "What's your point?"

"Emergency implies haste, Boyd. Dispatch, urgency. Other things and people *can* be more important than you. But does that cross your mind? No. I tell you to haul ass down here because Mom has a problem, and you waste time putting on a suit, like she's not important enough for you to be late to work." Spence was thinking that Boyd was proof you didn't have to love someone just because they were related by blood.

"I'm not like you, Spence. I can't go to work looking like . . . well, like you." Boyd gestured at Spence's rumpled shirt. "And stop acting like you're the only one who cares about Mom. I care as much as you do."

"I see. A dark blue suit and saying you care is your idea of compassionate conservatism?"

"Hysterical," Boyd said. "Send that one to Leno. Meanwhile, you're wasting my time with this juvenile rant. If this is such an emergency, why don't you tell me what the hell's going on?"

Spence looked around the hospital lobby. "Not here." He pulled his brother outside, through a cloud of smokers and over to a splashing fountain, where he told Boyd everything that had happened since he'd been thumped on the ear by the woman calling herself the heart fairy.

When Spence was finished, Boyd stuck out his lower lip. He squinted. "Hmmm, *tch*. So what do you think's going on?"

"I think somebody has bought his way to the front of the goddamn line, that's what."

"Hmmm. Any idea who?"

"*Who* doesn't matter! But it's somebody rich enough to have a helicopter, which I have on good authority is landing on the roof any second now." Looking up, he saw only a jet's contrail.

"Who's your source on that?"

"The heart fairy. She's one of the doctors on the transplant team."

"Hmmm, *tch*." Boyd folded his arms and tried to take charge. "I think maybe I should call my attorney, explore our options."

Spence stared at his brother for a moment, then yelled, "*I'm* your attorney!"

"Well, maybe I should get a new one. Somebody who's not so emotional."

"And what? File a lawsuit? Mom would be dead years before we got near a courtroom." Spence shook his head. "That's no good. We've got to do something." He stared accusingly at Boyd. "Or I'll be telling the kids how you let their grandmother die."

Boyd waved dismissively. "Don't be so dramatic. You're acting like a damn woman." He held his hands out, showing his palms to the ground. "Just calm down. Let's think this through for a minute."

"See, Boyd, that gets us back to the original point." Spence grabbed his brother. "This is an emergency! We don't *have* a minute!"

Boyd shoved clear of his brother's grasp, smoothing

his coat sleeves. "Well, we can't just go off half-cocked. We need some sort of a plan—otherwise this'll turn out like the rest of your life. Have you spoken with the head of the hospital?" Boyd glanced at his watch. "No, it's too early, I bet. Probably not in yet. Okay, options, options . . ." He tapped at the bottom of his front teeth with a fingernail. "Hmm, I really don't think there's anything to do except wait for another heart."

"Wrong." Spence grabbed Boyd by the arm. He did it so violently that Boyd couldn't doubt the seriousness of his brother's intent. Spence had a plan, and there would be no backing out. "Okay, listen up." There was a scheme in his eye. "Here's what we're going to do."

Before a heart is taken from the original owner for transplant into a new one, it must be stopped. Otherwise it will continue beating until it depletes the adenosine triphosphate that fuels it. Once depleted of ATP, the heart is finished. You can hit it with all the electricity and adrenaline and prayer you want, but that heart will never again beat nor ache nor be stirred nor anything else. Thus the need for cardioplegia, a solution of dextrose, monosodium glutamate/aspartate, tromethamine, and, most important, potassium chloride. Heart-stopping stuff.

After sawing the sternum in half and gaping the chest with the rib spreaders, Dr. Squires would pierce the pericardium to reveal Mardell's quietly beating heart. He would clamp the aorta and locate the sinoatrial node at the junction of the superior vena cava and the right atrium. He would place the needle between the clamp and the aortic valve. The perfusionist would then administer the cardioplegia via a roller pump, and Mardell's heart would stop.

A moment after Dr. Squires sawed the sternum in half, Agent Berger returned to the OR wearing a surgical mask. He had a grocery bag in one hand and some sort of high-tech device in the other. It was the size of a small beer cooler but looked like a prop from the set of *Men in Black II*. "When you get it out, you'll need to put it into this thing." Berger hoisted the compact container for the surgeons to see.

Dr. Squires glanced over his shoulder while turning the gear on the rib spreaders. The mere look of the device aroused Dr. Squires's imagination. "What do you have there?"

"Advanced prototype ECC," Berger said, referring to extracorporeal circulation. The perfusionist looked over the top of his bulky contraption. ECC typically meant a heart-lung machine, an unwieldy mechanism the size of a three-drawer filing cabinet that performed heart and lung functions during surgery. "Extends a heart's ischemic time indefinitely," Agent Berger said. "We've had a heart going for over five years in one of these things."

"What?" Dr. Squires's eyes widened in disbelief. He knew some biotech firms were working on warm-storage devices, but none were even close to going to market. Dr. Squires looked to Debbie and nodded at Mardell's chest. "Get that opened. I wanna see this." He walked over to

Agent Berger and looked into the container. It was like nothing he'd ever seen. The only parts visible were a series of flexible sterile tubes and a cradle of sorts for the heart. Dr. Squires assumed the actual works were hidden in the walls of the device. He was amazed by the miniaturization of the technology and the intuitiveness and elegance of the design. He knew instantly how to use it. He pointed at various tubes. "That's for the pulmonary trunk, that's superior vena cava, right pulmonary vein. Beautiful design."

"Yeah, you wouldn't believe some of the stuff we've got in our warehouse." Agent Berger puffed up a bit, as though he had invented the thing. He pulled a couple of sealed plastic bags from the grocery sack. They contained the sterile saline solution in which the heart would be suspended.

"Is this something the government is testing?"

"Nooo." Agent Berger shook his head. "This is old technology. We've had this since the early sixties. Works great. High gas transfer reserve capacity for superoxygenation; hollow fiber, cross-wound mat technology." Berger opened up a side panel like a used-car salesman popping the hood. He pointed at various features. "Computational fluid modeling, top-down membrane flow, all sorts of great stuff." He tilted the device to show a compartment on the underside. "Whole thing runs on a common lithium battery. He reached back into the grocery sack and pulled out several bottles containing a milky white liquid. He opened one bottle and poured the emulsion into the ECC's reservoir.

"Is that a blood substitute?"

"Yep. Little something called Hemo-Sub."

"I didn't think they'd even entered Phase III trials, let alone been approved."

"Most of 'em haven't," Berger said. "This was made at a DOD lab. They know how to get around some of those FDA hurdles. They tell me this stuff's a by-product of Teflon manufacturing, if you can believe that."

"Yeah, from what I read, it's a sterile perflubron emulsion made up of tiny particles suspended in a water-based solution. Liquid perfluorochemical particles like one-fortieth the size of red blood cells are surrounded by a surfactant. The PFCs dissolve and transport the blood gases." Dr. Squires looked at the bottle. "I'd sure like to get some stock in this outfit." He knew the global market for blood substitutes had been estimated around $5 billion a year.

Agent Berger snatched the bottle from the doctor. "Sorry, closely held corporation." He poured a couple more bottles into the reservoir. "Gotta get the temperature up on the liquids before you put the heart in."

Dr. Squires continued exploring the ECC device. "Sinus rhythm continues?"

"Long as the liquids stay around thirty-seven degrees Celsius." Agent Berger smiled and patted the side of the container.

Dr. Squires was astounded. "Why hasn't this gone to market, for God's sake?"

"Well, as you can see, we do use it on a limited basis."

"But this could benefit so many, I mean—"

Agent Berger held up a hand. "You know, Doc, I wish I could tell you the truth, I do, just to see your reaction. But . . . well, suffice it to say the government has its reasons."

"What possible reason could the government have for not sharing this?"

Agent Berger threw both his hands up in surrender. "Hey, they pay six hundred bucks for a ten-cent bolt! Who's to say why?"

"But this could revolutionize—"

"Doc." Agent Berger shook his head. "It's not going to happen. Now, you just get the heart out of that container"—he gestured at Mardell—"and get it into this one."

Dr. Squires huffed back to the operating table and resumed the harvest. "Doesn't make a damn bit of sense," he said. "Bad policy, if you ask me." He held out his hand. "Scalpel." He took out his frustration on the pericardium.

The FBI man opened his mouth to say something, but, aware of the consequences, he stopped. Still, it gnawed at him. It hurt not being able to tell the truth, not because he was an honest man but because he wanted people to know that he knew things they didn't. He wanted to swagger and leave their jaws slack. Probably some unconscious need for validation or some such thing. Regardless of the underlying psychological mechanism, Agent Berger wanted to shout out that he'd been to Area 51. *I've touched the craft myself,* he wanted to say. He was privy to the technology they'd pulled out and reverse-engineered and, oh, the marvels he'd seen.

Agent Berger noticed everyone's attention had returned to the harvest, whereas moments earlier he'd been the center of the universe. A sense of impotence overwhelmed him and broke him down. He had to say something, but he also had to be cool. He folded his arms and leaned against the wall. "But speaking of documentaries, any of you seen that one about Roswell?"

Unfortunately, just as Berger was saying that last word, Dr. Squires said, "There we go," as he made his final cut and plucked the heart from Mardell's chest cavity. Cupping the softball-size wad of bloody muscle in his hands, Dr. Squires carried it over to the ECC device. "All right, how do I hook this up?"

Forced to abandon his need for attention, Agent Berger reached over and hit a switch. A gentle hum issued from inside. "Put it in the bed." Dr. Squires did as instructed. "Now take the aorta and slip it into that sterile tube." He pointed at the tube in question.

"Do I suture it?"

"No, just bring it into proximity."

Sure enough, when the aorta came close to the tube, it triggered a response. The mouth of the tube wrapped around the end of the aorta like lips around a drinking straw, forming a perfect seal.

"Holy Mother," Dr. Squires said. "Like God Himself." He finished attaching the remaining veins and arteries and watched as the Hemo-Sub coursed through the heart and the machine.

Agent Berger closed the top. Dr. Squires and Dr. Robbins leaned over to look through the window on top of the carrier. Inside, like a living thing, the heart beat. Berger picked up the ECC device by the handle. "All right, let's get it upstairs. Got a bird waiting. Who wants to show me the way?"

"Let's go," Debbie said. Her knee-jerk reaction with any ischemic organ was to race for the elevators in a full sprint fueled by clichés. The clock was ticking, time was of the essence, life hung in the balance, and so forth. But this morning fate had raised the bet. Today Dr. Debbie Robbins was, by God, responsible for the heart of the leader of the free world. What a thing to have land in your lap, she thought as she raced down the hospital's wide hallway. Debbie couldn't help but see herself as a key player in this historic event. Sure, she knew that whoever actually transplanted the heart would get most of the press and be mentioned in the history books, but for the next few minutes the fate of the country was in her hands. Okay, Debbie realized that wasn't literally the case, since Agent Berger was the person actually carrying the thing, but figuratively at least . . . well, anyone would have to admit this was . . . this was damn inspiring. This was the sort of story she could dine out on for the rest of her life. *Did I ever tell you about the time I assisted in harvesting the heart for the president? Yeah, escorted it straight to the helicopter on the roof and you wouldn't have believed this FBI agent . . . Seriously, buy me a drink, I'll tell you about it.*

Agent Berger lagged behind, fumbling in his pocket for a cigarette. "Hey, Nurse Betty," he called out, hoisting the ECC device. "Slow your ass down. We got all the time we need."

"Oh. Right." Reality popped Debbie's balloon of heroic enthusiasm, and it wouldn't help much in the retelling of the story either. Taking a leisurely elevator ride to the roof sucked some of the punch out of the tale. Suddenly glum, Debbie mashed the call button for the elevator.

Agent Berger reached her side and snapped his fingers at his Zippo. Debbie snatched him by the wrist, just shy of lighting up. "Ever seen a lung transplant?" She blew out his flame.

"How the hell should I know?" said a nurse at the nurses' station, which made more sense than Agent Berger's asking the question, since most people who had seen a lung transplant were aware of it. The nurse was all but yelling into the phone. "It's not mine. What do you want me to tell you? Yes, I'll call security." The nurse hung up. "Hey, Dr. Robbins. Got a question. There's an incoming medevac two minutes out carrying an adolescent burn victim." The nurse pointed at the phone. "And I just got a call about an unauthorized helicopter on the roof, so the medevac can't land. Got any ideas?"

"Shit." Debbie could think of only one thing to do. "I'm on it." She grabbed the ECC device from Berger. "Come on, we're taking the stairs." She was down the hall like a sniper's shot, her action-sequence enthusiasm resurrected like a savior. She burst through a door under an EXIT sign and started the seven-story climb to the helipad. Owing to her work schedule, Debbie wasn't in as good a condition as she would have liked, but she figured she could beat Agent Marlboro to the top by about two heart attacks. Still, she was overly optimistic to start out taking the steps two at a time.

When Agent Berger reached the stairwell, he was already half a flight behind. "Hey, slow down, for Christ's sake! The kid's already burned. He can't get any worse." He considered stopping to light his cigarette, a little nicotine boost for the climb, but, thinking better of it, gave chase instead.

After six floors Debbie was slowing down, and, to her surprise, the wheezing FBI agent was only one flight behind her. "Ohhh, crap!" Debbie had reached a door with a sign on it. NO ROOF ACCESS. HELIPAD ACCESS VIA EAST STAIRWELL ONLY. Debbie turned around and charged back down the top flight of stairs, slamming Berger into the wall on her way.

"Hey!"

"Wrong stairwell, Wheezy. C'mon, we've got to hurry." Debbie burst into the hall on the ninth floor and charged toward the east stairwell. She made a graceful pirouette to avoid a wheelchair that lurched from a doorway. A little farther down the hall she hurdled a stack of linens that had fallen off an orderly's cart.

Agent Berger was doing his best to keep up, but he was running out of gas. He was ashen-faced and stumbling headlong down the hall propelled only by ego. He barked a shin on the steel footrest of the same wheelchair Debbie had dodged. "Oww!" Hobbled, yet determined not to be left behind by a woman, Berger reached down to rub his bone while still on the run. He looked up from his throbbing tibia just in time to see a swinging door hurled open by an emergency case on a charging gurney. The door hit flush on his forehead. The furious transfer of energy flipped Agent Berger upside down and backward with such violence that when the back of his head cracked on the linoleum, it woke someone from a dream one floor down.

Unaware that she'd lost her FBI escort, Debbie reached the door for the east stairwell marked with a sign: HELIPAD ACCESS. AUTHORIZED PERSONNEL ONLY. She took a breath and started the final climb. Just as she reached the last eight stairs, she looked up to the landing and saw someone, a man, wearing a surgical mask and full scrubs. "Hurry up," he said, reaching for the ECC device. "I'll take it from here."

"No, I got it," Debbie insisted. She was going to hog all the glory. "Get the door." But the man just stood there. Three steps to go. "Hurry!" Debbie yelled over the sound of the helicopter's rotor, but the man still didn't get the door. She reached the landing and leaned toward the man's ear. "There's a medevac with a burn victim incoming! We gotta clear the pad!"

"Right!" the man in scrubs yelled back. Then, sudden as a thought, he bent over and pulled Debbie's pants to her ankles.

This was approximately the last thing she had expected the man to do, and there followed a weird moment. Everything froze. She stared at the man, mouth opened. He peered back through the slit between his surgical cap and mask. She wanted to look, but she couldn't. She hoped she wasn't wearing the underwear she feared she was. Then, just as suddenly as the man had snatched down her pants, he grabbed the ECC device and took off.

In the flash of time before she could move—to pull up her pants and start after the thief—Debbie considered her reputation. Her mother had instilled in Debbie a deep respect for the significance of one's good name. "It takes a lifetime to build it but only a single moment to destroy it forever," she used to say. "Guard it jealously." Debbie's grandmother had weighed in on the subject as well, her advice taking the form of "And always wear nice underwear, in case you're in an accident." And now, against all odds, Debbie found herself suddenly enrolled in these two schools of thought simultaneously. In a bizarre firing of her synapses, Debbie realized that if she didn't retrieve the heart, her reputation would forever be that of the woman who let the president die while wearing cotton panties the front of which featured an iron-on replica of a yellow-and-black traffic sign that read SLIP-PERY WHEN WET.

Debbie pulled up her pants and started after the man in scrubs. "Hey!" she yelled. "You don't want to do that! Stop!"

"Can't! Got an emergency!" The man never slowed as he raced down the stairs, taking them three at a time, gripping the handrail with his left hand while holding the ECC in his right. He was two stories below Debbie when he reached the ground floor, exploded out to the side-walk, and skidded to a stop. Spence yanked the surgical mask off his face, revealing a look of where-the-hell's-my-getaway-vehicle? Then he saw it, way over near the door of the west stairwell. Thinking ill thoughts about his brother, Spence muttered, "Naturally."

Assuming Dr. Robbins would be blowing out the door any second, Spence took off for the truck. On the run, he looked over his left shoulder and saw he had a good lead on her. But what he didn't see was the dark sedan ramping over the landscaped berm behind him to his right. Spence darted into the road leading to the parking lot. That's when he heard the sedan crash to the asphalt about twenty yards behind him. He turned and didn't like what he saw.

From the sedan's passenger seat, Agent Hart casually nodded his head. "Pedestrian." Real cool.

"Got it." Rodgers jumped on the antilock brakes while surveying the range of evasive maneuvers available in the situation. It didn't take him long to conclude that with his rate of deceleration and the fact that the pedestrian was running pretty fast in the same direction they were heading—*boom*. Spence rolled up onto the hood of the sedan, somehow keeping a grip on the ECC. His face pressed against the windshield, one eye bugging at the two agents. Rodgers leaned on the horn. "Fucking moron! Watch where you're going!"

A hundred yards away Boyd was behind the wheel of Spence's old Chevy, twitching and sweating like Dick Nixon's upper lip. His eyes had been fixed on the stair-

well door until he heard the crash and saw his brother
rolling off the sedan's hood. Boyd turned the key, but the
engine wouldn't crank. Spence was running toward him.
"What're you doing?" He was yelling. "C'mon!" Boyd
tried again, but the engine just groaned like an arthritic
joint. He flooded it, then turned the key once more.
Boom! A gunshot. No, it was a backfire, and the truck
bucked to life just as Spence reached the passenger door,
still screaming. "Go! Go! Go!"

"The goddamn thing wouldn't start!" Boyd pressed
the squishy clutch to the floor and wrestled the stick
into gear.

Debbie was running as fast as she could toward the
old Chevy. "Stop! Somebody help!"

Boyd popped the clutch, and the truck jerked forward.

Spence held the ECC tight to his chest. "Christ!
Where'd you learn to drive?" Spence pointed at the
charging Dr. Robbins. "Look out!"

"You wanna drive or shut up? Pick one!" Boyd wasn't
an inherently skilled wheelman, and his automotive
training was limited to five hours of driver's ed, so he was
thoroughly unprepared for his present situation. But
these things he knew: First, he had to avoid the doctor
who was running straight at them; second, he couldn't
swerve left, as there was a dark sedan occupied by two
men in that lane; and third, he couldn't swerve right
because that would put him up on the sidewalk, which
was bound to be a moving violation of some sort, and he
didn't want to do anything to screw up his good-driver's
insurance discount.

As Boyd slowed to avoid even the appearance of reck-lessness, Debbie leaped onto the side of the Chevy and pulled herself into the bed of the truck, all the while yelling, "Stop! Somebody help!" She banged her fists on the roof of the cab.

"Who the hell is that?" Boyd asked.

"That's the heart fairy I told you about." Spence stuck his head out the window and yelled at Debbie. "Shut up!"

"Organ pirates! Help!"

"Well, this is just dandy!" Boyd screamed. "Stealing human organs wasn't enough—now we add kidnapping to this whole shitstorm." Boyd threw a fist, hitting Spence in the chest. "Idiot!"

"Ow. She wasn't this noisy before. And it's not like I invited her!"

The CIA agents watched as the two men in the truck exchanged a series of punches while the woman in the back continued screaming like a banshee. As the old Chevy approached them, Agent Hart picked up a digital camera and focused. *BinkBinkBink,* he captured some digital images of the alleged organ pirates. "I'm going to go out on a limb here," he deadpanned. "This might have something to do with the heart."

"Ya think?" When the truck had passed, Rodgers whipped a U-turn in the sedan, jumping the curb onto the sidewalk before rocking back onto the roadway.

"That lunch box the guy was carrying?" Hart began downloading the digital images into a paper-thin laptop. "Looked like Roswell technology."

"Get their plate number?"

"Running it."

"You see the split-tail jump in the back of the truck? I tell you what, I like 'em when they're agile like that." Rodgers nodded agreement with himself. "And those hospital outfits . . . shit, talk about easy access. You could tear off a quick piece in the supply closet and be back checking blood pressure in a minute."

"Speak for yourself." Hart pointed at the escaping truck. "Not too close."

They followed the old pickup at a distance. It turned onto a driveway tucked between two buildings. "Where'd this driveway come from?" Rodgers asked. "I didn't see this before."

"Maybe there's a way out of here without going over that berm."

"Yeah, but where's the fun in that?"

Ignoring the caterwauling in the back of the truck, Spence turned to his brother when he noticed the security guard racing out of the hospital ahead of them, his hand reaching for his gun. "Uh, Boyd? You remember earlier when we talked about the meaning of the word 'emergency'?"

"Shut up! You've ruined my life!"

"Well, in that case it won't hurt you any to *speed the hell up!*"

The sight of the approaching security guard put the fear of prison rape in Boyd. He floored the truck and took the turn out of the parking lot. All Debbie could do was drop to the bed of the truck and hope she didn't bounce out. "Slow down, you idiot!"

With a death grip on the steering wheel and eyes bouncing from the road to the rearview mirror to Spence, Boyd considered the familial consequences of turning state's evidence on his brother. "Now you see what I was talking about regarding your lack of a well-thought-out plan?"

"Shut up! Let me think." Spence hit his brother's arm.

"Oh! *Now* you want to think." Boyd hit back and kept an eye on Spence to see if he would retaliate.

But all Spence did was reach for the dashboard and scream, "Look out!"

Boyd looked in time to see the garbage truck backing into their lane. "Shit!" He slammed the brakes. They heard a dull thump, like a melon hitting a wall. It was Debbie. She had made the mistake of standing. When Boyd hit the brakes, she pitched forward, slamming her head against the cab of the truck. She collapsed like a folding chair in the bed of the truck as Boyd swerved to avoid the collision.

Spence glanced out the rear window at Debbie, lying quietly in the back. "Well, you solved that problem."

"Unless I killed her."

"True. But we still have one other problem."

"One?" Boyd was incredulous. "No, I'm guessing we have between fifty and a hundred problems."

"Whatever," Spence said. "But first we've got to go back to the hospital and get Mom. That's our main problem."

Boyd's eyes fixed on the rearview mirror. "Oh, Lord, not anymore." He crossed himself.

Spence turned and saw the flashing lights of the motorcycle cop. "Ohhhh, perfect."

Like a well-trained citizen, Boyd began to slow and pull to the side of the road. "I'm dead. Totally screwed. It's over."

Spence gestured down the road. "What are you doing? Keep driving! Buy us some time. Haven't you ever seen one of those high-speed chases?"

Boyd wasn't paying attention to Spence any longer. He was too busy imagining his future. *All my assets eaten up by legal fees. Connie will divorce me. I won't see the kids grow up. This wasn't part of my plan.*

"Okay," Spence said, trying to think. "Okay, maybe pulling over's the right thing to do. He probably just saw that bit where you swerved around the garbage truck. Let me handle it."

Boyd pulled to the curb. "Oh, God, Jesus." Like he was about to pray, but instead he hit Spence again. "I'm going to prison thanks to you! I'm going to be tossing salads! Do you know what that means? I saw it on HBO, and *it has nothing to do with lettuce!*"

A block behind, Agent Rodgers pulled over and grabbed the small duffel bag from the backseat. He snatched out a pair of binoculars and pressed them to his milky eyes while Agent Hart read from the laptop. "Okay. Truck's registered to a Spencer A. Tailor"—he tapped a few keys, then pointed at the screen—"who just happens to be the son of Rose Tailor, the intended recipient of the organ in question."

Rodgers lowered the binoculars but continued looking straight ahead. "So Junior there hears his mom's been screwed out of the heart and snatches it, not knowing what the deal is. Ain't that sweet?" Rodgers put the binoculars back to his eyes. "You do that for your mom?"

Agent Hart tensed and composed some words. "Failure to nurture. Don't talk about my mama. Makes me want to kill."

Rodgers stared at his partner for a moment. "I'll take that as a no."

The motorcycle cop dismounted his Kawasaki 1100 and cautiously approached the truck, inscrutable behind a pair of mirrored sunglasses. He was stone-faced and appeared to have spent an inordinate amount of time in the gym. Based on the beefy, Y-shaped torso and wasp waist, Spence figured the guy focused on upper-body work and likely used steroids.

As the cop approached, the sound of creaking leather from the knee-high boots, the gun belt, and the holster seemed to take the air from Boyd's lungs.

"Boyd, take a breath," Spence whispered. "Relax. He doesn't know anything."

The cop paused to glance in the bed of the truck where Debbie lay on her back, rubbing her forehead, moaning and rolling slightly, side to side. Spence was encouraged that this didn't seem to cause the cop any concern. He probably saw stuff like this all the time. He reached the driver's door and leaned over until Boyd's face was fully reflected in the sunglasses. After a long moment he spoke. "License and registration." His tone was as flat as his abs.

Boyd bit his lower lip to stop the quivering. It looked to Spence like his brother would start crying at any moment. "Please don't arrest me," Boyd whimpered.

Spence cleared his throat to get the cop's attention. "Officer, can we talk?" He gestured toward the back of the truck. The cop didn't object, so Spence got out and walked to the tailgate, where the cop joined him. When he got a close look at the cop's face, Spence decided he'd jumped the gun on the steroid speculation. Not only was this guy's face not marred by telltale acne, his skin was flawless. Spence looked at the cop's badge and name-plate. "Officer Bobb, is it? I suppose you may be wondering about . . . her." He gestured toward Debbie and spoke in low tones, like a consulting physician, which is what he looked like in his scrubs. "That's my brother's wife. She's a plastic surgeon, and . . . well, she's a full-blown alcoholic, there's no other way to put it. It's tragic, really, and this morning she screwed up a . . . uh, a boob job." Spence cupped his hands and indicated two very different-size boobs and locations. He nodded his head, hoping to elicit some empathy from the cop. He got none.

Behind the shield of his glasses, Officer Bobb tried to add it all up. One adult white male, nervous beyond his infraction, wearing a business suit that didn't match the truck he was driving. Another adult white male, this one wearing surgical scrubs and telling a far-fetched tale about the adult white female, also in scrubs, lolling about in the bed of said truck. He wasn't sure what to make of it, so he just listened, hoping for a clue, as the doctor continued talking.

"Anyway," Spence said. "My brother's just a wreck—the deductible on his wife's malpractice insurance is huge—so I was wondering, you look like a nice guy, maybe you could give him a break. Whaddya say?" Spence smiled gamely and waited for a reaction. All he got was the impassive stare. "No? All right, so you're gonna get us on, what? Possession of a loaded surgeon?" A nervous laugh from Spence. Officer Bobb turned his head slightly toward Debbie, then back to Spence, but never uttered a sound. "Just joking," Spence said before glancing at his watch. "Well, look, we've taken too much of your time already. You're obviously a busy man. I hope you didn't want to write him up, because it really was that garbage truck's fault back there."

A series of urgent beeps issued from the motorcycle's radio. Officer Bobb cocked an ear toward his radio while keeping an eye on Spence. "All units be advised of a 211 at Mulholland Memorial Hospital. Suspects are two white males, late thirties, last seen westbound on Selmer in older-model Chevy pickup. Possible kidnap victim. Approach with caution." Officer Bobb stepped away from Spence, muscles twisting into steel belts, his hand on the grip of his gun.

Spence held his palms out toward Officer Bobb in a calming gesture. "All right, now, relax," he said. "It's not what you think. We're not the criminals here. See, according to the charter of the United Network for Organ Sharing—"

For the first time in his brief career, Officer Bobb went for his gun, a Glock nine-millimeter. But he had trouble with the snap release on the thumb break, and when he finally got it off, his nervous energy sent the gun spinning out of the holster, tumbling through the air before landing on the street halfway between himself and Spence. A fleeting Mexican standoff followed as the two men stared first at the gun, then at each other, then back at the gun.

Finally the more desperate of the two made a move. Spence snatched the Glock off the asphalt and backed away while holding it on the paralyzed cop. This being the first time he had done such a thing, Spence stood mute, his mind racing for an opening statement. But before he could think of anything to say, Officer Bobb thrust his hands straight up in the air and shouted, "Don't shoot me! I'm gay!"

Spence lowered his head and squinted. "What?" Surely he had misunderstood. The cop must have said, *Don't shoot me today* or *Don't shoot me this way* or something. Spence couldn't get the baffled look off his face. "What?"

"It's true," Officer Bobb insisted. He was nodding vigorously. "I'm . . . gay." He put his hands over his mouth, then quickly raised them again. "Oh, my God, I can't believe I finally said it."

"Yeah," Spence said. "It's a shocker, all right." He looked around to see if they were being watched. "Now, do me a favor and put your hands down. And don't do anything stupid."

Officer Bobb lowered his hands, removing his sunglasses in the process. Pretty brown eyes. He exhaled like he'd just won a reprieve of some sort. "I can't believe how good that felt," he said. "I mean, what does it say about me that I had to be held at gunpoint before I could finally say it out loud?"

Spence honestly didn't know how to respond. "Look, I'm happy for you, really, GLAAD with two A's, but it turns out I've got a little situation here."

"Just don't kill me."

"I'm not going to kill you."

"Well, be careful, that Glock has a sensitive trigger."

"I'm being careful."

"Okay, fine. So what are you going to do now?"

It seemed like a good question.

5

Steal My Heart Away

Senator Check asked not what she could do for her country so much as she asked about the cost of the private jet on which she was presently luxuriating. "Beats the hell out of first class," she said as she stroked the lambskin upholstery. The jet in question was owned by one of her constituents, who assured her that she needn't worry about getting her own.

The senator was heading for a lunchtime fund-raiser at the Southeastern Bankers' Convention in Charlotte. Like every major-party presidential candidate, Senator Check had to raise three thousand dollars an hour every single day for eighteen months in order to buy a shot at the White House. It didn't leave much time for legislating per se, but such was the cost one paid to live in a free country.

There had been a minor revolt among citizens regarding this fact, which had led Senator David McSwain (D-North Carolina) to introduce the latest in a series of sweeping campaign-finance-reform bills. McSwain's legislation proposed to close loopholes created after the last such bill was undermined by language tacked on to an unrelated "taxpayer protection" bill that had broad support on both sides of the aisle and all but eliminated reporting requirements for the 527s or the so-called stealth PACs. Not for nothing did so many of these representatives have their substantial intellects sharpened at the wheels of the nation's finest law schools.

Senator Check had predicted that McSwain's finance-reform measure would pass the House by a slim margin but said that the opposition would poison-pill the legislation when it went to a conference committee. "It'll never reach the president's desk," Check told CNN. "That's the political reality."

Other representatives, meanwhile, made it clear that Senator McSwain would not even be named to any conference committee that considered his own legislation. Senator Buck Harter of Nebraska explained that since McSwain didn't sit on the Rules Committee, which had jurisdiction over the bill, he didn't have a legitimate claim to sitting on any committee that resolved differences between the House and Senate versions that might emerge. He refrained from saying "Nanner, nanner, nanner."

Appearing on Matt Christopher's popular political talk show, *HardHeads*, Senator Check said she agreed with Senator Harter's assessment. "Senator McSwain will have nothing to say about the fate of this bill," said Check, who was backing a rival measure—one that allowed for a return to unlimited soft-money donations and a "no questions asked" atmosphere—in the Senate.

Thanks to these and other public-spirited citizens, it was business as usual, and Senator Check was on her way to North Carolina to prove it.

Britton Belk, the senator's aide, was helping her with some new phrases for use at the fund-raiser, where the bankers would be asking about legislation she was to propose the next time she had a minute to get to the floor of the Senate. Britton leaned forward in her seat. "Senator, if they press you for details, just wink at them and say, 'Well, now, there's no need to get too deep in the weeds on this.'"

The senator nodded, then looked mildly confused. "What was the one you said about showing where the bear sat in the buckwheat? I like it, but can you put it in context?"

Before Britton could explain, her cell phone rang. She answered it, then handed it off to her boss, saying, "It's the SAS-SOG team."

Senator Check listened as Agent Hart filled her in on the situation, leading up to his saying, "And now it looks like they're kidnapping the cop that pulled them over."

The senator found that amusing. "Well, never thump

a free watermelon, that's what I always say." She looked at Britton, who gave her a perky thumbs-up for what she assumed was the proper use of the idiom. Senator Check then responded to Agent Hart's question about whether she wanted them to put the matter to rest by destroying the heart. "No," she said. "This way we keep our hands clean. You two just stick with them. Baby-sit. As soon as the president's people figure out where the heart is—*if* they figure it out—they'll send somebody after it. When they show up, your job . . . well, your job is obvious. Just keep my name out of it."

"Yes, ma'am."

"Oh, and one more thing . . ."

"Yes, Senator. I'll do that." Agent Hart flipped his phone shut and slipped it back into his black leather valise.

Rodgers noticed that his partner looked both confused and offended. "What's wrong?"

"She told me to be like a monkey on a bobwire fence," Hart said, a Muslim scowl crossing his face. "What the hell you think she meant by that?"

"Well, Senator Check's from Virginia," Agent Rodgers said. "It's probably some derogatory reference to the fact you're a nigger."

Agent Hart fixed Rodgers with his most severe black-militant scowl. Agent Rodgers met the glare with a racist squint before they both busted out laughing. "You're probably right," Hart said, wiping a tear on his sleeve. "I bet that's exactly it. She's one of them."

Agent Rodgers gestured at the kidnapping-in-progress. "Hey, they're moving the motorcycle." The word "motorcycle" triggered something for both men, and after they shared a knowing glance, they began laughing again. Silly, uncontrollable, gasping-for-air laughter brought on by a shared memory.

Although Agents Rodgers and Hart came from different divisions within the Department of Defense, the two had worked together dozens of times over the years and had become friends. They met early in their careers when they both volunteered to participate in army tests for a drug called quinuclidinyl benzilate. The army called it BZ. It was an anticholinergic agent that affected the peripheral and central nervous systems, a hallucinogen roughly a hundred times as potent as LSD.

The way Agent Rodgers told the story, he and Agent Hart had been brought together by Department of Defense directive 5141.2, which outlined the functions of the office of the Director of Operational Test and Evaluation (DOT&E) within the Department of Defense. Directive 5141.2 stated that one of the duties of the DOT&E was to "designate selected special-interest weapons, equipment, or munitions as major defense-acquisition programs." Among these "special-interest weapons" was quinuclidinyl benzilate, which, like all drugs (and weapons), had to be tested and evaluated for military uses.

No one's going to deny that medical researchers—from both the government and the private sector—have, on occasion, in pursuit of their goal, pushed the envelope, ethically speaking. Naturally, this envelope pushing was always done in a quest to learn, so that one day others might one day be healed. Or killed, as the case may be. It was in this spirit of medical adventurism that scientists injected live human cancer cells into chronically ill, debilitated, noncancer patients in the Jewish Chronic Disease Hospital case; that they gave the live hepatitis virus to severely retarded children at Willowbrook State Hospital; that they exposed American citizens to deadly doses of radiation. All to serve the greater good.

As to quinuclidinyl benzilate, the army had tested it in the 1960s at Edgewood Arsenal in Maryland, administering the drug to thousands of American servicemen. The testing program went remarkably fast, due to the fact that the army didn't waste any time telling the servicemen they were being experimented on in the first place. It turned out a fair number of the servicemen reported alarming adverse aftereffects, including severe birth defects in offspring and recurring psychotic episodes. It turned out further that in the wake of the Nuremberg Code, such testing procedures were frowned upon in U.S. courts of law.

Flash forward forty years after the original BZ experiments, and someone from the DOT&E had been charged with finding new ways to spend tax money. After pitching a proposal to an advisory committee within the department, it was agreed that what this country needed was a new BZ testing program. This time, however, in hopes of minimizing the frivolous lawsuits and claims of civil-rights violations, the army would use informed volunteers. Agents Rodgers and Hart were the first to sign up. The two men bonded after being dosed with the drug and set loose in a variety of environments, from marine boot camp to the It's a Small World ride at Disneyland to being participants in the Loretta Lynn Amateur National Motocross finals (hence their giggling at the word "motorcycle").

In all fairness, it had to be said that no one actually died as a result of these tests, and the collateral damage that occurred was deemed acceptable by military, motocross, and Disney standards. The actual design and purpose of the BZ experiment was eventually called into question, and upon review by a congressional oversight committee, the project received an increase of its initial budget. By then Rodgers and Hart had returned to their respective divisions within the Department of Defense, only to be reunited periodically, as they were now, in the form of a SAS-SOG team.

Rodgers finally gained control of his laughter. He dabbed at his eyes with a shirtsleeve. "Whew, I couldn't breathe there for a second."

Hart took a deep breath and tried to regain his composure. "Okay," he said. "All right. Under control."

Like a rascal, Rodgers looked at his partner and, in a comic nasal twang said, "Nigger."

They busted out laughing again.

At gunpoint, Spence had Officer Bobb stash his motorcycle in a hedge of bougainvillea. Spence then forced him to the cab of the truck. When he opened the passenger door, Boyd looked up for the first time since he'd handed over his license. Despite bleary eyes, Boyd couldn't help but notice that his brother was holding the cop at gunpoint. He blinked once as though it might help him better understand. It didn't.

"I had no choice," Spence said.

Boyd seemed momentarily to embrace the madness of the situation. "Yes," he said. "Of course. That's what was missing. Kidnapping a cop." Boyd extended his hand. "Hi, I'm Boyd Tailor. I see you've met my brother."

Officer Bobb noticed the deranged look in Boyd's eyes as they shook hands. "Are you okay?"

"'Okay' doesn't begin to describe what I am at this very moment, sir." Boyd sounded like he was drifting over the edge.

"Listen," Spence said. "'Under arrest' would describe you if I hadn't"—Spence paused to consider a new line of reasoning—"if I hadn't asked Officer Bobb here to join us in our attempt to assure that the lawful recipient of the heart"—he pointed at the ECC device—"does in fact receive said heart."

"Well, I'm no lawyer," Boyd replied. "But I think the salient point here is that you asked him at gunpoint."

"What?" Officer Bobb looked at the container. "What are you talking about? What's in that thing?"

"My mother's heart."

"Oh, my God." Officer Bobb's skin crawled. What had he stumbled into? Had these two lunatics cut out their own mother's heart? His relief at coming out was now undermined by the fear that he might end up carved into small parts and tossed into a dry ravine somewhere. The upside, however, was the opportunity this presented. If he managed to subdue these two psychopaths and bring them in, that would almost certainly soften the blow, to his father and his fellow officers, about the news of his sexual identity. *Wait a minute*, he thought. *The code was 211 (robbery) with a possible 207 (kidnapping). Nothing about a 187 (murder), let alone mutilation or ritual matricide, but then maybe the body hadn't been discovered yet.* Officer Bobb decided to play along and do nothing until he had more facts.

Spence nudged Officer Bobb with the Glock, urging him into the cab of the truck. He told Boyd to drive around the corner and find a secluded place to park. As they drove, Spence explained everything to Officer Bobb, complete with excerpts from the UNOS charter as well as citation of state laws regulating the legal allocation of human organs. "So there it is. Someone was trying to circumvent the law, and, as concerned citizens, we did the only thing we could to prevent the crime."

Boyd shook his head and muttered, "We."

Officer Bobb relaxed a bit. If the story was true—and it seemed unlikely someone would fabricate this—he probably wouldn't end up chopped into pieces. Still, he was pretty sure a crime of some sort had been committed, and if he could get these guys to surrender, it would be a nice feather in his cap. Hoping to calm his kidnappers, Officer Bobb said, "You know, I'm quite close to my own mother."

"That's touching," Spence said. "Now, we need to—" A low moan came from the bed of the truck, cutting Spence short. He gestured at Officer Bobb with the gun. "Help my brother move the doctor up here to the cab." Spence stood guard as the two men moved Debbie into the front of the truck. Spence then pointed at Officer Bobb. "Okay, now take off your uniform."

Officer Bobb pointed at himself as if to ask, *Me?*

"Look, I've got to go back to the hospital and get my mom. I figure no one's going to bother a cop, okay?" Spence nodded at Boyd. "Also, since I've got to leave the cowardly lion here to guard you, I figure you're less likely to run away if you're mostly naked."

Officer Bobb shrugged and began undressing.

Spence gave the gun to Boyd while he put the police uniform over the green scrubs. "It's not too late," Boyd said. "We can still call a lawyer and start plea bargaining."

"Trust me, it's way too late for that," Spence said as he put on the thick blue shirt. "You might as well get used to the idea that we're deep in the shit." After putting on the pants, Spence took the handcuffs from the belt and cuffed Debbie and Officer Bobb together through the steering wheel. He then reached behind the seat of the truck and grabbed a roll of duct tape and tore off a strip for Officer Bobb's mouth. He decided not to gag Debbie while she was semiconscious, but he told Boyd to do it if she woke up and started screaming.

Boyd found himself marveling at Officer Bobb's physique. There was virtually no body fat, and his muscles were defined but not bodybuilder grotesque. Boyd sat up a little and sucked in his fatty paunch. "Wow, you're in great shape," he said.

Officer Bobb smiled behind his silver gag. "Nnk vuuu." He looked into Boyd's eyes and thought he saw some kindness and acceptance. But he was unsure and, at the moment, wasn't in much of a position to explore the possibilities. He tried to say, "By the way, I'm gay," but with the duct tape it came out, "Hi na hmm, ommm ay."

Boyd had no idea what he'd said, but for some reason he looked at Officer Bobb's eyes and felt something. A brief squirming thing that stunted his sense of dread and panic for a moment, causing Boyd to smile. He glanced again at Officer Bobb's quadriceps and wondered what the bulging muscle felt like. This confused him more than anything else that had happened all day. But before he could really get in touch with these feelings, Spence nudged him and said, "Give me the keys to your Mustang."

White House chief of staff Martin Brooks longed for the good old days. He'd been there—well, at the tail end of them anyway—and he thought they could be recaptured yet. But to do so he had to get President Webster elected to another term. They had to implement a few more policies. He regretted things would never be idyllic, the way they once had been—as he had glimpsed them in his youth—but he knew they could be closer to it than they were now. And certainly closer than they'd ever be if the nation made the mistake of putting a woman in the White House. Good Lord, how had it come to this? How had it come to the point when a woman could challenge for the highest office in the land?

Martin Brooks came from an old California family that had done well in the mining industry going all the way back to the gold rush of 1848. His great-grandfather, Benjamin T. Brooks, got his start by conspiring with local law enforcement to frame and arrest independent miners who had hit pay dirt. Benjamin Brooks would take over the claims and kick a percentage back to the sheriff. By 1855 Brooks owned the largest mining company in California. Among the deeds that earned him robber-baron status was the fact that Benjamin T. Brooks regularly hired goons to murder union organizers who threatened the high profit margins of his mining enterprises. He became one of the richest men in the West and intimate with politicians.

Martin's father, Benjamin T. Brooks Jr., inherited vast wealth and, seeing the decline in gold production, moved the family fortunes into a more diversified portfolio, including petroleum refining and chemical manufacturing, where the fortune blossomed into Rockefeller proportions.

When Martin was a young man, his father took him to the Bohemian Club on the Russian River, just north of San Francisco. The Bohemian Club was an exclusive society of the world's most powerful businessmen and politicians. He remembered fondly his father's hand on his shoulder as they stood on the porch of one of the cabins built high in the redwoods as the bankers and kingmakers strolled the grounds below them. "These are our people," his father had said. "Christian men to whom God in His wisdom has given control of the property interests in this country." And Martin felt that was true. There was a kinship and a shared sense of destiny with these men. They were better and more deserving. It was in their blood.

This was where Martin had learned about politics, about the necessity of a ruling class. This is where he had learned to lament the demographic changes of the country he loved. Was a time, he remembered someone's saying, when you didn't have to appease the minorities, catering to the demands of the civil-rights people, the gay-rights people, the women's-rights people, and the labor unions. Goddamn unions. Was a time when all you had to do was select the candidate, set the machine in motion, and the office was yours. Was a time, was a time.

Martin Brooks was still a member of the Bohemian Club, and more than a few of his fellow Bohemians were counting on him to get President Webster reelected. Counting on him to keep that woman out of the Oval Office, just like women were kept out of the Bohemian Club. But that wasn't going to happen if they failed to get a heart for a transplant. And that explained why, after learning that things hadn't gone exactly as planned, Martin Brooks was crimson and shouting across the oblong mahogany conference table at the head of the FBI.

"What the hell happened? You said you had a good man on this!"

The head of the FBI grimaced. "Yes, sir, but I'm afraid the FIB SAD agent we had on the case was found unconscious with a severe head injury. He's in a coma."

"Jesus. So we're talking terrorists?" Brooks looked like he might have a stroke. The U.S. policy of refusing to negotiate with terrorists suddenly didn't seem like such a hot idea. "What's the thinking over at State?"

"We're pretty sure it's not Al-Qaeda," the man from the State Department said. "But we haven't ruled out Al-Jihad or Hamas."

"How could they even find out about this?"

"They have their ways, sir."

"Okay." Brooks pointed to another man. "What's NSA looking at?"

"FARC's a distinct possibility, sir. They took exception to our last policy change. But we're also looking into speculation that this might be a group of Buddhist separatists or antiglobalization extremists."

The head of the Secret Service shook his head. "Sir, all due respect. Given that it's the anniversary of the siege at Bald Knob, we have our money on a militia group based in Arkansas. You know how they like to use these dates as rally cries."

"What date?"

"Ten years ago today a farmer named Lester Barnett of Bald Knob, Arkansas, decided he'd paid enough income taxes for one lifetime. IRS disagreed and went to serve papers. He held them at bay for six hours before surrendering and paying the eighty-two dollars he owed."

"That's it? Nobody shot or killed or anything?"

"No, sir, they're pretty desperate for an excuse to rise up down there."

"I guess," Brooks said. "Okay folks, the security level on this is 'umbra.' That means no visible federal presence at Mulholland Memorial. Same goes for Secret Service and everybody else. If the media gets wind that something happened at that hospital and we were involved, we'll have too much to explain. So, if anyone gets media contact on this, deny. Deny. Deny. Deny." He poked the table with an index finger every time he said the word.

The rep from Secret Service asked, "What's going on in Los Angeles, sir?"

"We told LAPD to stand down and drop their investigation on the organ theft. As far as they're concerned, it's our baby. They have no comment for the press. Meanwhile, our fainting-spell story seems to have held. It ran its course in two cycles and is out of the papers. But somebody is bound to ask about it if we keep canceling and rescheduling his appearances. So, again, if your sources start asking about the president's health, deny, deny, deny. The president is fine and dandy. He's still resting, but he's working on the nation's affairs."

There were knowing nods all around the table. Then someone had to ask. "Sir, how is he, really?"

Brooks stood to leave. "Without a heart? Come November we'll be looking for new jobs."

Using the latest NSA-developed parabolic long-range microphone Agent Hart listened, from a block away, to the conversation between Spence and Boyd.

Rodgers was watching through binoculars when he reached a conclusion. "That doctor's got some nice tits, don't you think? A little smaller than I like, but still, I'd like to see her do the old squat and gobble up close." His hips seemed to grind in the car seat.

Agent Hart looked at him. "You're worse than a goat, did you know that?"

"All I'm saying is—"

Hart waved a hand to shut him up. "I don't want to know." He returned his attention to the argument between the Tailor brothers. There was some movement. Agent Hart put down the parabolic mike. "The younger one's going back to the hospital to get his mom and the Mustang."

Rodgers shrugged. "I'll stay and keep an eye on Nurse Nancy's nipples," he said. "You follow and keep him out of trouble."

Officer Bobb's uniform billowed around Spence's less developed chest. The waist was a bit of a squeeze, but the overall impression was all he needed. He looked like a cop. As such, he waltzed straight into the hospital and into an elevator without a hitch.

The security guard who hadn't given Spence a second

look roadblocked Agent Hart with his arm, then pushed him back. "Whoa," he said. "Visiting hours don't start till ten, bro." He crossed his arms and struck what he considered an intimidating pose.

"Bro?" Agent Hart sighed. "And what time do heart-stealing hours begin, ofay?" He pulled out his badge and just about rubbed it in the security guard's face. "I'm with the CIA, you stupid cracker, and to tell you the truth, I'm surprised you're still here after what happened earlier. I know for a fact if your ass had been black, you'd've been put out."

"CIA?" The security guard began to get a sense of his inadequacy.

"That's right. And I've got about ten ways I could kill you from this stance. You wanna try me? Pick a number between one and ten. Go ahead."

Despite his size advantage, the security guard could see the superiority in Agent Hart's face. It was demoralizing. Agent Hart was a reminder of everything he would never accomplish. He'd always wanted to be in the CIA or the FBI or something like that, but he didn't have the goods, so here he was, a minimum-wage rent-a-cop who couldn't pass the local police exam, let alone be a federal agent. All he could do was try to explain why he hadn't been able to stop the heart thieves. "Well, now, see, I was down here when I heard about it, and I ran out that door after them—"

"Yeah, and a lot of good that did anybody." Hart shook his head and gestured at the guard's gun. "I hope they didn't give you any bullets for that thing. Barney Fife like you wouldn't know what to do with it. I were you, I'd update my résumé." Hart pushed the man aside and headed to the elevators. The overhead display showed that Spence's car had stopped on the fifth floor. Agent Hart got into the next car and punched the button.

Five floors up, Spence was walking down a hallway heading toward his mother's room. Ahead was a group of doctors conferring with a man in a brown cardigan as they hovered over a patient lying on a gurney. "I think that would be premature," one of the doctors said.

As Spence passed the group, he recognized the guy in the cardigan. It was Dudley Chalmers, from the organ-procurement organization. "Aw, c'mon," he mewled. "Just let me peek in his wallet. If he's not a donor, I'm out of your hair." Spence turned to look at the man on the gurney. He'd never seen Agent Berger before, so he didn't recognize him, nor did he recognize the blood-filled swelling of his forehead as an acute hematoma.

Spence moved down the hall, glancing into every room, looking for something. Finally he ducked into one of the rooms and just as quickly came out pushing an empty wheelchair. He continued down the hall to his mom's room, looked around, then slipped in unnoticed. Inside, he found Rose, propped up in bed, smiling like a ninety-pound rag doll on Valium. Spence pushed the chair to her bedside, locked the wheels, then paused. *Now what?* he wondered. Rose was in the Land of Nod, so she couldn't move herself. That left Spence to go it alone.

He drew back the blankets and thrust his arms underneath her, failing to consider the design of the hospital gown. As his hands worked their way to the other side, Spence felt things that seemed unnatural for a son to be feeling. He didn't have time to worry about the creepy sensation, so he carried on. He picked Rose up and sat her in the wheelchair, then turned to get her overnight bag. When he turned back, his mother was sliding out of the chair like a stick of melting butter. He caught her just in time and lifted her back into the seat. He held her there while he looked around for something to keep her in place.

Outside, a moment later, Agent Hart saw Spence peer into the hallway before dodging back into the room. He emerged pushing his mother in the wheelchair, her arms bound to the armrests by Ace bandages, her overnight bag strapped into her lap. Now it was a simple matter of getting onto an elevator, going to the ground floor, and making it out the front door. They were halfway down the hall when things got complicated.

The security guard stepped off the elevator scanning his surroundings like a Secret Service agent working a rope line. Apparently Agent Hart's lesson in humiliation had spurred the guy into a more proactive style.

As they approached each other from opposite ends of the hallway, Spence leaned over to hide his face. He pretended to listen to Rose. "Yes, ma'am, I think you're right," he said.

"Excuse me, Officer," the guard said, forcing Spence to look up. "Have you seen any suspicious activity in this sector?"

Spence shook his head. "Nope, all quiet up here." He started to move ahead but the security guard stopped him.

"Have we met?" Something about the cop's face registered with the guard.

"Don't think so," Spence said, shaking his head again. "Listen, I need to get this lady down to, uh, radiology for some, uh, radiology stuff."

"Hey, wait a minute." The security guard pointed at Spence.

When he saw the dawn of recognition rising on the guard's face, Spence spun the chair sideways, cracking it into the man's shin.

"Ow!"

From his vantage point Agent Hart prepared for the chase he knew was coming.

Spence pushed down the hall as fast as he could, rounding the corner on two wheels. Rose's head flopped to the side as they made the turn. Agent Hart followed the security guard as he limped after the fugitives. To Hart's surprise the guard pulled his gun and yelled, "Everybody down!" A group of candy stripers screamed and scattered like squirrels when they saw the armed man leveling his gun at the cop behind the wheelchair.

Spence burst through a set of doors and into a hallway crowded with what looked like a bus wreck of hemophiliacs. It was a madhouse of misery and triage as doctors and nurses tended to the moaning overflow of patients sprawled on gurneys lined against the walls.

Spence shoved through this gauntlet and around the next corner, searching for another bank of elevators.

The security guard was gaining on Spence while Agent Hart was trying to figure out how to get ahead of the whole Keystone Kops chase sequence.

The security guard accelerated around the corner after Spence just as a young nurse was rushing in the opposite direction with a syringe intended for one of the emergency cases. The needle sank into the guard's chest, the momentum forcing the plunger to the hilt, pumping the full load of clear liquid into the man.

The horrified nurse recoiled as the security guard staggered backward to a wall, the syringe dangling from his chest like a game warden's dart. He looked down, gingerly removing the needle. Holding it between his thumb and forefinger, he stared at the nurse, aghast. "Good Lord! What was that?" His voice trembled.

The young nurse shrank from him. "Morphine?"

"How much?"

"A lot?"

"Oh, Christ." The security guard dropped the syringe and ran off, marionettelike, after Spence, who was rounding the corner at the far end of the hallway.

Rose was resting peacefully in the chair as Spence punched and punched and punched the elevator call button. "C'mon, c'mon!" He was bouncing on his feet like he had to pee when he saw the security guard fly around the corner and slam drunkenly into the far wall before gathering himself and continuing toward them like a boneless chicken.

The elevator door opened, and Spence hurried Rose inside. He punched at the "close door" button like a rat in a cocaine experiment. "C'mon, c'mon, c'mon!" The doors were coming together in slow motion as the security guard made a sluggish leap for the gap. Inside, Spence heard the unmistakable sound of a man's face smashing into the other side of an elevator door.

Amused, Agent Hart followed the spastic security guard as he barreled into the nearest stairwell in pursuit of his foe. Misjudging the first step, the guard stumbled ass over teakettle down the flight of stairs, ending in a heap on the landing. Agent Hart assumed that would be the end of things, but the morphine had minimized the man's pain response to the point of apparent invulnerability. When he saw the guard trying to scramble onto his rubber legs, Hart decided it was time to intervene. "Give it up, pal," he said, looking down from above. "You gave it your best shot."

The guard turned to see where the voice was coming from. His eyes seemed to absorb the light reflecting off the CIA agent, but his opiated brain was unable to process the information. As though suddenly remembering his job, the guard turned abruptly for the doorway and tried to resume the chase. But there was a problem. Agent Hart had him by the belt. It took a moment, but when the guard figured out the problem, he turned and floated an overmedicated punch that missed by several feet. Agent Hart responded with three blinding jabs to the head that seemed to get the security guard's attention more than anything. As the guard stood there swaying, Hart assumed a kung fu stance and made some accompanying noises. "Whaaaa! Eeeeyaaaa! Oyyyeeeee!" He launched a series of kicks to the guard's midsection, which backed him to the concrete wall of the stairwell but didn't take him down. To Hart's amazement the plucky guard shook off the assault and attempted a lethargic charge. Now, annoyed by the inconvenience of this entire scene, Hart machine-gunned a combination of martial-arts kicks and punches to the man's head, neck, and knees. When it was over, the security guard was bloodied but unbowed. His head wobbled as he gestured for Hart to "bring it on."

"Jesus, buddy, give it up." Hart reached into his coat pocket and pulled out what looked like a ballpoint pen. "You sure you're not done?" The guard came at him one last time. "Okay." Hart clicked the pen's button, and the crackle of a thousand volts echoed through the stairwell before ending the guard's shift.

A few minutes later Spence was in the hospital parking lot unraveling the Ace bandages that tied Rose to the wheelchair when a black man approached out of nowhere, admiring the Mustang. "Boy, oh, boy," he said. "That's the prettiest pony I've seen in a long time." He caressed the rear quarter panel. "Sixty-five?"

Spence looked at the man. He wore a dark suit, conspicuously thick black-framed glasses, and he had buck teeth like a beaver's, on which Spence couldn't help but focus. "I honestly couldn't say. It's my brother's."

Agent Hart slipped a hand under the front bumper, attaching a tiny tracking device, then stood and pointed at the interior. "Are those the original buckets? You know, you can drop the high-backs in on this with no problem. Mind if I look inside?"

Spence was using his teeth to try to loosen a knot in the Ace bandage. "Whatever."

Hart bent into the Mustang and slipped a bug under the dashboard. "Mmmmm, nothing smells like a pony, am I right?" His fake teeth nearly slipped out of his mouth as he spoke. He held them in as he stood up. "Don't suppose your brother would be interested in selling?"

"I doubt it." Spence got the knot untied and lifted Rose from the chair. "Do me a favor? Get the passenger door?"

Hart opened the door and smiled a goofy-toothed smile. "I guess I shouldn't be surprised. I wouldn't sell it either. Well, thanks anyway." He turned and walked off.

When Agent Hart got back to the sedan, Rodgers put down the long-range parabolic mike. "D'ja bug it?"

"Yeah," Hart said. "Tagged it, too." He put on an earpiece and tuned in the transmitter while Rodgers looked for a tracking signal on the computer. Hart shook his head as he listened to Spence and Boyd. "They're arguing about which car to take."

Rodgers held out his hands, pleading his case. "They've got to take the Mustang, right? LAPD's already ID'd the truck." He pointed at them. "And those boneheads know it. That's why they snatched the boy in blue."

"Yeah, but the owner insists they're not taking his baby."

"What're they gonna do, tie the old lady in the back like Granny Clampett? This is a no-brainer."

Boyd and Spence were standing on the sidewalk looking at the two vehicles. Rose was still zonked out in the Mustang. Debbie and Officer Bobb were in the cab of the truck.

"We don't have any choice," Spence said. He wiped the sweat from his forehead, then began taking off the LAPD uniform. "Jesus, I'm dying in this thing." After pushing Rose five blocks in the wheelchair, Spence looked like he had played a set of tennis in police blues. It was still early, but it was July, and the Santa Ana winds were blowing the rats out of the palm trees.

Boyd was adamant. "Forget it. The Mustang stays put. Period. I tell you what, why don't you steal a car? It'd be the smallest crime you've committed all day."

"I would," Spence said. "Honestly, that's a good idea, but since I'm not checked out on that, we're taking the Mustang."

"Nope."

"We've got to have room for both Mom and the hostages."

"Oh, yeah, I meant to tell you. I've changed my mind about the hostages," Boyd said. "My favorite part of this endeavor used to be the stolen heart, but now it's definitely the hostages."

"I'm glad to see you're keeping your sense of humor about this."

Boyd turned to his brother, his eyes pleading. "Listen to me. Listen to reason. Let's give up right now. We free the hostages. Let the cop take us in, throw ourselves on the mercy of the court. It's time to cut our losses."

Spence looked at Boyd, nodding as though the logic were seeping in. He glanced at the Mustang, then back at Boyd. "That thing got air-conditioning?"

As she prepared breakfast for the kids, Connie listened to what she considered the funniest morning radio show on the air. She still wasn't sure if the host was honestly right-wing or if he was being satirical. In any event she took a perverse pleasure in the show's extreme world-view. And every now and then she agreed with something she heard.

And Another Thing! was hosted by a splenetic man named Winston Archer. His syndicated radio show reached about 60 percent of the country. His goal was to penetrate another 30 percent and then sell his syndication rights for an estimated $40 million. He also broadcast a televised version of his show in the afternoons. Winston Archer didn't plan to change anyone's mind on anything—he knew that wasn't the point of these kinds of shows; all he wanted to do was make a buck without breaking a sweat. Winston Archer preached to the choir and didn't let facts get in his way. Indeed he frequently made up statistics, not only because it was fun but also because he knew he'd never be disproved on the air.

"And another thing," Winston Archer said, his voice always rising on the second word. "We're talking about the duty of the American citizen to vote. Let's take a call. Nick, you're on the air," Winston said. "What's on your mind?"

"Yeah," Nick said. "I always thought voting was a right, not a duty."

"What are you, a communist or something?" In the background the "audience" laughed as if Winston Archer had said something funny. The show's producers used an array of canned laughs, boos, gasps, and other taped reactions to give the listening audience the sense that they weren't alone in their prejudices. "Listen, my fellow traveler," Winston said, "the right to vote is a blessing and a duty, and you ought to be thrown in jail if you don't exercise it!" The audience applauded.

"And if the choices offered by the parties are unacceptable?"

"That's easy. You pick the one who is least unacceptable and thank the good Lord you weren't forced to take the other guy! Remember, you can't complain if you don't vote!" The canned audience hooted and hollered its approval of the popular banality.

"Let me ask you something," Nick said. "Say you go to the grocery store and you find all the vegetables rotten and the meat spoiled—do you have to buy something, or should you be free not to shop at that store?"

"But there aren't any other stores in our system!"

There was a pause on the line. "Are you arguing with me or agreeing?"

There was another pause. "What's your point?"

"All I'm saying is, the only people who don't have a right to complain are the ones who don't pay taxes. If you don't vote, but you're willing fund the system others vote on, I say you can complain all you want."

"Hey, Nancy," Winston said to his in-studio producer. "You're supposed to weed out the crackpots! Audience, whaddya say?"

"Booooo!" The audience howled its disapproval.

"You're outta here!" Winston disconnected the caller. "We don't need your libertarian negativism!"

The canned audience yelled, "Amen, Archer!"

"Hey, Nick, if you're still listening, I got a statistic for you. Forty-five percent more Russians turned out to vote in their 1996 presidential election than Americans did in that same year. I think that tells you all you need to know about whether you should vote! Anyway, whew, the wackos are out there, aren't they? Stay with us. When we come back, we'll discuss some interesting legislation that would allow public schools to segregate deviants and biological errors from the rest of our children." The canned audience hooted and whistled. "You won't believe what some people are saying about this!"

Connie rolled her eyes at the radio sideshow. She actually knew people who had AMEN, ARCHER bumper stickers, and it wasn't just the anti–Mark Twain contingent.

Boyd Jr. shuffled into the kitchen and grabbed a handful of bacon. "Hey, Mom, where's Dad?" He slid the strips of warm pork into his mouth.

"He went to the hospital. Gramma Rose is having her operation today." She cracked three eggs and scrambled them in the hot animal fat.

"Cool. Can I get her old heart in a jar?"

"We'll see, honey."

6

Heart of the Matter

Boyd's 1965 Mustang wasn't what it used to be. According to its previous owner, the car had come off the line with a 289 V-8, an automatic three-speed transmission, 3.80 rear end, and drum brakes. When Boyd bought it, it had a 302 V-8, a four-speed tranny, 4.56 full posi rear, and four-wheel disk brakes. The paint job was new but loyal to the original Wimbledon white roof and poppy red body. The interior was all new white vinyl with red trim.

The car harked back to a more innocent time. A time when *The Fugitive* was one of the most popular shows on television. A time when "Help Me Rhonda," "I Can't Help Myself," and "Help!" issued from the AM radio, which was one of the few things still factory-original with the car. But, most important, it harked back to that more innocent time when neither Boyd nor Spence was being hunted by the Federal Bureau of Investigation or the National Security Agency.

They were on I-5 approaching the northernmost reaches of greater Los Angeles. After the raving panic of the previous hour, a relative tranquility had settled into the cramped interior of the Mustang. For Boyd, who was driving, it was a sort of quiet dread, a calm before the storm that would end life as he knew it, probably in a hail of gunfire, widowing Connie. Whoa. He hadn't thought about that. What if he was killed? Oh, he'd made sure Connie and the kids would be taken care of, but the thought of never seeing them again was crushing, the thought that he had kissed Connie good-bye for the last time was— *Wait. I did kiss her good-bye this morning, didn't I?* He wasn't sure, and that bit of doubt brought to the fore something that had lurked in the back of his mind for too long. *Have I been a good husband? Did I deserve to have a woman as good as Connie? She's going to be so disappointed when she finds out what I've done. Jesus, that's an understatement. She's going to think I've lost my mind!* Boyd began to count the ways in which he felt he failed to measure up.

For Spence, who was riding shotgun with Officer Bobb's Glock in his lap, the calm was an opportunity to focus and try to figure how in hell he was going to save his mother's life and then, maybe, his own. He wished he knew more about criminal law.

Officer Bobb was sitting behind Boyd wearing only

his briefs. At first he couldn't bring himself to put his uniform back on, because Spence had gotten it so sweaty. Now, with his full, muscular body folded like a contortionist's into the back of the tiny car, it was simply too hot to consider it. He struggled to lean forward to look at the dashboard. He mumbled something through the duct tape while nodding at the air-conditioning.

"Sorry," Boyd said. "That's all she's got."

Officer Bobb slid back into the semibucket of the rear seat, where his sweat was pooling, still stunned that he had come out the way he had. He was stewing in an uneasy gumbo of anxiety and relief as he imagined the conversation he would have with his parents. He was pretty sure his mother already knew—in fact, he would bet she'd known since he was a little boy, even though she'd never said a word. But his father. Oh, God, telling his father wouldn't be easy.

He looked at his right hand, which was cuffed to Debbie's left, forming a sort of seat belt for Rose, who, being the smallest passenger, was perched on the hump of the rear bench seat, still dozing peacefully on benzodiazepam.

Debbie was behind Spence trying to figure out what to do. Since being moved to the Mustang, she'd been feigning unconsciousness waiting for an opportunity to do something. She wasn't sure what, but it seemed that she should have a plan of some sort in the event a chance presented itself. She didn't think Spence and Boyd were dangerous men—just desperate to help their mother. Still, desperate men were capable of— Debbie had a sudden thought. The thing she was supposed to remember. But what the hell was it? She almost had it but, just like that, gone. Damn it.

"I say we drop them off in Palmdale," Boyd said out of the blue.

"What?" Spence said. "Are you nuts? We gotta think basic hostage strategy here. We need bargaining chips in case we get caught. Besides, they'd tell if we let 'em go, and we'd be in custody before we got out of the county." Spence looked at Officer Bobb. "You'd tell, right?" Officer Bobb nodded. "See? Plus, Mom might need the doctor."

"The doctor's in a coma!" Boyd pounded the steering wheel. "Christ on a crutch! What statutes apply here? Like the Lindbergh Law? What's the story on that? Can they execute you for kidnapping?" Boyd's face soured momentarily before expressing curiosity. "Do you get a choice? I think I'd prefer lethal injection, or is Florida lethal injection and it's gas in California?" He hit Spence. "You're the lawyer, you're supposed to know this kind of stuff!"

"Would you stop worrying?" Spence said. "We only execute the poor in this country."

Officer Bobb made some noises like he wanted to say something. Figuring it couldn't hurt, Spence reached back and pulled the tape off his mouth. "And the retarded," Officer Bobb said. "They execute the retarded down in Texas."

"That's right," Spence said. "But only poor ones, and not as often as they used to. Still, since you're not a poor, retarded Texan, Boyd, you need to stop worrying about that. Besides, we didn't kidnap the doctor. She jumped in of her own accord."

"But you kidnapped a cop, you . . . *idiot!*"

"Well, technically, you *both* kidnapped me," Officer Bobb said. "So you'll both be, uh, tried on that. Sorry."

"Hey, can I add something?" It was Debbie, sitting up, an eggplant bruise on her forehead, her eyes bright with fury. She had a plan.

Spence turned without considering his hostage's potential attitude. Debbie's punch landed square on his nose. Blood spurted out, spilling on to Spence's scrubs. "Ow! Crap!" Now he looked like a working surgeon.

The sudden display of violence frightened Boyd, and he nearly lost control of the Mustang. The car swerved onto the shoulder.

"Boyd! Stay on the road!" Spence screamed as he groped around the floor and the console and the glove compartment until he found a napkin. "Jesus, that hurt!" He twisted the napkin and stuck it up his nose just as Boyd regained control of the car. "Why the hell'd you do that?"

"You kidnapped me!" Debbie began struggling wildly, reaching for Spence's throat, the handcuffs wrenching Officer Bobb's wrist.

"Ow! Hey, watch the hand, please."

"Let me go!"

Spence snatched the Glock from his lap, jerked around, and jammed it onto the tip of Debbie's nose. She froze, eyes crossed. Spence glared at her, his jaw set, the bloody napkin a red stalactite dropping from his nostril.

He peered over the gun's sight and spoke frankly between clenched teeth. "I'd appreciate it if you wouldn't mess with me right now. I'm having a really bad day."

Joshua Whitcomb, president and CEO of the pharmaceutical juggernaut Lumpkin-Whitcomb, smiled at his friend from the Food and Drug Administration and said, "As you know, Jim, our new erectile-dysfunction drug, Mycoxaflopin, has a potential market estimated at two billion dollars. Naturally we're very excited about that. But we're even more excited about the vital societal benefits and the significant impact it will have on our local economy."

White House chief of staff Martin Brooks spoke up. "Oh, a huge impact. Staggering," he said with a knowing wave of his hand. "Increased tax base, lower unemployment . . . classic trickle-down situation, everybody wins."

They were meeting in the Oval Office. Seated around the coffee table with Brooks and Whitcomb were Dr. Jim Thomas, director of the Office of Blood Therapeutics Research and Review—a division of the FDA's Center for Biologics Evaluation and Research—and, as it happened, a Yale classmate of both Brooks and Whitcomb.

Jim nodded. He understood. He'd been with the Center for BE&R for twenty years. In fact, Jim was less than a year from retiring from the FDA and was looking forward to cashing in on his years of experience with the regulatory agency by taking a lucrative job in the pharmaceutical industry, possibly even with Lumpkin-Whitcomb. "Josh," he said, "I know we're on the same page here. My only problem—the one I wanted to discuss with you today—is that research assistant's memo citing the test results indicating Mycoxaflopin causes life-threatening kidney damage."

Joshua Whitcomb's expression changed to reflect his concern on this matter. "Yes, well, of course we've seen those test results, Jim, and, quite frankly, the numbers just aren't supportable."

"Completely unsupportable," Brooks said. "The president agrees."

Jim Thomas shook his head. "Well, we can't have that."

Martin Brooks held up a thick, bound document. "Now, according to this report from the Senate ad hoc bipartisan blue-ribbon panel on erectile dysfunction, the occurrences, in clinical studies, of kidney damage among Mycoxaflopin patients were *comparable to placebo.*" Brooks stressed those last three words. "You can't flag Mycoxaflopin with numbers like those. That's bad science. It's the sort of thing that prevents good medicine from getting to the market, and that has a negative effect downstream on the economy."

Jim seemed thankful to receive the report. It would support his position in case things blew up in his face. And he could always deny knowing that the blue-ribbon panel consisted of Lumpkin-Whitcomb's board of directors, many of whom were qualified to make scientific judgments of this nature absent any conflict of interest— which of course wasn't absent.

Martin Brooks continued, "Jim, you know this administration was elected in part because of our promise to trim bureaucracy. Hell, we're the antibureaucracy administration. We want to make government less intrusive and obstructive to the private sector. To put it plainly, the president would like to see the FDA start acting more like a partner with the pharmaceutical industry rather than an adversary. Do you know what I mean?"

Jim nodded. He understood. "Of course the research assistant has been reassigned, Marty, but the memo . . . well, you understand I'm concerned about the Freedom of Information Act. And I was wondering if you had any thoughts about that."

"I'm sure you can find some way to make sure it's not FOI-able, Jim. And we'd like to see you chair any public FDA hearings on the matter to make sure no one cites it. We don't want Health and Human Services to look like they're dabbling in bad science."

"Nooo, of course not." Jim Thomas knew that if Lumpkin-Whitcomb's sales numbers were right, Mycoxaflopin would kill nearly four hundred users, most deaths involving kidney damage, in its first year of sales. The thing was, though, he also knew that recently passed legislation capped the amount of punitive damages for which corporations were liable in product-liability and wrongful-death lawsuits, so profits from the sales of Mycoxaflopin would far exceed the cost of settling with the families of the dead. Jim tapped the report from the Senate panel on erectile dysfunction. "Well, based on the research and recommendations contained in this, I'm sure we can generate a memo saying causality is indeterminable. That shouldn't be difficult."

Martin Brooks gestured at his friends. "I like a problem solver." He stood, indicating the end of the meeting. "Jim, I think this has been an unusually fruitful discussion."

"Yes," Joshua agreed. "It's been extremely helpful, and I'd just like to mention how much Lumpkin-Whitcomb appreciates your candor and your concern on this issue. And let me reiterate my invitation to you should you decide to move to the private sector." There were smiles all around as they shook hands and asked about one another's wives and children. Brooks then walked Joshua and Jim to the door, where they said their final good-byes.

As soon as they were gone, Martin Brooks's assistant, Grant, emerged from the shadows. "Sir, you're due with the Fed chairman in ten minutes."

"Walk me to the car." As the two men headed down the hallway, Martin Brooks turned to Grant. "Are we making *any* damn progress finding that heart?"

"Sir, we learned they escaped in a beige Chevrolet pickup, but we haven't been able to locate it yet."

"Christ Almighty." He gestured toward the ceiling. "Damn sky's full of birds they tell me are capable of reading people's retinas, but we can't find one beige Chevy. What good does that do us?"

"Yes, sir. Of course we're still looking."

But it didn't matter. The truck would never be found,

and it wasn't the fault of American intelligence-gathering satellites. Turned out that ten minutes after the Tailor clan took off in the Mustang, the truck had been stolen by a gang of professional car thieves and was currently being parted out in a garage in East L.A.

"So," Brooks said, "we don't have any description of the vehicle the terrorists are in or where they're heading? Hell, they're probably in Mexico by now. Or they're heading east on I-10 or north on I-5 or going up the coast on Highway 1 or the 101 or— Shit, what're we going to do, shut down every highway and interstate in Southern California? How the hell would we explain that?"

"Sir, we'll start by expanding the search to recently stolen and rented vehicles."

"Brilliant. And make sure we've got a good eye on the border crossings at San Ysidro and Tecate."

"Yes, sir."

Brooks stopped when they reached the door leading outside. "Has anybody taken credit for this yet?"

Grant shook his head. "Not yet, sir."

"How the hell are we supposed to know what they want if they don't tell us who they are or why they've done what they've done? Fucking amateurs. All right, make sure we're tapped in tight at all the news orgs. I don't want this to sneak past us. Anything else?"

"Sir, I thought you might appreciate this. The heart? It came from a black man."

"Hmmmm." Brooks paused to consider the political implications of this. "That's good," he said. "If, by some damn miracle, this happens to work out, we'll end up with a JFK and Martin Luther King Jr. all sewn up in one package."

"Yes, sir, that'll deliver the Volvo Conservatives and the Urban Midscales, all right."

For just a moment Martin Brooks wondered about the feasibility of getting a Hispanic kidney, but he let it go. He was too busy as it was. "All right, what else?"

"We picked up a point in the latest polls, sir, so we're only down one."

Brooks smiled. "Man's in a coma and he gains a point." He shook his head. "Things might not be as bad as I thought. Anything else?"

"That's it, sir." Grant opened the door for his boss. "Your car's waiting."

Martin Brooks stepped outside and headed for his black Yukon XL. There was a group of reporters standing behind a rope line by the main driveway of the White House still making notes after an impromptu news conference with the secretary of the interior, who had met with Brooks just prior to the meeting with Thomas and Whitcomb. Martin Brooks smiled and waved at the press. *Jackals, every one of you*, he thought.

When they saw the chief of staff approaching his car, they called out his name. "Mr. Brooks! Mr. Brooks!" One of the reporters yelled a question about President Webster. "Why has he rescheduled all his meetings and public appearances?"

"Well, first of all, he *hasn't* rescheduled all his meetings. He's cut back, yes, but he's been out a few times. You must have been napping." He smiled. "I won't tell your boss if you won't." He winked.

"There are rumors that your office has been in touch with Dr. Nichols at Bethesda. Have those contacts been in regard to the president's heart?"

"Well, of course. We don't want to leave any stone unturned. But the president's fine. I was just in a meeting with him. He looks great, by the way." *He says he wishes you'd all get an anthrax-laced letter in the mail.*

"What about claims that the president needs a heart?" one of them yelled.

Martin Brooks snapped his head straight. "I'd say that's an unfair characterization. What about the underprivileged children's literacy program? Heck, I'd say the president's all heart. Now, if you'll excuse me. I have a meeting with the Fed."

It was against Mulholland Memorial policy, but one of the respiratory therapists needed a smoke, so she sneaked into the stairwell to have a cigarette. That's where she stumbled across a heap of flesh that was formerly the security guard. With smoke curling into her eyes, the respiratory therapist gave him a cursory examination. He was still breathing, his bleeding was superficial, and he didn't appear to be in any pain whatsoever. The respiratory therapist figured the security guard wouldn't be any worse off by the time she finished her cigarette than he was at the moment, so she took her time and enjoyed.

After crushing out her butt, she returned to her office and put in an anonymous call for help.

They laid the security guard on a gurney and rushed him to the ER, where the attending physician eventually declared the man comatose. About half an hour later there were several more people crowded into the trauma slot to confer over the man's body. "What the hell happened to this guy?" one of them asked.

The attending physician looked at his clipboard. "Tox report shows morphine. My guess is our security man here was shooting up in the stairwell. Afterward he missed a step, stumbled down the stairs, landing on his face several times along the way. Never felt a thing."

"Sure made a mess of those teeth," a resident said. "Did they find his rig?"

"They're still looking for it, but it's like trying to find a needle in a haystack of cigarette butts. You know how trashy those stairwells are."

A man who had been hunkered over the security guard's body stood up and yelled, "Woo-hoo!"

"Whatcha got there, Chalmers? Organ-donor card?"

When in the course of human events a politician is invited to be on a television talk show, it becomes necessary for her to wear something that will appeal to voters. On the flight back from the Charlotte fund-raiser, Senator Check was trying on different outfits. She had passed on the urbane Evelyn Stokes pantsuit with its black matte jersey halter top and matching black crystal skirt.

She had also rejected, as too risqué, the black, lizardskin-belted bustier and zebra silk organza bias pants ensemble by designer Brian Meehl, an outfit the trades had hailed as "startlingly original trashy chic."

The door to the bathroom was cracked open just enough for the senator to carry on a conversation with her assistant, Britton Belk, who was standing outside trying to explain President Webster's recent one-point gain in the polls. "It's a sympathy point," she said. "The public feels sorry for him because he fell down and got his head stepped on and the whole thing was broadcast around the world, making him look like a fool. The media consultants call it the 'poor guy' response. Gerald Ford made hay with the strategy for years. They sold him as the lovable klutz, and the public bought."

Senator Check's face appeared in the crack of the doorway. "You're saying Ford wasn't a klutz?"

"Senator, I don't think anyone that physically inept would ever reach breeding age."

Her face disappeared. "Boil it down," she said.

"As long as the public perception of President Webster is that he's clumsy but otherwise physically viable, a majority will vote for him. It's the value of incumbency."

"So you're suggesting I bite the sidewalk every time I see a television camera?"

"No, ma'am, the consultants tested that. They found it to be a turnoff to voters in key electoral states, though they couldn't tease out the reason for the underlying double standard. I think your best tactic is to take advantage of your television appearance to counter Webster's surge in the polls."

Senator Check thought about it a moment. She smoothed the front of her jacket. "Fine," she said. "I'll take a leak on Matt Christopher."

"Yes, ma'am," Britton said. "I think now's the right time."

Back in Washington, Senator Check arrived at the television studios wearing a Donna Karan black wool layered jacket and a black wool gauze skirt with silver pinstripes. Dominating yet chic in a middle-of-the-road sort of way.

The senator was making her twenty-third appearance on *HardHeads with Matt Christopher*, one of those pundit outlets where political adversaries sat across the table from one another barking like dogs on opposite sides of a fence, never finishing a thought or providing verifiable evidence to support their claims. On occasions when there was only one guest, the host would throw out a series of questions, interrupting the guest before he or she could finish giving a single complete answer. The most notable aspect of the program was the way in which it created the illusion that intelligent people were engaged in an ideological debate.

The host, Matt Christopher, had the dark-haired swagger of a man who wasn't accountable for anything. He tended to lean forward on crossed arms, a combination of bluster and family money. "Welcome to *HardHeads*," he barked coming out of the intro. "My guest is Senator Peggy Check of Virginia. In addition to being the first viable female presidential candidate since Elizabeth Dole, Senator Check is a member of the Senate Commerce, Science, and Transportation Committee, which has oversight for Internet regulation, which is what we want to talk about today. So. Are we ready? Let's be HardHeads!" Matt turned from the camera to his guest. "Senator Check, let's begin with the Internet Regulatory Freedom Act. It's designed to eliminate unnecessary FCC regulation that would increase the cost of Internet service to end users. Now, your committee seems intent on castrating this legislation, and a lot of Americans would like to know why."

"Well, Matt, let me start by—"

"How about let's start with some reasonable justification for a bloated and inefficient bureaucracy impeding the American public's access to the Internet?"

"I think we need first to examine why we have federal regulation at all. Most people are aware of—"

"The classic examples. Salinger's gaffe about the navy's shooting down TWA Flight 800. FBI, Pentagon, and federal air-safety investigators all discredited his missile theory after the July '96 crash. NTSB chairman Hall called Salinger's allegations 'irresponsible.'"

"And rightly so. Another—"

"Three years later the PairGain Technology fraud. April sixth, PairGain common stock closed at eight-fifty per share. April 7, bogus merger report posted on the Internet prompts a buying frenzy pushing the price up to eleven twenty-five per share."

"So you can see—"

"What I can see, and what I think most people see, is the federal government imposing repressive regulations on Internet use while citing two aberrations, and old ones at that."

"Well, how about a more—"

"How about a more recent example, Senator?"

"Okay, yesterday—"

Matt slapped his hand on the desktop. "Now you're talking!"

"Yesterday I was on my way to meet the majority leader when I saw a television news broadcast reporting an anonymous-source rumor—"

"An anonymous-source rumor! We love those!"

"A rumor that President Webster's recent fainting spell was actually a heart attack and—"

"Senator, wait!" Matt looked like he might flip over backward in his chair. "Are you saying the president had a heart attack? The whole fainting story is a lie? That the current administration is involved in a cover-up? Those are explosive accusations!"

"I'm not accusing the current administration of anything, Matt. If you'll—"

"Then what's your point? Why bring me this bone if I can't chew on it a little?"

"Because it's an example of what we're talking about vis-à-vis the need for Internet regulation and—"

"That's my point exactly! Go ahead, Senator."

"I was shocked that this uncorroborated statement about the president's health was out there. My staff tracked the source, which turned out to be nothing more than a comment posted on a Web site that—"

"That's wild! What's the address?"

"Oh, it's www dot, uh, something dot whatever, but that—"

"Sounds like one of those conspiracy-nut Web sites where everyone posts three-hundred-thousand-word manifestos about the Trilateral Commission and the Freemasons running the world. I love those! All these yahoos out there weaving conspiracies that don't even make sense—like Queen Elizabeth being in cahoots with Bavarian Illuminati and child-sex-slave traders in the Far East. Is that the sort of thing you found at this site?"

"Well, there was a claim on the site about an alleged incident this morning—"

"An alleged incident? Those conspiracy nuts allege the wildest things!"

"Yes, at Mulholland Memorial Hospital in Los Angeles, where—"

"What was the allegation? It sounds like that's where the meat is on this bone."

"Matt, I'm telling you, this was beyond the pale. Crazy stuff like the president needing a heart transplant, so the NSA or the FBI was sent to get a heart for him—"

Matt pounded a fist on the table, grinning to beat the band. "This is great!"

"—accused them of stealing the heart from some sweet old lady who was supposed to—"

"In other words, a complete fairy tale."

"Absolutely, but the story somehow got picked up by

the networks without anyone's vetting it. As far as we know, it's a total fabrication, and that's my point."

"That's your point exactly!"

"The Internet needs to be regulated because it is such a potentially empowering medium but at the same time it's ripe for abuse, and—"

"But you agree that everyone should have access to it at a reasonable price?"

"Of course, but we must provide some protections for—"

"Otherwise, you're saying stories like this one, rumors and alleged incidents, not stories, about the president having a heart attack and the government stealing a heart might receive television news coverage which ends up lending the claims unwarranted legitimacy?"

"Exactly."

"Senator, your theory sounds pretty far-fetched to me. I mean, what does your committee propose? That they can legislate a certain level of cynicism? You can't stop gullibility with laws any more than you can stop racism. I mean, if we haven't learned anything in the past fifty years, haven't we learned that? But I think we'll have to take that up on another show, because we're out of time for this segment. Senator, thanks for being here."

"My pleasure, Matt."

"*HardHeads* will be right back!"

Traffic was at a standstill. Spence was staring at the bumper of the car in front of them. It was covered with stickers. One of them read EVERY VOTE COUNTS!* Below that the asterisk explained: (*MAY NOT APPLY IN ALL STATES).

They'd been in the Mustang for nearly an hour trying to get out of Los Angeles. Perversely, the farther they got from the center of town, the more the traffic slowed, as if there were some sort of gravitational pull caused by the density of celebrities. They started out on the 405, and, after they'd merged with I-5 at the north end of the San Fernando Valley, the radio traffic reporter finally mentioned the half-hour-old multicar pileup that lay eight miles ahead. That explained the crawl. Spence told Boyd to take Highway 14 and head into the desert. Into the sun. In July.

Debbie said, "Mmmmm." Then, perhaps to clarify, she continued by saying, "Rrrgd efft dvrft." After her earlier outburst Spence had cuffed Debbie's hands behind her back and slapped her in the face with a strip of duct tape. For the past hour she'd been wiggling around in her seat saying things like "Rrrgd efft dvrft," which one would assume were wry observations about the skill level of her kidnappers. Debbie was about to say something else when she realized she wasn't in much of a position to be casting aspersions, seeing as how she was still genuinely chagrined that her own plan—the alpha and omega of which had consisted of punching Spence in the nose—had been so ill conceived. However, in her defense, she thought it only fair to keep in mind that this was her first time as a kidnap victim. The only undeniably embarrassing thing was that she had essentially volunteered for the job.

Meanwhile, Boyd was at the wheel, tied off and main-lining despair. His pupils were fixed on the road ahead like it was the only future he had. What had he done to deserve this? he wondered. This was no small rebuke by fate. This was a prison-yard assault, and he would just have to bend over and take it dry, as it were. *Connie is bound to leave me after this. And where will I be then? I'll be lost, that's where. And it's my own damn fault. I wasn't there as much as I should have been. God, I can't believe I made that comment at dinner the other night about settling for what you can get. She's the one who settled. I've got to call her and tell her how sorry I am.* Boyd obsessed like this for another mile or so before punching Spence in the chest. "You moron!"

Spence recoiled. "Ow!" The vibration throbbed up to his nose. "Stop hitting me!" He didn't think his nose was broken, but it sure hurt. "Like this is what I wanted to happen." Spence turned to look at his mom in the back-seat. She looked peaceful, if not exactly in the pink. He wondered if she would look so serene lying in her casket, which is where she'd be pretty soon if she didn't get the heart transplant. He thought about that. She would be dead soon. His mother would be dead. D-e-d. Soon. Death. Death. Death. Till death do us part. Death was nature's way of saying howdy. What was the Fran Lebowitz quip? *There is no such thing as inner peace. There is only nervousness and death.* Spence looked out the window to the side of the road and saw trash. Miles of it. Cigarette butts, broken bottles, used diapers. *The things people will throw out the window of a moving car,* he thought. Then a possum. Dead. Spence looked away, yet he couldn't help but wonder if it was an omen.

About three minutes later it happened again. Boyd took the exit off I-5 onto an elevated transition road, sloping and curved high above the ground, carrying traffic to Highway 14. Then the sign: CLARENCE WAYNE DEAN MEMORIAL INTERCHANGE. Like everyone else in the world, Spence had seen photographs of this otherwise indistinct crescent of concrete after the 1994 Northridge earthquake. Clarence Wayne Dean was the LAPD motorcycle officer who plunged to his death in the darkness after the quake had caused a section of the elevated roadway to collapse. A good guy on his way to help. Now he was dead. The Grim Reaper was taunting Spence from the roadside like a morbid hitchhiker, his bony thumb held high in the air.

Spence held his own hand in front of the air-conditioning unit, one of those under-the-dash installs in the '65 Mustang with the fifties sci-fi cone-shaped chrome air vents. He looked to see that the vents were pointed his way. "Does this thing even work?" He wiped the sweat from his face. The sun was barely up, and it was already eighty-eight degrees.

Officer Bobb leaned forward, touching Boyd's soft shoulder. "Yeah, we're really not getting anything back here."

"Get off my case about the AC," Boyd barked.

"Sorry," Officer Bobb said. "Whatever. I'll just stay in my underwear." He looked at Rose. "It's a good thing she's wearing this thin hospital gown. At least she won't die of heatstroke."

Spence turned to glare at Officer Bobb. "Hey," he said, offended. "Do you mind?" He slowly turned back around and looked at the long road that lay ahead of them.

Both the Senate and the House have armed-services committees with general oversight of U.S. military forces. The authorizing subcommittee in the Senate for much of the Department of Defense's Research and Development was the Senate Subcommittee on Emerging Threats and Capabilities. The comparable subcommittee on the House side was the Armed Services Subcommittee on Military R&D.

Like the rest of Congress, the armed-services committees deal primarily with two types of bills: authorization and appropriation. Authorizing legislation gives a federal department or agency permission to spend money and set policy direction; appropriation provides the actual money.

And that's where the fun begins.

Each year Congress passes the Department of Defense Authorization Act. Section 103 of the act pertains to the U.S. Air Force. In the most recent DOD Authorization Act, Congress approved the following appropriations for procurement for the air force: (1) for aircraft, $11,968,371,000; (2) for ammunition, $789,808,000; (3) for missiles, $3,878,915,000; (4) for *other procurement*, $9,724,527,000.

Now, granted, $10 billion didn't procure as much *other* as it used to, but there were senators and representatives from both parties dedicated to ensuring that some of that *other* was spent in their home districts. And it was in this spirit of reaching across the aisle to pass the pork that the project known as CP-1 was born.

The project was named after the recently divested program known as Heliborne Prophet, which was the Armored Cavalry Regiment commander's principal signals-intelligence and electronic-warfare system. That system in turn had been named for the Prophets—Delta Company, 104th Military Intelligence Battalion, Fourth Infantry Division, and the unit it was reflagged from, the 522nd Military Intelligence Battalion, Second Armored Division, who were known as the Original Prophets.

CP-1, or Colossal Prophet-1 was touted as an innovative blend of technologies. Part V-22 Osprey, part Bradley Infantry Fighting Vehicle, part Ford Pinto, all run by a Windows Operating System. It was more than two hundred feet long and, in theory, exceeded every aircraft ever built in every statistical category, from maximum takeoff weight to top speed to armament to highest per-unit cost. It was capable of circling half the globe without refueling and was said to be invisible to all types of radar and heat-seeking missiles. It was a marvel of aeronautical engineering that brought together technologies from highly profitable corporations all over the United States, all of which happened to be major contributors to both parties of the democratic process as currently practiced. But more amazing than its third-generation stealth technology was how it disappeared on paper under the words "other procurement."

Today's unveiling of the CP-1 had brought together the Republican senator from New York and the Democratic senator from Georgia, the chairman and ranking minority member on the Emerging Threats and Capabilities subcommittee respectively, along with representatives from Texas, California, and Michigan who sat on the Armed Services Subcommittee on Military R&D. Also present were two dozen air force officials and project managers, as well as the CEOs from Northrop Grumman, Boeing Military Airplanes, Vought Aircraft, and General Electric Aircraft Engine Group, General Atomics, Data Device Corporation, Varo LLC, and dozens of other defense contractors.

After a surprising rash of budget overruns and completion delays, the final development cost on the CP-1 would be $457 million. Estimated production cost was $298 million per aircraft. Once the CP-1 was a proven entity, sales in the hundreds of units were projected. Welcome news to many thousands of working voters in California, New York, Georgia, Michigan, and Texas.

Today's unmanned flight was at a highly restricted airfield in a dry lake bed in the Mojave Desert. It was part of the R-2508 Complex, a tri-service testing range used by the DOD for research and development of weapons-systems technology. R-2508 was comprised of the Fort Irwin National Training Center, the Naval Air Warfare Center Weapons Division at China Lake, and Edwards Air Force Base.

It was early, and the dignitaries were in the grandstand with binoculars. Someone made a stirring speech in the crackling desert air, and then the huge doors to the hangar opened and the CP-1 emerged. It was a machine of mythic proportions. A wingspan the likes of which no one had seen since Howard Hughes's "Spruce Goose." It was black and seemed to absorb the early-morning desert sunlight. With its sharp angles and oddly reflective surface, it looked to be sculpted from obsidian. The CP-1 taxied to the end of the runway and began spooling its massive General Electric F-101-GE-102-XL turbofan engines, burning the first of the sixty thousand gallons of military aviation jet fuel on board.

The senator from New York stood a little bit taller when he thought about the enormity of the contributions to his political party made by some of the corporations represented here today. He turned to his friend and colleague, the senator from Georgia. He smiled. "Is this a great country or what?"

7

Save Your Heart for Me

Spence looked at Rose, then at Boyd. "Do you think it's okay she's still out?"

Boyd shrugged. "Probably better if she stays that way."

This time Spence punched Boyd hard enough to bruise. "Don't even think it," Spence said. "And I swear to God, if you say it again, we'll pull over and I'll kick your fat ass from here to Fresno. Jesus." His shook his head.

Debbie added her two cents. "Mrft kuuhn ehlks!"

Officer Bobb looked at her and wondered why he didn't find her attractive in a sexual way. She *was* attractive. So how come that didn't trigger anything? He looked again. Well, okay, she wasn't beautiful. Her lips were a bit thin, and her hair was a mess. Still, most guys would go for it, but not him. He didn't get it. What was it? Was it a gene? A chromosome? Something that had happened in his childhood? Was it something he could change? Did he want to? It was all so confusing. Maybe, he thought, in a weird way this whole kidnapping thing could turn out to be just what he needed. A chance to think things through, find out who he really was.

Highway 14 traversed a broad swath cut through the Angeles National Forest, though just by looking you'd never guess you were near so much as a tree farm, let alone a national forest. The hardworking people who supplied La La Land with an ever expanding workforce had to live somewhere, even if it was row upon row of tract housing, like dog kennels. Spence wondered how the owners could tell their houses apart.

Half an hour after turning on to Highway 14, the Mustang struggled over Soledad Pass before plunging into the grit that was the Antelope Valley, home, in the 1950s, to Frank Zappa and Captain Beefheart. Two hundred years before the Mothers of Invention, however, it was the home of the Kitanemuk, Chumash, and Shoshone Indian tribes. The area had been a hunting ground for antelope and, as irony had it, an escape route for bandits.

Spence stared out the window as they passed the factory-outlet stores, fast-food joints, and auto malls sprouting like warts among Joshua trees, creosote bush, and jimsonweed. Then a billboard caught his eye. A picture of a high-school cheerleader and words spelled out in letters two feet tall: I WASN'T READY TO DIE. CAN YOU HELP CATCH MY KILLER? There was her name and a number to call if you had information leading to the arrest and conviction of the guilty. Right there on the roadside. Lord, what a gruesome route they were on, Spence thought, like the Antelope was the Valley of the Shadow of Death. His mother's death. Spence turned and saw Officer Bobb dabbing the perspiration from Rose's forehead. "How's she doing?"

"Still sleeping."

"How 'bout Mike Tyson?"

Debbie tried to yell, "Ooh uff urhfff!"

"She's still pretty pissy," Officer Bobb said. He looked at her face. *Would it hurt her to wear a little makeup?* he thought. Debbie turned and looked at him like she had something to say, but he avoided eye contact and instead looked out the tiny triangular window on his side of the car. She wiggled violently to get his attention. He looked at her again and saw she wanted to communicate somehow. Probably wanted to plan an escape. He just shook his head and turned back to the window.

Debbie was baffled. Exactly who was this nearly naked man? And why was he nearly naked? She'd tried to make eye contact with him so they could conspire, but he seemed uninterested, lost in his own thoughts. Still, she had to give him this: He had great skin. A complexion she would kill for. Nonetheless, he wasn't a lot of help under the circumstances. *Fine,* she thought, *I'm on my own.*

They were in heavy traffic. Debbie was looking for a way to signal one of the passing cars, but with her hands cuffed behind her and Spence's seat pushed back, she was pinned down. She couldn't even press her taped mouth to the Mustang's puny back window. *Just be patient*, she thought. An opportunity of some sort would present itself sooner or later.

They drove through Palmdale and then Lancaster, where Spence saw another billboard. This one featured a smug crocodile smoking a cigarette and the words 400,000 TOBACCO-RELATED DEATHS A YEAR. The reptile, being the tobacco industry, was saying, "Too bad. They were some of our best customers." Spence finally had to smile. He knew these reminders of death were everywhere if you just looked for them. He was simply hypersensitive at the moment, owing to the fact that his mother was in the backseat reaching for the knocker on death's door.

After Lancaster they drove the twenty miles along the western border of Edwards Air Force Base before arriving at the town of Mojave. A crossroads. "Now what?" Boyd asked.

Spence consulted his map. "The choices are 58 West to Tehachapi and Bakersfield, which gets us back to I-5 and Highway 99. If we take the 58 East, we go to Barstow. If we stay on the 14, we end up in Bishop and Mammoth. That's no good." He studied the map for a moment. "The 58 East gives us the most options. It'll take us to I-15 and I-40."

Boyd turned east and floored the Mustang. He noticed the fuel gauge leaning to the left and thought maybe he should just let the car run out of gas. If he couldn't get Spence to agree to surrender, maybe that was his best bet. Get arrested by the Auto Club. "So, boy genius, let me ask you," Boyd said. "Where're we going at ninety miles an hour, and what the hell are we going to do when we get there?"

Debbie chuckled darkly behind the duct tape as she shook her head.

"The doctor's mocking us," Spence said in dejected tones.

"And why not?" Boyd asked. "We're highly mockable."

Spence was beginning to wonder—really wonder—what the hell he was going to do. He knew he'd done the right thing. He just didn't know what the *next* right thing was.

"Mmmmphhh," Debbie said. "Trksph jes ejoibit rrrr."

"Did you hear that?" Boyd looked at Spence. "She said we should pull over, call a good lawyer, and start plea bargaining immediately."

"Mmmmmmphhh," Debbie said. "Blijj pfftrw rrrr."

"No, she's saying how sorry she is for breaking my damn nose." All of a sudden Spence reached back and yanked the tape off Debbie's mouth, figuring she could yell all she wanted out in the desert.

"Owww! God, that hurt."

"Yeah?" Spence pointed at his nose. "You oughta try one of these."

Officer Bobb noticed that Debbie's downy blond mustache had been removed with the duct tape. An improvement. But he wondered if it would grow back thicker.

"Yeah? Well, your brother almost killed me with his

stunt driving back . . . there." She paused, trying to gather her wits and thoughts and some air. She nodded toward the dashboard. "Hey, can you turn up that AC? It's really hot back here."

"Look," Boyd said. "This car wasn't meant for driving across the Mojave in July. At this speed, with this transmission, we're revving at fifty-two hundred rpm, which means we're probably burning out the compressor." His smile demented somewhat. "If you think it's hot now, just wait."

Debbie sat back. "Thanks, that's comforting." Debbie wiped her face with her sleeve, then leaned forward again to speak. "I'm just going to get to the point here, so if you'll forgive me for saying so, you two are screwed." She made a face she hoped would convey how serious she was. It consisted mainly of raised eyebrows and staring. She looked back and forth between the men. "Do you have any idea whose heart that is? Any idea? I mean, you can't possibly know. We wouldn't be here if you did."

"You're wrong," Spence said. He pointed to Rose. "It's hers."

Agent Hart had been quiet ever since they left Los Angeles. But finally, as Agent Rodgers turned to follow the Mustang onto Highway 58, Hart spoke. "The health maintenance," he said cryptically. "Organization my ass." There was a philosophical pause. "Hippocratic what?" Very dramatic.

Rodgers squinted. "Huh?" He looked in the rearview mirror.

"I told you. It's haiku, motherfucker."

"I know it's haiku," Rodgers said. "I just didn't get it. The health maintenance? What's that about? Say it again." His eyes glanced back at the mirror.

"No. It's the whole HMO thing." Agent Hart cupped his hands as if holding the poetry. "The health-maintenance organization my ass, don't you see?" He shook his head. "Forget it. I don't want to talk about it anymore."

"I know what it's about. I just want to hear it again."

"You don't get it."

"I do." He checked his side mirror. "It's a comment on the current state of the health-care industry."

"I don't want to talk about it."

Rodgers shrugged then nodded at the mirror. "Can you believe this son of a bitch in the SUV?"

"He's still on your ass?" Hart turned around and looked.

"Yeah, I'm tapping my brakes and whatever, and the moron just . . . looms."

"Big son of a bitch, too," Hart said. "What the hell is that anyway, that's gotta be eight thousand pounds? Seats about fifteen? And how many in there? One? They shouldn't let the public drive those things." He shook his head. "Well, you know what they say: big car, little dick." He picked up his binoculars and looked at the poppy red Mustang half a mile ahead of them. He turned up the volume to hear their conversation.

"*Right, fine,*" Debbie said. "*In the best of all possible worlds it's your mom's heart. But I'm here to tell you that's*" *not the kind of a world we live in. And I can't believe you two don't know that. Now, I hope that what I'm about to tell you will scare some sense into both of you. Maybe it won't but, here goes . . ."*

"Oh, this ought to be good," Rodgers said.

"I was about to put that heart aboard an FBI helicopter so it could be flown somewhere so they could transplant it into the president."

There was a pause before Spence said, *"What, like the president of Exxon-Mobil or something? See, Boyd? I told you it was some rich son of a bitch."*

"No," Debbie said. *"The president of the United States."*

The CIA men heard Boyd and Spence yell, *"What!"* Simultaneous with the exclamation, they saw the Mustang's tires lock up and skid to a stop in a cloud of blue smoke. Reacting instinctively, Agent Rodgers slammed on his own brakes, pitching the two agents forward. A rapid series of events then unfolded. The SUV hit them like a tank. They shot backward, then forward violently. Their air bags deployed, throwing them backward again. There was a brief hissing as the air bags deflated, followed by the sudden roar of the SUV as it passed them, horn blaring, as it took off down the highway.

"Hey," Agent Hart said, "I thought air bags weren't supposed to deploy in rear-end collisions."

Boyd had brought the Mustang to a dead stop in the fast lane. Cars were speeding past on the right, their drivers honking and yelling. Boyd sounded like a eunuch when he turned to Debbie and said, "As in 'Hail to the Chief'?"

Debbie nodded. "As in."

"Holy, holy, holy." Boyd was mesmerized by the depth of his trouble. The SUV roared past blasting its horn. The driver threw something out his window at them, snapping Boyd from his daze. He took his foot off the brake and accelerated. For a moment everyone was quiet, absorbing the information. After about a mile Boyd said, "The president of the United States." He paused, as if weighing the words. "President Webster." Boyd was doomed. "Did you hear that, baby brother?" He hit Spence again. "Are you satisfied now?"

Spence didn't respond to the punch or the questions. Was this possible? The implications seemed to paralyze his thought process.

Debbie leaned forward, hands behind her. "You've got to give it back. Do it now, and I'll tell the police you didn't kidnap me."

"We *didn't* kidnap you!" Spence insisted.

Boyd began muttering. "So if President Webster dies, it'll be John Wilkes Boothe . . ."

"Yes you did!"

". . . Lee Harvey Oswald, and the Tailor brothers."

"No, you jumped into the truck on your own."

"Won't Mom be proud?"

"Boyd, Mom will be dead if we turn ourselves in."

"And God help me, what is Connie going to think?"

"Look," Debbie said, "I understand what you're doing. I do. I can almost get behind you on this, but, I mean, you're talking about all the resources of the federal government out to get you. I mean, you saw the FBI agent . . ." Debbie paused, wondering where he'd disappeared to during the chase.

"I didn't see any FBI agent," Spence said.

"He was escorting me to the roof."

"Right," Spence said. "The FBI let me get away." Debbie opened her mouth to respond, but she didn't have an answer. Spence gestured at the ECC device. "And if that was going to the president, how come there's no sign of the CIA, NSA, Secret Service, FBI, ATF, U.S. marshals, or anybody else?"

"And nothing on the radio," Officer Bobb added.

Debbie didn't have an answer to that either. "Uh, well . . ."

Officer Bobb looked at her. "It's a good question."

Debbie turned and glared at the nearly naked man. "And just who the hell are you?"

"I'm Officer Bobb," he said. "I'm a policeman."

"Uh-huh." Debbie nodded at him. "And where are your policeman pants?"

"It's hot!"

Debbie turned back to Spence. "All right, listen, you've got a seriously ill woman here whom you obviously care about, yet you're hauling her around in the Mojave in an old car with bad air-conditioning."

"Hey! I don't want to hear another crack about the AC."

Debbie said, "What are you going to do? Stop at Mel's

Truck Plaza in Barstow where they do free organ grafts with every western omelette?"

Spence shook his head. "I haven't figured that out yet."

"No. Clearly. And that's not your biggest problem," she said. "The heart only has about another hour before it's completely useless, so if I were—"

"An hour?" Boyd turned to look at Spence. "We've only got an hour? What in the hell are— We're more than an hour from—" He hit Spence again. "Congratulations. You killed Mom *and* the president."

Spence smirked. "She's lying again," he said. "Like when she told me everything was going to be fine. The ischemic time for a heart is six hours." He hit Boyd. "Didn't you read any of the literature on this?"

"I was busy," Boyd said.

Spence pointed at Debbie. "So you're either a really bad doctor or you just lost your credibility." He shook his head. "The president's heart, my ass. I guess that tells us all we need to know." He turned to his brother, his confidence surging. "Boyd, I think you can relax about the feds."

Agent Hart looked like a black actor in whiteface as he tried to blink the cornstarch from his eyes. The air bags, which had hit them like powder puffs at two hundred miles an hour, now hung limp from their deployment modules like two sad, gray bosoms, leaving a dusty white reminder that looked funnier on Hart than on Rodgers.

Agent Hart climbed into the backseat of the sedan as Agent Rodgers continued driving down the highway. Rodgers ripped the shriveled nylon teat from the steering column. "What the hell was I supposed to do?" He wiped his face then gestured ahead. "We're following these yahoos—I can't go chasing a goddamn hit-and-run."

Agent Hart rolled down the back window on the driver's side and leaned out to assess the damage. The hot desert air blew the cornstarch from his skin. The rear end on that side of the sedan was badly damaged.

"How's it look?" Rodgers asked.

"Not too bad." Hart spit.

Rodgers sniffed the air. "Do I smell gas?"

Hart leaned farther out the window and noticed a trail of fluid in the roadway. "Yeah, we're leaking a little," he said. "Otherwise we're in pretty good shape." Just as he said it, one end of their mangled bumper dropped to the concrete and started fishtailing behind them, kicking up sparks. "Uh, check that," he said. "We have a small problem."

Rodgers glanced in the side-view. "Should I stop?"

A spark ignited the trail of gasoline. *Wuuuuufff!* The back end of the sedan burst into flame.

"No time for that," Hart said. He grabbed the small duffel bag on the backseat before scrambling to the front. "Grab the laptop!" He kicked open the door. "Bail out!"

Rodgers jerked the flaming sedan off the road like a steel-belted meteor, driving it into the desert scrub. He grabbed the black leather valise on the seat. "One, two, jump!" The two men leaped from the burning car.

"Yiiiiiiieeee!" They got lucky and hit a sandy patch devoid of cacti. The blazing Chevy continued into the desert for a hundred yards before the gas tank exploded. A moment after that, there was another explosion. Except it wasn't really an explosion so much as it was a launch.

It was a Stinger RMP Block II with advanced imaging focal-plane array, roll-frequency sensor, and a ring-laser gyro. It shot out of the trunk at supersonic speed, propelled by a dual-thrust, solid-fuel rocket motor. It flew on a horizontal plane toward a highly restricted portion of Edwards AFB. Within a half second of launching, the Stinger's passive infrared sensors had locked in on the heat signature of the CP-1's eight General Electric turbofan engines, which were spooling up for takeoff. The fully armed, thirty-five-pound missile was approaching from directly behind, homing on the red-hot exhaust ducts. The CP-1's defense system, sensing the incoming missile, immediately launched decoy heat-source flares and other countermeasures, all of which landed on the runway like flaming turds.

The senator from New York pointed. "Look! Fireworks!" Giddy as a child.

Though no one in the grandstand saw it, the Stinger, relying on advanced flare-rejection processor technology, flew straight into the exhaust duct of one of the jet engines, triggering the contact fuse and detonating the fifty-seven thousand gallons of jet fuel.

The White House press secretary was in Martin Brooks's office, hoping to convince the chief of staff of the importance of taking a more controlling approach with the media. "Sir, we're getting blowback from Senator Check's comments on *HardHeads*. The press is running with the rumors. And someone is writing a story about a possible 'shadow government' in bunkers somewhere."

Martin Brooks seemed to weaken at the news. "Goddamn vultures," he muttered. He wondered how much one man could take. And, more to the point, why did *he* have to be that one man? Huh? When did Martin Brooks ever apply for sainthood?

The press secretary was hoping for a more comprehensive response than "Goddamn vultures," but none seemed forthcoming, so he continued by saying, "They're poking around at Mulholland Memorial, sir. It's just a matter of time before they find out about the heart we seized."

That brought Brooks to life. "There was no heart seizure!" he shouted. "Why would we need a heart? The president simply fainted! We can't say that enough, even to ourselves!"

The press secretary hated when Mr. Brooks slipped into denial. "Sir, sooner or later it's going to come out. It always does. And we need to be ready."

"What if we ignore them?" Like they'd just go away.

"Sir, let me paint a picture for you," the press secretary said. "After Senator Check's appearance on *HardHeads*, the press is looking into everything. Somebody is going to find something. Then on Sunday morning's shows, someone, when asked about the rumors, will float a notion for the amusement of the audience. A mere hypothetical, you understand, that's how they'll put it. Pure conjecture, they'll insist, but 'What if,' they'll say, 'what if the president didn't really faint?' Everyone on the guest panel will pick it up and toss it around like a rugby ball. What if the president—who did, after all, have heart surgery a few months ago—what if he had a heart attack and now he needs a transplant? And, better yet, what if the federal government stole one for him? That's what they'll say, sir, and, even jokingly, someone will quote them, but context will be unclear, and the hypothetical will seem like a claim of fact, and it will get into print, and people will believe it—and what do we do then?"

Brooks threw his hands up. "We laugh! We call them conspiracy nuts and tell 'em to stop watching Oliver Stone movies. We issue a flat denial. With overtones of outrage."

"Sir, the new polling numbers show Senator Check up by two points. We have to be more proactive."

Brooks stood and began to pace. "Tell them the president's fine, you saw him play a round with his chief of staff this morning." He paused. "No, wait, that sounds like we're queers. Just say he'll hold a press conference tomorrow afternoon to address the matter."

The press secretary couldn't hide his surprise. "Is he well enough for that, sir?"

"What difference does it make? We just want to get through this news cycle with the notion that he is."

"Fine, then tomorrow we'll cancel it because of an emergency meeting with the Joint Chiefs or something."

"Exactly."

"Sir, all due respect, but think about Nixon. Or Reagan. Or Bush. Or Clinton. Or the other Bush. The denial strategy won't work forever."

Martin Brooks looked away, thinking. "Maybe we can start a war," he said. "That's worked before."

"*Wag the Dog,* sir?"

"It's just a thought."

All right, so I lied," Debbie said. "The heart's got about five hours left," she lied again. She figured as long as she didn't tell them about the ECC device, this fiasco would be over before sundown, assuming Spence would give up when he thought the organ was no longer viable. Debbie opened her mouth to lie again, but before she could, there was a huge explosion somewhere off in the desert. The shock wave rocked the Mustang, frightening Boyd to the point that he drove onto the shoulder before jerking the car back onto the road. "What the hell was that?"

They looked to the south as a massive fireball mushroomed to the sky. "That's Edwards Air Force Base," Officer Bobb said. "They're probably testing a new weapon system."

"It seems to work," Spence said.

Debbie stared at the dust and black smoke curling over the desert. Her tone was tentative when she said, "That was too small for nuclear, right?"

Spence shrugged. "Probably, but it's a moot point. If it was nuclear, we're already screwed, radiation-wise."

Cramped in the back of the Mustang, Officer Bobb

had to lean down to look out the window. "Nuclear testing's mostly done underground now, the way I understand it," he said.

"Radiation poisoning's a nasty way to die," Debbie said. "I've seen pictures."

Just then Spence heard something. He cocked his head at a high-pitched keening coming from the engine. "Jesus, what is that?"

Boyd hit the dash with a fist. "That's the sound a compressor makes when it's burning out, goddamn it!" He held his hand in front of a vent. The air grew warmer. "This is just great," he said as he opened his window. "If the government doesn't track us down and kill us, we'll be dead of heatstroke or dehydration."

"I thought we agreed to stop worrying about the feds since we exposed Dr. Pinocchio here and her pattern of deceit," Spence reminded him.

"What pattern?" she asked. "I lied about the heart's ischemic time. Let's get past that, shall we?"

"You also told me everything was going to be fine."

Debbie shrugged. "A figure of speech."

Officer Bobb pointed at the instrument panel. "Is your gas gauge right?"

Spence leaned over to look. "Wasn't this thing full when we left town?"

"Hey, we've got five people packed in here, and until ten seconds ago we'd been running the air-conditioning the entire time. We're probably getting eight miles to the gallon."

"Christ, that's worse than an SUV."

"Yes, and another good reason for lifting restrictions on coastal oil exploration here and in Alaska."

"Sure, according to the Grand Old Petroleum party, but—"

Debbie tapped Spence on the shoulder with her chin. "Fascinating as this discussion on energy policy is, I hope you don't mind if I direct your attention back to the issue at hand."

"Right," Spence said. He looked at the ECC, then at Debbie. "What are you, a second-, third-year surgical resident? You can do the transplant, right? I mean, not legally, since you don't have a license yet, but from a practical basis? You have the technical skills, right?"

Debbie had never seen such a naked display of lunacy. "Of course I can do it," she said. "All I need is a pocket knife, a bullet, and some whiskey."

Spence pruned his face.

"We'll use the jack as a rib spreader."

"This isn't helpful."

"As compared to kidnapping." Debbie paused. "Spence, your delusional manifestation is called magical thinking."

"Look," Spence said, "I don't know what we're going to do, okay? But I do know that without the heart, Mom dies. Now, since no one knows where we are or what we're driving, at least we've got a chance. We just have to find a way to get the heart, I don't know, installed."

"Installed." Debbie didn't know if she was more amused or amazed. "There are one hundred and seventy transplant centers in this country, and even if we weren't speeding away from the nearest one, do you think you can just show up and have somebody pop in a hot ticker? Please. You're not that stupid. Just turn around, and we'll do whatever we can to find your mom a new heart."

"With her blood type? She'll die waiting, and you know it."

"Well, this road trip will almost certainly kill her."

There was a long silence while Spence looked at his mom. She stirred a bit and made a mumbling noise, emerging from the benzodiazepam. What would he tell her when she came to? Sorry, there was a mix-up at the hospital? A mix-up? Like someone put onions on the burger when you said no onions. This wasn't a mix-up. This was a death sentence. Well, Spence wasn't going to let her die without his trying, even if what he was trying bordered on insanity. He looked at Debbie. She seemed to be waiting for a response. Spence didn't know what to do or say. He was, simply, scared.

Officer Bobb dabbed the sweat on Rose's forehead, then looked at Debbie and asked, "What if it was your mom?"

The question hit her like a foul ball, and she remembered the thing she'd been trying to recall ever since she woke up. She felt that sting in her nose that always came before she cried, but she fought it back. Her mouth opened like a tiny coin slot, but nothing came out. Now it was Debbie who didn't know what to say. How could she have forgotten? She quickly decided that in light of the insanity of the past hour or two, she could forgive herself for not remembering. Still, this changed her perspective. "All right," she said. "In the interest of my patient, I'll go along on your magical-thinking mystery tour. But you've got to uncuff me."

"No more outbursts?"

"Whatever," Debbie said.

"No, not 'whatever.' I want to know you're not going to throw any more punches." Spence held up the key to the cuffs.

"Fine."

"Deal?"

"Yes, deal. Jesus. I only hit you once."

"Yeah, but you lie on a fairly regular basis."

"I'm sorry," she said. "I'm just trying to end this. I promise to behave."

She seemed sincere enough, so Spence relented. "Turn around," he said. Debbie struggled to twist around in the cramped space. Spence reached into the backseat and unlocked the cuffs. He put his hand to his mother's forehead, then her cheek. "Is she all right?"

Debbie took Rose by the hand and checked her pulse. She lifted an eyelid and looked for pupil response. "She's okay, but she's getting dehydrated. We need to get some fluids in her."

Spence put the handcuffs in the glove compartment, then turned back to face Debbie. "We have to stop at the next gas station anyway. We need gas and something to eat. And a transplant surgeon. Right? How do we get one?"

Debbie looked at him. He seemed completely serious. "You realize you're insane?"

"No, I'm desperate," Spence said. "That's different. So how do we get a surgeon?"

"You look in the Yellow Pages under 'Not Going to Happen.'"

"Hey, I got hostages," Spence said. "I bet I can make it happen. All I have to do is threaten to kill you, and you can bet we'll get a surgeon."

"Kill me?" She nodded at Officer Bobb. "Why not threaten to kill him?"

"He didn't punch me in the nose."

Officer Bobb smiled at Debbie. "My mom used to say you catch more flies with honey than vinegar."

Debbie shook her head in disbelief. She looked back at Spence. "You need more than a surgeon," she said. "You need a first assistant, a scrub nurse, a circulating nurse, a perfusionist, and an anesthesiologist, minimum. And you need an OR. And you can't exactly rent them like party rooms or something. At least I don't think you can."

Spence thought for a moment. "Listen, in a country where you can buy anything from kidneys to congressmen, I can damn sure hire a heart surgeon with a private operating room."

"Okay, maybe you can," Debbie said. "I don't know. They haven't covered that part of heart surgery in the classes I've taken. But even if it is possible, you're talking about something for the ultrarich—we're talking like J. Paul Getty or Bill Gates rich. So, okay, if you had that kind of money, I suppose we might be able to pull this off. Otherwise why would a surgeon be willing to risk everything he or she—"

"We?"

"What?"

Spence smiled. "We. You said 'we might be able to pull this off.' Or was that another figure of speech, like 'everything's going to be fine'?"

"Don't be so damn literal," Debbie said. "And don't be pissed at me. I'm not responsible for any of this. I was—"

"You're right."

Debbie was surprised at Spence's admission. "Oh, okay."

"You're right that nobody's going to perform this surgery out of the kindness of their heart." Spence turned to Boyd. "What's the typical asset-to-debt ratio of a surgeon? Aren't they notorious for being poor money managers?"

"It's not uncommon," Boyd said warily.

"That's what I thought. You got your PDA?"

Boyd knew where this was going. "Ohhh, no. Forget it. Not going there."

"Don't have any choice." Spence pointed out the window. "Pull in at that gas station."

Martin Brooks was dismayed. He'd just received a call from the chairman of the Emerging Threats and Capabilities subcommittee, who was carrying on about some sort of mishap with a military project out at Edwards Air Force Base. Brooks told the senator he was too busy to deal with pork-barrel snafus at the moment. They set up a meeting for the following week, and Brooks returned to his current dilemma.

His jowls sagged as he looked over the bluebooks from the NSA, Secret Service, FBI, and the other agencies that had weighed in with theories on who was responsible for stealing the heart and leaving the FIB SAD agent in a coma. Unfortunately, there was no consensus. The various agencies were offering enough theories and circumstantial evidence to explain the participation of two dozen unrelated terrorist organizations. One senior national security adviser had even proposed a unifying conspiracy theory positing that the groups were working in concert, a scenario Brooks figured was about as likely as the American public's electing as president an intellectual black lesbian on an independent-party ticket.

Brooks shook his head sadly. *We're going to hell in a foreign-made handbasket,* he thought. In his estimation this particular failure by the American intelligence community was a symptom of bigger problems. How could such a highly funded juggernaut of satellites, Internet spying, and a network of human assets be so obtuse? Not only were they unable to say who had committed the terrorist act, they couldn't even figure out how the information about the heart had leaked out in the first place. Brooks thought he knew the answer, and it angered him. His blood boiled when he thought about how diluted the employment pool had become as a result of all the affirmative-action legislation passed over the last forty years. Agencies that once ran like pure water were now muddy as the Mississippi. African-Americans, Asian-Americans, Mexican-Americans. *Whatever happened to American-Americans?* he wondered. And he didn't mean the Indians. The way Brooks saw things, it was this dilution that was responsible for so much of what was wrong with this country.

He took a moment to regret the passing of the Old America. *My Lord,* he found himself thinking, *if the soldiers who stormed the beaches at Normandy—men like my father—could have seen what America would be like at the start of the twenty-first century, they would not have got fifty yards up the beach. Indeed,* he thought, *they would have given up in disgust.*

But Brooks couldn't give up. He didn't have that luxury. He had a nation to save. He had to find the answer no one else could. He had to consider what all those mutts had failed to consider. Who, besides foreign governments and the world's terrorist organizations, stood to gain from the president's death? It seemed unlikely the other side had the balls for a move like this. And the Greens were too disorganized, too passive, too poor. Then a thought. Maybe they'd been looking at this from the wrong angle. What if the people responsible didn't care, or even know, that the heart was bound for the president. What if, instead of terrorists, it was the family who had been expecting to get the heart in the first place? Jesus H. Jones. It was almost too obvious. He grabbed a secure line and hit the speed dial for his buddy, Howard Phillips, the SAD A-Dic at FBI. "Howard? It's Martin. Do we know who was supposed to get that heart?"

"Yeah, hang on." There was a pause as he accessed his database. "Woman named Rose Tailor."

"She have a father?"

"Long deceased."

"Husband?"

"Ditto."

"Siblings?"

"One sister, too old to do anything about it."

"Children?"

"Two sons."

There was a pause. "Well, I think it's time we pay those boys a visit."

8

Stop Dragging My Heart Around

I t was an uncommon sight. Two men in suits trudging through the Mojave Desert like they were on their way to make a presentation. Agent Rodgers had the duffel bag, Hart was carrying a black leather valise that had survived the leap from the burning sedan with only cosmetic damage. "I don't care what they say, dry heat is plenty hot."

"I'm not disagreeing with you," Hart said. "My point is, they're different. That's the thrust of my argument. I did this destabilization op in the Congo River Basin once. The humidity?" He shook his head. "You want to talk about hot? I got one word for you: fuck."

"Oh, I don't doubt it." Rodgers slipped his coat off

and glanced at the sun, shading his eyes. "But all things being equal, you can actually die quicker in the desert than in the jungle."

"Huh." Hart sidestepped a creosote bush. "Is that right?"

"It's true. I took a two-week desert-survival course out here a few years ago."

"That marine course?"

"Yeah. Colonel Raphael."

"I hear that's a good one."

"Oh, yeah," Rodgers said. "Learned all sorts of stuff: what you can eat, what's good for sunburn, the range of thermoneutrality."

Agent Hart reached into the valise and pulled out an impossibly small digital ranging scope. He scanned the horizon as Rodgers talked.

"Animal tissue can function only in a narrow range of temperatures," he said. "Exceed the range, animal dies. Four or five months of the year—and this is one of them—the daily temperature out here exceeds the range."

"Of thermoneutrality."

"Exactly." Rodgers loosened his tie. "Most of your desert mammals and reptiles are crepuscular, only active at dawn and dusk. That's why we're not likely to see any rattlesnakes or Gila monsters."

"Good to know." Hart tapped Rodgers on the shoulder. "Hey, what about peyote? Does that grow out here?"

"It does. But I haven't seen any."

"Well, keep your eyes open."

Rodgers gestured at the desert with his free hand and said, "You know, General Patton trained over a million troops out here for World War II."

Hart was peering through the digital ranging scope again. "No, I did not know that." He stopped and pointed at something Rodgers couldn't see. "But I do know where we're getting our next ride."

Connie was still listening to Winston Archer's radio show as she finished her coffee. "Coming up after the break, proof positive the first gun lock was invented by a homosexual."

The canned audience chimed in with "Amen, Archer!"

Connie had a guilty laugh, then shook her head. *That's a bit much*, she thought. *Still, it's kind of funny.* Connie was no extremist but she believed the Second Amendment gave everyone the right to own a gun, even if they didn't belong to a militia. Connie didn't go to NRA rallies or gun shows, nor did she own a sinister cache of weapons. She owned a single Sig-Sauer P225, and she liked to do a little target shooting every now and then. She kept her gun safely locked away and, despite temptation, never took it to school-board or parent-association meetings.

Connie looked at her watch and decided she could start making calls about tonight's vote. The moment she picked up the phone, the doorbell rang. She turned and yelled upstairs, "Boyd Jr.!" No response. She yelled again:

"Someone's at the door!" She turned down the radio and waited for a response. Nothing. "Erica!" Nada. Connie shook her head. Damn kids. Probably up there with headphones on, listening to songs illegally downloaded from the Internet. Oh, sure, she had tried to tell them it was stealing, but the concept of intellectual-property rights was lost on them.

"It's not like we're going into stores and leaving without paying," Erica had said. "*That's* stealing."

Connie wanted them to understand the concept, but she also knew she had to choose her battles. And she wasn't going to lose sleep over a few cents in unpaid royalties, especially for those vile rap acts.

The doorbell rang again. Connie put the phone down and screamed louder, "Boyd Jr.! Erica!" Then a loud knock. "All right, all right," she muttered as she stalked to the front door. Squinting one eye, she looked through the peephole and saw a handsome young man in a nice dark suit.

Just then Boyd Jr. came thumping down the stairs with an MP3 player in his hands and headphones clamped over his ears. "Mom, there's somebody at the door."

"Thank you, Professor Einstein, I know." She smoothed the front of her outfit and opened it. "Hello." She smiled pleasantly. "Can I help you?"

The man smiled pleasantly back. He was younger than Connie, only slightly bigger. "Yes, I'm looking for Boyd Tailor," he said.

"And who, may I ask, are you?" Connie tried to out-pleasant him with a big squinty-eyed smile and tilt of the head.

The man reached into his pocket and showed his badge long enough for Connie to read it. "Agent Sandlin, FBI." He slipped it back into his coat, then smiled again. "Is Mr. Tailor here?" He looked over Connie's shoulder and saw Boyd Jr., his head bobbing to some hip-hop.

Connie felt an ugly turn in the pit of her stomach. "No, he's not," she said with her smile still in place. "What's this in regard to?" She couldn't imagine an answer that would be a relief. When the FBI shows up at the door, something bad isn't far behind. She just hoped it wouldn't take long. Her schedule was too tight today.

"Ma'am"—he returned her smile with yet another one and gestured toward the living room—"let's step inside to discuss this." He made a firm move to walk past Connie. She let him pass, not wanting her neighbors to see what-ever might happen. She knew how they talked.

"You really with the FBI?" Boyd Jr. asked.

"That's right, son."

"Now," Connie said, "what is this about?"

"You may not want your son to hear this, ma'am." Agent Sandlin's eyebrows suggested that Boyd Jr. go to another room.

Connie kept smiling as if her perfect teeth could make the bad news disappear. And what could Agent Sandlin be but bad news? Obviously, something was very wrong, and Connie figured that whatever it was, Boyd Jr. was going to hear about it sooner or later. She copped an attitude. "I tell you what," Connie said. "You don't worry about my son, how's that? Now, why don't you tell me why you're asking about my husband?"

"Ma'am, we know your mother-in-law was scheduled for a heart transplant this morning."

My God, Connie thought. Just last week Winston Archer was talking about this sort of invasion of privacy by the government and how they'd find ways to use the information to their advantage. She assumed he was exaggerating. "And how do you know that?" Connie asked indignantly. "Medical records are supposed to be private."

"Ma'am, we're the FBI. We know pretty much whatever we want to when it comes to matters of national security." He wasn't a big guy, but he had a certain forcefulness.

Connie's hackles went up. "And what does my mother-in-law's heart transplant have to do with national security, for heaven's sake?" Her mind was racing. The FBI was in her living room talking about national security and private medical information. Either this had a very funny punch line—*Whoops, sorry, ma'am, just a wacky mix-up!*—or it was a We-interrupt-this-program-special-report about to happen. She looked at Agent Sandlin. His face didn't say wacky mix-up.

"Ma'am, we have reason to believe your husband is involved in a conspiracy to assassinate the president."

Boyd Jr.'s eyes popped wide. "Holy shit!"

Connie spun around. "Boyd Jr.!"

"He's right, ma'am."

"That's absurd," Connie said. "You can't be talking about *my* Boyd. He wouldn't conspire to bad-mouth the president, let alone kill him. This has to be a mistake."

"Nonetheless," Agent Sandlin said. He changed his posture to imply a threat. "I'll need you and your children to go ahead and come with me."

Connie thought again of Winston Archer and things he had said. Maybe he wasn't doing satire after all. "Is that a request?"

"No, ma'am."

Connie stared at Agent Sandlin thinking, *Damn. It was all going so good. We were on our way. Everything was on track, working out perfectly. And now this guy wants to ruin it all?* "Well, okay," Connie said. "Let me get my purse." She put her hand on Boyd Jr.'s head and gave it a rub. "Honey, you keep the nice FBI man company. I'll be right back."

Boyd Jr. waited until his mom left. Then he looked up at the FBI agent, all devious. "What'd Dad do?" Like he was glad to know his dad was in trouble instead of him.

"I can't say."

Boyd Jr. thought for a moment. "Have you ever shot anybody in the eyeball? I bet that would be cool."

Agent Sandlin gave him a sideways glance. "Where's your sister?"

"How'd you know I had a sister?"

"We know everything."

Boyd Jr. turned and yelled up the stairs: "Erica!"

Erica came downstairs just as Connie returned to the

living room with her purse. "Well, then," Connie said, chirpy as a sparrow, "are we ready?"

"What's going on?" Erica asked.

"You're coming with me," Agent Sandlin said.

"Who're you?" Erica asked.

"He's with the FBI," Connie said as she reached into her purse, presumably to get her keys. "But we're not going with him."

"What's that, ma'am?" Agent Sandlin turned to look.

Connie pulled her Sig P225 from her purse, assumed a two-handed firing stance, and said, "Kids? Frisk him."

Boyd parked the Mustang in the shade by the gas pumps. Spence refused to let anyone go inside, lest they call the police. Instead he went in, bought water and fruit juice and snacks, and brought them back to the others. Rose was showing signs of life as the benzodiazepam continued to wear off.

From the backseat Officer Bobb said, "Hey, can we at least get out and stretch our legs?"

"Only if you put on your pants," Spence said. He tried tucking the Glock in his waistband, but scrub pants don't have much grip, so he just held on to it. While Officer Bobb struggled into his uniform in the confines of the backseat, Debbie climbed out of the Mustang. Spence pointed at her. "Don't try to run off," he said. "I got enough problems."

Debbie looked around at the bleak surroundings as she stretched her back and legs. *We're in the middle of nowhere*, she thought. *Where am I going to run? Into the*

vast . . . brownness? Through all the prickly brown plants?
To those brown mountains in the distance? Even the air
seems brown out here. "Don't worry," she assured Spence.
"I'm not going anywhere." The only thing not brown was
all the trash. Beer cans, cigarette butts, and Styrofoam
food containers blowing by like tumbleweeds. Debbie
was surprised by the ugliness. She had heard people wax
poetic about the beauty and majesty of the desert, but
they must have meant a different one. The Mojave, at
least around Boron, California, had all the appeal of an
ashtray in a bikers' bar.

After a moment Boyd's whining caught Debbie's ear.
"They'll trace it through my password," he said. "I'll get
fired."

Spence grabbed the PDA from his brother. "And
what's more important, your job or your mother?"

"It's more complicated than that," Boyd said, falling
back on the scoundrel's reply to any question the answer
to which was indeed simple.

This exchange redirected Debbie's thoughts from
desert aesthetics to the question Officer Bobb had raised
earlier and the subsequent thought that had been trou-
bling her ever since. What if it *had* been her mother?
Would Debbie have let the government take the heart?
Would she have absconded with it? And if so, then
what? And if not, what did that say about her? Everything circled back to her mother and led Debbie to beat
herself up a little more for forgetting that today was her
mother's birthday. Her sixty-fourth. In her entire life

Debbie had never forgotten it. She'd celebrated every one of her mom's birthdays until today.

Meanwhile Spence was trying to get Boyd's PDA to work. He stabbed repeatedly at the screen with the stylus but wasn't making any headway. "This stupid thing doesn't work!" He began shaking it like a can of soda.

"That won't help." Boyd snatched the PDA from Spence and, with a few deft pokes of the stylus, logged in to his bank's system, complaining all the while about inadequate bandwidth.

Spence clapped him on the back. "Shut up and find a surgeon with poor money-management skills," he said.

There were several candidates, each with heavy outstanding student-loan balances, enormous mortgages, new loans on eighty-thousand-dollar luxury cars, alimony, child support, and staggering piles of high-interest credit-card debt. The problem with the first three candidates was location, location, location. Michigan, Connecticut, and Florida were simply too far to drive, but a fourth option presented itself in the form of Dr. Norman Speyburn of Salt Lake City's Brigham Memorial Hospital. Spence wrote down the doctor's particulars, then pulled out his cell phone.

"So, boy genius, what do you plan to say?" Boyd asked.

"I have no idea," Spence said. "But generally speaking, people who already have food and shelter are motivated by fear, greed, and sex. I'm going to start there."

"Yes," Boyd sneered. "Perhaps he'll do the transplant in exchange for a sex act."

"Okay, we can rule that one out. But that leaves us with fear and greed, so I'm optimistic."

"What about love?" It was Officer Bobb, leaning against the car, a romantic tone in his voice.

Spence shook his head. "People do all sorts of stupid things for love, I'll grant you, some even criminal. But in my experience fear and greed are the greater motivators."

"You kidnapped me for love," he said.

"No, that was out of fear."

"Of what?"

"Of being beaten, shot, or framed for something."

"No, it was because you love your mother."

"No, that's why I stole the heart."

"Exactly."

"But that wasn't a crime," Spence said. "The heart belongs to her. You can't steal something that belongs to you."

Officer Bobb nodded. "Yeah, I see your point."

"Well, I don't," Debbie said. "What crime do you plan to ask this doctor to commit?"

Spence shrugged. "I don't know. You're the one who said a doctor would be risking his career to do this. I assumed it was a crime of some sort. Or have we caught you in another lie?"

"It may well be a crime," Debbie said. "I don't know the laws in Utah. But I suspect that the licensing board or the hospital's transplant committee would have something to say about it." She shook her head. "I just can't imagine why this guy would agree to do this."

The truth was that, unlike most foreign countries, which had national screening boards reviewing every transplant performed, the United States relied on hospital transplant-review committees to look for illegal transplants, by which was meant any transplant done with a brokered organ, as compared to those obtained through proper channels. Some U.S. hospitals, especially those having a bad fiscal quarter, might employ a sort of look-the-other-way policy when it came to a brokered transplant, which is what it would appear to be if you just called up a surgeon and said you had both an organ and a transplant patient and was he free this afternoon to pop it in? All the hospital would need was to have the buyer and a seller sign documents attesting that no money had changed hands for the organ. Once you had those, the truth was irrelevant.

Unfortunately, Spence didn't know any of that, nor did he have time to learn. So he had to wing it. After a few moments Spence dialed the number. "Yes, Dr. Speyburn, please. Yes, tell him it's . . . Dr. Peters from the Centers for Disease Control. It's urgent." Spence covered the mouthpiece, looking at Boyd. "Going to start with fear and close with greed," he said. "Hello, Dr. Speyburn? Yes, first of all let me confess. I'm not with the CDC. I'm calling on behalf of the, uh, the Gates Foundation." Spence paused. "Yes, I'm sure you're busy. So are we. But this isn't a fund-raising call. In fact, it's rather the opposite." He paused again. "Well, let's not be coy, Doctor. Given your financial position, you're going to want to take my call." Spence listened for a moment. "My name isn't important. The name that's important here is Bill Gates. Yes, that's right. That Bill Gates."

Dr. Speyburn apparently expressed some skepticism as to the authenticity of the caller's claims. "All right, how's this for starters: 078-05-1120. Rebecca Hovart. Thirty-nine eleven Oakdale Drive." Dr. Speyburn recognized his Social Security number, his mother's maiden name, and the address where his children lived with his ex-wife. "We can find out anything we want because we can look into virtually every computer on earth, since we made the software and built the back doors. Shall I continue? Fine," Spence said. "We've done our research, and we came to you at Mr. Gates's request. Hmm? Oh, it's Mr. Gates's mother, I'm afraid, advanced dilated cardiomy-opathy. Naturally, he doesn't want to lose her. Now, Doc-tor, as you know, sometimes the rules must be broken and . . . well, this is one of those times. Everyone we've spoken with said you were the best man for the job."

Spence spread the flattery on thick and followed with a convincing speech regarding the vast amount of com-pensation for the doctor and his team. Then, returning to the fear part of his scheme, he made it clear it would not be in Dr. Speyburn's best interests either to say no to the world's wealthiest man or to contact the authorities. When Spence finished, he paused for Dr. Speyburn's response. "Well, fine, then," Spence said. "We should be there late this afternoon." He hung up and turned to Boyd and Debbie, gesturing with the gun. "Saddle up. We're going to Salt Lake."

The group turned to head back to the Mustang when Rose's weak voice emerged from the backseat. "Spencer? Is that a gun?"

The two agents could hear it from a quarter mile away. Rodgers turned to Hart and said, "Did you know the human threshold for pain caused by sound is around a hundred twenty-five decibels?"

"No," Hart said. "Can't say I knew that."

"It's true. A jet engine hits about a hundred fifty. At around two-thirty dB an average human will chew a leg off to escape the noise. We did the studies. We know this."

The noise grew louder. As they emerged from the desert scrub at the edge of the parking area, they could barely hear themselves think. Throbbing like a migraine, a custom-painted 1990 two-door G-20 Chevy Van was the only vehicle in the rest area. The agents could see the van vibrating with each sonic boom going off inside like syncopated bombs.

The near side of the van was decorated with a psychedelic rendering of what looked like Bob Marley riding a skateboard through a black hole in the Western Spiral Arm of the Milky Way Galaxy. Flanking the image on one side were the words THEY SHALL NOT MAKE BALDNESS UPON THEIR HEAD, NEITHER SHALL THEY SHAVE OFF THEIR BEARD. LEVITICUS 21:5. On the other side were the words BETTER IS A DINNER OF HERBS WHERE LOVE IS, THAN A STALLED OX AND HATRED THEREWITH. PROVERBS 15:17.

Agent Rodgers looked at his partner. "Whaddya make

of that?" He had to yell to be heard over the booming sound system.

Hart shook his head. "Hard to say. Religious types misinterpret Scripture more often than they get it right." He pulled his gun and racked a cartridge into the chamber. "And a high percentage carry weapons. I'll take the driver's side." He paused, pointing at Agent Rodgers. "But remember, thou shalt not kill, unless it's at the behest of some branch of your government." He smiled, then walked around the van and saw another airbrushed image. This one was a white kid riding a skateboard, dreadlocks flowing behind him as he skated off a cliff toking on a joint. Underneath it said JED X, U.S. OPEN FREESTYLE CHAMPION '02. The rest of the van was covered with dozens of sponsor logos: Menace, Droors, Evol, Plan B, Zooyork, and on and on.

As Agent Hart eased up along the driver's side, he touched the van and felt the throbbing. He got to the door and looked in the window to see a kid, early twenties, his head bobbing to the music. He had a long braided goatee, bleached-blond dreadlocks dropping from underneath a black wool cap. On the left side of the kid's face Hart could see three upper-ear cartilage spikes, a half dozen two-gauge captive bead rings along the helix, and an earlobe stretched wide enough to hold a silver disk the size of a quarter. He was wearing a pair of wraparound sunglasses and had enough tattoos and piercings to make Agent Hart wonder if everyone's nervous system worked the same way.

Hart saw Rodgers looking in the window on the other side. The kid lit up a joint, oblivious that two men were watching. Agent Hart put his hand on the door handle and nodded at Rodgers. After a silent count to three, they simultaneously jerked the doors open and leveled their guns.

Jed X was so startled he sucked the joint into his throat. He pounded the steering wheel as he lapsed into a spastic coughing fit, spewing a cloud of exotic smoke.

Agent Hart screamed something but was drowned out by the massive sound system. He leaned in and killed the music. "CIA!" he yelled again.

Following a desperate guttural wretch, Jed X finally dislodged the joint, launching it onto the dashboard. He threw his hands up in surrender. "Yo, G, chill, we can deal wit' it."

"We're commandeering this vehicle!" Rodgers shouted.

Jed X made some sort of ganglike hand gestures as he spoke. "Ay yo trip, homes, don't get your jammy all hard, I'm game, ite? You and Jake jus' hop on the side and cool your burners."

The two agents kept their guns on Jed X. They exchanged looks. "What?"

"Get in."

Had Dante lived in the twenty-first century, the street layout of Washington, D.C., might have ended up about five-sevenths of the way down the spiraling cone to hell, set there as punishment for those who daily committed the mortal sin of government upon millions of innocent citizens.

Britton Belk was there now, driving a black SUV, the vehicle of choice among D.C.'s power brokers. More than the Lincoln Town Car ever could, the black SUV with tinted windows said, *I'm rich enough to squander money and resources, and I'm so big that I'll literally kill you if you get in my way*. Britton was trying to get Senator Check from Capitol Plaza to Adams-Morgan for a lunch meeting at Cashion's Eat Place. It was geographically impractical, given the traffic, but the food made it worth the hassle. "Fine," Britton said into the hands-free phone. "Just keep us informed." She disconnected the call, then leaned on the horn, demanding that someone move.

Senator Check was looking at results from the most recent poll. "What's the margin of error on this?"

"Ninety-five percent confidence interval with a three percent margin of error."

"So we're either down two, up two, or tied?" The senator shook her head at the modern political equivalent to reading entrails. "I told you to take Sixteenth," she said.

"Yes, ma'am." Britton cursed the street layout of the capital, which made about as much sense as the politics rendered in the grand buildings a mile to the south. There were few, if any, straightforward ways of getting from A to B in the entire town, thanks in large part to a conspiracy of one-way streets, no-turn signs, and construction on every road you needed to travel. For those so timid as to obey mere signs, the result was to be sent circling deeper into the city when all they wanted was to escape to Virginia or Maryland. But Britton hadn't become a senator's aide by being timid. She was prepared to make a left or run a light or do whatever else it would take, but first the cars in front of her had to move. She honked again.

The senator gestured vaguely at the phone. "So what'd they say?"

"Oh, they had some car problems." Britton craned her neck looking for an escape route.

Senator Check closed her notebook and tossed it into the backseat. "What happened?"

"He wasn't specific, but he said they're back on track and everything's under control."

"They're still in the Mojave?"

"Yes, ma'am, and no rivals in sight. Said it looks like they're free and clear."

Senator Check shook her head as she thought of the infamous Phoenix memo, Wen Ho Lee, Robert Hanssen, the McVeigh document snafu, and a string of other FBI screw-ups. "I sometimes wonder how this country ever achieved all it has." She looked at her watch. "You better pick up the pace or we're going to be late."

"Yes, ma'am." Britton leaned on the horn again and made an intimidating move that involved breaking whatever laws there were about driving on sidewalks.

As they made the turn onto New Hampshire Avenue, Senator Check allowed herself to start feeling optimistic about her chances in November. With President Webster either dead or so feeble he couldn't campaign, and with his party lacking any other viable candidate, the White House seemed like a real possibility. The senator slipped into a dream where Peggy Check was in charge. The first woman to be president of the United States. She would seize power for all the other women who had tried, failed, and been forgotten. She would do it for all the women who had been laughed at, ridiculed, and humiliated for daring to run for the office. She'd do it for Victoria Woodhull and Shirley Chisholm and Lenora Fulani. She'd do it for Jeane J. Kirkpatrick, Geraldine Ferraro, and Liddy Dole. She'd do it for her own mother, who told her she could be the president if she wanted.

Britton leaned on the horn again, startling the senator back to reality, where she was still merely a woman who happened to be an elected official in a nation run by men. There was still plenty of business to take care of before Peggy Check could start picking her cabinet.

As a member of the Banking, Housing, and Urban Affairs Committee's Subcommittee on Financial Institutions, Senator Check was on her way to meet with Senator Mike Richardson to discuss a financial-services bill. Under the guise of updating, for the second time in five years, the nation's Depression-era banking rules, the bill was designed to allow insurance companies, brokerage houses, banks, and credit-card companies to merge and create what their marketing people liked to call financial supermarkets, conjuring the image of customer convenience. It would also allow them to amass and share reams of private data, everything from customers' incomes, investments, possessions, and credit ratings to summations of where they ate dinner, what hotels they used, and what their medical expenses were. Additionally, if a consumer's bank and health-insurance company were affiliated, a loan officer could punch a button and see if the customer had any health problems before deciding whether to award a mortgage and at what rate.

From the financial-services industry's point of view, it was a fine piece of legislation. But even the best legislation faced opposition, so the senators were meeting to see if they could reach across the aisle and bring the two sides together.

The senators and their assistants arrived at Cashion's at the same time and were seated at their usual table in the elevated section of the room. Senator Richardson ordered an appetizer of pork rillettes served with a salad of locally grown mâche. Senator Check went with the avocado and grapefruit with a poppy-seed dressing. The two assistants ordered the salad of roasted beets, walnuts, and aged goat cheese with mixed greens. After some small talk Senator Check speared a wedge of grapefruit and waved it toward Senator Richardson. "My people tell me this sort of information sharing is going to be a terrific convenience for customers." She sucked the fruit off the fork.

Senator Richardson nodded once, slowly. "Yes, but consumer advocates are worried about the privacy implications. They're demanding an amendment. And I think they have a point. Consumers want some control over how their personal information is used."

Senator Check pointed across the table with her fork.

"Well, all right. Let's roll up our sleeves here and show some leadership. What if we amend the bill?" She stabbed at her salad, then made a sweeping gesture with some avocado. "Add an array of privacy protections."

Richardson swallowed some of his pork. "That's all my constituents are asking."

"Good. I know we can reach an understanding if we just put our heads together and do what we were elected to," Senator Check said. "And, in the interest of saving everyone some time, we took the liberty of sketching out a few new ideas." Britton handed an outline of the proposed consumer protections to Senator Richardson's assistant.

As he read the document, the others returned to their food. After a minute Richardson's assistant set the document on the table and looked up. "An oyster's got more teeth," he said.

Senator Check templed her fingers and struck a reflective pose. "I think it would be preferable to characterize this amendment as more centrist than the original draft."

Richardson's assistant wiped a dab of goat cheese from the corner of his mouth. "There's nothing enforceable in this. It's a sham. It leaves consumers with virtually no control over their personal data."

"Well," Senator Richardson said, "I think 'virtually' is the key word here." The senator seemed to measure each word as if it were a diamond. "It would have been foolish to come in expecting to get everything we wanted. So we get a little and they get a little, and that's how things work. And though no one gets what they consider the perfect law, we end up with something everyone can live with. What's the expression, 'Perfection is the enemy of the adequate'? I think that's how we have to look at this."

"It's all about compromise," Britton said.

"Finding the middle ground," Senator Check added.

"And leadership," Britton said earnestly as she hoisted her water glass. "To which I would like to propose a toast."

They clinked glasses just as the entrées arrived. Aromatic plates of buffalo hangar steaks, pearly pan-roasted halibut, grilled guinea-hen sausage, and crab cakes.

Richardson's assistant's disappointment in the legislative process was subdued as soon as he took a bite of his lunch. It might have been the best thing he'd ever tasted. After a few more bites he got to looking at the bright side of things. Next year his boss would be able to say he was the one who had forced the compromise banking bill. Most people wouldn't remember what the bill was, much less that the amendment was a toothless hag. They would just read the direct-mail brochure and see that Senator Richardson had stood up to the banking interests. It wasn't much, but it would be worth something at certain fund-raisers, and that's all that really mattered.

The waiter stopped at their table. "How is everything?" he asked.

Senator Richardson's assistant looked up and said, "Fabulous." He pointed at his plate. "How do they make these sausages?"

The waiter smiled and said, "You don't want to know."

Except for when they inserted the catheter, President Webster was comfortable and happy. In fact, he hadn't been this relaxed in decades. Like someone had turned off the pressure spigot. His staff was treating him as if he were in a coma, and he could think of no reason to disabuse them of that notion. Feigning unconsciousness was the best idea he'd had in years. He just lay there, sleeping whenever he wanted. The country was doing fine without him.

Physically, the president felt pretty good. Though his heart wasn't what it used to be, he was perfectly lucid and taking advantage of all the downtime to take stock, to reflect on his career and, indeed, on his profession as a whole. Depending on where his thoughts took him, the president had to be careful not to laugh or cry, lest someone notice he was possessed of a consciousness sufficient for fund-raising. Yet he couldn't help but crack a smile when he overheard Martin Brooks say something about the current campaign. It made him think of George Bernard Shaw's line about how "democracy substitutes election by the incompetent many for appointment by the corrupt few."

In the president's experience it was all too true. He'd been out there pressing the flesh year in and year out. He'd met the people. Some were earnest and well educated, a few were crackpots, but most of them were so frazzled by daily life they just wanted to be soothed by a familiar tune. They just wanted to hear that the candidate was focusing on the issues. The candidate intended to face the challenges of the new millennium while encouraging economic growth and reforming the government. They wanted to be reassured that this representative would reach across party lines because he was there to serve the American people, to fight for working families, and to put children first, since their future was at stake. And of course they wanted to believe. The president knew that Americans had a deep and amazing capacity for belief in their political system. A faith made all the more wondrous in light of the history of American politicians.

Like many elected officials, President Webster loved Americans, the whole crazy lot of them. They were mostly hardworking, generous people who did their best when it came time to cast a vote. The president believed there were two kinds of citizens, the ones who voted their pocketbook and the ones who tried to vote the issues. Most of them voted their pocketbook, believing that one candidate would improve their lot in life whereas the other would be their financial ruin. The logic was faulty, of course, but it had been handed down generation to generation, so the people clung to it. President Webster knew better than most that it didn't matter which white man of privilege was in the White House. He had once said, "Look. If you're wealthy when a candidate takes office, you'll be wealthy when that candidate leaves office, assuming you don't lose the money yourself. Conversely, if you're poor when a candidate takes office, then, absent your own efforts to improve your position, you'll be poor when that candidate leaves office. We politicians might make it slightly easier or a little more difficult to improve your net worth, but most of the work is up to the people."

Then there were those who tried to vote the issues. It was a fool's errand, but that didn't stop them. President Webster knew that in an increasingly complex world, truly educating oneself on the issues was impossible. Thus the issue voters, to a greater extent than not, made largely uninformed decisions each time they cast a vote. It wasn't their fault, of course. There were only so many hours in a day, and after taking care of personal obligations, who had time to read the transcript from the hearing before the Senate judiciary committee's subcommittee on antitrust, business rights, and competition, which examined the competitive implications of so-and-so's proposed purchase of the such-and-such orbital satellite slot? Or to read the bill to amend Title 5, U.S. Code, to provide for the establishment of a program under which long-term-care insurance would be made available to federal employees? Who had the time or expertise to digest these or any of the dozen or so similar documents created every single day in Washington? No one, that's who. The voters, faithful if not fully informed, had to rely on special-interest groups to do all the reading and evaluating and advising. It was a messy system, fraught with conflicts of interest most of which the voters would never be aware. Yet—and this was both the good news and the bad news—it was the best system of government in the history of the world.

President Webster smiled inwardly, happy to have participated in such a grand experiment, and for a fleeting moment he thought it might be fun to get back in the game for one last round. Put one final spur to the horse. Take advantage of the perks he'd worked so hard to earn. Besides, he'd be a laughingstock if his last act in politics were to lose to a woman. So it was that President Webster, in a moment of enlightened self-interest, began to wonder how the search for that heart was coming.

And then, as if Martin Brooks had been reading his mind, President Webster heard his chief of staff say to someone, "You know what? We need a contingency organ."

9

Only Love Can
Break Your Heart

As she stood there listening to Spence tell lies to Dr. Speyburn, Debbie gave herself another psychic punch in the stomach for forgetting her mother's birthday. It was only then, with her ego doubled over from the jab, that Debbie realized the fault in her reasoning, since obviously she *had* finally remembered the birthday. So what was this signal she was getting? Why was she beating herself up like this? It dawned on her that her heart was trying to communicate something, but her brain had interfered, redirecting the heart's message into mental self-abuse about her weak character. But was that the message? That she wasn't an admirable person? No. She decided not. The brain had screwed up. So Debbie listened for a moment, a little closer this time. And she realized her heart was trying to convey sadness. She wasn't mad for forgetting. She was sad she wasn't going to see her mother on her birthday for the first time in her life. Debbie looked out over the desert and tried to convince herself it didn't matter.

Just then Spence hung up the phone. He turned to Boyd and Debbie, gesturing with the gun. "Saddle up," he said. "We're going to Salt Lake."

The group turned to head back to the Mustang when Rose's weak voice emerged from the backseat. "Spencer? Is that a gun?"

When he heard his mother's voice, Spence had a minor panic attack. What would he tell her? The truth? He wasn't sure what the truth was, except that someone had tried to take the heart she was supposed to get and that he had subsequently recaptured the organ and, depending on your point of view, he had either been joined by two concerned citizens or he had kidnapped two people in the process, one of whom was a cop. How would she react to that? More important, how would her heart react? And even if Spence told a convincing lie, what if Debbie or Officer Bobb started talking about being kidnapped? That would surely do her in. Or Boyd? What if he spilled the beans in an attempt to get their mother to talk Spence into giving up? Spence might have worked himself into a psychotic break over the possibilities, except that he noticed none of the others were on the verge of saying anything. In fact, upon hearing her trembling voice, everyone quietly turned to look at Rose as if she were a freshly hatched chick.

"Spence?" Her voice was growing weaker.

He quickly put the gun behind his back, leaned down to the car, and spoke gently. "Hi, Mom. How are you feeling?" The others gathered behind him, peering over his shoulder.

Rose's eyes closed slowly. "Wooooozy," she said. Then she drifted back to sleep.

"Mom?" She didn't answer. Spence turned to Debbie. "Is she all right?"

Debbie squeezed into the back of the Mustang and gave Rose a quick exam. "She seems fine. It's just going to take her a couple of tries to come out of the drug."

Spence thought for a moment, then pulled the gun from behind his back, pointing it at the group like a reluctant Edward G. Robinson. "Okay, here's the deal. We can't tell her the truth. I'll make something up, and you guys play along, all right? When she comes to and starts asking questions, we—"

"Put the gun away." Officer Bobb said it in his no-nonsense cop voice. "None of us is going to run off into the desert, and even if we did, you're not going to shoot anybody. And it won't do your mother's heart any good to see you holding a bunch of strangers at gunpoint, so just put it up and let's get this show on the road."

Boyd was strangely taken by the way Officer Bobb had said it. He didn't threaten Spence or try to act tough. And what he said made sense. He had a nice, deep voice that Boyd found comforting, and his shoulders were broad and seemed reliable. Boyd was glad, in a way he didn't understand, that they'd been forced to bring him along.

Spence hesitated, considering Officer Bobb's point. "Right," he said. "You're right." He looked at the gun, unsure what to do with it. "But, you know, it's weird. When you're holding a gun and telling people what to do, you just naturally wave it around. Now, everybody get in." He gestured at the car with the gun. "See? Like that."

Boyd put the Mustang onto Highway 58 heading east. It was ninety-one and getting hotter. As soon as they were on the road, Officer Bobb took his shirt and pants off again. Boyd took off his tie and unbuttoned his shirt. Spence pulled a map from the glove box. "All right, we're coming up on Barstow, we'll take I-15 from there to Salt Lake."

Debbie reached forward. "Can I see the map?" Spence handed it to her. She squinted as she looked at it, mumbling as she calculated. "Okay, it's about five hundred miles to Salt Lake. The heart's good for another four and a half hours, right? So that means we'll have to average a hundred thirty miles an hour and pee out the window. Oh, and we can't stop for gas. Wastes too much time." She handed the map back to Spence. "Otherwise your plan's great."

"She makes a point," Boyd said.

"We'll never get there in time," Officer Bobb added.

Spence grabbed the map and studied it for a moment. They were right. The drive was impossible if the heart was good only for another four and a half hours. Spence kept staring at the map, but it went blurry as he took a moment to focus on his situation. He was pretty sure Debbie was lying about the FBI and the president, since they hadn't seen so much as a highway patrol unit, let alone the CIA or Secret Service or ATF. He found it hard to believe that the federal government could be that inept. But even if it wasn't the president—if it was just some big swinging dick and they weren't in imminent danger—what were the odds this Dr. Speyburn would come through for them instead of just calling the cops or just not being there?

The choices weren't good, but Spence had to make one. Giving up was a virtual death sentence for Rose. Continuing might not be much better. But what if Speyburn bought it? What if he was waiting for some of that Microsoft money in Salt Lake? Even if he wasn't, Spence thought, what would happen if they just showed up at a hospital with a heart about to expire and the patient who UNOS said was supposed to get it? They'd have to operate, right? Hospital policy would likely be guided by liability issues, so which presented the greater liability, doing the transplant or not? What would they do, let the heart and, by extension, the patient die? Spence's eyes focused on the map again. He stabbed a finger at it with the force of an idea. "Look, we can be in Vegas in two and a half hours. We'll fly from there. It's probably not an hour to Salt Lake. We're there with time to spare."

Debbie was starting to feel sorry for him. After all, he just wanted to help his mother. She felt a bit embarrassed over getting so excited earlier about the idea of having some vague celebrity attach to her as a result of her actions in delivering the heart for the FBI. It had seemed like the right thing to do at the time, especially with the threatening FBI guy, the head of the hospital barking at her, and the helicopter on the roof. It hadn't smelled completely kosher, but Debbie was told what to do, and, just as she'd been trained, she did it reflexively.

But now, removed from the chaos of the moment, it was obvious to Debbie that the government had no right to kill this woman, which for all practical purposes is what they would have done had Spence not acted on his own. The government was simply wrong. She wasn't an ethicist or an attorney, but it struck her as morally and legally and obviously wrong.

And here's this one guy, willing to fight for what was right. He had to assume going in that he was up against big odds, but not as big as the entire federal government. Debbie felt a pang of respect for Spence. This was the most heroic thing she'd ever witnessed. All of a sudden Debbie wasn't so sure whose side she was on. She considered telling Spence about the ECC device, telling him he had plenty of time to get to Salt Lake. But something stopped her. That bit of information was the only advantage she had. She couldn't imagine the situation where it might be the bargaining chip she needed, but she figured it would be better to have it then than to give it up now.

Boyd, meanwhile, drove on, silent and mired in disbelief. He was thinking about how fast things had changed and how little control he had over if, when, and how things did. Just yesterday he was a guy with a future. A guy with a good job, good kids, and a good wife. A wife he had neglected. A wife who was a wonderful mother to his children. A wife he had certainly disappointed. But now all that was gone. Now he was Richard Kimble, on the road with his brother the serial kidnapper. He still had a future, but it was far less Optimist Club than it had been.

While they all were lost in their own world of considerations, Rose opened her eyes. She looked around and took in as much as she could. Then, still slightly groggy, she asked, "Boyd, honey, where are we going?" Boyd's eyes jerked to the mirror. The rest of them turned in their seats. "What about my operation?"

Boyd looked to Spence, who said, lamely, "Mom? How are you feeling?"

She shook her head slightly. "What happened?"

"Uh, there was a rolling blackout," Spence said.

Rose crinkled her face. "What?"

Joining his brother's lie, Boyd nodded and waved a hand. "Yeah, you know, the whole energy crisis. No power. They couldn't do the operation. Goes to show how we really need a more coherent energy policy in this country." As if Rose, who had expected to wake up in a hospital bed with a new heart in her chest but instead found herself sitting in the back of a sweltering Mustang, wearing a hospital gown, between two strangers, one of whom was nearly naked, might be baited into a discussion about federal energy policy instead of one about the lifesaving heart transplant she was supposed to have received.

Rose was confused, and not just because of the benzodiazepam. Much as she loved her sons, she knew they weren't the two brightest stars in the sky. *Bless their hearts,* she thought, *the bigger brains went to others.* And, okay, maybe she shouldn't have been drinking when she was pregnant, but no one had told her back then. Still, her boys had done fine for themselves by many standards. Granted, Boyd was in a job he couldn't put his heart into and Spence had always been so much more concerned about fighting for causes that she worried if he would ever take the time to find a nice girl and settle down. But what could she do? He was a big boy now and had to take care of himself. "Rolling blackouts?" She tilted her head to the left the way she always did. "That doesn't make any sense, for Pete's sake," she said. "The hospital has its own generators."

Spence was turned around in his seat, facing Rose. "The doctors didn't want to take a chance. So we're going to Salt Lake City for the operation." He tried to sound as cheery as he could. "Electricity's good there." He paused before he said, "You know those Mormons." He chuckled.

Debbie looked at him as if to say, *You know those Mormons?*

"Well, why aren't we flying?" Rose asked.

"You know, that's what I asked," Spence said. "And . . . well, you explained it earlier," he said, pointing at Debbie. "And I thought you did a great job, so why don't you"—he pointed at Rose—"do it again?"

Rose looked at Debbie, who smiled before putting on her doctor face. She reached into her head and pulled out "Deep vein thrombosis. Even though the flight's not very long, on balance we decided that driving to Salt Lake was the best plan we could come up with." Debbie glanced at Spence as she said the last part.

Rose turned to face Debbie. "You seem familiar, dear. Who are you?"

"Oh, I'm sorry. I'm Dr. Robbins." She offered her hand. "Debbie Robbins. I'm a surgical resident at Mulholland Memorial. I saw you briefly this morning. How are you feeling?" She took Rose's hand and felt her pulse.

"Light-headed," Rose said.

"That's the benzodiazepam wearing off." Debbie opened a bottle of water and handed it to Rose. "Here, you need to get some fluids in your system."

"Thank you, dear." Rose took a swallow, then turned to her left. She smiled politely at Officer Bobb and, with a quick downward glance, said, "Young man, you're not wearing any pants."

"Yes, ma'am. It's just so hot."

"It certainly is," Rose said, leaning forward. "Boyd, dear, could you turn the air-conditioning up? We're not getting anything back here."

There was a noise, like creaking wood, as Boyd's teeth ground together.

"By the way, I'm Officer Randall Bobb." He held up his shirt to show his badge. "I'm with the Los Angeles Police Department." He sat up straight, proud. "And I'm gay." He smiled.

Rose wasn't sure how to respond to that. She smiled politely and said, "Well, you certainly have the legs for it."

"Oh. Really?" Officer Bobb hadn't intended to tell Rose he was gay. It just came out. He decided he wouldn't tell anyone else.

Boyd, meanwhile, felt something curious within himself, and he looked in the mirror. "Did you say you were gay?"

"Yes, and it's thanks to Spence that I finally came out."

"Well, good for you," Rose said. She didn't know what he meant by that, and she started to wonder if maybe Spence was looking for a nice young man instead of a nice girl. *He has always been sensitive,* she thought, *and as long as he's happy.* Rose sipped again from the water bottle and watched the desert blur past for a moment, thinking. Her face grew serious. "Well, you all must think I'm confused from these drugs or that I'm just plain stupid."

Spence tried to act innocent. "What are you talking about?"

"Spencer Tailor, I know when I'm being lied to. Do you want to try again?"

Despite having lost visual contact with the Mustang half an hour earlier, Rodgers and Hart seemed unconcerned as they cruised down Highway 58. Jed X was driving, equally nonchalant, as if he'd picked up a pair of friendly hitchhikers instead of having been carjacked. Rodgers was in the passenger seat staring at the big green spiderweb tattoo centered on Jed X's right elbow. It spread up and down his arm and annoyed Rodgers for reasons beyond his ken.

Agent Hart was in the back, hunched over, looking at something in the valise.

Rodgers turned and cast a jealous eye at the custom interior and contents of Jed X's van. Skateboards, mounted like rifles in a gun rack, angled against the back walls like wheeled shingles. Long boards, short boards, plywood, Fibreflex, all with gleaming custom trucks and personalized paint jobs ranging in theme from pseudosatanism to the praise of hemp. Helmets, knee pads, elbow pads, wrist braces. Weapons and armor for a different kind of fight.

Agent Rodgers sighed. This was the sort of thing he had been denied as a kid. While his father made sure there was no long hair or dope smoking, his mother refused to allow him to participate in any activity that might result in physical harm. *No football or baseball or hockey for you, young man.* He was forced to learn chess and piano, and for that he'd been taunted and teased and eternally tormented. He remembered one day staring out his window at neighborhood kids playing football when one of them raced and dodged the length of a field without being touched. He wondered what it must have felt like to score. To be the hero. To put points on the board. To be cheered. But it was something his mother never allowed him.

Jed X noticed Agent Rodgers admiring his boards. "Yo, you old school or what?"

Rodgers made a disparaging noise as he gestured at the skateboards. "Games are for losers."

Jed X shrugged. "Awww, now, c'mon, G, show me a l'il love."

Agent Hart looked up from the valise. "They're still eastbound," he said. "But we need to close the distance if we want to keep our client comfortable."

Rodgers nudged Jed X with his gun. "Give it some gas, Cheech."

Jed X glanced into the valise and saw what looked like a radar screen. "'Sup with the Lojack, yo?"

"GPS," Hart said. "Designed, funded, and controlled by the Department of Defense."

"Yo, check it, homes, you droppin' the science like it's all hush-hush, but, shit, they got all that bling bling in the new Lex." Jed X nodded seriously. And he was right. GPS had become optional equipment for luxury cars, whose owners apparently found themselves having not the slightest idea where they were at such an alarming rate as to make GPS seem like a great idea. Jed X pointed at the screen. "Yo, dog, that show where we at?"

"You wanna know where *you* at, look out the damn window," Hart said. "This tells me where someone else is."

Jed X nodded for a moment before waving a hand at Agent Rodgers. "Ay, yo, trip, I gotta ax, how long this gon' take? Whatever we up to. See, I'm supposed to be thowin' down at the Darwin Games pretty soon." He swaggered in his seat. "Been polishin' a fresh Benihana blunt-slide nose bonk triple-backhand ollie to a double lutz-out."

Rodgers stared at him, stone-faced.

Jed X, reading more into the stare than existed, explained his radical notion. "Yo, gotta guard my grill." As if that explained everything. "Whole thing kicks tomorrow."

"Yeah? Where?" Not that Rodgers really cared.

Jed X started to say something, then stopped. He looked down the road and thought for a moment. "Somewhere," he said. "Rock Springs or Glenwood Springs or Colorado Springs. Someplace with a 'Springs' in it. I wrote it down somewhere."

"Idiot."

Jed X stabbed a couple of gang gestures in the air. "You betta step off, Jake! Gettin' all federal up in my face, shit." He motioned toward the past. "I was just marinatin' back there with my Scooby Doo, and you slip up all Five-O and jack my ass." He shook his head. "That's some no-diggety shit." He seemed genetically obligated to angry posturing and violent hand gestures with every utterance.

Rodgers wondered if Senator Check would object to his killing Jed X and leaving him in a shallow grave in the desert. Probably, he figured, but there was no reason she had to know about it. He was just going to broach the subject when Agent Hart leaned forward from the back, smiling. He pointed out the front window. "There they are."

Connie was doing the best she could under the circumstances. Her schedule had been shot to hell by the FBI. She'd left messages for Boyd at his office and on his cell phone, which for some reason seemed to be out of range or something. She considered calling the police but on second thought decided they'd be compelled to frown on her holding an FBI agent hostage, so she called the only other person she could think of who might be in a position to help.

Agent Sandlin was in the living room, seated in an ersatz Louis XVI–style balloon-back chair demonstrating one of the many uses of duct tape. He was bound but not gagged, so there was nothing to hide his worried expression, which reflected the fact that his first job evaluation was scheduled for the coming week. "You're making a big mistake," he said to Connie.

"Well, someone is anyway." Connie had the phone in one hand. She was on hold. She plucked her earrings off, setting them on a faux Italian carved beech console table next to Agent Sandlin's gun and badge. "Yes," she said into the mouthpiece. "I'd like to speak to Winston Archer, please." She rolled her eyes in exasperation. "Yes, I'll hold." She wandered into the kitchen with the phone. The Bundt cakes were cooling on a rack.

Erica was sitting on the stairs looking at Agent Sandlin. "I bet you feel pretty stupid," she said. Agent Sandlin glared at her.

A second later Boyd Jr. came bouncing down the stairs with a high-powered squirt gun. "This is so cool," he said, squirting Agent Sandlin's lap. "Look! He peed his pants."

"Hey, stop it," Agent Sandlin said. "It's a crime to wet a federal agent."

"No it's not," Erica said. "That's stupid." She didn't appreciate having her intelligence underestimated.

Boyd Jr. squirted Agent Sandlin again. "Wouldn't it be cool if we made Dad give us a bigger allowance to keep our mouths shut about all this?"

Agent Sandlin shook his head. "Your parents are going to prison for a very long time."

Boyd Jr. looked up the stairs to his sister. "Cool."

Erica nodded. "Yeah, maybe the social workers will let us go live with Uncle Spence."

"Oh, yeah. That'd be cool."

"He'll be in prison, too," Sandlin said with a dark expression. "If he's still alive."

Erica took offense at the FBI agent's cheap tactic. She grabbed the squirt gun from her brother, then aimed it at Sandlin. "You know, taped to that chair? You don't scare me much." She squirted him in the face.

Sandlin spit and sputtered. "You better hope I don't get out of this chair," he said.

Connie wandered back from the kitchen. She had been connected with an associate producer. "Well, I know this is going to sound crazy, but I've got something of a situation here, and I thought Mr. Archer might be able to help."

Boyd Jr. slid down a few steps and looked out between the banister posts as if he were behind bars. "Have you ever tortured anybody?" he asked Agent Sandlin.

"Untie me and I'll tell you."

"Can't. You're not tied up." Boyd Jr. smiled. "You're taped." He looked at Erica. They both rolled their eyes. "Duh." Boyd Jr. took the squirt gun and wet the FBI man some more.

Agent Sandlin had a sudden and black thought about how federal snipers in past standoff situations had inadvertently shot and killed children.

"Well, here's the thing," Connie said. "I have kidnapped—though that may be too strong a word for it—uhhh, let's just say I have an FBI agent here who tried to remove my children and me from our home without any apparent cause."

Agent Sandlin motioned with his head for Boyd Jr. to come closer. "I'll give you ten thousand dollars to undo this tape."

"Liar." Boyd Jr. seemed skeptical. He wet Sandlin's lap some more.

"I swear." Sandlin was beginning to sound desperate.

Erica bloomed with inspiration. "I have a better idea," she said. She tapped her brother on the shoulder. "C'mon." They ran upstairs together and went to Erica's room.

Connie grew excited as she reached the climax of her story. "That's the really weird part. Apparently they think my husband and his brother stole a heart they say President Webster needs for a transplant." She paused. "That's exactly what I thought. 'Cause it was just a fainting spell, right? So why would he need a heart?" She paused again. "Wonderful," she said when the associate producer put her on hold. Connie turned to Agent Sandlin. "That seemed to get her attention."

"This is going to end badly," Sandlin said.

"We'll see," Connie said. She turned her attention back to the phone. "Yes, hello, Mr. Archer, my name is Connie Tailor, longtime listener, first-time caller."

Martin Brooks was not having the best morning of
his life. It had started at eight with polling data showing President Webster's job-approval rating down three
more points since the reported fainting spell. Around
nine Brooks learned that someone, assumed to be terrorists, had absconded with the heart intended for his
boss. An hour or so later he got word that Senator Check
was on television denying nonexistent rumors about
White House involvement in the disappearance of a
heart intended for a little old lady not far from Pasadena.
Forty-five minutes after that, he learned the press was
nosing around Mulholland Memorial Hospital. Some-
time later it dawned on Brooks that perhaps it wasn't a
terrorist act at all but rather an act by a desperate family member trying to keep a loved one alive at the
expense of the current administration. If that were the
case, the family had the benefit of a three-hour head
start. And finally, not five minutes ago, the Press Information Office reported a phone call from one of Winston Archer's producers asking for comments on an
allegation by a Los Angeles housewife who claimed to
have an FBI agent captive in her home after he came to
arrest her husband on charges of domestic terrorism in
connection with an attempt on the president's life.

The only good news Brooks had received was that the
intern with whom he'd been sleeping had agreed to
accept a job at the Justice Department in exchange for

keeping her mouth shut about their affair. So the morning wasn't a complete loss.

Still, Brooks had decisions to make and little time to make them. First he decided to get the president flying west in case they managed to find the stolen heart. That way less time would elapse between its reacquisition and its transplant. But since he knew there was a chance they might never find Mardell's heart, Brooks had earlier set in motion a backup plan, which explained why his assistant had just walked in and said, "Sir, the contingency organ is here to see you."

For a moment Brooks allowed himself the luxury of thinking his luck had finally changed. He knew the odds were slim they would find a local candidate. In fact, over the past few days Brooks had come to know exactly how slim those odds were. He had learned that with liver and kidney transplants there were tissue-match considerations, but with a heart transplant the only thing that mattered was blood type. The ABO system, Brooks now knew, was the best-known method for the classification of blood, which was divided into four types: A, B, AB, and O. Eighty-five percent of the U.S. population was either type A or type O, 10 percent were type B, and only 5 percent were AB. A concomitant classification method called the Rhesus system further divided the four types into Rh positive or Rh negative, depending on the type of Rhesus antigen present in the red cells. Eighty-five percent of all blood was Rh positive. In other words, Brooks knew that finding someone with AB-negative blood was a

major pain in the ass. And though there was no practical
way of testing the notion, since the ABO system had
been in existence only since the 1930s, the odds were
good that President Webster was the only AB-negative
chief executive in history.

Just my luck, Brooks thought.

However, thanks to a combination of public records
and assistance from friendly insurance companies,
Brooks knew the blood type of virtually every person
born in the United States. Under normal circumstances
that wouldn't be particularly helpful, but when trying to
locate a potential "volunteer" for a heart transplant, such
information was invaluable.

Not wanting to pluck a rare AB-negative taxpayer at
random from his or her home just yet, Brooks had his
assistant begin the search in-house, looking at all
branches of the military as well as the records of anyone
working for any of the federal police agencies. They
found several candidates, but only one they could get to
the White House within the required time frame.

Grant entered the chief of staff's office with the "volunteer." "Mr. Brooks, this is Staff Sergeant Kravit,
United States Marine Corps."

Staff Sergeant Kravit snapped to attention.

Brooks liked what he saw. "Relax, soldier," he said.
"At ease." The marine clasped his hands behind his back.
Brooks turned to his assistant. "Leave us, please." After
Grant closed the door, Brooks propped himself on the
corner of his desk. He looked at Staff Sergeant Kravit.
"Son, what did your CO tell you about this mission?"

"Nothing, sir. Classified."

"No idea?"

"No, sir."

Excellent, Brooks thought. Gung ho. Trained to take orders, no questions asked. "Son, this is a rare day in your life. Your chance to fully serve your country has finally arrived."

Staff Sergeant Kravit snapped back to attention. "Excellent, sir. Semper Fi, sir!" He never even considered what Mr. Brooks meant by his use of the word "fully."

Brooks slowly moved off his desk and began pacing, hands clasped behind his back. "As with anything of this magnitude, there's good news and there's bad news."

"Sir, yes, sir!"

"The good news is, you're going to become president of this country."

This was so far out in left field Staff Sergeant Kravit couldn't even see it. He broke his rigid posture for the first time as he looked at the chief of staff. "President, sir?"

"That's right, of the United States." He waited for Kravit to say something, but nothing came from the soldier's open mouth. "The bad news is, it won't be all of you."

"How's that, sir?"

Brooks turned quickly and leaned into the young man's face, barking, "Staff Sergeant Kravit, are you prepared to die for your country?"

"Sir, yes, sir!"

"Lemme hear you say boo-yaa!"

"Boo-yaa, sir!" His face turned red and started to twitch.

Brooks stared at Staff Sergeant Kravit for a long time. He could tell the young man was willing to make the ultimate sacrifice. "At ease, soldier. You're a good man." The marine stood rigid, never looking askance, as Brooks explained. "There's no guarantee your service will be required; you're just our backup position. We'd rather not waste all the money we've spent training you."

"Sir, yes, sir!"

"Good. Any questions?"

Eyes fixed on the far wall, Staff Sergeant Kravit spoke. "Sir, may I have an hour to put my things in order and say good-bye to my mom?"

Martin Brooks was touched. He paused before nodding. "Permission granted, son."

"That's my point," Spence said. "The hospital in Canada simply admitted the kid and treated her. They didn't demand proof the family could pay, let alone proof they were Canadian citizens, which they weren't. And when they found out the kid was American, did they throw her onto the street? No. They contacted HMOs in the States, none of which would take her, since she didn't have insurance. So Canada is taking care of the kid because our HMOs won't."

"You're misplacing blame," Boyd said. "It's not the job of HMOs to take care of the kid, it's the kid's parents' job." Boyd assumed a patronizing tone. "Why is it liberals always demand warm and fuzzy solutions to life's problems? And why do they expect the government or the private sector to provide them? It's so naïve." He shook his head. "People die."

"And the poor should die in disproportionate numbers?" Spence said.

"Everybody dies," Boyd said. "The poor don't have a corner on the market."

"Your argument is that people should die if they can't afford insurance? Like it teaches them a lesson or something?"

"You're missing the point," Boyd said. "What were the kid's parents thinking? How smart is it to have children if you can't afford to insure them in a society that effectively delivers medical care through a system of insurance carriers?"

"Effectively?" Debbie leaned forward. "Insurance companies cap what they'll pay to treat particular diseases. I've seen a lot of people die of AIDS after insurance carriers stopped paying for treatments after only fifty thousand dollars."

"That's tragic, but—"

"If any of them had been hit by a car, they'd have paid up to half a million dollars," Debbie said. "What does that tell you? Of course, if they *weren't* insured and got hit by a car, most hospitals in this country wouldn't even admit them. I assume you've heard of patient dumping?"

"Yeah, well Congress is working on a patients' bill of rights."

"I've read it," Spence said. "And as Gail Collins at *The New York Times* wrote, 'the patients' bill of rights is to health-care reform what a gnat is to aviation.'"

"Yeah, yeah, and your argument is HMOs should go bankrupt treating illegal aliens. What happens then?"

"First of all, the kid was from the U.S. Secondly, if HMOs went under, we might find our way to providing health care for our citizens."

"Not that I don't enjoy a spirited political discussion," Rose said as she adjusted her immodest hospital gown. "But I'd still like an answer to my question."

"We're getting to it," Spence said. Hoping to distract Rose from the question she had asked a hundred miles earlier, Spence had started a string of medical-ethics arguments with his brother.

"Would someone just tell me what's going on?" Rose dabbed a tissue at her sweaty neck.

Boyd was frustrated after losing all the arguments. He was looking for a way to retaliate against Spence. So he glanced into the rearview mirror at his mom and said, "Someone tried to steal the heart, so Spence stole it back."

A moment passed as Rose tried to make sense of the words. "What?" Rose looked at Debbie, then at Officer Bobb. Both looked a bit sheepish but nodded.

Caught short by Boyd's unexpected confession, it took Spence a moment before he thought to hit his brother. "Ow!"

"You idiot!" Spence turned around in his seat. "Now, Mom, don't worry. I can explain."

A calm settled over Rose. "Who would try to steal it?"

"We're not sure," Spence said.

"Yes we are," Debbie said. "It was the government."

Rose shook her head. "What do you mean, the government?"

"President Webster didn't faint the other day," Debbie said. "He had a heart attack." She lifted the ECC device. "And he needs this heart." Debbie noticed for the first time a red light on top of the ECC device. It was blinking. She didn't recall seeing that before. Debbie looked at the LED screen. It said: LOW BATTERY.

"But that heart is rightfully mine." Rose looked at Debbie, her disbelief yielding to anger. "I waited my turn. They can't just take it." She turned to face Officer Bobb. "That's just wrong."

"Yes, ma'am," he said.

"We don't know it was for the president." Spence gestured at Debbie. "She says the FBI was at the hospital, but I never saw them. All we know is, the hospital was going to give it to someone else, so . . . I took it back, and now we're going to Salt Lake for the transplant."

"I tried to talk him out of it," Boyd said. "I told him I thought we should contact the authorities."

"Yes, dear, I'm sure you did." There was disappointment in Rose's voice. Boyd had always been the type to cover his own ass before considering others.

Her attention still focused on the ECC device, Debbie reached forward and tapped Spence's shoulder. "We have to stop."

"We don't have time to stop," he said. "We have to get to Vegas."

"If we don't stop, getting to Vegas won't matter." She pointed to the ECC device. "We need a new battery."

"For what? The thing's on ice." For the first time since the ordeal began, Spence took a closer look at the device. It was obviously more high-tech than an ice chest. He looked up and saw Debbie's chagrined expression. "Don't tell me we've caught you in another lie."

10

How Can You Mend
a Broken Heart?

Rolling along a quarter mile behind the Mustang, Rodgers and Hart listened as Debbie explained how the ECC device worked. Jed X listened, too, though what he heard might as well have been a discussion about subatomic-particle theory. "Yo, J. Edgar, drop summora that science on my ass. 'Sup with a warm-storage device, yo?"

Rodgers yanked on one of Jed's dreadlocks, then pointed down the road. "You know what, rasta boy? Your job here is to follow that Mustang. Period."

Jed X jerked his head. "Oh, it's like that?" He gestured angrily with exaggerated fingers and punctuating stabbing motions. "Now you gon' dis my locks? 'At's cold. I ain't said nathan 'bout *yo* damn do." He stabbed a gesture at Agent Hart. "And you with the sorry-ass fade."

"They're pulling in, Snoop Dogg." Rodgers pointed at the gas station. "Park at the other end of the lot."

As Boyd pulled up to the gas pumps, Jed X steered the van to a spot at the far side of the gas station. One after the other, Boyd, Spence, Debbie, Rose, and Officer Bobb climbed out of the Mustang like sweaty clowns. Boyd went to top off the tank while the others headed inside. Debbie and Spence walked ahead of Officer Bobb, who helped Rose dodder across the parking lot. When they were out of earshot, Spence turned to Debbie. "This is what, the third or fourth lie we've caught you in? How do I even know you're a doctor?"

"Look, I could have kept my mouth shut. I could have let the battery and the heart die—and then where would you be?"

"You're right," Spence said. "I'll submit your name to the Nobel committee."

Inside the store they went to the battery display. Debbie lifted the ECC device over her head, looking at the underside for the battery compartment. "Looks like it takes a three-volt CTB32 lithium. About the size of a thick dime, I'd guess."

Spence looked at the carousel of batteries. He spun it around slowly, reading the model numbers. "Here's an ECR2320. Will that work?"

Debbie looked, then shook her head. "Too big."

Spence continued searching the rack. "Here's a

thought. How do you replace the battery without the heart stopping?"

"Good question." Debbie shook her head. "Knowing the government, they failed to take that into consideration."

"Wouldn't it just start beating again?"

"Not likely. We'd need to jump-start it." She looked at Spence. "Did you think to bring a defibrillator?" Spence glared at her. "No? Well, maybe we can use jumper cables or something."

Spence made one final spin through the carousel. "It may be a moot point," he said. "They don't have the battery we need." He looked at the ECC device, then at the doctor. "So what do you suggest?"

"Well, the FBI guy said as long as the liquids stay around thirty-seven Celsius, the heart keeps beating, so even if it's slow, we're okay. But sooner or later the battery's going to die and the temp's going to drop."

"Then what?"

"The heart stops, and we'll have about four hours."

"Before the heart's useless?"

"Pretty much. Once it stops, we'll have to do things the old-fashioned way." She turned to the clerk. "Where's your ice?"

Sitting quietly in the van in the parking lot watching his kidnappers watch the people from the Mustang, Jed X was aware he was involved in some sort of secret government operation. As this was his first, he wasn't sure about certain protocols. So after a few minutes Jed X made an inquiry. "Ay, yo, trip, I'm gon' for some corn dogs and Oreos, yo. You want a Big Gulp or somethin'?" He was reaching for the door when he felt the gun pressed against the side of his neck, right in the eye of a weeping-skull tattoo.

"Hands on the wheel. Now."

Jed X complied quickly, then looked at Rodgers. "'Sup with the 'tude, yo? No need to wet my ass just 'cause I wanna get my snack on."

"Hungry's better than dead."

Jed X conceded the point. "Word."

Another minute passed before Agent Hart turned and glanced out the back window. What he saw made him jerk so hard his teeth snapped. "Fuck!" He whirled and tore into the duffel bag.

Rodgers turned and saw the black Suburban screech to a stop. "Holy shit! What happened to our intel? Jesus! Hurry!"

"Yo, dog, why you trippin'?" Jed X turned and saw Hart screwing a silencer onto a small semiautomatic. "Whoa, G, you oughta get your AK if you fixin' a step-to." As Jed X was considering how phat that sounded, he saw a man climb out of the Suburban wearing a full desert-camo outfit. He carried a weapon neither Rodgers nor Hart had ever seen. A long barrel, balanced stock and grip, connecting to a tube and a tank of some sort. "Damn!" Jed X said, with one of his hand-stabbing gestures. "That bee-atch is strapped for some shit."

Hart pointed at the man's weapon. "Holy Mother! What the hell is that? That's gotta be NSA stuff. And I'm not wearing a damn vest."

"Vest might not stop whatever that is," Rodgers said.

"Word up." Jed X folded his arms in defiance and watched.

The man in camos was heading straight for the store, no dawdling. A big, grim-looking son of a bitch, eyes hidden behind wraparound mirrors.

Rodgers turned to Hart. "Go!" he shouted. "Now!"

Hart threw open the van's side door and moved with as much stealth as the situation allowed. He reached the man before anyone in the store could see whatever was going to happen. "Hey," Hart called out. He had one hand raised, one behind his back.

The man in camos looked up, an emotionless pit-bull face. "You talkin' to me?"

Hart's hand came from behind his back. *Pwip! Pwip!* Hart's first two shots hit abdomen and chest, stopping the man's progress. He began slumping forward but seemed determined not to stop. *Pwip!* The third shot stood him back up, Hart advancing on him the entire time. The man raised his weapon and squeezed off a shot just as Hart reached him. *Fup!* The shot missed Hart by an inch before something neon green splattered in Bob Marley's hair on the side of Jed's van. As Hart slung the man's arm over his shoulder and started to drag him around the side of the building, someone in the black Suburban threw it into reverse and floored it. Hart couldn't get a clean shot at whoever it was. They were gone in a hurry. Hart propped the man against the building's back wall before returning to the van.

Jed X had watched the whole thing as if it were a music video. "Damn, you smoked that punk-ass bitch," he said when Hart returned to the van. He pretended to be firing a pair of guns. "Gettin' loose with the deuce-deuce." He imitated the dead man, with his head lolled to the side. "Ole 'Bama out there kickin' it in the gansta lean now."

Hart slapped the side of Jed X's head. "Would you shut up?" He slammed the van door shut and grabbed the duffel bag.

Rodgers pointed at the interior side of the van. "The hell was that? It didn't penetrate."

"Don't know, never seen it," Hart said as he dug urgently through the canvas bag. "Green liquid. Chemical, biological, who the hell knows? It's on the side of the van. I didn't get any on me."

"What?" Jed X glanced in his side mirror, irritated. "That janky-ass camo boy got some shit on the side of my ride?" He got out of the van to look. There was a watery green liquid splashed on the airbrushed Bob Marley. "Punk got Bob's plats all green. Damn." He touched the emerald liquid, then rubbed his fingers together. "Shit better wash off." Jed X sniffed at his hand as he returned to the driver's seat.

Hart pulled something from the duffel bag and tossed it to Rodgers. "Here."

"You don't wanna wait?" Rodgers asked.

"Hell no, I don't wanna wait," Hart said. "You wanna wait?"

"I guess not."

Jed X watched as the men opened the kits, each of which contained two unusual-looking hypodermics. They were bright yellow sealed units with no finger flanges at the base. Rodgers and Hart popped the tip protectors off the needles and looked at each other. "One, two, go." They jammed the autoinjectors into their thighs. The sudden release of an inert gas within the sealed hollow barrel pushed the plungers, forcing nerve- and biological-agent antidotes of atropine and pralidoxime chloride and God-knows-what-else into their muscles.

Rodgers's eyes rolled back in his head. "Yow!" He rubbed his thigh.

Jed X was sitting in the driver's seat shaking his head. "Hey, yo, James Bond, check it. The green stuff?" He held up his finger. "Looks like you capped yourself a paint-ball busta." Rodgers and Hart exchanged disbelieving expressions. Jed X shook his head. He had to laugh. "Y'all a pair-a scary muthafuckas."

Air Force One, of which there is a pair of two, are Boeing 747-200Bs modified for in-flight refueling and advanced communications systems. The planes also feature a custom interior configuration including an executive suite as well as a special section outfitted with equipment for medical emergencies. The aircraft are maintained by the Presidential Maintenance Branch and are assigned to Air Mobility Command's Eighty-ninth Airlift Wing at Andrews Air Force Base, minutes south of Washington.

At Martin Brooks's direction, President Webster had been spirited from the White House and slipped on board via the catering truck that serviced through the rear door of the aircraft. Now, with the four GE CF6-80C2B1 jet engines spooling up, Martin Brooks was in the executive office of Air Force One waiting for the arrival of Staff Sergeant Kravit and his heart.

Grant finished a phone call and approached his boss. "Sir, I'm afraid the contingency organ is AWOL."

"What about his escort?"

"Bound and gagged in the trunk of his car, sir."

Brooks took a moment, frowning, then looked up at his assistant. "What's your blood type?"

"O-positive, sir. Sorry."

"Me and you both," Brooks said. "All right. Find me another one, and tell the captain to get this thing in the air."

Once they were airborne, Grant worked the phones, setting in motion the search for a second contingency organ and collecting information regarding the whereabouts of the heart taken from Mardell Coleman. By the time they had cleared Virginia airspace, Grant was ready to report to his boss. He flipped his phone shut and returned to the executive office, where he found Martin Brooks staring out the window. "Sir, we can't make a connection between the heart and any known terrorist group. The best evidence points at the family."

"All right, so we—"

Grant's phone rang. "Excuse me, sir."

While Grant took the call, Martin Brooks looked out the window and thought about those long-ago days at the Bohemian Club. He remembered his father's paraphrasing Barry Goldwater. "Extremism in the defense of your goal is no vice," he would say. Then, misconstruing Vince Lombardi, "Winning isn't everything; it's the only thing." Martin Brooks knew the real quotes but preferred the ones his dad used. He tried to live by them.

"Sir," Grant said as he put his phone down, "they used a Visa card to buy gas."

"The Tailors?"

"Yes, sir."

"Where the hell are they?"

"They were at a convenience store near Barstow, sir. But that was a couple of hours ago. We made contact with the cashier at the store. He said they were in a red '65 Mustang."

"I thought they were in a brown pickup truck."

"Turns out Boyd Tailor owns the Mustang."

"Why are we just learning this?"

"Snafu at the DMV, sir. It happens."

"Christ. All right, which way were they headed?"

"The attendant wasn't sure, sir."

"Well, what are the options?"

"If they left Los Angeles on the 10 East, then went north on I-15, they'd have to be going west on the 58, heading toward Bakersfield or Reno. Or they could have backtracked onto I-40, which puts them eastbound probably heading for Flagstaff, then maybe south to Phoenix. Or they could be heading north toward Vegas."

"Is that it?"

"No, sir, those are just a few of the scenarios. They could have left L.A. through the Antelope Valley and be circling back, heading for San Bernardino."

"What the hell for?"

"Loma Linda Medical Center, sir. Terrific cardiac staff. That's where they did the Baby Fae baboon-heart transplant back in 1984."

"Sounds more like a vet hospital."

"Of course, they *could* continue south to San Diego or even Mexico. We're also looking into charter flights out of all the small airfields out there."

"Let me see if I got this right," Brooks said. "The best information we have is that the people with the heart might be in a red Mustang going either north, south, east, or west?"

"A 1965 Mustang, sir. That narrows it down considerably."

"How much road are we looking at?"

"Over a thousand miles, sir."

"Well, what're you waiting for? Get some birds in the air."

Senator Check was working on the speech for the next fund-raiser sponsored by the Association of Southern Petroleum Producers. Her assistant had given her a new list of expressions to work into her repertoire, and she felt like she was starting to get the hang of it. She looked up when Britton came into her office. There was a bounce in her voice. "Hey, check this out," she said. The senator slipped on her bifocals and read aloud from her notes, "'While President Webster has said he means to push for the oil and gas tax credit legislation, "mean to" don't pick no cotton.'" She looked over the top of her glasses. "Not bad, huh?"

"That's perfect, Senator, but we just got some information."

Senator Check glanced quickly at the phrase list. "Well, cut the tail off the dog." She winked. "That means get to the point."

"Yes, ma'am, and brilliantly, if I might say so." Britton handed a document to the senator. "The White House figured out the Tailor family has the heart. And worse, they have a general idea where they are and what car they're in."

"What about our SAS-SOG team?"

"They're still following and waiting for orders."

Senator Check waved the document at Britton. "What's this about?"

"That's an unconfirmed report Air Force One recently left Andrews heading west. I contacted Air Mobility Command. They flatly denied it."

"So we'll take that as a confirmation."

"Yes, ma'am."

"Okay, Brooks will probably scramble choppers out of Nellis to scout for the Mustang. Tell the SAS-SOG team to get the Tailors into a new vehicle ASAP and report back"—she glanced again at her list of phrases— "quicker than a cutworm on a cabbage leaf."

Britton paused on her way out the door, an uncertain expression on her face.

Senator Check wrinkled her nose as she looked at the idioms. "Is that right?"

Rodgers pinched the evidence between his fingers like a soggy grape skin. "A paintball?" He flipped the withered thing out the window to the ground, then muttered, "People walking around with weapons like that. Unbelievable."

"Yo, cuz." Jed X smirked. "You and your road dog here is what's unbelievable." He mimicked the way they had stabbed the autoinjectors into their thighs like cartoon spies. Then, with all seriousness, he nodded toward the side of the building, "D'joo really ghost that Jethro?"

Rodgers started to answer but stopped. He bunched up, squeezing his eyes shut as the side effects of the atropine and pralidoxime began to manifest. Too much light poured in through abnormally dilated pupils. A wave of nausea and dizziness came and went. Rodgers reached over and wiped his green fingertips on Jed's shirt. "English is—what, your second or third language?"

Jed X lapsed into a gesticulating rap. "Hey, yo, I'm comin' correct and all 'bout it. I got it in check, gon' shout it."

Rodgers smacked Jed X upside the head. "Yo, shut up."

Agent Hart gestured for both of them to shut up. He

was struggling with double vision and tachycardia while talking on the phone with Senator Check. He took shallow breaths, trying not to hyperventilate. "Right," he said. "We'll do that now." He flipped his phone shut and dug back into the duffel bag.

"Do what right now?" Rodgers asked through a dry mouth.

Hart nodded at Boyd's car. "Get 'em out of the Mustang."

"What happened?"

"They ID'd it." Agent Hart removed something from the bag. It was green and pliable, like a gob of wasabi. Working it between his palms, he rounded it into the size of a golf ball, then inserted a detonator that looked like a computer chip, smoothing over the dimple left behind.

"Is that enough?" Rodgers sounded skeptical.

Hart shrugged. "Don't want to blow the gas pumps."

Rodgers nodded. Looking around, he saw only a motorcycle, apparently belonging to the store's cashier. "So then what? Not a lot of other vehicles to choose from out here," he said. "What do we do, offer them a ride?"

Hart shook his head. "No. We can't insert ourselves into their situation. Has to be the other way around."

Rodgers mulled it a moment, then nodded. "I guess he'll kidnap us."

Hart nodded. "If we're his only choice." He pulled a tiny radio transmitter from the bag, then motioned toward the store. "Keep 'em inside for a minute."

Rodgers headed for the store. Agent Hart had Jed X drive over to the gas pumps and park between the Mus-

tang and the store. Hart slipped out of the van, popped
the Mustang's hood, and placed the doughy green stuff
on the engine block. He closed the hood, hopped back
into the van, and told Jed X to drive to the far side of the
lot again. Once they were parked, Agent Hart looked at
his tattooed driver. His left arm was covered by a full-
color fantasy tableau featuring a swirling collection of
mutant creatures that reminded Hart of a poster for a
creepy circus sideshow. "All right, Queequeg," he said,
"here's the deal." Hart pointed toward the store. "Those
folks are going to ask us for a ride, and we're going to give
them one. If they start inquiring about who we are, you
just say I'm your coach and my partner is your, uh . . .
sports psychologist."

Jed X nodded slyly. "Yo, G, I know we down low, an'
that's cool, long as I gets to my games in time to get all
crunk and clock me some serious ducats."

Agent Hart reached over suddenly and pinched one
of the stainless-steel dog bones that pierced Jed X's
eyebrow. He gave it a sharp twist.

"Ow, ow, ow, quit it!" He swatted Agent Hart's hand
from his face. "I said I'd play along!" White as Pat Boone.

"Good." Hart fixed him with his hardest Miles Davis
glare. "Long as we're on the same page, I ain't gotta bust
a cap in your weak-ass crown."

As Hart tormented Jed X, Rodgers ambled into the
store. He paused at the newspaper rack by the door and
bent over, feigning interest in the front page. He kept his
peripheral vision on Boyd, who was standing nearby
looking out toward the gas pumps. Glancing up at the

convex security mirror, Rodgers saw Spence remove a sack of ice from the freezer. After a moment he and Debbie headed for the cash register, where Rose and Officer Bobb were cooling themselves under the air-conditioning vent. As Rose was still wearing only the hospital gown, Officer Bobb stood behind, guarding her modesty.

"What do we owe you?" Spence asked the cashier.

When Boyd took a step toward the front door, Agent Rodgers casually stopped him, gesturing out toward the Mustang. "Nice car," he said. "Is that a '66?"

Like a proud father, Boyd was cheered by the stranger's interest in his baby. "Nope, she's a '65."

Rodgers nodded. "She's a beauty. My dad had a '64 and a half. Red with white interior." His voice took on a nostalgic softness. "I loved that car."

"He still have it?"

"Nah, he traded it in a long time ago."

"Too bad," Boyd said.

"Yeah." Rodgers assumed the expression of a sudden thought. "Hey! You wouldn't by chance be interested in selling, would you?"

Boyd opened his mouth to say something when he saw a flash of light followed by the hood of his Mustang shooting straight up in the air. "Jesus!" The explosion started a ferocious fire, consuming the engine as if it were a gas-soaked rag. Boyd's eyes bugged wide. He pushed Agent Rodgers aside and went racing out to his car. "Call 911!" he yelled.

The others ran out of the store as if pulled in Boyd's wake. The cashier raced for the gas-pump shutoff valve.

Boyd kept yelling, "911!" He got as close to the car as the heat allowed, but there was nothing he could do. Flames had spread to the interior and were curling out the windows, licking the roof. The paint blistered. The car was done. Boyd let out a terrible noise. It sounded like someone was kneecapping a howler monkey.

Agent Rodgers materialized at Boyd's shoulder, trying to offer comfort. "Aw, man. That's a shame. You insured?"

Boyd's head moved slightly, approximating a nod.

Rodgers clapped him on the back. "Well, there you go. It's not a total loss."

There followed a great deal of confusion as Officer Bobb attempted to douse the fire with a Class B fire extinguisher, the perfect tool for gasoline, kerosene, and common organic-solvent fires. Unfortunately, Agent Hart's incendiary device was a proprietary pyrophoric organometallic reagent that not only burned at two thousand degrees but also reacted violently with carbon dioxide, which happens to be the sole ingredient in Class B fire extinguishers. Fortunately, no one was hurt in the ensuing explosion. It did, however, put Officer Bobb off trying to save the rest of the car.

As that bit of insanity unfolded in front of his eyes, Spence assumed a weird calm. He wasn't used to making decisions like the ones he was having to make on this particular day, let alone make them so frequently, but he was starting to get into a groove. Spence found himself focused and quite clear that he had to make a choice. Quit or forge ahead? There were plenty of reasons to give up, not the least of which was the fact he was trapped in the middle of the Mojave with his getaway car currently being reduced to hot scrap metal.

Spence glanced to where Rose was standing. He could tell that she hadn't given up. She looked as defiant as he imagined possible for an old woman with heart disease whose hospital gown was flapping in the parched desert air. A smile of resolve crossed his face as he thought about her indignant response when told that the government had tried to usurp the heart that was rightfully hers. He tried to imagine what his mother would do if the situation were reversed, if one of her children needed the heart. Would she stop at anything to see the right thing done?

Spence walked to where Boyd and Agent Rodgers were standing, staring at the burning Mustang. Boyd looked at Spence, resignation in his voice. "Well, baby brother, now what?"

Spence looked around the parking lot. "I'm working on it." He saw a motorcycle and Jed X's van. He turned to Agent Rodgers. "That your van?"

"Yeah."

"Got air-conditioning?"

Rodgers nodded.

"Where you going?"

"Uh, west," Rodgers said.

"Not anymore." Spence reached under his shirt and pulled out the Glock. "We have to get to Las Vegas." He pointed the gun at Rodgers.

Rodgers calmly put his hands up. "You can have the van. Just don't hurt us."

"Us?"

"I'm not alone," he said. "Just take the van and let us go."

"I can't let you go," Spence said. "I've gotta kidnap you." Then, waving the gun like an admonishing finger, he added, "But don't tell my mom."

Winston Archer was of two minds when he arrived at Connie's house. Skeptical on the one hand that the woman's outlandish claims were true, hopeful on the other that they were. Winston and his producer reached the front door and rang the bell.

Connie, who had consumed two pots of coffee, greeted them like an overcaffeinated June Cleaver. "Hi, Mr. Archer? I'm Connie Tailor, it's nice to meet you. Thank you for coming."

"Pleasure," he said. "This is my producer, Nancy Mitchell."

Connie and Nancy shook hands. "Won't you come in?" In an attempt to dress the situation up with some hospitality, Connie offered Bundt cake and coffee. They declined. Connie then led them to the living room, pointed at Agent Sandlin, and said, "There he is."

Archer looked at the man duct-taped to the chair. "And you say he's with the FBI?"

Connie sensed Mr. Archer's skepticism. "That's what he claims." She pointed at the faux Italian carved beech console table. "He had that badge and that gun. You decide."

Archer examined the evidence, then walked over to Sandlin and looked down at him. "You really FBI?"

Sandlin nodded grimly. "Yeah."

"So if I call the local office and talk to your supervisor—"

The agent shook his head. "This one's off the books."

"Ahhhh." Archer raised an eyebrow. "Well, can you tell me about the president and his heart?"

Sandlin just stared at him.

Archer turned and pointed at Connie. "But you told her." Like he was insulted.

Sandlin gestured toward the window. He could see a man setting up the microwave antenna on Winston Archer's remote truck. "That was before I knew this was going to be televised."

"Are you sure you don't want some Bundt cake? It's fresh."

Mr. Archer smiled. "And it smells wonderful, Mrs. Tailor, but let me ask you about your mother's operation."

"Mother-in-law."

"Fine."

Connie told the whole story, from Rose's wait on the organ-transplant list to her scheduled operation to Spence's early-morning phone call.

Winston Archer and his producer listened without interruption, measuring Connie as she spoke. She seemed sincere, and that certainly appeared to be an FBI agent taped to that chair. "Mrs. Tailor, what did they say when you called the hospital?"

"They said the operation had been canceled. When I started to ask questions, they put me on one of those automated phone-routing systems until it disconnected me."

"Ah." Nancy Mitchell gestured at the phone. "May I?" She reached the media-relations department at Mulholland Memorial and confirmed to her satisfaction that something extravagantly screwy had happened, something so baroque in its nuttiness that she knew it would deliver the remaining 40 percent of the nation's radio and television markets if Winston Archer officially broke the story.

Connie and Winston stood there awkwardly, smiling at each other, then looking away, until Nancy hung up the phone. "So," Connie said, "what do you think?"

Nancy pulled a document from her briefcase and waved it at Connie. "I'll need you to sign this."

Connie signed the release form and gave it back to Nancy. "Now what?"

Mr. Archer looked at Connie, sincere and thoughtful. "I think we'll have some of that Bundt cake."

Boyd Jr. walked into Erica's room and quietly shut the door. Erica looked up from the computer screen. "What are they doing?"

"Eating cake," Boyd Jr. said.

Erica rolled her eyes. "That is so lame." She looked back to the computer. "Dad and Uncle Spence are, like, running from the cops, there's an FBI agent taped to a chair in the living room, and Mom's down there serving cake to that stupid radio-show guy."

"He's on TV, too," Boyd Jr. said.

"Whatever." Erica made one of those judgmental noises that only young girls can get away with making. "That is sooooo Martha Stewart."

"Is there anything about Dad in the news?"

"Not yet," Erica said. She swiveled in her chair and pointed at a shoe box on her bed. "Gimme a picture with Dad and Uncle Spence."

Boyd Jr. looked in the shoe box. It was filled with family photos. He picked one that made him smile. He showed it to Erica. "This was your birthday party. Dad looks funny."

"I think he was dizzy from spinning around," she said.

Boyd Jr. watched for a second. "What're you doing?"

Erica put the photo on her scanner. "Making gif files."

"Oh." Boyd Jr. watched for a moment before losing interest. "You want some cake?"

11

Expressway to Your Heart

Rose was staring at Jed X like he was something escaped from the circus. She pulled Spence close, never taking her eyes off the nose studs, lip rings, and tattoos. "Are you sure about this, dear? I think that young man has a something stuck through his tongue."

"Mom, we're working with a short list of options here."

"I suppose you're right." She held the back of her hospital gown closed behind her and moved toward the van's sliding door.

"Holy shit!" They all turned when they heard the voice of the cashier coming from the far side of the building. Rodgers and Hart assumed he had come across the dead man in camos after throwing the shutoff valves.

The cashier rounded the corner at a full sprint. When he saw Spence holding the gun, the kid began weaving toward his motorcycle, trying to make himself a difficult target. Jumping onto his bike, he got it started in one kick. He popped it into gear and raced off into the desert like a drunk stunt driver.

"I wonder what that was all about," Rose said.

There was much shrugging of shoulders and shaking of heads before Spence began herding everyone into the van. Rodgers and Hart climbed in first, followed by Boyd and Officer Bobb. Rodgers tried to peek down Debbie's shirt when she climbed in, but he had a bad angle.

In addition to the wall racks holding Jed X's skateboards, the custom interior featured four adjustable captain's chairs in two rows in the front with two overstuffed sofas bolted to the floor in the back. Rodgers and Hart took the captain's chairs behind the front seats while Officer Bobb and Debbie settled onto the middle sofa, leaving room for Rose between them. Boyd squeezed his way to the sofa by the rear doors.

Spence helped his mother into the van. "These folks were nice enough to offer us a ride. I think we should take it."

"They're driving us all the way to Salt Lake?"

"No, just to Vegas. We can catch a flight from there."

Rose took her seat between Debbie and Officer Bobb. She folded her arms, striking a derisive pose. "Oh. So we're not worried about the deep vein thrombosis anymore?"

Spence knew he was busted, but he just kept talking.

"Well, we're trying not to worry too much about anything at this stage." Hoping to appear optimistic, he smiled, nodded, and gave a thumbs-up before closing the van's side door. He pushed Jed X toward the driver's seat, then went around and got into the passenger seat with the ECC device. He turned to face the back. "We all ready, then?"

Agent Rodgers made a dramatic gesture out of pointing forward, like some hokey scoutmaster at the start of a field trip. "Wagons ho!"

"Ay, yo, trip, who you callin' a ho?"

Rodgers stared at the skateboarder. "Just drive," he said.

Jed X could see a threat in those milky eyes, so he put the van in gear and gassed it onto the highway. Then, just to annoy Rodgers, he said, "Would it hurt you to give just a l'il love, hmmmm? Just a taste for the X man?"

Rodgers suppressed the urge to hurt Jed X and said to the others, "By the way, I'm Bill Casey." He gestured at Jed and Agent Hart. "This is my nephew and his sports psychologist, Dr. Colby."

As introductions went around, Boyd stared out the rear window, watching the flames consume the Mustang. Officer Bobb reached over the back of the sofa and tapped Boyd on the shoulder. "I know it's not much, but I'm sorry. It was a great car."

Boyd gave a grateful nod. He took some comfort in the warmth and strength of Officer Bobb's voice. "Thanks. I appreciate that."

Spence turned the air conditioner on high, holding

his hand in front of the vent. "Oooooh, doesn't that feel nice?"

Debbie wondered if Rose was going to press the thrombosis issue or if she was just going to surrender to the madness and take whatever came. She handed Rose her water bottle. "Are you feeling okay?"

"To tell you the truth," Rose said, "I feel like I'm being played for a fool."

Ignoring her comment, Spence half turned in his seat, speaking over his shoulder. "Mom, can you feel that air?" He bounced a little in the plush captain's chair. "Sure is more comfortable than the Mustang." Spence turned to Jed X and gestured at him in general. "Hey, let me ask you, which hurts more, the piercing or the tats?"

"Spencer Andrew Tailor." Rose didn't have to raise her voice to silence everyone in the van. They all had mothers who did the first-, middle-, and last-name thing.

"Oooooh." Jed X snickered. "You busted now, boy."

"Tell me the truth," Rose said. "You kidnapped all these people, didn't you?"

Spence turned around, feigning surprise, amusement, and offense. "Where did you get . . . how on earth . . . what makes you think . . . ?" Spence didn't want to actually pose an entire question to her, lest she answer it and put him back in the position of having to explain, so he just held his hand in front of the vent and said, "Is this cool air getting back there?"

"Spencer." Rose pointed at Officer Bobb's waist. "Randall doesn't have a gun in his holster. I saw you holding a gun earlier. Now, it does not take a mathematical genius to put two and two together. If you were telling the truth about someone trying to steal the heart and you stole it back, then I imagine someone tried to stop you, someone like a police officer or one of the doctors." She looked at Officer Bobb and Debbie in turn. "And you being . . . well, being you, rather than give up, you might have thought kidnapping was the right thing to do." She leaned over to Debbie and said, "He's always had a highly developed sense of right and wrong."

Spence looked out the window for a moment. He wondered if there was any point in continuing the charade. He decided there wasn't. He spun his captain's chair around to face the back. "Okay," he said, "here's the deal." Spence told her the whole story, how he'd taken the heart from Debbie and how Debbie had jumped into the truck and Officer Bobb had pulled them over, heard the radio call, pulled his gun, and dropped it, and how Spence had picked it up and then after the Mustang blew up he was more or less forced to commandeer Jed X's van—so, yes, he admitted, technically he and Boyd had kidnapped everyone in the van, except Debbie who, he continued to maintain, had come along on her own.

During his explanation Debbie interrupted to offer alternative interpretations to some of Spence's assertions. She reiterated her claim that the FBI had come to take the heart and said her friend at Bethesda Naval Hospital had told her the heart was for President Webster. Rodgers and Hart tried to look shocked by everything they heard.

Spence wagged a finger at Debbie. "Well, that's the first I've heard about the guy at Bethesda. You didn't mention him before."

"Wait a second." It was Agent Rodgers, going for incredulity. "You're saying the federal government stole the heart your mother was supposed to receive?" He looked at his partner. "That's unbelievable."

"Psh, wouldn't surprise me a bit," Agent Hart said. "Name one recent administration that hasn't committed some sort of crime."

"Well, you have a point, but to take this nice lady's heart? That strikes me as beyond the pale."

"As compared to the Tuskegee Syphilis Study?"

"Well, you're mixing apples and oranges there, I think. For example—"

"Do you mind?" Spence turned his attention from the two men to Rose. To his surprise, she was sniffling. She dabbed a tear with the sleeve of her hospital gown. Spence wondered if she was crying because she was ashamed that her son had gone bad or because she was frightened by her impending death or for some other reason. "I'm sorry, Mom," he said. "I didn't know what else to do."

"No. It's not that." Rose shook her head and looked at Spence with moist eyes. "It's just . . . I'm so proud of you."

Spence scratched the back of his neck. "Really?"

Rose nodded. "You've risked everything," she said. "For me." She lowered her eyes, then glanced ever so slightly toward the back of the van. "Not everyone would do that."

Silence filled the van as all eyes turned furtively toward Boyd. "What?"

"Nothing, dear," Rose said. "I still love you."

Boyd shook his head like a wet dog. "No, no, no. Don't give me that," he said. "That's not what I'm talking about." He leaned forward, pounding his hand on the back of the sofa. "I don't believe this! You think I don't love you just because I'm not willing to go on a crime spree? Is that what you're saying? You think that's a proper standard?"

"I never said that, dear. I'm sure you love me. It's just that you show it in a . . . different way than your brother."

"What's that supposed to mean?"

Spence sensed the conversation veering off in an unnecessary direction, so he said, "Hey! We're almost in Vegas." He pointed at a sign marking the Las Vegas Corp Limit. "Let's see if we can find a traffic report." He reached for what he assumed to be the radio.

Jed X saw it too late. "No!" He tried to block Spence's hand but was too slow. Spence had turned on the sound system with its six Vulcanator Series 1,200-watt amplifiers, which blasted at roughly 165 decibels. "**GONNABONEDATBITCHWITHA—**" Jed killed the power a second after it came on. The resulting silence was as startling as the sonic boom a moment earlier. Jed X looked at Spence. "Ay, yo, dog, don't mess wit nuttin', ite?"

Spence looked at him. "What?" He stuck his little finger in his ear and wiggled it around.

When Jed reached for another button on the dashboard, they all threw their hands to their ears. But he turned on the radio at a normal volume and tuned down the dial until he found a traffic report. He gestured at the radio. "Yo, here's a coochie droppin' some Cronkite."

As he listened to the traffic report, Spence looked at the map he had bought at the last stop. "All right," he said when a commercial came on. "Looks like it's clear sailing to the airport."

"You can't always trust those traffic reporters," Hart said darkly.

Spence was about to turn the radio off when the announcer said, *"This is a special report from KLAV News. The KLAV Eyewitness Action News Team has learned that syndicated radio and television talk-show host Winston Archer announced he would not be broadcasting from his studio today. Instead he is broadcasting from an unidentified residence somewhere in greater Los Angeles. According to Archer, the FBI arrived at this residence attempting to take a mother and her two children into custody, claiming that the woman's husband and his brother were involved in an attempt on the life of President Webster."*

"Holy shit!"

"Spencer!"

"They've got Connie and the kids."

Boyd made a low moaning noise as his head landed on the back of the sofa. "Oh, God, what have I done?"

"It's unclear how or why the conservative talk-show host became involved in the situation, but, according to an unnamed source within the local FBI office, the whole thing, quote, smells like a hostage situation, end quote."

"Well, it sounds more like Connie and the kids have them," Agent Rodgers said.

"Oh, my" was all Rose could say.

Agent Rodgers turned to her. "Don't worry, ma'am, as long as the media's there, I'm sure the FBI won't do anything to harm anyone."

"Yeah, let's all pretend Waco was an aberration," Agent Hart mumbled.

The radio announcer continued by saying there were rumors that the alleged attempt on the president's life was somehow connected to an incident at Mulholland Memorial Hospital in Los Angeles. Here they played the sound bite of Senator Check on *HardHeads* in which she denied she was suggesting that the president had suffered a heart attack and that the White House was perpetrating a cover-up with the alleged fainting spell.

Rose leaned forward. "Spencer, I think you owe Dr. Robbins an apology."

"For what?"

"You said she was lying about the FBI. It sounds to me like she was telling the truth, now, doesn't it?"

Spence looked at Debbie, who held her hands in the I-told-you-so position, though she didn't speak.

"Well," Agent Rodgers said, "I stand corrected."

"See?" Hart nodded sagely. "That's what I'm talking about."

"The woman, whose identity Archer has so far refused to release, claims the FBI in effect canceled her mother-in-law's heart transplant. Her implication being that the FBI had taken the heart for President Webster. A spokesman for

Mulholland Memorial had no comment, and the White House said the entire scenario was ludicrous and that the media was trading in nothing more than rumor and innuendo. Vice President Osborne, reached in Malaysia, where he is on an international trade mission, said he was unaware the president had fainted. He went on to say he would recommend the formation of a blue-ribbon panel to make suggestions for ways to improve the nation's organ-distribution network."

Spence turned the radio off and thought about what he'd just heard. His mind went first to the legal implications. He felt Rose's claim on the heart was solid, but he had no idea what sorts of extralegal directives might obtain in such unusual circumstances. Were there laws governing something like this? Was this civil, criminal, state, federal, or all four? Regardless, Spence knew it would require expert legal help in what was clearly a narrow area of specialization, and an interesting one at that. Still, fascinating as it might prove to be from a jurisprudential perspective, Spence quickly abandoned this line of thought. The legal issue would take years to resolve and would have no bearing on what happened in the next few hours. He'd deal with the legal later. First he had to deal with the medical. He glanced at the ECC device. It had slowed two beats per minute.

Out of the corner of his eye Spence saw a highway patrol car heading the opposite direction. He prepared for the worst, but the officer never looked their way. It gave Spence a vague sense of optimism. Despite the news report confirming Debbie's claims, despite his brother's opposition, despite everything, Spence was beginning to believe they might actually pull this off. Sure, the entire situation was fantastic by any measure, and he found it almost impossible to fathom they had escaped from the FBI and whatever other federal police agencies it seemed likely were looking for them. But here they were, speeding through the outskirts of Las Vegas without a cop in sight, save, of course, Officer Bobb.

"Listen." Agent Rodgers put a firm hand on Jed X's shoulder. "I just want to say—speaking for my nephew here, as well as my associate—I just want you to know we don't consider ourselves kidnapped, okay? After hearing all that . . . well, as far as we're concerned, we volunteered to give you a ride, wherever you need to go."

"That goes for me, too," said Officer Bobb, giving Rose a reassuring pat on the leg.

"Whoa, dog, I gotsta get to my games." Jed X glanced at the mirror and saw Agent Hart pinching the skin of his eyebrow as he mimed the painful removal of Jed's dog-bone piercing. "But ain't no thang, you know, if Uncle G says we gon' bounce, we gon' bounce. We just gon' deal wit' it, knowhat'msayin?"

"More or less," Spence said as the others nodded vaguely. What a weird trio this was, he thought, but, hey, a gift horse, right?

"Yo, cuz, here's ya MIA." Jed X pointed at the exit sign for McCarran International Airport. "Ya want me to slow the roll down that strip?"

Spence shook his head. In light of the news, he figured the feds were bound to be monitoring airports. "No,

keep driving north." He looked at his watch. "But faster."
It was a long way to the Great Salt Lake.

The Kiowa Warrior came out of the clear blue sky.
Dispatched from Nellis Air Force Base outside Las Vegas,
the Bell OH-58D followed Interstate 15 on its search
mission for Boyd's Mustang. The chopper was heading
for Barstow at 140 miles per hour. Once there, the pilot
could choose between continuing south on I-15, heading
west above Highway 58, turning east to follow Interstate
40, or taking a chance on any of a host of smaller state
and county roads and highways. Needle in a haystack.

Eventually the pilot spotted something. It was the
smoldering remains of a vehicle at the gas station where
Boyd Tailor had last used his credit card. The pilot set
the helicopter down in the middle of the highway. "Go!
Go! Go!" A four-man team deployed and set about secur-
ing the area. Two men charged into the store, weapons
ready. One checked behind the counter. "Clear!"

The other went down the first aisle. "Clear!"

The first man checked the walk-in cooler. "Clear!"

His partner came up the second aisle. "Clear!"

The utility closet. "Clear!"

The third aisle. "Clear!"

"All clear?"

"All clear."

A second two-man team checked the building's
perimeter, where things were less clear. The moment
they saw the camo-clad corpse with the exotic weapon
propped against the wall, they fell back. "Looks like

bioterrorism," one of the soldiers said into his radio. "Better fly in the space suits."

While they waited for the hazmat team, the pilot got on the radio with his superiors.

"What about the vehicle?"

"Hard to say," the pilot responded. "It could have been a Mustang. Not much of it left."

"Can you tell which direction it was facing?"

The pilot looked again. "Negative. Tell you the truth, I'm only guessing it was a car based on its position by the gas pumps. Whatever it was, it burned hot, like maybe it had help."

"What about store employees?"

"Negative, sir. No one here but the corpse on the side of the building."

When the news reached Martin Brooks somewhere over the Ohio Valley, it felt like someone branding his intestines. It made him want to hit something or spit or curse, but he kept it inside, further aggravating his ulcer. His ire seeped into the phone. "In other words, not only do we not know whether to continue looking for the Mustang or some other, unknown vehicle, but we don't even know in which direction to be conducting the pointless search, is that about it?"

"I'm afraid so, sir. We'll just have to wait for them to use a credit card again."

Brooks flipped his phone shut, then popped two antacids. He chewed slowly as he appraised his world, as a cow with its cud. He looked out the window at the tiny homes and cars and people below. He could see toothpick telephone poles with black threads stretched tight between them, threads bringing the latest news updates into the tiny homes to the tiny voters below. *What are they watching?* Brooks wondered. *Whose story do they prefer? What do they want to believe? How do we control them?*

Brooks knew that all the networks had picked up the story after Winston Archer broke it. Within thirty minutes Archer's live truck had been spotted and the media frenzy had begun in earnest. Boyd Tailor's house was under full media and FBI siege. Without any new comments from the White House, and lacking any details beyond those Archer was reporting, the various news outlets were spinning yarn faster than Rumpelstiltskin.

The anchors from the different news organizations were intoning distinct—and increasingly exciting—variations on Winston Archer's claims. The most popular spin on the story was that of government malfeasance. Did the White House lie about the president's health? Did he need a transplant? Did the government attempt to take a heart that rightfully belonged to someone's grandmother? Had they sent federal agents to detain a woman and her two children as leverage against the extended family? And if they hadn't, what good were they? The talking heads had plenty to chew on.

Because live shots of Boyd's upper-middle-class house made for drab television, some news directors were augmenting their coverage with footage from previous government-citizen standoffs, everything from grainy film clips of the shootout with the Symbionese Liberation Army to the Waco conflagration to hastily produced reenactments of Ruby Ridge. Other, less well funded news orgs had taken to showing excerpts from *Dog Day Afternoon*.

The White House press secretary, meanwhile, continued sticking to the original story, the words "deny, deny, deny" still ringing in her ears. She was loyal and would stick with it to the end, even though she knew that doing so would hasten the end's arrival.

Brooks knew this, too, so he was working on a new strategy. But he needed guidance. He tried to imagine what his father would have done, or his grandfather, but it didn't help. They'd had the good fortune to be born into an era without cable and satellite television and a hyperaggressive media that used the First Amendment like a blunt instrument to destroy good men and institutions. They'd had it easy. Martin Brooks didn't. His guidance would have to come from elsewhere, like consultants or a poll, the latest of which had President Webster down two points.

Brooks knew they had three problems, four if he counted the poll. First was President Webster's health. Second was that the administration had been caught lying about it. Third, and most problematic, was getting busted for trying to steal the heart from the intended recipient. Brooks felt singled out when he learned that the recipient was someone's grandmother. "Just my luck," he had said. "Just my goddamn luck."

Air Force One bounced on a swell of turbulence, then smoothed out. The chief of staff ran his fingers through his thick white hair and rubbed his oily palms together. He decided to go see his friend in the back, find out how he was doing. He pushed up from his seat and walked out of the office, heading down the aisle toward the rear of the plane. "Grant!" he barked.

His assistant appeared at his side and fell into step, cell phone stuck to his ear. "Call me when it's secure." He flipped the phone shut. "Sir, we just got a bit of good news."

"I'll take it." Brooks used his tongue to pry a chip of antacid from between two teeth.

"NIH has located a new contingency organ."

Brooks seemed to perk up a bit. "Well, that's something. Where?"

"Glendale, California, sir. Unfortunately, they said it's not ideal."

Brooks spit the chip of antacid onto the floor. "It's still beating?"

"Yes, sir."

"Then it's ideal. Send a team for it and get it on a jet."

"Already on the way, sir."

"Good. Meanwhile, we need to run our story through the spin cycle."

"Yes, sir. We do seem to be coming across as the bad guys." He cleared his throat. "How do you want to handle it?"

"Aggressively." They stopped outside a closed door near the rear of the plane. Brooks paused to compose his thoughts, then leaned close to speak with his aide. "Look, if we're going to win this war, we have to start by winning the battle for public opinion." He stared into Grant's eyes. "It doesn't look good right now, but we have something important going for us. We have history on our side," he said.

"And destiny," Grant added. "We can't shortchange our fate, sir."

Despite everything, Brooks allowed himself a smile. His spirits were buoyed by Grant's embrace of Manifest Destiny and all that came with it. It wasn't something he saw much among Grant's generation. The kid's ideology was a source of reassurance. It gave Brooks reason to believe the future could be like the past, that things in this country could return to the way they once were. If they could just get one more term, maybe the Grants of the world would still have a chance. The chief of staff felt a surge of optimism, and he didn't want it to end, but the plane bucked on another hump of turbulence, calling him back from his reverie. "Well," he said to the door more than to Grant, "here we are." He eased the door open, and the two of them went inside.

It was a small room. There was a hospital bed in the center. President Webster lay silent and still in the middle of the bed, his head elevated slightly. The two men looked at him, then at the doctor hovering nearby.

"How is he?"

The doctor shrugged. "About the same."

"He sure looks good," Grant said, out of respect.

"Still needs that heart, though."

"Yeah," Brooks said. "We're working on that."

"What about those new artificial hearts?" Grant asked. "I hear they've almost perfected them."

The doctor shook his head. "He'd have to take blood thinners."

Grant looked at Brooks. "So?"

Brooks nodded at the president. "With his ulcers he'd bleed to death before you could say 'New Hampshire primaries.'"

"Oh." *Bummer,* Grant thought.

Brooks leaned down and whispered to his boss. "Hang in there, old friend, we're going to take care of you. Just stick with us a little longer."

President Webster thought he smiled, but it was only in his head. His muscles weren't actually responding to his thoughts. Still, he had reason to smile. If his trusted friend said he was going to take care of him, then take care of him he would. Things would be all right. He'd be back in business for that last hurrah. Sure, he'd be a lame duck, but that was the beauty of it. That just took the pressure off. If he could get reelected, he could turn it into four years of the best golf, whiskey, and cigars anyone ever had. And he felt he *could* get reelected, too. He had a terrific staff. He had incumbency, and, best of all, he still looked good. Or so he heard someone say.

Brooks looked at the doctor. "Do whatever you have to, just keep him going." He turned and left, with Grant trailing closely. They walked back toward the front of Air Force One. "So what were we talking about?"

"Having history on our side, sir."

"Oh, right. All we have to do is apply the lessons learned. First of all, think about Ronald Reagan. His numbers were pedestrian at best until John Hinckley tried to impress that actress. But what happened after he survived the attempt on his life? His numbers soared, that's what. So that's lesson number one. Lesson number two is Richard Nixon. What was it Harry Truman said?" Brooks squinted as he remembered the quote. "'Dick Nixon is a shifty-eyed goddamn liar. . . . He's one of the few in the history of this country to run for high office talking out of both sides of his mouth at the same time and lying out of both sides.'"

Grant's face soured. "That judgment was harsh, unfair, and partisan, if you ask me, sir."

"You're damn right it was. But it didn't matter, and that's the lesson. The public *knew* Nixon was a shifty-eyed goddamn liar. That's who they wanted. Hell, John Q. knows politics isn't patty-cakes. So they elected a guy they knew could play the game. And you know what? He'd have finished his second term if it hadn't been for those goat-fucking mongrels from the *Post*."

Grant was starting to see the angle. "So our decision not to disclose the truth about the president's health was a matter of national security. Our only concern is this nation's well-being. And sometimes that is best served by lying to the public." He held his hand up immediately. "Though we'll find another way to say that."

"Clearly. And anyone who doesn't understand that doesn't know shit from apple butter. And the truth about the stolen heart is this." Brooks stopped when he reached the main cabin of the aircraft. He turned around and poked at the air with his finger. "That heart was designated for the president from the moment the donor was admitted to the hospital. It never got into the UNOS system. It was never intended for anyone, let alone someone's grandmother. That is a myth, no, a lie started by the liberal media. And these people who stole the heart—"

"Are attempting to assassinate the president." Grant balked, his face frozen in regret. "Sorry to interrupt, sir."

"It's okay." Brooks held his hands out wide and smiled. "I think that's our starting point. Get that smoothed out and call a press conference."

"What do we say about Archer and the FBI standoff?"

"Obviously a publicity stunt. And we don't comment on publicity stunts, except to say Winston Archer is a shameless opportunist."

"He was an awfully big supporter in the last election."

"That's right, he was. But what is he now?"

Grant understood. "He's a turncoat, sir. And a shameless opportunist."

Brooks winked at Grant. "Be sure the FBI is on the same page with us there. If they really have a man in a hostage situation, make sure they deny it."

"Yes, sir."

"Oh, and get the head of UNOS on the phone. We don't want him going on TV contradicting us."

Grant's phone chirped. He looked to his boss for permission. "Sir?"

"Go ahead." Brooks motioned for him to answer.

Grant took the call. It lasted a minute. When he finished, he looked at his boss. "That was the press office. They're getting questions about a big explosion out at Edwards Air Force Base. Something about a fifteen-billion-dollar jet that blew up on the runway? They want to know our position."

Brooks felt the acid begin to churn again. He fished another antacid from his pocket and popped it into his mouth. "Deny it," he said. "Deny everything."

Five minutes after Spence told him to drive faster, Jed X fell in behind a Corvette with a radar detector and cruise control set on ninety. Along with a couple of other cars, they formed a convoy speeding north on I-15. Spence periodically tried to find news updates on the radio, but they were quickly beyond reach of signals from Vegas stations, and the only other formats in the southwest corner of Utah were country, Spanish, and oldies. Eventually he turned the radio off.

The effect was interesting. Soothing. Without constant news updates and with no one visibly giving chase, it was impossible to maintain the urgent fear of a fugitive. There was no sense of danger. There was only fatigue mingling with a vague sense of hope on the one hand and real dread on the other. For a while no one spoke. The hum of the tires on the freeway seemed to lull everyone into a contemplative mood.

Agent Hart stared at the red-and-blue scorpion etched on the back of Jed X's neck, thinking, *Tattoos and piercing. Self-mutilation as art. The chicks must dig it.*

No, that's no good. How about ink, deep in the skin. Sub-cutaneous penance? Or just plain stupid? Hmmm, no. Too judgmental.

Spence was looking at the map. They weren't far from the interchange with I-70, the road east to Denver. Salt Lake was about two hundred miles north of that. Spence glanced at the speedometer. If they maintained ninety the whole way, they'd arrive with time to spare and everything would be fine. He thought about that. *Yeah. Sure. Everything is not going to be fine. Can't be. World doesn't work that way. Even assuming this Dr. Speyburn is on the up-and-up—and what are the odds of that?—there's the small matter of the federal government's interest. So Mom gets her heart and lives to see her sons prosecuted for God-knows-what crimes. Okay, so this wasn't my best idea, but what the hell else was I going to do? Right is right, and Mom was on the list. She was next. The heart is hers.* He glanced down at the slowing ECC device, then at Rose. She looked tired, or worse. *What if these are her last hours? Shouldn't we be talking about the important stuff we never talked about when there was ample time? And what's wrong with us that all those things go unsaid until those last moments? But what would we say? There aren't any confessions to make, no apologies to demand, no dramatic revelations explaining some dark moment in family history that's been festering in either of our subconscious-nesses sending us deep into denial and therapy. Not that we were perfect, but maybe, compared to some families, we were closer to it. We know she loves us, and she knows we love her, and what else is there? I suppose I could thank her.*

Maybe that's what we get to do. That's what the last moments are for. We get to thank her. Thanks for teaching us, for nurturing us, for showing us how to be good people. Now go on your way knowing you've done good. Have we ever thanked her for the thousand things she did?

Spence found himself thinking back to the first funeral he ever attended. He was a little boy. His mom had helped him put on his little suit as she wiped his tears. *We want to pay our respects,* she'd said. *He deserves that, don't you think?* Rose carried a Bible and walked with Spence into their backyard, where the mourners had gathered. It was a small service, not only in the sense that there were only five mourners but also in that they were all under four feet tall. They were Spence's friends from the neighborhood, gathered together to say good-bye to Mr. Fuzzy, the hamster.

When she saw how devastated Spence was at the death of his first pet, Rose organized the service. It was nondenominational, as was Mr. Fuzzy. Boyd was there because his mother had asked him to be kind to his younger brother in his time of grief. Boyd accepted that responsibility and even dug the hole. Rose put Mr. Fuzzy in a tiny box and presided over the service, allowing everyone to say a few words. Spence didn't want to cry in front of his friends, but he couldn't help it. Boyd put his arm over his little brother's shoulder as they stood by the tiny grave.

Spence never forgot his mother's words that day. *He was a fine hamster and a good friend. He liked carrots and never pooped outside his cage,* she said solemnly. *May*

God bless his fuzzy soul. Spence put a piece of carrot in the little box, then set the box in the ground, then gently covered it with dirt.

Spence glanced back at Rose again. She seemed to be resting. She tried to take a deep breath, thinking *Should I be feeling my heartbeat like this? It seems to be . . . I don't know, off somehow. Am I dizzy? It's hard to tell. My hands feel clammy. Should I say something? No. I don't want to make a fuss. I'll be fine.*

Officer Bobb was staring at the back of Spence's head. *It's not as if I woke up this morning thinking this would be a great day to come out of the closet. But, boy, when he pointed that gun at me and I said the words— whew! I have to thank him when this is all over.* Officer Bobb shook his head when he thought about how his life was going to change now that he could admit who he was. The magnitude of it was disquieting, and he knew that to reconcile the truth and lies and fears and joys he was facing would take years. He knew he wasn't going to resolve the new complications of his life during the next few hours. He was happy just knowing he could start working on it when this escapade was over. Assuming they weren't all killed by their government.

Debbie was wondering if she had violated the Hippocratic oath. *"That I will exercise my art solely for the cure of my patients, and will give no drug, perform no operation, for a criminal purpose, even if solicited, far less suggest it." Could this be construed as criminal purpose? I'd be done before I got started. That wouldn't be fair. All those years of medical school, wasted. Not to mention the student loans. Is there some way out of this mess?* She looked at Spence. *And what's going to happen to this guy? He didn't ask for this. What do they expect people to do?*

Boyd was thinking about Connie. He couldn't believe he had put her in this situation. Worse yet, he realized the situation didn't stem from his actions but rather from his inaction. His cowardice had forced Connie to take a hostage. *And not just any hostage,* he thought. *An FBI agent. Probably put the kids in charge of torturing the poor bastard. Fine. Let them earn their allowance while using their natural talents. And like that's not enough, she somehow got Winston Archer, of all people, involved. Lord help me understand. Winston Archer? If there's anyone on earth more likely to antagonize the federal government into ramming tanks into my home and burning it to the ground, I want to know who it is. But why Winston Archer? I know she listens to his prattling on the radio, but she also watches CNN, yet Wolf Blitzer isn't at the house. So what gives?*

Agent Rodgers gazed ahead at the endless path of concrete that lay in front of them. He tapped Spence on the shoulder, pointed out the windshield, and said, "See that?"

"The overpass?"

"Yeah. Ever wonder why those things are so overbuilt?"

As they passed underneath the thick concrete structure, Spence shook his head. "Can't say I have."

"To withstand bombing." Rodgers nodded. "One of the first things an enemy goes for is bridges." He looked at Spence and nodded some more. "To slow troop movements. I mean, that was the thinking when they built these."

It was true. In 1919 Lieutenant Colonel Dwight Eisenhower spent sixty-two ass-numbing days as part of the United States Army's first transcontinental motor convoy. Given two months to think, it dawned on the future president that should the nation require rapid and massive movements of troops and equipment to defend its shores, it would be screwed. But what could he do? He was just a twenty-nine-year-old riding across a vast country in a truck.

As fate would have it, twenty-some years later Eisenhower was the U.S. commander of the European Theater of Operations. As such, he couldn't help but notice how much faster Allied convoys moved on Germany's multilane autobahns as compared to the roads on the rest of the Continent. These two events, plus Eisenhower's election, more or less led to the creation of the National System of Interstate and Defense Highways, vast stretches of concrete designed to aid in the movement of troops and matériel and speed the evacuation of cities in case of attack. They would also serve to facilitate interstate commerce as well as provide billions of dollars' worth of contracts for politicians to dangle in front of contractors as a way of encouraging them to participate in the democratic process. Not that anyone would suggest that any sort of a kickback scheme might have come from such an arrangement.

As Agent Rodgers pontificated on the interstate sys-

tem, a disturbing thought crept into Boyd's mind. *I wonder if Connie is attracted to Archer? Not his lunatic brand
of politics, but him.* Boyd's imagination shifted into over-
drive. *Oh, my God, is she having an affair with that right-
wing media-clown whore? No, she wouldn't do that. She's
too honest for that, too loyal. But maybe she's thinking
about it. Maybe after so many years with me she's casting
about for alternatives, someone who could put a little
excitement in her life, someone with flair and showman-
ship and syndication rights. And who could blame her?*

Rodgers rubbed his chin. "I think it was 1950, Congress approved six hundred million dollars for highway-
construction programs. Six years later they authorized
another thirty-two billion, setting up a permanent Highway Trust Fund."

I'm completely irrational, Boyd thought. *The stress
from all this is making me crazy. I can't believe I thought,
for even a minute, that Connie might be having an affair
with Winston Archer. I must be losing my mind. She
probably called him because she had nowhere else to turn.
She probably figured the police would side with the FBI,
so she called the media. Smart and savvy. God, I love her.
If I had just kissed her on the way out the door. I suppose
I could have put my foot down and told Spence no at the
hospital, but I didn't. I'm weak that way, I guess. I wonder
what Connie ever saw in me to begin with.*

"Then in '73 Congress passed the Federal Aid Highway Act authorizing eighteen billion dollars. They passed
the Intermodal Surface Transportation Efficiency Act in
'91, which was, like, one hundred twenty billion dollars

for building and repairing highways, but which also encouraged states and localities to develop mass-transportation systems to reduce urban highway congestion."

"Which any commuter in L.A. will testify was money well spent," Spence said.

"Well, the plan didn't take population growth into account," Rodgers said with a shrug. "The recent Transportation Equity Act for the Twenty-first Century included another hundred and seventy-four billion."

Boyd was trying to make sense of his world. *Let's see. Spence called, Connie woke up, answered the phone, and gave it to me. Spence said there was an emergency and I had to get to the hospital. So I got up and put on my suit. Connie was in the kitchen drinking coffee, and I said I'd call when I knew what was going on and that I was going straight to the office from the hospital, and then I left. Shit. I did. I left without kissing her good-bye. I just walked out the door.*

"Adjusted to current values, the total cost for the interstate system is around six hundred billion dollars."

Debbie leaned forward. "For how many miles?"

"Just over forty-five thousand."

"So," Agent Rodgers concluded, "it's thanks to Dwight Eisenhower that the United States has the best highway system in the world."

"Yeah." Agent Hart sucked on his teeth. "And at thirteen billion dollars a mile, it had better be."

Debbie sat back and said, "Are those numbers right? I can't do math in my head, but isn't thirteen billion times forty-five thousand a lot more than six hundred billion? Isn't it, like, trillion?"

Hart shrugged. "Whatever."

Debbie tried for another moment to do the math, then gave up. "How do you know all this?"

Agent Rodgers smiled modestly. "I get the Auto Club magazine."

All right, I've got to get a grip on myself. We're here. We've done what we've done, and we were right for doing it, Boyd thought. *I know that. This is my chance to show Connie—or am I trying to show myself?—that I'm not Mr. Milquetoast, that I'm willing to do the right thing instead of the prudent one. I just hope she can forgive me for it.*

Debbie and Spence were still looking out the window at the interstate when they came to a bridge. They both saw the sign at the same time. The black silhouette of a car weaving on a yellow background. And the words SLIP-PERY WHEN WET. Spence thought for a moment, then turned slowly to look at Debbie. She turned to look at him, and their minds went back to the landing of the hospital stairwell. Debbie started to say something, then stopped. A moment later she pointed at Spence and said, "Look, I work like a hundred hours a week. I don't have a lot of time for laundry." She nodded. "Just so you know."

"Okay." Spence smiled.

"They were a gag gift! It was the only clean pair I had left."

Spence held his hands up. "I didn't say a word."

"Well, you better not."

"I was just wondering who—"

The discussion was interrupted by Rose, moaning in agony.

"Rose?" Debbie turned urgently. "Are you okay?" Rose winced, clearly in pain.

Spence turned. He could see the suffering in her expression. He reached back and took her hand. "Mom? What is it? Are you all right?"

Rose looked up with as much dignity as she could muster and said, "I really have to pee."

12

Searching for a Heart

In the fall of 1950, with the White House undergoing renovations, President Harry Truman set up shop across the street at Blair House. On November first of that year, in a poorly conceived attempt to advance the cause of Puerto Rican independence, Oscar Collazo and Griselio Torresola tried to assassinate President Truman.

The two Puerto Rican nationalists approached Blair House from opposite directions, intending to shoot their way in. A gunfight ensued. White House police officer Leslie Coffelt fired a shot. It hit Torresola in the side of the head, killing him instantly. Officer Coffelt was wounded during the attack and later died. Oscar Collazo was shot, captured, and eventually sentenced to death, but a week before his scheduled execution, Truman commuted his sentence to life imprisonment. Twenty-seven years later President Jimmy Carter further commuted Collazo's sentence, setting him free. Collazo returned to Puerto Rico, where he lived for the next fifteen years, never having to buy a single shot of rum.

Prior to this the Secret Service had been concerned primarily with the suppression of counterfeit currency. However, after the attempt on Truman's life, Congress enacted Public Law 82-79, which permanently authorized Secret Service protection of the president, his immediate family, the president-elect, and the vice president, if he wished.

Spurred by a loose interpretation of 82-79, Martin Brooks called the Southern California field office of the U.S. Secret Service. It took half an hour for two agents to make the drive from downtown Los Angeles to Glendale, California. Agent Shuman pulled the black sedan to the curb in front of a two-bedroom home facing the Verdugo Mountains. The house was done in the local style that real-estate agents called "authentic Spanish," which meant a red tile roof and faux adobe exterior. The lawn was well tended. "Nice landscaping," Shuman said.

Agent Pomus looked at it. The lawn and flower beds were manicured, trimmed, weeded, sprayed, and fertilized into an unnatural beauty. "God, I hate yard work," he said. "That's why I live in a condo. Got one of those mow-and-blow crews comes in and takes care of all that shit." The two men got out of the car and walked slowly toward the front door.

Agent Shuman shook his head. "I tell you, what I hate

are those blowers. Use a damn broom or a rake, know
what I mean? That's how I did it when I was a kid. Those
damn blowers are loud as all hell, and all they do is blow
shit into the street for five minutes before it blows back
into the yard. Meanwhile, all the dust comes into my
house. And the fumes coming in the window? Shit. You
might as well run a hose from your car exhaust. One
time, I swear I thought I was gonna asphyxiate." They
reached the door. Agent Pomus rang the bell. His partner
continued his harangue. "My neighbor's yard crew came
in at seven last Saturday morning, sounded like the goddamn Mexican air force landing next door. I went out
there with my gun and got that straightened out quick."

"That's a good way to meet the disciplinary committee," Pomus said as he rang the bell again, then knocked.

"What, a buncha illegals gonna call the cops? I'd have
INS over there long before LAPD showed up. You know
how long it takes those guys to respond."

Pomus nodded, then said, "Let's check the backyard.
She's probably out there weeding with tweezers."

They walked around the side of the house, past perfectly tended beds of liatris, salvia, and talinum, all
thirsting in the California heat. Rounding the corner,
they saw her at the far end of the yard. Tucked underneath a floppy straw hat, she was sweating over a bed of
campanula and penstemon. She was in her sixties and
scooting along close to the ground on a wheeled gar-
dener's cart made of green and black plastic. As the
Secret Service agents approached her from behind, they

saw her reach for a one-gallon hand sprayer. She began pumping the plunger.

"Excuse me," Agent Shuman called out.

The woman stopped pumping and turned to face them. There was a cigarette wedged in the corner of her withered mouth, the filter caked with red lipstick. She set the sprayer down, squinting suspiciously at the two men in their dark suits.

Shuman leaned toward Pomus and murmured, "Looks like my mother-in-law."

Pomus nodded, then spoke to the woman. "Are you Daisy Austin?"

Daisy stood, resting gloved hands on her tool apron as if it were a gun belt. "Who the hell's asking?" Her voice like one of Marge Simpson's sisters.

They flashed their identification. "I'm Agent Shuman. This is Agent Pomus. We're with the U.S. Secret Service. Will you come with us, please?"

"I will not."

Shuman could smell her bourboned breath from five feet. "Don't make this difficult, ma'am."

"Go fuck yourself," Daisy said.

The two men exchanged a look, then shrugged. Agent Pomus stepped forward and grabbed Daisy's arm. "Let's go, lady."

"Get your filthy hands off me!" In one deft motion Daisy snatched the saw-toothed angle weeder from her tool belt and raked the shark's teeth across the top of Agent Pomus's hand, tearing a jagged, bloody gash.

"Son of a bitch!" Pomus jerked backward, his blood watering the lawn.

Agent Shuman lunged, grabbing Daisy's right hand. "All right, lady—" was all he said before she plunged her two-pronged Jekyll weeding fork into his lungs. Agent Shuman dropped to his knees, gasping.

Daisy stood there, looking down at Shuman as if he were so much crabgrass. She tightened her grip on the weeding fork and considered her next move. She didn't notice Agent Pomus regrouping behind her. A second later he came at her again, knocking her to the ground this time. The weeding fork flew from Daisy's hand, leaving her momentarily unarmed. She groped around until she found the pesticide sprayer. She thrust the wand toward Pomus's face and pulled the trigger. Pomus took a dose of malathion into his sinuses and began to gag. He was on all fours, producing excessive saliva and drooling like a Saint Bernard.

Shuman was still on the ground trying to force air into his collapsed lung when he felt Daisy climbing on top of him, pinning him down. With the cigarette still dangling from her lips, she pressed the weeding fork to one of his eyes. She leaned close. "A one-eyed man walks into a bar, orders three bourbons, says, 'Put 'em all in my hat.' The bartender says—"

All of a sudden Daisy's eyes bugged out and her whole body spasmed. She lost her grip on the weeding fork, then went completely slack, slumping to one side. Agent Shuman pushed her off and saw Pomus holding his taser gun, the wires trailing to the dart in Daisy's back. "You didn't want to hear the punch line, did you?"

Senator Check sat back, propped her feet on her desk, and laced her fingers behind her head. She closed her eyes and listened to the voice of her dreams. *Madame President*, it said in tones oddly reminiscent of Marilyn Monroe's. The words poured over her brain like warm caramel, settling sweetly into the folds. Until this moment she hadn't allowed herself to think it. Not really. But now, up two points in the polls and with Winston Archer stirring up a major media stink, Peggy Check began entertaining the far-fetched notion that not only might the United States be on the verge of putting a woman in the White House but that *she* was that woman.

Senator Check thought about how—less than a month ago—she had begun to accept her role as a sacrificial lamb, an offering to the left wing of the party. Another distaff casualty on the road to equality. A way to raise money from new sources for the next candidate in the next race. The political consultants were unanimous in their opinion that President Webster would be reelected, and a man would continue doing a man's job.

But a funny thing had happened on the way to the White House. Things changed. And that had Senator Check smiling.

Politicians do all sorts of stupid things, she thought. And every now and then they get caught. But more often they get caught covering things up. And when that happens, a different clown gets to run the circus.

After Winston Archer broke the news and the government denied his claims, the public wasn't sure what to believe. But given a choice between assuming that the White House was telling the truth or that it was guilty of something . . . well, with history as a guide, the choice was obvious. So now, in Senator Check's mind, it was just a matter of time before *she* made history.

She glanced at a framed photo on her office wall. It was taken at a black-tie function years ago. The red-nosed Speaker of the House stood in the middle wearing a tuxedo and a single-malt grin. Peggy Check was on his right. Peggy's mother was on his left, august and elegant in a black evening gown. The pride on her face resonated even in two dimensions. But she wasn't proud that she was standing next to the Speaker of the House—she'd had her picture taken with many of the rich and powerful—her pride was invested in her daughter.

Staring at the photograph, Senator Check recalled a formative event. Fourth grade. Her class went on a field trip to the local fire station, where young Peggy Check resolved to become a fireman. But she came home disappointed. She went to her mother in tears. "I want to be a fireman, but the chief said it's not a job for a lady."

Her mother bristled. "Listen to me," she said, wiping Peggy's tears away. "Never, ever let anyone tell you you can't do something. Especially a man. You can be anything you want if you work hard enough."

Men had told Peggy's mother what she could and

could not do. "You need to learn to submit to the natural order of things, young lady." She wanted to study the law, but her father had laughed. "Nonsense. Everyone knows women don't have the critical faculties necessary for law school." She had a brilliant mind, but she lacked the will to demand her rightful place in the world. "Now, be a good girl and bring me some coffee."

Peggy's mother instilled in her daughter the idea that the only limits in life were the ones you put on yourself. One might not be able to defeat the old boys' network today, she would say, but one could infiltrate. And, once inside, one might accomplish all sorts of things in time that might otherwise never be accomplished. That would be the best way to help this great nation achieve what it was capable of.

You can be anything you want. Her mother's words still echoed in her ears.

Could I be the president?

Yes. You could even be the president.

And now, looking at that long-ago photo, Peggy honestly believed it was true. She could be the president, just like her mom had said. But Senator Check knew, as all politicians did, that she couldn't have everything. Even if elected, she could never share the victory with the woman who had made her believe it was possible in the first place. Her mother was in a care facility now, staring into space and into faces with the same blank eyes, her agile mind and bristling fury gone, lost to Alzheimer's. But, by God, Peggy could do it in memory of her mother. She would be the nation's first nurturing, maternal, *incorruptible* leader and the most powerful woman on earth.

But only if President Webster were out of the picture. Senator Check began to rethink her strategy on the heart. All the media attention increased the likelihood someone would spot the fugitives and turn them in. If they recovered the heart in the next couple of hours and managed the spin well enough, Webster just might win reelection. She gave it a moment's thought and decided that the best thing was to have the SAS-SOG team throw a monkey wrench into the Tailors' progress.

A brisk knock on the door made the senator jump. She pulled her feet off her desk as Britton Belk entered the room. "What is it?"

"Senator, you're needed on the floor." The senator's face begged for more information. "For the vote," Britton said.

"I'm busy," she said. "Is it important?"

"Your annual cost-of-living raise."

"Oh." She smiled and hurried off to the chamber.

The media coverage bloomed like a virus. It had been months since anyone famous had been properly disgraced, and the public was starved for it. People wanted a scandal. So they huddled around their television sets as if they were campfires, waiting for juicy details to emerge and warm them. Ratings would soar and ad rates would rise. The news would suffer, the news divisions would thrive.

Winston Archer glanced over his shoulder at the

house behind him, then back at the camera, serious and confiding. "From the outside this looks like any other home in an upper-middle-class neighborhood." He tilted his head just so, implying an informed skepticism. "But what about inside?" Archer took a few crab steps toward the house, gesturing. "The federal government says it was a virtual training camp for domestic terrorists." He looked at the ground, then back at the camera, his eyes narrowed. "A Brentwood Tora Bora, if you will." A beat before the eyebrows arched. "I'm Winston Archer, and today I'll take you inside." He turned to point. "Behind that closed door, to reveal the shocking truth." He froze, staring into the lens. "And we'll be back, right after this."

A moment passed before his producer said, "And we're in commercial." Nancy looked at her stopwatch. "We've got three minutes. Let's reset for inside."

"How was that?" Winston asked as he removed the lavalier mike from his tie.

"'A Brentwood Tora Bora'?" Nancy made a disapproving face. "That wasn't in the script."

"I was improvising. It seemed like a good image."

"Maybe to you."

"What, too chilling?"

"Too old. Nobody remembers the reference."

"That's crazy. I remember it."

"So do I, but *they* don't. The great unwashed *they* has the attention span of a twelve-year-old with ADD. You might as well reference the Vietnamese tunnels of Cu Chi."

"The what?"

Nancy shook her head. "Look, we don't have time to argue. Do me a favor: Don't improvise when you've got a script."

"I'm going to have to improvise if your expert doesn't show up." Archer shot a glance at his watch. "Where the hell is she? She was supposed to be here half an hour ago."

"She'll be here. Relax." Nancy looked at her stopwatch. "We're on in twenty. Let's get set, everybody!"

Not for the first time was a neighborhood in West Los Angeles under siege by police and the media. There were fourteen remote trucks and enough microwave transmitters to cook a cow. Police and media helicopters circled overhead. Two large black panel trucks with SWAT painted on their sides blocked the road at either end. The rest of the street was choked with LAPD cruisers; a Bureau of Alcohol, Tobacco and Firearms mobile headquarters; and a couple of FBI combat-engineering vehicles.

The rear doors on the SWAT trucks burst open. An FBI Hostage Rescue Team deployed, taking up predetermined positions around the Tailors' house. The FBI sniper went to his perch on a roof across the street. Moving down the sidewalk toward his position, the sniper passed the line of reporters doing their stand-ups with the Tailor house in the background. One after another he heard snatches of their reports.

Fox News: ". . . question we're asking is, domestic terrorist or government run amok?"

CNN: ". . . consequently the director of Homeland

Security has issued a new color to the color-code alert system to represent previously unpredicted—"

E!: ". . . a recent poll by the Snack Food Association, twenty-five percent of Americans cite President Webster as the chief executive who, quote, best personified cool ranch tortilla chips, unquote."

MSNBC: ". . . asking if lessons were learned at Waco, and, if so, will they be applied? And what about rumors of sexual exploitation? John's in the studio with renowned—"

CNBC: "The story you won't believe! The video you have to see!"

Over the past hour or so, Connie's emotions had run from disbelief to fear to terrible anxiety. She had been worried about Boyd, Rose, and Spence out there somewhere being hunted like mad dogs. She had been worried about what would happen to her children if this played out the way she feared. She'd also been worried about herself. Connie had never even been pulled over by a cop, let alone spent the night in jail. She was a bad candidate for a lengthy prison sentence. But now, surrounded by the insane media posse, Connie felt some hope. As Archer's crew filled her house with cameras, boom mikes, and monitors, Connie began to feel better. Her worry thawed under the hot lights, and she realized her best chance of saving herself and her family was through the media, however biased. She turned to Agent Sandlin, gesturing at the equipment. "Can you believe all this?"

He stared at her for a moment, then shook his head. "Yeah," he said flatly. "It's our fifteen minutes, all right." He couldn't believe his career was about to go swirling down the toilet on national television.

"You don't sound too excited about it."

"It's not exactly a résumé builder."

Connie considered Sandlin's position and decided to change the subject. "The producer said they're bringing in an expert on hostage situations. That should be interesting."

Agent Sandlin could see himself now, guarding a warehouse from midnight to eight.

Across the living room Nancy Mitchell was watching the dozen television screens set up to monitor the other news networks. She wanted to be sure they received credit from anyone using their feed. "Hey, Winston," she called out. "Take a look at this."

Archer came in from the kitchen and saw the picture. "Turn up the sound," he said.

". . . *seen here wearing a disguise.*" It was the picture of Spence from last Halloween.

"Hey," Connie said. "That's my brother-in-law."

"*His brother, shown here*"—a picture of Boyd popped onto the screen—"*may also have altered his appearance in an attempt to evade the law. If you see either of these men, do not attempt to apprehend. . . .*"

Connie sat up a bit, surprised and smiling. Her Boyd had struck fear into other men's hearts. He was considered dangerous. He was out there fighting for principles, the risk be damned. It tickled her no end. *Just when you think you know someone,* she thought. She had never been so proud.

"Goddamn it," Archer groused. "I thought we had an exclusive on this. How the hell did they get that photo?"

Nancy shook her head, unbothered. "Probably got into the brother's house. Don't worry about it. It's still our story."

There was a commotion at the front door, diverting everyone's attention. Connie saw several people orbiting around a middle-aged woman. She was well dressed and somewhat familiar. Famous somehow. An actress? Connie wondered. No. A model? No. Winston and Nancy walked over to greet her. After the pleasantries Nancy turned and announced that the hostage consultant had arrived. She led the consultant into the living room to make introductions. "Connie? Agent Sandlin? I'd like you to meet Patty Hearst."

Jed X pulled into the rest area and parked between a couple of recreational vehicles.

"All right," Spence said, "we're going to take a quick breather. Get out, stretch our legs, use the facilities. I'd appreciate it if no one tried to escape." He held the gun up, weakly. "I still have this." Spence sounded tired for the first time that day.

While Debbie helped Rose to the rest room, Jed X stood by the side of the van sniffing the air. Someone was frying something somewhere. He emerged from between the two RVs, scanning the horizon until he saw the catering truck. He nudged Spence. "Ay, yo, trip, corn dogs."

"In a minute," Spence said, grabbing Jed's arm. "We're going to the bathroom first." The six men herded into the restroom. Boyd was the last one in. The only open urinal was the one next to Officer Bobb. Boyd stepped into the gap and unzipped. He let out a long, deep sigh as he relieved the pressure on his bladder. His head tilted back in a moment of pleasure. Then, leaning forward, he put his free hand against the wall and began to relax. A moment later, without his thinking about it, his gaze drifted over toward Officer Bobb's tackle.

Officer Bobb turned slowly and looked toward Boyd. "What do you think?"

"I wasn't looking!" He sounded more offended than embarrassed.

Officer Bobb shook his head. "What do you think about the odds of us getting to Salt Lake? Getting Rose the transplant?"

"Oh." Now Boyd sounded embarrassed. "I thought you thought I had looked—" He looked again, then jerked his eyes away, his curiosity threatening to over-power him. "But I didn't. I mean, I wouldn't. Why would I?" He zipped up and wiped his hands on his pants. "I'll be outside." On the way out, Boyd paused to look at his reflection in the dull sheet of metal that served as a mir-ror. He wasn't proud of what he saw, and he slouched out of the room.

Rodgers and Hart finished, then wandered out into the bright Utah sun a second behind Boyd. It was hot, but not as bad as the desert. They strolled to a shade tree and watched Boyd as he walked to the catering truck. A moment later Debbie and Rose exited the ladies' room and headed back toward the van. After they passed, Rodgers nudged his partner and gestured at Debbie. "I decided," he said. "I'd definitely do her."

Agent Hart looked down and spit. "You'd do a tailpipe if it was wet."

Rodgers grinned.

Agent Hart's cell phone rang. "SAS-SOG Two." He paused. "Hello?" He moved a little to his right. "Wait, you're going Martian on me." He moved to his left. "Can you hear me now?" He slapped the phone. "Call me back." He snapped the phone shut. "God, I hate these things."

Jed X, Boyd, and Officer Bobb were at the catering truck, loading up on snacks.

Spence and Debbie were sitting with Rose at a picnic table. "We're almost there, Mom. Think you can make it?"

Despite the weak, fluttering sensations in her chest and her own doubts, Rose winked at her son. "I plan to live long enough to cast my vote against that goddamn President Webster." Rose turned and touched Debbie's arm. "Pardon my French."

Debbie smiled. "I'm going to vote against the son of a bitch, too," she said. "Just for you."

Spence shook his head in mock dismay. "Citizens forced to vote against candidates they *don't* want in office instead of voting for the ones they *do*."

Rose held up an index finger. "I believe it was Shakespeare who said, 'There's small choice in rotten apples.'"

She paused, then said, "Of course, I wasn't going to vote for him anyway. I like that Senator Check." Rose looked off to the middle distance, nodding thoughtfully. "It would be so nice to see a woman in the White House before I die."

Debbie looked over at the tree where Rodgers and Hart were lingering in the shade. Hart had his phone to his ear. He was twisting and turning and bending in different directions. She assumed he was trying to improve his reception. Agent Rodgers seemed to be leering in her direction with one hand wiggling in his pocket. Debbie turned to Rose. "Would you like something from the snack truck?"

"No, I'm fine. Randall said he would bring me some water."

Debbie nudged Spence. "Walk with me?"

"Sure." He patted Rose's arm. "We'll be right back."

They headed for the catering truck. Incongruous in their blue-green surgical scrubs, they ignored the stares from passersby. "So," Debbie said, "in your wildest dreams did you think you'd get this far?"

"In my wildest dreams I didn't think I'd have to."

Debbie nodded.

"She was on the list," Spence said. "The heart belongs to her."

"Yeah, I know." Debbie looked back at the two men in the shade. The black man was shaking his cell phone in what looked to Debbie like pure fury. She couldn't be sure, but she thought the white guy was wiggling his eyebrows at her. She'd been curious, maybe even suspicious, about them from the start, but now they were beginning to give her the creeps. She didn't think they belonged with the skateboard kid. Their story, their looks, and their interactions didn't mesh. Skateboard coach and sports psychologist? It didn't pass the sniff test. Debbie turned to Spence. "What do you think about those guys?"

Spence shrugged. "I don't know. They've been pretty cooperative. More than I'd be, I think. Why?"

She nodded toward Agent Hart. "How do you know he's not calling the cops or the FBI or something? And if he isn't calling the cops, how come?"

"He said he was calling the tournament director to let him know they couldn't make it to the games. Said he didn't want to lose his deposit. Besides, after they found out about the government's involvement, they offered us the ride. They didn't have to do that."

"Exactly. Did you ever think they're being *too* cooperative? Something about them just seems weird. I mean, I don't know. You think the white guy is really the kid's uncle?"

"I hadn't given it much thought," Spence said. "You think the black guy's the uncle?"

"I don't think any of them are related. But, I mean, think about it. Who wears a suit to a skateboard tournament?"

"Don't know, never been to one."

Debbie issued a frustrated sigh. "I've never been to the queen's coronation, but I bet nobody wears cutoffs." She shook her head. "It just seems weird."

"Unlike the rest of our situation."

At the catering truck they bought drinks and a sandwich, then walked to a picnic table near the fence at the edge of the rest area. They sat down and split the sandwich. Spence took a bite, then put his hand in front of his mouth as he said, "By the way, I'm sorry about all this." He swallowed as he gestured at the world around them. "The kidnapping and"—he pointed at Debbie's head—"your bruise there."

"Bruise? More like a subdural hematoma. Any minute I might lapse into a coma." Debbie paused. "Hey, I'm rapping!"

"Yeah, well, I'm sorry, but—" He gestured at the world again, this time with an air of futility. "But what're you gonna do?"

Debbie nodded as she ate her half of the sandwich. She looked at Spence for a moment. "Yeah, I'm sorry about your nose, too. Still hurt?"

"Throbs a little. How's it look?"

"Like Karl Malden's." She smiled. "Kidding. It looks pretty good considering how hard I hit you."

"Yeah, that was a decent punch."

"Thanks." Debbie studied him for a moment. She liked the way he touched his nose, gingerly and deft, like a physician. She wondered how his fingers would feel touching her back. Spence used the muscles of his face, testing for pain around his bruised nose. The contortions made Debbie smile. "You know," she said. "This is probably the Stockholm syndrome talking, but I think I'm, uh, starting to . . . side with you." She pinched her fingers together. "Just a little."

"Yeah, but only because the other side is worse."

She nodded. "Could be." As Debbie finished her half of the sandwich, she looked past Spence to an older woman standing about ten yards away. Something about the woman was familiar. She was in her sixties and seemed to be talking to someone in the field beyond the fence, though no one was there.

Spence took the cellophane sandwich wrapper and folded it in half as he spoke. "So you think this Dr. Speyburn can pull this off? I mean, getting an operating room and a surgical team and all?" He folded the wrapper in half again, then looked up. Debbie's eyes were still fixed on the woman behind him. Spence reached over and touched Debbie's arm. "Paging Dr. Robbins."

She looked back at him. "Hmm? Uh, no. I was just watching this woman." Realizing what made her seem familiar, Debbie pointed. "My mother had a dress just like that." Her voice softened as though mystified. "I mean exactly like that. She's been standing there for a while, just talking."

Spence turned to look. He could see what Debbie couldn't. There was a small white cross in the ground in front of where the woman stood, just at the fence line. It was a memorial, presumably for a loved one who had died, most likely on the interstate. "She's talking to her daughter," Spence said, though he hadn't thought to say it. The words just came out. "She's saying, 'Don't worry.

Everything's fine. I know you're thinking about me. And it's okay. You can let go now.'" Spence had no idea why he'd said it—it was as though someone had spoken through him.

Debbie listened, nodding solemnly at the words that seemed to be for her. She felt goose bumps rising on her arms. She wanted to ask Spence to ask the woman a question, but she didn't want to interrupt what she believed was happening. Debbie had always been open to such things but had never had the experience. She'd never courted it, but neither had she resisted.

Debbie saw death every day, and every time she saw it, she sensed that it wasn't the end. There was a similarity in the last words people uttered and things the next of kin often reported feeling just after the moment of death. Debbie didn't pretend to know what the afterlife was, whether there was a forked road leading to heaven or hell or if it was something less structured. Whatever it was, she had long believed in the possibility of connecting from the other side. Now she knew.

Debbie saw the woman bend to lay something on the ground. Flowers. Then she turned and headed for the parking lot, smiling and looking at peace with the way things were. Spence and Debbie watched her walk past, get into her car, and drive away.

They sat under the blue Utah sky absorbing whatever it was they had just experienced. After a quiet moment they looked at each other, and something passed between them. "What made you say those words?" Debbie asked.

"I have no idea," Spence said, truly mystified.

Debbie stood slowly, lifted by her disbelief. "I'm going over there."

"I'll go with you." Spence, who previously would have described himself as a devout skeptic, didn't know what had happened, but he was having a hard time denying that something had. The word "occult" came into his mind, but he dismissed it. It wasn't right. This was more supernatural or spiritual or, more likely, something for which he lacked the vocabulary.

They walked to where the woman had been standing. Looking down, they saw the flowers she had laid at the cross. Debbie took a sharp breath. "Oh." It was almost a whisper.

"What is it?"

"Gloves of Our Lady." She said the words softly, conjuring a spectral image in Spence's mind.

He assumed she was talking about the flowers. The blooms were a couple of inches long, wide at the mouth, tapering to the stem, like tubular bells, crimson above and paler red below. "They're pretty," he said. But Debbie's reaction clearly went beyond admiration for their beauty.

"Those are my mom's favorite flowers." She looked at Spence. "But they don't grow around here."

"Huh." It was the only thing he could think to say. Spence started searching for a way out of this weirdness. His rational tendencies insisted there was a sound explanation for what had to be a series of chance events that added up to the eerie moment they'd just shared. He considered the evidence. First of all, the dress. If it was, in fact, like one Debbie's mother owned, so what? There were bound to be hundreds or even thousands of identical dresses out there. So much for that. Next he tried to dismiss the flowers. No telling how many people considered Gloves of Our Lady their favorite, so that didn't amount to anything, right? But what had made him say those words? He had to rationalize. Well, people do it all the time, don't they? You see someone talking, but you don't know what they're saying, so you make something up based on how they're dressed and the context they're in. The words he'd said didn't mean anything to Spence. They simply struck him as the sort of words someone might say to a loved one who had "gone on." He figured the words didn't mean anything to Debbie either. But he had to know for sure. "I hate to ask," he said, "but . . . the words?"

"Yeah," Debbie said absently.

"They don't mean anything to you, do they?"

"Yeah. They do." Debbie looked at Spence. "Today's my mom's birthday," she said. "And I've been thinking about her and worrying that I wouldn't be with her." She gazed back at the cross. "In my entire life I've never not celebrated it with her . . . until today."

Spence gave her a sheepish look. "That's my fault, I'm sorry. Is she in Los Angeles?"

Debbie turned back to Spence. "Yeah. Forest Lawn," she said. "She died eight months ago."

13

Inarticulate Speech
of the Heart

Debbie felt a great and sudden sense of relief. She also felt a sense of wonder and connection and, she had to admit, weirdness. She gestured at the spot where the old woman had been moments ago and quietly said, "That was my mother." She looked at Spence, her voice pitching up in excitement. "Well, not her exactly, but the dress and the flowers and the words were hers. They had to be, don't you think?"

The last thing Spence wanted to discuss was the elephant that had just charged into the room. His logic refused to entertain the possibility of contact from beyond the dark veil. He kept thinking, *There are no such things as ghosts*. Still, he didn't see any point in denying what Debbie clearly believed to be true, so he just said, "Okaaay."

Debbie sensed his skepticism. "What's the matter, you don't believe in that sort of thing?"

He held up his hands. "I just don't like to argue about things I can't disprove."

"But you don't even know why you said those words. You said so yourself." She pointed at him. "You have to admit, something just happened."

"Look, if you believe that was your mother telling you to let her . . . spirit go and to stop worrying, that's good enough for me."

"Don't be patronizing."

"I'm not. I'm just . . . I'm just not sure what happened, that's all I'm saying."

"I just told you what happened. What else do you need?"

"Well, I'm a stick-my-hand-in-the-wound kinda guy," Spence said. "I'm partial to having proof of something before I swear to it."

"Some things don't lend themselves to proof. What about faith?"

"I'm all for it, but it doesn't hold up in court."

She smiled. "You know, I'd understand if it was just some story I told you, but you felt it. I know you did. I saw the look on your face after you said the words. Why can't you admit it?"

"Admit what? That your mother just sent you a message from the hereafter?" He shook his head. "The only thing I know for a fact is that you're insisting it was her."

"Can you admit you don't know why you said what you did?"

"Fine. I'll stipulate to that. But that doesn't prove anything."

"Fine, whatever."

"I'm not saying something didn't happen, just that there's no way to prove it."

"I understand your position."

"Good. So can we change the subject?"

"Fine."

"I want to ask you a personal question."

"Okay."

"You don't have to answer."

"Right."

Spence hesitated before saying, "Were you with your mother when she died?"

The question caught Debbie off guard. She hadn't thought about that moment in a long time, and she wasn't sure it was any of Spence's business. But when she realized he was seeing himself in that position in the near future, she said, "Yes, I was. Mom had been in the hospital for a while, and once she realized she wasn't going to get any better, she asked her doctors to let her go home to die in her own bed. So I took her home and sat with her for a couple of days before it was over."

"Did you talk to her? You know, about . . . stuff?"

Debbie nodded. "We talked about a lot of things."

Spence looked over to where Rose was sitting. "The reason I ask is, I've been thinking I might be close to having that conversation with my mom, and I don't know what to say or what to ask. Seems like there are so many things you never talk about when they're alive. So I just wondered what you talked about, that's all."

Debbie understood. In a way she felt sorry for him. She could see how scared he was and how he was trying not to let it show. And she wondered if the subtext was that he was beginning to give up hope that he could save his mother. "Just tell her you love her," she said. "That's all anyone needs to hear."

Winston Archer's agent was on the phone. "I love you!" he shouted. "Ratings are through the roof! We've cleared another twenty-three stations, and the syndicate is putting together a new proposal for us. Now, don't hold me to this," he said, "but this could go north of fifty million."

The late-night talk-show writers were busy turning the scandal into jokes for that night's monologue. The all-news networks had suspended format in favor of full-time coverage of breaking events. Matt Christopher had come in early to talk with a handsome and well-dressed young Democratic congressman who had once sat on a House select subcommittee on domestic terror issues. As far as politicians were concerned, this was a bipartisan issue. If the public started to entertain notions about limiting what they were allowed to do in order to be reelected . . . well, they were all screwed.

Matt put a hand to his ear. "I'm told we've just received a new photograph of the fugitives—"

"Terrorists, Matt. These men are domestic terrorists."

"Excuse me, Congressman. You're exactly right. Terrorists."

"We can't emphasize that enough."

"So this is the latest photo we've received. And I'm told this is an exclusive. Winston Archer does not have this one, so stay with us." There was some confusion as they waited for the photo to appear on-screen. Matt Christopher laughed nervously. "Boy, this is like doing live television in the old days, isn't it? Oh, wait, here we go." Matt pointed at the monitor showing the photo. "Congressman, it looks to me like this photo was taken at—what would you say?—a birthday party?"

"I'd say that's what it's meant to look like, Matt, but, as you know, our subcommittee heard expert testimony on terrorist cells staging traditional American celebrations in order to attempt to blend in."

Matt shook his head in wonder. "Fascinating. What else can you tell us?"

Squinting his eagle eyes, the handsome congressman used a pointer to indicate something on the screen. "Look in the background. You see that?"

Matt leaned forward in disbelief. "What are those? Kids? Children?"

"Exactly. Experts say this is one of the ways they recruit."

A big smile. "Holy cow!" Matt sat back, slapping the tabletop on his way. "You serve a little ideology with the cake and ice cream, and the next thing you know, they're strapping a bomb to themselves and strolling into the capital, is that it?"

"It's terrifying."

"That's why we call them terrorists, isn't it?"

"And that's why I'm suggesting to party leadership that we make a formal request to Congress for the formation of a bipartisan, blue-ribbon panel on ways to increase federal spending on homeland security while lowering taxes and keeping the economy strong while at the same time protecting Social Security and Medicare."

"That's sweeping legislation, Congressman."

"The war on terror isn't over yet, Matt. In fact, just about an hour ago the House passed a resolution authorizing a two-million-dollar reward for the capture of these terrorists."

"Amazing how fast Congress can act when they stop the partisan bickering and get behind something."

"Where we find common ground, we see no reason not to move forward quickly," the congressman said. "And since we had a scheduled vote on a cost-of-living increase, we tacked on the reward resolution just to save the taxpayers a little money."

"Terrific strategy," Matt said.

The congressman shrugged demurely. "It's what we do."

"Now, if you don't mind, let's return our viewers' attention to the photo for just a moment. As you can see, one of the men is blindfolded."

"Yes, we assume that's part of a terrorist training exercise."

"Certainly one of the most chilling photographs I've ever seen."

Boyd was the one blindfolded. Spence had his hands on Boyd's shoulders, spinning him around for a go at pin the tail on the donkey at Erica's last birthday party. It was one of a dozen photos Erica had offered for sale to news organizations via bidding on eBay. So far she'd earned $14,500, which she was splitting seventy–thirty with Boyd Jr.

By this point the nation had given its full and fevered attention to television coverage of the breaking scandal. The functions of the free market and the power of niche marketing having trumped legitimate news coverage long ago, viewers could find a spin to pander to their every political predilection. The liberal-biased press was sticking to the government-run-amok angle. The conservative-biased press ran with the domestic-terrorist story. Each was selling a lot of soap to a different demographic. Citizens were watching at home, at work, at electronics stores—anywhere there was a television set.

Dale Benson was a perfect example. Dale was a law-enforcement officer from Amarillo, Texas, and a zero-tolerance kind of guy. He leaned toward a conservative interpretation of events, just as he leaned toward his tiny television screen to get a better look at the pictures they were showing of the terrorists. "Son of a beachcomber," he mumbled. He wanted to say "son of a bitch," but he had a zero-tolerance policy toward cursing. He took his binoculars and looked out the nearby window, then back at his television screen. "Heck if it ain't," he said.

Dale's wife, Betty, glanced up from her magazine. "You say somethin', hon?"

"Uh, yeah, the kids all outside?"

"Yeah, out there runnin' around, I expect."

"See if you can't get 'em on in here, would ya?"

Betty put down her magazine and stepped outside. She whistled as if calling dogs. Dale walked over to a cabinet and pulled out his old Smith & Wesson Chief Special, a snub-nose .38 with a Crimson Trace Laser-grips sight. He picked up his cell phone and dialed 911. "Hello? Yeah, I got some information on them tare-ists."

"Just tell her you love her," Debbie said. "That's all anyone needs to hear."

"Thanks." Spence nodded. "When the time comes, that's what I'll do." He checked his watch, thinking they ought to get back on the road. But he was also thinking that he wanted to kiss Debbie. And he thought she was looking at him like she might be thinking the same thing. But Spence was worried because he had a terrible track record of getting signals wrong. Was this the right moment? It was either perfect timing or the worst thing he could do. He never knew. But if not now, when? *Screw it,* he thought. *What's the worst that could happen?*

Spence finally started to lean toward her when he heard a voice say, "You two. Hold it riiiiiight there." Debbie and Spence looked up to see a steel beam of a man holding a gun on them. It was Dale Benson and his .38. "I know who you are and what you've done." He wiggled the gun. "Now, get up."

Debbie and Spence looked at each other, then stood

slowly. When Dale saw the Glock in Spence's hand, he tensed to snapping. "Jiminy!" He crouched into a firing stance. "Drop that and get your hands up!" Dale kept his gun on Spence as he eased over to disarm him.

"Take it easy," Spence said. "You've got it all wrong."

"Shut up!" Dale backhanded Spence. The .38 opened a gash on his cheekbone. "I don't need you telling me who's got things wrong."

"Hey!" Debbie took a step forward but stopped when Dale threatened to open her cheekbone, too. "Creep," she said as she turned to look at the cut on Spence's face. "You might need stitches." She gave him her napkin. "Keep pressure on it." She looked at Dale. "You didn't have to do that."

"Just want you to know I mean business." Dale tucked the Glock in his waistband at the small of his back. "Now we're going to gather your friends together and wait for the authorities to get here." Dale gestured toward the picnic table where most of the others were now sitting with Rose. "Just head on down that way."

Boyd was the first to see them. He pointed at his brother's bloody cheek. "What the hell happened?"

"Watch your mouth," Dale said. "I don't like that kinda language."

Agent Hart turned around and saw the man with the gun. "Who the fuck are you?"

Dale shoved Spence and Debbie toward the others, then turned the gun on Hart. "I hear another foul word outta your mouth and you'll find out exactly who I am, boy."

"'Boy'?" Agent Hart shot to his feet. "Did you just call me 'boy'?"

Dale squinted. "Rhymes with Chips Ahoy." He thumbed the hammer back on his .38 and turned it square on Agent Hart. "Now, sit."

Hart considered drawing on the guy, but he knew revealing his weapon would raise questions Senator Check preferred not be raised. So he sat back down, hoping to find another solution to the problem.

"I'm Sheriff Dale Benson of Amarillo, Texas." He nodded toward his Winnebago. "I was just sitting in my RV there, watching the news, when I saw the pictures of you two." He wiggled his gun at Boyd and Spence. "Found out there's a nice little reward for your capture. So I called the authorities, and we're just gonna wait till they get here."

Hart was incredulous. He pulled out his phone. "You got a clear signal out here?"

"Shut up." He turned to Spence. "Is this alla ya?"

Spence saw Rodgers down at the catering truck getting coffee. He didn't have any reason to think Rodgers could save them, but he saw no reason to point him out either. "Yeah, this is all of us."

Dale stood there with a curious expression. In all his years of law enforcement, he'd never seen such a mismatched assortment. An old lady in a hospital gown, a tattooed freak with blond dreadlocks, a Nation of Islam–looking black man, a flabby white guy in a suit, a muscular guy in a police uniform, and what looked like a pair of surgeons. "What are y'all supposed to be, the Village People?"

"Ay, yo, Dick Tracy." Jed X jerked a gang gesture with his hand. "Why you be dissin'—"

Dale turned the gun on Jed X. "You! Shut up!"

"Whoa, Jed X can't get no love nowhere."

Dale Benson shook his head, looking to Officer Bobb. "You really a cop?"

"LAPD."

"And you're helping these folks?"

"That's right. And you might as well know, I'm gay." He hadn't intended to say it. The words just kept coming out of his mouth.

Dale looked disgusted. He stared at Officer Bobb for a second. *California*, he thought. Then he gestured at Boyd. "I wouldn't have been surprised if this one here was a nancy, but not you."

Boyd took offense but was too frightened to speak up.

Rose, however, stood abruptly. She stepped forward, pointing at Dale angrily. "Young man, that is terribly rude," she said. "What would your mother say? You apologize this minute or—" Rose stopped and made a gasping sound as her hands fell to her side.

Spence thought she might collapse. "Mom?" He caught her and guided her back to the bench where she'd been sitting. "What's wrong?"

Rose had difficulty swallowing. "I . . . don't know." Her face was losing all color. Everyone circled around her.

Debbie feared the worst. "Does your chest hurt?"

Rose barely shook her head. "No, but . . ." She took a shallow breath. "I feel . . . faint."

"Give us some room," Debbie said. "Let her breathe." She put her fingers to Rose's neck, feeling for the carotid.

"Now, y'all just hold it right there," Dale warned as he waved the gun around. "I don't know what you're trying to pull here, but—"

Jed X stepped toward the sheriff. "Hey, yo, lady's sick. Don't need you comin' in all cock diesel wavin' your paddle. 'Ite?"

Dale turned on Jed, cracking his chin with the butt of his gun. "I told you to shut up!"

Jed staggered backward, his chin split and bleeding.

Rose put her hands to her throat. "My neck feels so . . . full." She closed her eyes.

Debbie instinctively reached for her stethoscope, but it wasn't around her neck. She groped for pockets she didn't have, looking for anything to help deal with the situation.

Spence put his hand on Debbie's arm. "What do you need?"

"A hospital would be nice," she said. Without equipment to do a diagnosis, Debbie was shooting in the dark, but she had to do something. Rapid heartbeat, lightheadedness, and Rose's characterization of fullness in her neck. Arrhythmia.

Boyd peered down at his mother. "What's wrong with her?"

"Ventricular tachycardia," Debbie said, making the diagnosis. "Get her in the van!"

Boyd and Officer Bobb picked Rose up and carried her.

"Hey, stop. What are you doing?" Dale followed along, desperately trying to maintain control of the situation. He didn't want to lose that reward, but he didn't want to start shooting people either. "All right, I told you not to try anything else, and here you are, tryin' something. So just everybody hold still for a minute. I don't wanna have to hurt anybody."

"Honey?" It was Dale's wife calling from the Winnebago. "What's going on?"

Dale turned and yelled, "It's okay. Just get the kids in the RV!"

Debbie couldn't believe it. They'd escaped an FBI dragnet only to get caught by some hard-ass yahoo on vacation who didn't know half the story and wouldn't believe it if he did. On top of that, she now had two wounds that needed suturing and a sudden cardiac episode to deal with. She needed a miracle, like having a dose of Class IB antiarrhythmics drop from the sky. Then it hit her. She put her hand to her face in disbelief. "Oh, my God."

"Watch your language," Dale said. "I don't like that kind of talk."

"Gloves of Our Lady." Debbie felt goose bumps return to her arms, and she looked at Spence. "Get those flowers!" She pointed back to where they'd just been.

Spence was ready to do whatever she said, like *Elevate her feet* or *Boil some water*. But *Get those flowers?* "What?" It didn't compute. "Why?"

"Trust me!"

Spence turned and ran back to where the cross was stuck in the ground.

"Hey! Where're you going?" Dale felt he was losing control.

Debbie looked to Agent Hart, pointing at the catering truck. "Get some hot water!"

"Right." Hart took off in the opposite direction. He figured this dumb cracker with the gun wouldn't know what to do with hostages scattering every which way. The more confusion, the better their chances of pulling something off.

"Now, hang on a second!" Dale was starting to sound desperate. He pulled the Glock from his back, so he had a gun in each hand pointing in two different directions.

Officer Bobb was afraid the guy would panic and start shooting. Then he noticed Hart saying something to Rodgers down at the catering truck. He hoped they were working on a plan, and he didn't want Dale to see them talking. "Hey, Sheriff," he said. "Just take it easy."

Dale turned to look at Officer Bobb. "Shut up! Don't try to distract me."

Officer Bobb pointed at Spence. "Relax. He's not going to run off. I mean, where would he go? He's just getting those flowers."

"He's going to the coroner if he don't get back here pretty quick," Dale said.

When Officer Bobb glanced over at the catering truck, Rodgers was nowhere to be seen. Hart was hustling back with a Styrofoam cup full of hot water. A second later Spence returned with the flowers. "Tear the leaves up and put them in the water," Debbie said. "Like tea."

"All right," Dale said, trying to regain control. "One more of you runs off and I'm gonna have to—" Dale stopped when he felt something hard poke him in the back.

"I'll tell you what you're gonna have to do," Agent Rodgers said from behind. "Real easy, now, you're gonna loose your grip on those guns and let my friend take 'em from you."

Dale felt the wide barrel against his spine. It felt like a shotgun, probably sawed-off given how close the man was standing. He figured his wife and kids were looking out the RV at the whole thing. He didn't want them to see him cut in half by a twelve-gauge blast, so he let the black guy take his guns.

Agent Hart stuck both guns in Dale's face. "You gonna call me 'boy' now?"

Dale shook his head, but he didn't look scared.

"You did the right thing," Rodgers said from behind Dale. "I didn't want to have to use this." He nudged Dale's spine one more time.

Dale turned around slowly and looked down to see if he was right. "Awww, man." He slumped. The barrel of the shotgun turned out to be a saltshaker with the top screwed off.

Rodgers winked at him. "I'm telling you, that sodium will kill you."

Spence smirked as he handed the Styrofoam cup to Debbie. He looked up to Agent Rodgers and said, "Thanks."

Rodgers shrugged. "Anything for Mom. How's she doing?"

Debbie held the cup to Rose's lips. She sipped the hot liquid. "This tastes awful."

"I bet," Debbie said.

"But I feel a little better." She sipped some more. "It could use some sugar."

Officer Bobb leaned down to pick up the leafless stem of flowers. He gestured with them at the pale green brew Rose was sipping. "What is this?"

"Foxglove," Debbie said. "The source of digitalis, or at least it used to be. Strengthens heart contractions."

Spence looked a bit confused. "You called it Gloves of Our Lady."

"That's what my mom called it," Debbie said.

"It's also called Fairy Thimbles," Boyd added.

Dale turned slowly and stared at Boyd with disgust. "You people." He shook his head.

Boyd seemed ashamed and defensive. "I saw them at a flower show once," he said. "With Connie. My wife."

As they tended Rose, Debbie and Spence kept looking at each other. They were both thinking the same thing. *What do you suppose happened back there?* Though neither of them said it. After a moment Spence stood slowly. He gazed off into the distance. "Uh-oh," he said, cocking his ear toward the interstate. "Sirens. We gotta get outta here."

"You might as well give up," Dale said. "I told the authorities all about your hippie van. You wouldn't get two miles in that thing, all painted up like that."

Spence looked at Dale, then at Dale's Winnebago. "You're right," he said, taking the Glock from Agent Hart. "We'll have to take something they're not looking for." He gestured at the Winnebago. "All right, everybody in the RV."

"Yo, yo, yo, whassup?" Jed X complained that bailing on his ride would set him back a phat load of scrilla, but at the same time he knew he'd be playing Rodney King with the Kojaks if he stayed. So he grabbed his favorite boards and piled into Dale's RV with everybody else.

Rodgers jumped behind the wheel, cranked it, and gassed it up the merge ramp. As they pulled out of the rest area, Hart looked out the back window and saw a dozen Utah highway patrol units screaming into the rest area. They surrounded Jed's van, holding it at gunpoint, and began negotiations through a bullhorn.

Meanwhile, Spence gathered Dale, his wife, and their six boys into the back of the Winnebago. "All right," he said, holding up the ECC device. "For all you new kidnappees, here's the deal."

Martin Brooks held the phone away from his mouth so he could yell at it. "Tell 'em to go hump themselves" were his exact words. "I don't give a shit! GAO's a bunch of bean-counting pissants. We're the goddamn White

House. We don't have to tell them where he is if we don't want to. We don't have to tell anyone anything!" He listened for a moment, his exasperation growing. "No! He's the *chief executive*. Not telling is his *privilege*. Hence the term 'executive privilege.'" He rubbed his eyes with one hand as he listened some more. "Jesus Christ! Who cares if they sue? We'll be dead and gone before any of us sees the inside of a courtroom. Besides, all we need to do is win the election and get a pardon."

Grant tapped on the door to the stateroom and peeked in. The chief of staff gestured for him to enter. "Okay, okay, okay," Brooks said. "Look. Tell them he is in an undisclosed secure location." He paused. "Because we've determined there's a credible terrorist threat against him! That's why!" He listened some more. "No! We don't have to tell them what the threat is. Telling them would jeopardize the president, compromise national security, and undermine the power of this office, which we intend to preserve at all costs. Got it? Good!" He slammed the phone back in its cradle and looked up at his assistant. "What is it?"

Grant smiled. "We found them, sir. They're in Utah."

Brooks perked up. "In custody?"

"No, sir."

His perkiness faded. "Why not?"

"We don't know what they're driving."

"Yet we know they're in Utah?"

"Someone called in to collect the reward, sir. Said they were in a rest area on I-15, somewhere between

Fillmore and Leamington. By the time we got someone on the scene, they'd fled."

"Terrific." Martin Brooks consulted the map on his desk.

"But now we know what they were driving after the Mustang burned up."

"Does that help us?"

"It doesn't, sir."

"I didn't think so." He traced his finger along the line representing I-15. "Ah, there's Fillmore."

"It was a custom-painted 1990 two-door G-20 Chevy Van, sir. Belongs to a professional skateboarder who calls himself Jed X."

"Fascinating." Brooks opened a drawer and removed a file. "How many transplant programs in that part of the country?"

"You wouldn't think many, sir."

He pulled a document from the file, looking for the answer. "There are three," he said, closing the file. "LDS Hospital, University of Utah, and Brigham Memorial. All in Salt Lake."

Grant leaned down to look at the map. "Sir, we could scramble some assets out of Hill Air Force Base, here in Ogden." He pointed at a dot north of Salt Lake. "They could set up an interstate roadblock, grab the heart, and—"

"No. Too public. Makes deniability problematic." Using the last joint on his thumb, Brooks measured something on the map. "They're only, what, a couple of hours out?" He began to nod slowly. "We'll just let them bring it to us. Surprise them at the hospital and do the transplant right there. No muss, no fuss." He looked up and pointed at Grant. "Divert the pilot to Salt Lake."

"Yes, sir." He turned to leave, then stopped. "What should we do with the contingency heart?"

"Have them meet us there," Brooks said. "She still might be useful."

As a member of the Senate Select Committee on Intelligence, Peggy Check had eyes and ears in all thirteen agencies comprising the U.S. intelligence community. However, due to a complex array of political allegiances, some of the eyes went blind periodically and some of the ears deaf. The once vaunted spirit of interagency cooperation—which never really amounted to much beyond the press release—had given way to business as usual. So while Senator Check might be unable to get any useful information from the Defense Intelligence Agency about what the Secret Service was up to, she could turn to the NSA to find out what Army Intel knew about the status of a given FBI operation. Thus did she discover what the White House knew and what their plans were in relation to the Tailor clan. As a result of that information, she called her field agents.

Rodgers was behind the wheel of the Winnebago when his cell phone rang. Spence was standing in the doorway of the bulkhead that separated the RV's cockpit from the living room area behind it. Rodgers answered his phone in a weird, singsongy voice. "Hellooo?"

Senator Check hesitated. "Is this . . . you?"

"Yes it is."

"Aren't you supposed to answer 'SOG Two' or some-thing?"

"I'm afraid we're unable to at the moment."

"Ohhh, you're with our friends, then?"

"That's right, and we're terribly sorry. My nephew really wanted to be there for the games, but we had some car trouble and . . . well, bottom line is, we're not able to make it." Rodgers looked at Spence, who shrugged an apology for the inconvenience. "I hope that doesn't cause you any problems," Rodgers said.

A thought occurred to the senator. *Is he speaking in code?* All previous communication had been straightfor-ward, but for some reason she now felt as if she'd been thrust into an espionage thriller. She pictured Robert Redford on the other end of the line, then changed him to Alec Baldwin. *If he's speaking in code, I guess I should, too.* She gave it a moment's thought before saying, "In other words, the team's not ready to play due to injury, and we need a new game plan?" She was pleased with her sports metaphor.

Agent Rodgers had no idea what she was talking about. He assumed someone had walked in on her and the sports thing was the best she could come up with. "I think I'm losing you," he said. "Can you repeat that?"

After hearing his partner's phone ring, Agent Hart came in from the living room area. Spence looked at him and said, "I think it's someone from the skateboard tour-nament." Hart nodded as he squeezed past Spence and took the front passenger seat. It was big and soft, and it swiveled.

Senator Check thought she'd lost the connection. "Are you there? Hello?"

"I'm still here," Rodgers said. "Can you hear me now?"

Senator Check spoke in hushed tones. "Yes, listen carefully," she said, switching her picture from Alec Baldwin to Andy Garcia. "Your Uncle Sam knows where you're going, and he's planning a surprise party for your arrival. Do you understand?"

"I'm not sure," Rodgers said. "Can you say that again? I didn't get it all. We're in the middle of Utah. Reception's really bad."

Hmmm, maybe he wasn't speaking in code, she thought. Senator Check noticed the clock on her desk and realized she didn't have time for any more games. "Okay, when you said you're not able to make it to the *games* and you hope that doesn't cause any *problems,* were you trying to tell me the mission is compromised somehow?"

Marveling that someone so dense could rise to the office of senator, Rodgers chuckled lightly and said, "Not at all. But thanks for asking."

"So what you said a second ago makes sense at your end but not at mine."

"That's right."

"And it's not code."

"No, no, of course not."

Andy Garcia vanished, replaced by one of those vaguely sinister-looking character actors whose name you never know. "Okay, then. Fine." And she proceeded to explain the situation.

Rodgers hung up a few moments later. He held up the phone, looking at Spence. "Tournament director."

Spence nodded. "Listen, I'm sorry we screwed up your schedule."

"Forget about it," Hart said. "He's young, and there's always next weekend. Besides, like my mama used to say, we all need a few lessons in disappointment along the way."

"Yeah, well. I appreciate your help." Spence gestured toward the back of the RV. "You guys need anything? I'm gonna go check on Mom."

"No, we're fine," Rodgers said.

Spence turned and stepped through the doorway into the living room area.

Rodgers shut the door behind him. "That was our client," he said, hoisting the phone again. "Things have changed."

Hart looked out the side window, checking the mirror. "We got incoming?"

"No, nothing like that. We just need to throw a monkey wrench in the works, slow down our progress. Make sure we don't get to Salt Lake anytime soon."

Hart nodded as he considered his options. "You know the tank layout on something like this?"

Rodgers gestured at the dashboard. "From the gauges I'd guess this thing's got one for gas plus a small reserve and a tank for propane to run the fridge and the stove."

Agent Hart opened the glove box and grabbed the

owner's manual. He flipped to the index. "Let's see, tanks, tanks, tanks . . . here we go. Black water, fresh water, gray water. Ah, fuel, page ninety-two." He flipped to the page and read for a moment. "Shit. If I'm reading this right, the fuel tank's a mile from the black-water tank." He stuffed the manual back into the compartment. "I'd have to use a pretty big charge to get from one to the other." He shook his head. "Guess I'll have to improvise."

"I'm sure you'll think of something."

"Yeah." Hart grabbed the duffel bag then headed toward the bathroom, passing through the living room, where Rose lay on the sofa. Spence was sitting on the floor next to her. Boyd, Officer Bobb, Debbie, Dale, and Betty were standing or sitting around as furniture allowed. "Don't mind me," Hart said before pointing down the hall. "Restroom this way?"

"Next door on your right," Betty said.

"Thanks." He paused and pointed out the window. "You really do get a nice view from here." He smiled and nodded, then turned and went down the hall to the bathroom. The door was locked. He rattled the handle. "Somebody in there?"

"Yo, yo, yo, I be bouncin' out in a sec, OG. Just gotta empty my clip, 'ite?"

Hart leaned against the wall and waited. He looked to the far end of the RV. Dale and Betty's six boys were in the bedroom. They were working on coloring books, playing Nintendo, and having pillow fights. Hart could hear the conversation in the living room. Debbie was doing most of the talking, trying to convince the Bensons to join their cause—or at least not to cause any trouble. "I'm telling you the truth," Debbie said. "The heart was supposed to go to Mrs. Tailor." She pointed at Rose, who nodded weakly. "Then the FBI came in and tried to take it."

Dale listened carefully, three fingers pressed to his cheek while his little finger rubbed up and down on his lips, occasionally touching his nose. He mulled over all the facts Debbie had recited and then, with the ire of a man betrayed, slammed his hand down on the arm of his chair. "Damn guvmint!" He looked to Betty, then Debbie and Rose, holding up a hand. "Forgive my language, ladies, but that burns me up." He pointed at Spence. "And I'm sorry I hit you like that. You gonna be all right?"

Spence touched his wound. "I'll be fine."

"But what about the news?" Betty asked, pointing toward the television. "They're saying these men are plotting to kill the president."

"That's crazy," Debbie said. "Did they say how?"

"Uhhh, no," Betty admitted. "They weren't specific. In fact, they said the White House issued a statement that they couldn't go into details on that without compromising national security in general and the president in particular."

Debbie couldn't believe it. "They're saying that on CNN?"

"CNN?" Dale snorted his disapproval. "They don't do news anymore," he said. "They used to, before they got bought by that entertainment company. Now all they talk about is celebrity reaction to what people in the news are wearing. I was trying to find that Winston Archer," Dale said, pointing at the television. "I usually like his take on things, but I hadn't been able to pick up his show out here. Not all the stations carry him, you know."

Betty pointed at the ECC device. "The heart's in there?"

"Yeah."

Betty wiggled a finger at it. "What's it mean when the red light stops blinking?"

Spence grabbed it and looked at the LED screen. It said BATTERY FAILURE.

14

Heart of Gold

With the battery dead, the ECC device could no longer keep the artificial blood warm. Once the Hemo-Sub dropped below thirty-two Celsius, the heart would simply stop. "Bring me the ice!" Debbie shouted as she scrambled to get the sterile saline solution into the container. "What time is it? Somebody mark the time!"

Spence brought the ice and packed it into the ECC device as instructed. "Is it going to be all right? You think it's still viable?"

"We've got about four hours," Debbie said, all business.

Agent Hart watched from the hallway, still waiting to get into the bathroom. He put his ear to the door. He heard Jed X coughing. He rattled the doorknob again. "Hurry up in there, circus boy."

"Yo, chill, homeskillet. You ain't gotta be allupinit like 'at." A second later the bathroom door opened, and Jed X emerged in a small cloud of smoke. To his left he saw the serious gathering in the living room. To his right, at the back of the RV, were the kids playing in the bedroom. He smiled at Agent Hart. "Peace. Out." He headed to the back.

Hart slipped into the bathroom and locked the door. He gave the room the once-over, deciding where to start. He looked under the sink for useful household chemicals. There was a nearly empty bottle of Windex and some 409, both of which were useless to the task. Next to that was a box of something called Stool-Sweet, some sort of septic-tank additive promising the obvious. Unfortunately, the active ingredients of Stool-Sweet were not specified, and the inactive ingredients weren't of any help to the CIA. Hart stood and opened the medicine cabinet, where he found three bottles of grit-covered sun block (SPF ratings of four, fifteen, and thirty). There was a nearly spent tube of toothpaste with tartar control and whiteners, some expired aspirin, a tin of Band-Aids with a rusty hinge, and a bottle of rubbing alcohol. "Hello," he said.

Hart looked into the dry toilet, then found the foot pedal that opened the trap. He wedged a bar of soap in near the trap's hinge to keep it open. He pulled a cigarette and a pack of matches from the duffel bag. He lit the cigarette, then pushed a fresh match through, near the filter, until the tip touched the paper. Then he emptied the bottle of isopropyl into the black-water tank. Next he tried to balance the cigarette on the toilet seat so that when it burned down and lit the match, it would topple into the tank, igniting the alcohol. But the motion of the RV kept rolling the cigarette side to side. He needed something to stabilize it, so he reached back into the duffel bag and pinched off a bead of the doughy green pyrophoric reagent. He made two smaller beads from that and stuck them to the lip of the toilet seat on either side of the cigarette, stabilizing it. He wasn't sure if the heat from the burning cigarette would ignite the material, but he'd find out soon enough.

Satisfied with his work, Agent Hart paused for a moment. He was breathing through his mouth, staring at the smoke as it curled off the cigarette poised on the edge of the toilet. Thin blue eddies vanished in the bad air. Hart's dark eyes drifted along the length of the cigarette, past the filter, and then down into the darkness of the black-water tank. Staring into the shithole, trying not to breathe through his nose, he began to reflect on his life's work. He'd met interesting people and been to some exotic locations. He'd learned some things about the world, had picked up some useful skills, and he'd served the country he loved. For the past twenty years he'd followed orders, doing all he could to protect democracy and freedom. He didn't have much to show for his troubles—a modest pension and a few thousand in savings. But he had his poetry. He would always have that. "Do not be alarmed," he whispered. "I'm a trained professional. I make things go boom."

A nasty turf battle was unfolding at the hostage scene. It all stemmed from a botched bank-robbery negotiation two years earlier, which had resulted in a wave of unfavorable publicity, a union squabble, and the creation of two separate federal emergency-response groups. Now the head of the Federal Crisis Management Team refused to coordinate with the head of the Federal Crisis Response Unit, so the field commander put in a request to meet with the tactical supervisor to discuss replacing the current negotiation foreman.

The public-information officer, meanwhile, was taking advantage of the lack of progress to give television interviews to anyone who asked. He hoped to parlay the exposure into a network job offer. "There are three different types of hostage situations," he explained. "There are deliberate sieges, spontaneous sieges, and anticipated sieges. My understanding is that this is a spontaneous situation."

"But an FBI spokesman has said there is no hostage situation. They're saying this is a publicity stunt by Winston Archer."

"Really?" This was news to the public information officer. "If it is, it's a good one."

Once it was apparent that talks between the two hostage-negotiation teams had reached a stalemate, a nonunion hostage consultant with military psych-ops experience was brought in to deal with what might or might not have been a hostage situation. Within thirty minutes an elaborate sound system was set up around the perimeter of the Tailor house. A dozen Altec Lansing Voice of the Theater loudspeakers, each the size of a large sofa, were connected to an equal number of Crown power amplifiers bridged to mono to push a thousand watts per speaker. With the last wire connected, the psych-ops guy gave the signal for everyone to put on OSHA-approved ear protection. "Everybody ready?" When he pushed the start button, Paul Anka assaulted the Brentwood neighborhood with his 1974 hit "(You're) Having My Baby."

Winston Archer almost flipped backward out of his seat when the sound system began blasting outside. He was rattled but was determined to continue. So he yelled, "Connie, tell us more about your husband!"

"He's very sweet!" she screamed. "And he loves his mother a great deal! That's the only reason he did this!" Winston nodded thoughtfully at the words he couldn't hear. Connie cupped her hands together and continued yelling, "I know he'd hate for me to say this on television, but he's very sensitive and loving!" She looked at the camera. "Boyd, honey, if you're watching this, I want you to know I love you!"

"Thank you, Connie!" Winston Archer turned to Agent Sandlin and shouted, "Can you tell us why you were sent here?"

Agent Sandlin seemed unaware the question was aimed at him. He just sat there mouthing the words to the song.

Outside, the crowd stampeded out of the way of the deafening loudspeaker system. Those running into the street had to dodge a couple of incoming Suburbans. The SUVs bullied their way to where most of the television crews were camped. Once they were parked, several well-dressed black men and one black woman got out and assembled in front of the vehicles. "Who's in charge here?" one of the men yelled, hoping to be heard over Paul Anka's aching ballad.

Realizing who had arrived, the press rushed over. A reporter shouted, "Reverend! Why are you here?"

The reverend waited until all the television cameras had a clear line of sight. He began to thunder, "We are here because the black community is tired of being excluded from these talks and we could not, with a clear conscience, allow it to go on any longer! We are not here in support of one side or the other," he hollered. "We are simply here to demand some participation and representation in the negotiation!"

"Reverend! What does the black community have to do with this situation?"

"As in so many aspects of this great nation, the black community has *everything* to do with this!" The reverend turned and held an arm out. The black woman who had arrived with the entourage stepped forward, anguished. The reverend put his arm around her shoulder. She dabbed a tissue at her eyes as the reverend shouted,

"None of us would be here were it not for the black community, for it was a black man who, literally, *is* the heart of this matter! I am not saying a black man is *at* the heart of this matter. I am saying a black man *is* the heart of this matter. And that man's mother is here to demand some justice!"

Jed X was sitting on the bed surrounded by Dale and Betty's six boys. They were fascinated by his inverted vertical labrets, his dermal punches, and especially his tattoos.

The youngest pointed at one on Jed's arm. It seemed to be a rendering of a skeleton in a Canadian Mountie outfit rubbing his face with a beaver. "How come this one looks so funny?"

Jed X laughed. "Yo, lil G, my best dog did that with a homemade tat machine when he got outta juvey." The child's eyes grew wide. "Yo, check it, homes taped a slot-car motor to the side of a hollowed-out ballpoint, at the top, knowhati'msayin? Then he wrapped a guitar string around the motor arm and ran it through the pen so it stuck out about this much." Jed held his finger and thumb about a sixteenth of an inch apart. "Then he hooked the motor to a nine-volt battery, 'ite? Motor arm spins 'round and moves that string in 'n' out *muy pronto,* yo. Then my whodi dipped it in the ink and got allupinit." Jed X stretched his skin, skewing the skeleton's smile. "But, yo, it helps if your man's got some da Vinci skills."

"Word," the oldest son said.

"Does it hurt?" asked the next youngest.

Jed X pulled up his pant leg and pointed at a tribal band. "Oh, I got squicked when my dog carved this. Fact, I 'bout went out when he started slingin' the ink." Jed X looked down the hall just as Agent Hart was exiting the bathroom. "Yo, Skinny G," he called out. "Whassup?" He cupped a hand by his ear. "We didn't hear no flush, knowhati'msayin?" The kids laughed.

Agent Hart turned and moved to the front of the RV. He stepped through the doorway in the bulkhead and closed the door. He sat down, put on his seat belt, then looked at Rodgers. "Shouldn't be long."

The two CIA agents were expecting only a small discharge of energy, more noise and smoke than anything, so the magnitude of the explosion surprised them almost as much as it did the others. It blew the bathroom door off its hinges and started a galloping fire in the middle of the Winnebago. Apparently there was a radical chemical reaction wherein the active ingredient in the Stool-Sweet acted as a catalyst to the isopropyl and the pyrophoric reagent. Rodgers threw open the bulkhead door and yelled, "What the hell was that?"

There was major panic in the main cabin as everyone reacted to the explosion and the fire. "Mom!" The children's voices called through the smoke and flames.

Betty screamed, "My babies!" She and Officer Bobb ran to the hall but were stopped by the flames and the hideous stench. "Oh, my God!" Betty covered her face and started to run into the flames, but Officer Bobb restrained her.

"Pull over!" He yelled to Rodgers. "Stop!"

Betty was hysterical, fighting to get away from Officer Bobb, but he was too strong. Dale grabbed the small fire extinguisher from the kitchen and exhausted its contents, to no avail. The flames and smoke were getting thicker. "Mom!" They could hear glass breaking and imagined the intense heat shattering the full-length mirror on the back of the door to the bedroom where the children were.

Rodgers pulled the Winnebago down Exit 236 and stopped. He didn't want to be in that RV when the gas and propane tanks blew. "Everybody out! Go! Go! Go!" Dale grabbed Betty while Officer Bobb helped Boyd and Spence get Rose out.

Betty was screaming. "My babies!"

Rodgers and Hart herded everyone away from the Winnebago. One of them yelled to Dale, "Where's the gas tank on this thing?"

Dale pointed. "Above the axle."

"How big?"

"Eighty gallons."

"Jesus!" Rodgers waved his arms. "Everybody back up!"

"But my babies!" Dale had to use all his strength to move Betty away. She was wailing and struggling to escape, willing to charge back into the blazing Winnebago. "Let me go!"

"Somebody go around the back!" Dale yelled.

Spence, Boyd, and Officer Bobb were carrying Rose farther from the RV when a thought occurred to Spence. "Oh, shit!" He turned and charged back toward the burning RV.

"Spencer, no!" Rose put her hand to her mouth and began to pray.

Holding his breath, Spence disappeared into the smoking Winnebago for a few seconds before emerging with the ECC device. Stopping to take a breath, Spence heard Jed X yelling, "Yo, yo, yo! Need a little 911 back here!"

Spence ran to the back of the RV, where Jed X was climbing out the shattered rear window with the last two kids hanging on his back. The others were standing anxiously below, waiting for their brothers. As Spence reached up to take one of them from Jed's back, Betty and Dale arrived. "My babies!" Betty and Dale scooped up two kids each and ran like hell.

Spence led the two older boys across the road to where the others were waiting. When they reached safety, they turned to look for Jed X, but he had vanished. They exchanged glances, wondering what had happened. A second later the fuel tank exploded. A massive fireball boiled out the rear window as they watched in horror. Simultaneous with the explosion they heard what sounded like a war whoop. They looked. It was Jed X surfing the tube of the fireball. He was tucked low, riding his favorite board. Pushed by the shock wave, Jed X landed thirty feet away. He hit the road so hard the dark-side of the deck burred the asphalt. But the board had major pop. Jed executed a gnarly mute grab tweaked frontside 9090, followed by a wicked tic tac. He road-tucked and carved over to where everyone was waiting, ending with a 180 pop shuvit and kickflip. He bounced off the board and landed with his arms held out to his side. "Yo!"

"Whoa!" the youngest one replied. The others cheered and clapped and mobbed their hero. Betty joined in, smothering Jed X with kisses, praise, and unending gratitude.

Dale saw Jed's bloody hands. He'd cut them climbing in and out of the broken window, saving the kids. Dale pulled a clean handkerchief from his pocket and cleaned the blood and glass from Jed's palms. "Son, I'm sorry I hit you earlier. I had bad information. I hope you'll forgive me."

"Yo, we good." Jed shook his slightly singed head, then pointed at Agent Rodgers. "See? That's all I'm talkin' 'bout. Just a l'il love, youknowhati'msayin'?"

"I *don't* know what you're saying, son, but you're all right in my book," Dale said.

Rodgers nudged his partner while nodding toward the flaming RV. "What the hell did you use?"

Hart shrugged. "Hey, you wanted a monkey wrench."

Spence was staring off to the east at the Mount Nebo Range of the San Pitch Mountains. He wondered what else could go wrong. Boyd walked over. "Well, baby brother, you got us this far. Now what?"

Spence turned and gazed at the smoldering RV. "I don't know." Then he turned back to his brother. "I honestly don't know."

When Air Force One landed in Salt Lake, the press was there to meet it. Martin Brooks could taste the contempt bubbling up from his gut as he looked out the window and saw the microwave antennas. There was no point in asking how the press knew they were coming. Either he had an internal leak or someone in air-traffic control was dating a reporter. Secure in his own staff, Martin Brooks turned a gimlet eye on the control tower. "Goddamn radar jockeys." Wondering if there was a way to retaliate against NATCA, he turned to his assistant and said, "Who do we own on the Labor and Pensions subcommittee?"

Grant tilted his head slightly and said, "Who do we own?"

"I said 'Who do we *know*?'" Brooks waved his hand. "Oh, forget it."

"Yes, sir." Grant checked his watch. "Sir, the contingency organ will be landing in about ten minutes. I think we should address the media in the terminal so we don't have to answer any questions about that."

Brooks looked out the window again as Air Force One glided across the apron. "Would that there was a way we'd never have to answer any of their questions," he said absently.

"Well, sir, technically, the First Amendment simply allows them to ask. It doesn't require you to answer."

Brooks turned slowly and pointed at Grant. "Yes or no. Do you still beat your wife?"

Grant was caught off guard. "I'm not married, sir."

"I know that, you idiot." Brooks made a conciliatory gesture toward Grant. "I'm sorry," he said. "The point is, they let the questions serve as accusations. The answers don't matter. What's implied by the question is assumed to have some basis in truth. If you don't answer, the public assumes you're hiding something. If your answer denies the implied accusation, you're assumed to be lying. It's a no-win situation."

"It's an outrage, sir. Something the Founding Fathers should have considered when they framed the Bill of Rights." Grant's political passions were inflamed by the thought that a bunch of shortsighted colonists in powdered wigs could hobble a great man like his boss, and from the grave no less. "Sir, you know how much I love this country," Grant said. "But, if you don't mind my saying so, I can't help but wonder how much better things would be if we had more control over the press. I mean, you're trying to save the republic." He pointed out the window at the media throng. "And what are they doing? They spend their time trying to trick you into saying something scandalous."

Brooks shook his head sadly. "It's ever been thus," he said.

"It's a disgrace, sir. You're going to go out there and they'll start demanding answers about why you're here and where's the president and what happened out at Edwards Air Force Base and—" Grant caught himself. "I'm sorry, sir. I get carried away sometimes when I see how they treat you."

"It's okay." Martin Brooks smiled broadly, touched by Grant's show of affection. He knew the kid didn't really want to rewrite the Constitution. It was just his way of showing his loyalty. "Don't you worry, son. I can handle them." He put his arm around Grant's shoulder. "*We* can handle them."

"Yes, sir, I know you can."

They were walking toward the front of the plane when Martin Brooks stopped without warning. His eyes shifted left and right as his thoughts ran to a conclusion. He turned to look at Grant. "You know, what you said just now, about the questions they're going to ask?"

"Yes, sir?"

"Gave me an idea." He clapped Grant on the back. "Yessir, a helluvan idea."

"It did?"

"Yes, indeed. We don't need to change the Constitution to control the press. We have all the control we need." The certainty of the claim buoyed Grant's spirits. Martin Brooks stuck out his chin and shot his cuffs. "How do I look?"

Grant reached over and straightened the chief of staff's tie. "Like a leader, sir."

"Atta boy! Now, just watch this."

A few minutes later they were in the main terminal. Martin Brooks screwed on a smile and faced the press. "Mr. Brooks! Mr. Brooks!"

He pointed at a reporter who said, "Mr. Brooks, where is President Webster? Is he with you?"

"As we've said before, the president is in an undisclosed secure location." Brooks was calm and assured, his tone matter-of-fact but agreeable. Grant stood behind his boss and to the side, nodding all the while.

"Is that because of the credible threat your office referred to earlier?"

"Exactly."

"Is there any connection between that threat and the incident at Edwards Air Force Base?"

Brooks leaned forward on the podium, serious. "Yes, we are now looking into possible connections between terrorist organizations and the CP-1 explosion."

"Earlier your office denied there was—"

He cut the reporter off. "We received new information." As if the answer were obvious.

"Mr. Brooks!"

The chief of staff pointed to another reporter.

"Is your visit to Salt Lake related to the CP-1 investigation?"

"No, believe it or not, we actually have people who investigate these things for us." His tone and his smile implied that the reporter should go back to reporter school before asking another stupid question.

"So why are you here?" a different reporter asked.

"I'm here on official business, specifically in regard to legislation that would require farmers to sell or lease their water rights to the federal government if they participate in a specific conservation program. We think that sets a terrible precedent. The president strongly opposes the use of federal dollars to encourage farmers to give up their water rights. As we've said all along, this is the family-farm administration."

"So your visit here has nothing to do with—"

"Look, I just told you why I'm here. Now, if you think you're entitled to know about any personal matters I may be dealing with while on this trip, just ask. It's none of your business, but I know you feel entitled to ask. So go ahead." There was a moment of silence as the press corps tried to think of personal questions to ask.

Grant watched with growing fascination. He thought the misdirection with the answer about the CP-1 was the helluvan idea. But now he could tell his boss had a second card up his sleeve.

A reporter called out, "Could you give us a hint?"

Martin Brooks hung his head for a moment before looking up with the expression of a man about to confess. "The truth is that while I'm here, I'll be seeing a specialist," he said. "A doctor." A murmur rippled through the press corps as they wondered what sort of disease they were looking at. "It's a personal issue," Mr. Brooks said. "A little embarrassing, I'm sure you'll be happy to know." He shrugged as if he couldn't understand their fascination. "I was hoping not to go public with this but, fine. You want transparency? Well, how's this?" He shoved a hand in a pocket and looked at the reporters as if to suggest they should all be ashamed of themselves. "While I'm here, I'll be undergoing some tests to see if I qualify for a Phase III test of a new product being developed by Lumpkin-Whitcomb Pharmaceuticals."

"Mr. Brooks?" A young reporter raised his hand. "Are you dying?"

Brooks smiled in a grandfatherly fashion as he peered over the tops of his glasses. "Why, no, but thank you for your concern." He cast a wistful gaze toward a camera. "No, the truth is, I'm suffering from erectile dysfunction."

Talk about your sound bite. If the press was agog, Grant was purely astonished. It was only now that he understood the whole strategy. The CP-1 announcement would send half the press racing to the Mojave Desert looking for connections between terrorist organizations and the destruction of an experimental military aircraft. Brooks's claim that he was participating in a medical experiment would provide cover for their visit to the hospital. Meanwhile, the rest of the press would be so busy scrambling to write personality pieces about how brave Martin Brooks was to admit he was a candidate for Mycoxaflopin that the heart-seizure story would probably drop below the fold.

Grant shook his head. He knew it wasn't true, yet this great man had stood there in the full glare of the media and said he couldn't get it up. It was not only a brilliant strategic move, it was the greatest act of courage and sacrifice in defense of liberty Grant had ever seen.

The chief of staff looked pleased with himself. "Are there any questions?"

"Mr. Brooks! Have you spoken with Bob Dole?"

"There's nothing prettier than a boiling-liquid, expanding-vapor explosion," Rodgers said, somewhat wistfully. "Beautiful as all hell."

"Armageddon heat./Fireball mushrooming upward./ Orange, black, and gold," were the words that came to

Agent Hart as he watched. The blast, along with the fire, caused the RV's propane tank to fail, which triggered the boiling-liquid, expanding-vapor explosion about which Rodgers and Hart had spoken so lyrically.

Following the fiery blast, a procession of six children, three men in dark suits, two surgeons, a married couple, a cop, an old lady in a hospital gown, and a big kid covered in tattoos could be seen walking down a road in the middle of nowhere as if searching for an Italian film director.

They were heading for a coffee shop one of the Benson boys had spied just up the road in the hamlet of Mona, Utah. Spence, Boyd, and Officer Bobb took turns carrying Rose, who was by now too tired to walk. Jed X gave piggyback rides to the kids one after the other. Dale, Betty, and Debbie brought up the rear.

The coffee shop was a quarter mile up State Road 54, where it intersected with old U.S. 91. The 91, which ran parallel to I-15 from Nephi to Goshen, was known locally as the Mona Road and was the main drag through this community of eight hundred people none of whom were currently at the coffee shop with the big hand-painted sign that read POLLY'S JOE.

The parking lot was empty, but the lights were on inside. A woman in her late forties, in a starched waitress outfit, leaned on the counter reading a paper. Above her in the corner, a muted television blinked from one image to the next. When the door opened, ringing the little bell, the woman looked up. She had few expectations beyond having to answer the usual question about the whereabouts of the bathroom and, no offense intended, the nearest McDonald's, too. But as they kept coming, one after another, until sixteen of them were standing there, dressed in all manner of outfits, her expectations evolved. The woman pointed at Spence, recognition flashing in her eyes. "Hey." She pointed up at the television, where, to her surprise, she saw a detailed cross-section of a flaccid penis on one half of the screen and Martin Brooks making his embarrassing announcement on the other. She looked back at Spence. "You're the guy!"

Spence hung his head momentarily, wondering if the woman was about to leap toward phoning the cops. If she did, Spence wasn't sure he had the will to stop her. "Well, I'm not the guy with the penis problem."

"No! You're the guy who—" The woman saw Rose and pointed at her. "Hey! You're his mother!" The woman hurried over to Rose. "You must be exhausted." She offered Rose her arm for support and led her to a booth. "You sit down right over here," she said. "My name's Polly. Can I get you something, ma'am?"

After serving coffee and homemade pie, on the house, Polly allowed as how she'd been following the news stories about their plight and was rooting for *them* to get the heart and the president be damned, though she didn't use that word because, although she was no longer a practicing Mormon, Polly had her standards. She went so far as to apologize for not having a car they could take. "I loaned it to a friend who had to go to Spanish Fork on some business," she said. "Otherwise I'd drive you there myself."

Polly, it turned out, was no big fan of elected officials, her antipathy springing from the completion of Interstate 15 in the mid-1980s. She pointed at a line on the horizon and said, "That stretch out there from Yuba Lake up to Payson was the last part of the interstate to be finished in Utah."

Agent Rodgers, standing behind the others, raised his hand slightly. "Did you know the Virgin River Gorge section of I-15 was the most expensive stretch of freeway ever built in the United States?"

Polly nodded. "That's true," she said. "Those four miles cost nearly fourteen million dollars."

"It's breathtaking, though," Rodgers said. "A very pretty drive."

"Oh, yes, that's true." She waved a hand at the interior of the restaurant. "Anyway, my father built this place in '72 and named it after me. Ten years later, when the Utah DOT announced they were finally going to finish the interstate, the people here in Mona got pretty excited, figuring it would revitalize our little economy." Polly held up a finger. "Now, the DOT had two choices," she said. She leaned over and huffed some fog onto the window. She drew lines in the moisture as she spoke. "They could overlap I-15 onto this stretch of old U.S. 91, or they could bypass us, which didn't make as much sense from a budget or an engineering point of view. But the next thing you know they were surveying a quarter mile that way." She pointed toward the freeway. "So we looked into the land titles, and guess what? All that property up there had been bought up over a span of about ten years, all by some corporation nobody'd heard of. It turned out to be a shell corporation with a whole bunch of off-the-book partnerships or something. Finally came to find out the board of directors of the corporation were the partners of the same law firm that just so happened to represent some close personal friends of our duly elected senator and a former business partner of his, who just so happened to have been head of the Federal Highway Administration, though I'm sure that's all just a coincidence," she said. "Still, that pretty much drove a stake through the heart here. All the money that comes up and down that interstate? Goes to those franchised joints and the gas stations at the next exit, all owned by guess who?" Polly shook her head again. "Put a lot of people out of business and put a few in the grave, too, including my parents."

"Look," one of the kids yelled, "the fat guy's on TV!" Everyone looked up to see a family photo of Boyd hoisting a carving knife at Thanksgiving.

Polly pulled the remote from her pocket and turned up the volume. "*. . . has been a low-level employee at a branch of First Santa Monica National Bank for several years.*"

"I'm a goddamn vice president!" Boyd turned on the kid. "And I'm not fat!"

Boyd's photo was replaced by one of Spence. "*His younger brother was the founder of the Westside Poverty Law Center, a radical left-wing legal-aid organization whose mission was to sabotage legitimate business interests with frivolous lawsuits on behalf of the so-called poor."*

Debbie cracked a smile and nudged Spence. "That's you?"

"Yeah, well." Spence shrugged. "They make it sound better than it is."

Ten minutes later Polly emerged from the kitchen with a tray held high over her head. "Here we go," she said. "Who had the BLT?"

Officer Bobb raised his hand. "That's me."

"There you go, handsome."

"Thanks, but I should tell you, I'm gay." He just couldn't stop telling people.

Polly nodded thoughtfully, then leaned down to Officer Bobb. "Huh, you might wanna keep that under your hat while you're in Utah."

Jed X and the kids devoured hamburgers while Spence, Boyd, Officer Bobb, and Debbie sat with Rose, trying to figure out what to do next. With their options limited by a lack of transportation, it didn't take long for despair to arrive. Though no one would say it, it seemed the end had come.

"Mom, I'm sorry," Spence said. "I really screwed this up."

"Would you stop? We'll be fine." Rose glanced at her reflection in the window. "I don't feel nearly as bad as I look." She turned, smiling, to gaze at her sons. "I'm very proud of you both. You did your best. That's all anybody can ask."

"You deserve better," Boyd said. "That's all."

"Sweetheart, I'm okay," Rose said. "Goodness, I've got no complaints, none at all."

Spence watched her as she spoke. She was an old lady. Her face was creased and tired.

"I've had a fine life," Rose continued. "Grandchildren, a loving husband, and two wonderful sons who love their old mom so much they'd . . . well, that they'd do this." She gestured at their current circumstance.

Her hair thinned to wisps. Her hands fragile as bird's bone.

"Even if it ends here, I still come out ahead."

She was pale and drawn, yet there was a sparkle in her eyes that wasn't yet dimmed.

"Besides, I'm not dead yet. I'm just a little tired."

Spence thought of his earlier conversation with Debbie, about what he should say when the time had come. He reached over and put his hand on Rose's. "I just want you to know." Their eyes connected. "I love you," he said.

She smiled and said, "I love you, too." She gave him a look as if to say she was fine and to stop worrying. "Now, if it's all right, I think I'd like to lie down for a minute."

They left her alone in the booth so she could stretch out. Polly brought a tablecloth for a blanket. Boyd and Spence moved several booths away and sat. "You know," Boyd said, "for a while there I really thought you were gonna get us to Salt Lake." He held his fist out toward his brother and said, "You did good."

Spence smiled and bumped his fist against Boyd's. "Thanks. I had to give it a shot."

"Yeah," Boyd said. "I just wish I'd thought to do it." He poked his finger at the tabletop. "Or at least gone along when you had the idea."

Spence snorted a little laugh. "That's funny. I was just thinking I should've taken your advice." He glanced over his shoulder at Rose. "My bulb doesn't look so bright at the moment."

"It was the right thing to do."

Spence rubbed his eyes for a second, then looked out the window. "You know what I was thinking about?" He gestured to the south. "Back there? I was thinking about Mr. Fuzzy's funeral. Remember that?"

Boyd's head bobbed. "Yeah, I do," he said. "When was that? A hundred years ago?" Now his head shook. "God, I hadn't thought of that since . . . I don't know when. What made you think of that?"

Spence stared at his brother. "What made me think of a funeral?" A tone of disbelief.

Boyd got it a moment later. "Oh. Right." He pointed a few booths over. "Mom."

"Yeah, Mom."

"Listen. I really don't want to start talking about Mom and funerals," Boyd said. "Not just yet. Not in the same sentence. I'm the executor of her estate, and that's more work than I've got time for right now."

"You'll have plenty of time in prison," Spence said.

"Good point," Boyd said. "And now that we've got

that figured out, let's talk about getting to Salt Lake for that operation."

Spence looked out the window at the empty parking lot. "And what makes you think we can pull that off?"

Boyd pointed at his brother. "You do."

15

Take This Heart of Mine

Debbie checked the time again. She'd been drinking coffee for an hour. Her kidneys ached. Assuming the heart was still viable, it had only two and a half hours left. The parking lot was still empty. On the horizon, smoke rising from the burning RV. She readjusted her focus in the window and studied the reflection of Spence and Boyd sitting in their booth. All the hope seemed to have faded from Spence's face, while Boyd looked like he was trying out for cheerleader as he worked to rouse his brother into leading one final charge.

After finishing another cup of coffee, Debbie headed to the restroom. It was at the end of a hall on the far side of the restaurant. She was three steps down the hall when someone stepped in behind her. "Hey, Doc." It was Agent Rodgers, from out of nowhere.

"We need to talk," he said.

She heard something unsavory in his voice, so she kept walking.

He come down the hall after her. He raised his voice. "I said we need to talk."

Debbie paused by the pay phone between the two restroom doors. *I knew it! I knew there was something creepy about this guy*. She still didn't know what it was, but she didn't like it. She glanced over her shoulder and said, "Can it wait?" She pointed at the restroom door. "I gotta go."

"This won't take a sec." Rodgers smiled without parting his lips. "There's something you should know."

She turned to face him. "What's that?"

He nodded back toward the booths. "I'm afraid the Brothers Karamazov out there have reached the end of their road."

"What's that supposed to mean?"

Rodgers slipped a hand into his coat. "Let me put it this way," he said. "The RV didn't just happen to explode."

"No?" She wondered what his hand was doing inside his coat.

Rodgers sighed philosophically. "What was it Gary Hart said?" He looked up at an angle. "'In politics, nothing of consequence happens by coincidence.'"

Debbie squinted and shook her head. "What're you saying?"

Rodgers pulled his hand from his coat and showed Debbie his badge. "My friend and I are with the CIA." He raised his eyebrows. "Special Activities Section." Like she'd be impressed.

"Oh." She was both surprised and not. "And you're working for . . . ?" She held her hands out as if for the answer.

Rodgers slipped his badge back into his coat. "The taxpayers, I guess. You tell me."

Debbie had a bad feeling. The man's body language and tone were insinuating a threat or blackmail or something. And she had to wonder why—if the guy was really with the CIA—why was he telling her? She couldn't think of any good answers, so she decided it was best to keep him talking until someone else who'd had too much coffee came down the hall. "So why'd you blow up the RV?" Its political implications being unclear to her.

"Here's a better question," Rodgers said. He put a finger in Debbie's face. "What are you going to say when you get called to testify in front of the committee about all this?"

"What committee?"

Rodgers picked at something between his teeth. "Look, you've seen the news." He flicked something gray off his finger and pointed back toward the coffee shop. "Those two boys out there are in deep shit." He propped an arm on top of the pay phone. "When this is all over, there are going to be some closed-door hearings and somebody's going to prison. That is, if they don't commit suicide first, which happens sometimes in situations like this." He shrugged.

"There have been other situations like this?"

"More than you'd think," Rodgers said. "And when those people on the Senate Subcommittee for Emerging Threats start grilling you about your part in all this and threatening your career as a doctor before you even get your license, well . . ." He shrugged again. "I was just thinking about how I'd hate for that to happen and how I'm in a unique position to testify on your behalf to see that it doesn't." Rodgers took a step toward Debbie, smiling his hookworm smile. He began to rub her arm. "I might even be persuaded to make you out to be the hero in this mess." As Debbie backed up, Rodgers stepped closer until his pelvis pressed hers to the wall. "But I'd need a little incentive to make sure I got my facts straight."

Debbie could feel the trap closing. Over the last several hours she'd stopped thinking about the implications of what she'd done, or, more precisely, she hadn't thought about how it could all be misconstrued, especially by professionals. And if this creep was really with the CIA, he could screw her bad, which was apparently what he had in mind in a more literal sense at the moment. Shit. Debbie thought about Spence and Boyd and Rose and the others, but she didn't have to think about them very long. She stared at her shoes for a second. Then she raised her eyes to Rodgers and let out a sigh of relief. "I am so glad this is over," she said. "I'll do whatever you want."

Because they were promoting the idea that there was no hostage situation at the Tailors' home—at least not one involving one of their agents—the FBI wanted the least number of reporters on the scene in case something unfortunate occurred, which seemed a likely eventuality. Unfortunately, the presence of the reverend and his entourage served only to brighten the media spotlight. Thus the FBI was engaged in a second negotiation inside one of the FBI's SWAT vans.

"Exactly how much justice are you and Mrs. Coleman looking for, Reverend?"

"As you know, my constituency is the desperate, the disinherited, the disrespected, and the despised," he said.

"Right. How much?"

"They are restless, and they seek relief!"

"Can you just give me a number?"

The reverend cupped a hand to his odd-looking ear. "Do I hear the call of litigation and mitigation or that of celebration, indemnification, and diversification?"

"Reverend, there aren't any cameras."

"We must emancipate lest we be forced to adjudicate. We should seek to alleviate, not to emasculate."

"How about I write a number on this piece of paper?"

"Throughout this process the black community has been compromised, victimized, and dehumanized!"

The FBI agent handed the piece of paper to the reverend.

The reverend looked at the number, then at the FBI agent.

"How's that?" The agent hoped to put this to bed right now.

"I believe at this price she would take my advice," the reverend said. "And for justice this would suffice." Then, leaning forward, more quietly he said, "But there is the matter of expenses."

"Fine," the agent said. "Whatever."

A few moments later the reverend stepped out of the FBI SWAT van into the blasting music. He gathered his entourage and Mrs. Coleman and headed for his Suburban. As they walked, the reverend leaned over to Mrs. Coleman and said, "Man, I hate that song."

The psych-ops DJ had segued from the irritating Paul Anka ballad to Bread's tiresome 1972 hit, "Baby I'm-a Want You."

"Lord, you ain't kiddin'," Mrs. Coleman said. "I don't even know what that means. How can you be 'a want you'? Don't make a damn bit of sense." They climbed into the SUV and drove away.

Inside, Connie was sitting on the sofa, like a guest on a talk show that happened to be taking place in her living room. She looked at the framed picture on the end table, Boyd kissing her on Mother's Day five years ago. The photo made her think back to this morning when Boyd had left the house. She hadn't kissed him good-bye. Connie put her hand to her mouth, surprised and disappointed in herself. She looked at the photo again and hoped Boyd was all right. Her dangerous man. She thrilled at the notion. She missed him, and she wanted that kiss.

Winston Archer, meanwhile, was struggling to carry on his interview. "Welcome back to America's Heart Held Hostage," he shouted into the camera with a quick glance at his watch. "Hour four of our national crisis! During the break Agent Sandlin decided to acknowledge his connection with the FBI as well as to give us some insight into this shocking situation! What can you tell us?"

The camera cut to a tired and disillusioned Agent Sandlin. Bitter at having been disavowed by his bosses, he was ready to talk. "It started early this morning," he yelled over the tepid vocalizations of David Gates. "I was—"

The bay window in the living room suddenly shattered. Agent Sandlin felt his scalp burn as the sniper's bullet grazed his head. "Yiii!" He wanted to dive to the floor, but he was still duct-taped to the chair. "Cut me loose!" he yelled.

Winston Archer shot to his feet and began skittering around the living room like a water bug. "Holy Jesus! Did you see that?"

Connie saw blood trickling past Sandlin's ear. She screamed and ran into the kitchen.

Archer pointed at the shattered window, then at the hole in the wall. "Scott! Zoom in on that bullet hole. Right there! Right there! Can we have a replay on that? Holy Jesus!"

Anticipating another shot from the sniper, Agent

Sandlin was bobbing and weaving as best he could while taped in the chair. "Somebody cut me loose, goddamn it!"

Nancy Mitchell pointed at the window. "Somebody close those curtains," she shouted. "Where's the replay? Do we have it? C'mon people!"

As the tape operator in the remote truck worked to get the tape cued up, Connie returned from the kitchen with paper towels and some carpet cleaner.

Still wiggling, Agent Sandlin whimpered, "Please, somebody help me."

A moment later the tape played back in slow motion on televisions across the nation. Winston Archer stood by pointing at the screen, narrating frame by frame. "There! You see his head snap back a little. Then the shot hits here." He pointed at the hole in the wall. "Wow!" He beckoned the cameraman over. "Let's get a shot of the wound!" Archer grabbed Agent Sandlin's head and held it still. "Zoom in on this! Boy, if that had hit you square . . ."

Nancy Mitchell had a thought. "Hey, can we work up some graphics showing what would have happened if that shot had hit his head better?" She paused. "Like a melon exploding or something like that?"

Agent Rodgers pushed open the door to the ladies' restroom. "Let's go in here." He nudged Debbie into the restroom, palming her ass as she went by. "That's nice. You work out?"

Debbie knew there was only one way to do this, so

she touched herself and sounded flattered. "I'm glad you like," she said, turning around to face him. She stroked his tie and let her hand drift toward his belt. "You know what? I've been watching you ever since we met." She ducked her head like a schoolgirl. "It's true. Even with that suit on, I can tell you've got a great body."

Rodgers glanced down at himself. "No kidding?" Even more than most men, Rodgers needed to be flattered.

"I don't kid about that kind of thing." Debbie arched an eyebrow and bit her lower lip, which seemed to catch Agent Rodgers's eye. "So tell me, what kinds of things do you like to do? I mean, sexually."

"Let me show you." He grabbed Debbie by the hips and pulled her toward him, but she pushed away playfully.

"No, no, no. Slow down," she said. "I'm looking for the right place."

Rodgers slapped the front of the sink. "How 'bout in front of the mirror?" He started to undo his belt.

Debbie shook her head. "No. I wanna do this right," she said. "I wanna be the hero." She winked as she took him by the belt buckle and led him toward the stall. "In here," she said, an eager look in her eyes. "With what I got in mind, we're going to need some leverage." She backed into the stall, licking her lips.

"Ohhh, baby." Rodgers let himself be led into the stall like a congressman, the blood rushing from one head to the other.

"You know what?" One of Debbie's hands rubbed Rodgers's chest while the other rubbed farther south. "I wouldn't be at all surprised to find out you have a really big gun." She found them both simultaneously. "Ooooh, I was right." She jerked his belt off and put it between her teeth. She stepped up onto the toilet seat and pulled the drawstring out of her pants, the bow waiting to be undone. Rodgers stared straight ahead. "I know what you want," Debbie teased, her hips grinding toward his face.

Rodgers nodded, too beguiled to speak.

Debbie put her hands tenderly on both sides of his face. "Undo the string," she whispered. Rodgers started to reach for the bow. Debbie slapped the side of his face playfully. "Not with your hands," she said. "With your teeth." She made a nasty snapping sound with her mouth.

A wild look flashed in his eyes. As he leaned forward, Debbie seized his hair and threw his head down into her knee, which was coming up hard and fast. Rodgers's head popped up like a jack-in-the-box, his nose bloody and broken. Debbie grabbed his tie and jerked his head left. One of his retinas detached when his head hit the wall the first time. She jerked his head to the right. The stall shook again. Debbie was about to punch his larynx when she noticed he had lost consciousness. She let go of his tie. He collapsed, cracking his chin on the edge of the toilet. She looked down at him. "How's that for incentive?"

Debbie worked quickly to hog-tie Rodgers with his belt. Then she stuffed his mouth with toilet paper to keep him quiet. She took his badge and his gun, an AT-32, stainless steel, single action, semiauto. She looked at it and wondered what the hell she was going to do next. She figured the other guy, the "sports psychologist," was almost certainly armed. *I can't just go out there and shoot him*, she thought. *So what am I going to do? If I try to disarm him and something goes wrong . . . Shit. All right. Just wing it.* She turned to leave, then stopped. *But first, pee.*

Agent Rodgers began to regain consciousness as Debbie washed her hands. He flopped around on the floor like a trout, trying to break free. Debbie kept an eye on him as she took a paper towel from the dispenser. As she dried her hands, she put a foot on Rodgers's head, pinning him down. "You probably have a concussion," she said. "You should see a doctor first chance you get."

With the gun in one hand and the FBI badge in the other, Debbie looked into the hallway to see if "Dr. Colby" was looking for his partner. He wasn't. She came out of the restroom holding the gun behind her back. At the end of the hall she stopped to peek around the corner. She could see Rose's feet poking out of the booth where she was resting. Jed X and the Benson kids were at a long table off to the side. Betty and Dale were at the counter talking to Polly. The others were in the booth between the window and the beverage-refill station. Spence and Officer Bobb were sitting next to each other, facing toward Debbie. Boyd and Agent Hart had their backs to her. *At least I've got that going for me,* she thought.

At first Debbie considered trying to get the attention of Spence and/or Officer Bobb in order to do some sort of pantomime to explain the situation. But, she realized, if "Dr. Colby" turned to see what they were looking at, she'd be busted and the element of surprise would be lost. After a moment she decided to stroll over casually, revealing the gun only at the last second. She planned to put the gun to "Dr. Colby's" head and say something along the lines of *One false move and I'll blow your brains out.* It was cliché, obviously, but what the hell, she didn't have time for original. Besides it had a nice, forceful ring. Then it occurred to her that if she had to shoot, the bullet might pass straight through and hit Spence or Officer Bobb. So she decided to put the gun on the crown of his head, pointing down, and say something along the lines of *One false move and I'll blow your brains down your esophagus,* which was not only original but also had the nice ring.

She stepped out of the hallway, into the main dining area. That's when she saw the big yellow bus in the parking lot. Painted on the side were the words THE CHURCH OF JESUS CHRIST OF LATTER-DAY SAINTS. There were no other customers in the coffee shop, so Debbie figured the bus had just arrived. Sure enough, before she took another step, the bus doors opened and out stepped ten of the tallest and whitest men Debbie had ever seen. Following them were assorted men and women of various heights and shades of white. It was a ward basketball team, along with the coach and some parents, on their way home from a Mormon summer-league tournament. Debbie stared. At least two of the guys were seven feet tall. Debbie figured this would affect her plan, though for the life of her she wasn't sure how. Taking a few more steps, she got close enough to hear Spence say, "All right, as soon as they're in here, we'll get the keys and go."

"We have to kidnap them," Boyd said matter-of-factly.

Agent Hart turned around, casually looking for his partner. Debbie smiled innocently and kept walking toward the booth. Agent Hart turned back to the table. With one hand he pulled a napkin from the dispenser while his other hand casually reached into his coat and pulled a Ruger KP97. Spence, Boyd, and Officer Bobb didn't know what to think when they saw him pull the gun. They had no idea he was armed. Hart covered the .45 with the napkin, then pointed it across the table. "You two. Hands flat on the deck. Now."

Spence and Officer Bobb exchanged a glance, but did as they were told.

"What about me?" Boyd sounded slightly wounded when he asked.

"Not particularly worried about you," Agent Hart said as he leaned across the table. He took the Glock and the Smith & Wesson from Spence and put them in his lap.

"What are you doing?" Spence was as baffled as the others. "We can get to Salt Lake now."

"Order yourself an omelette." Hart scowled across the table. "Nobody's going anywhere."

From her position Debbie couldn't see what was going on. But based on everyone's expression and body language, she figured Hart had pulled a gun and disarmed Spence.

Boyd looked at the two guns in Hart's lap. His heart began to race. This was it. His opportunity. He would get only one chance. He had to make the grab and fire a shot in one quick move. And the shot had to be good. There would be no room for cowardice and little for error. After a moment's thought he realized he needed a partner. He made eye contact with Officer Bobb. Boyd's eyes darted to Hart's lap, then back to Officer Bobb. Boyd moved one hand over the other, hoping to convey the notion of grabbing. His eyes went back to Officer Bobb to see if he understood. He seemed to.

The little bell rang when the door opened. The Mormons, about thirty of them, began pouring into the place, filling empty tables and ordering things with no caffeine.

Spence was trying to understand. "You've had a gun all this time?" He held out his hands. "Who are you working for, and why wait till we get this far—"

"Now!" Boyd and Officer Bobb made their moves. Boyd thrust his hands into Agent Hart's lap, distracting the CIA agent more than a little.

At the same time Officer Bobb pinned Agent Hart's gun hand to the tabletop. "Get the guns!" he yelled at Boyd.

Spence, who hadn't seen any of this coming, was so startled all he could do was watch as he pressed himself into the corner of the booth, trying to get out of the line of fire. Everything happened in a few seconds. As Boyd and Officer Bobb made their play, Debbie pulled the AT-

32 from behind her back. A scene flashed in her mind: She put the gun on the crown of Hart's head, yelled, "*Esophagus!*" and pulled the trigger. His head exploded, spraying brain, skull, and esophageal tissue everywhere. Debbie looked at the gun, then at the man's head. She couldn't bring herself to do it.

Spence saw Debbie holding the gun and wondered where it had come from and why she wasn't using it. He pointed at the gun and yelled, "Do something!"

"I'm trying!" Still she didn't do anything.

Meanwhile, with both hands fumbling in Agent Hart's lap, Boyd knocked the Glock to the floor before managing to grab the Smith & Wesson. He turned it on Hart but, in his panic, couldn't find the safety.

Agent Hart snatched a fork with his free hand. He stabbed at Officer Bobb's arm, the one holding Hart's gun hand. Officer Bobb pulled out of the way just in time. Unfortunately, in doing so, he had pulled the gun toward himself and there was nothing he could do to stop Hart from pulling the trigger. It sounded like a crack of thunder in the little coffee shop. Officer Bobb jerked when the bullet hit his flank, but he managed to keep a grip on Hart's hand.

Unable to figure out the safety on the Smith & Wesson, Boyd simply hammered it into the side of Agent Hart's head.

A second later Officer Bobb lost his grip on Agent Hart. His hands fell instinctively to his wound. Without even looking, Agent Hart deflected Boyd's next blow, then turned the gun on him. "Guess I should've been more concerned about you," he said. He was about to pull the trigger when the fires of hell descended upon him, or at least that's what it felt like. He dropped his gun and let out a sound so awful it might have curdled the artificial blood. Debbie had poured an entire steaming pot of coffee down his back.

Spence grabbed the Ruger and turned it on Agent Hart, who let out another horrible screech when Debbie poured a pitcher of ice water down his back to start the healing.

Boyd shoved Hart out of the booth and onto the floor. Debbie pinned his head down with her foot. "Those are severe second-degree burns," she said. "You'll want to have those looked at as soon as possible." Boyd took the handcuffs from Officer Bobb's belt and cuffed Hart's arms behind his back.

"Hey, Doc." Officer Bobb held up one of his bloody hands. "Could you take a look at this?" Debbie went to check on his wound.

The Mormons were staring in stunned silence. In fact, they wouldn't have been any more slack-jawed if Hyrum and Joseph Smith had walked in and ordered cocktails.

Boyd looked at the Mormons and knew someone had to take control before they recovered from the spasm of violence and ran screaming from the building. He looked at his brother. "Do something," he said.

Spence held out his hands. "Like what?"

"Oh, for crying out—" Boyd took the AT-32 from Debbie and stood up on a chair. He smiled. "If I could have your attention for just a moment? This is a kidnapping. If you'll all just follow my brother back out to your bus, we'll be on our way, and no one will get hurt." Boyd gestured with the gun and liked the way it felt.

The Mormons complied with Boyd's request. They were mostly cooperative, possibly sensing the opportunity to proselytize to a captive audience. Spence stood at the door of the bus, gently herding the Mormons back in. "Really sorry," he said. "Oh, watch your head." There was a commotion somewhere in the line. "No pushing," Spence called out. "I'll explain everything." A moment later Boyd was steering the bus back onto I-15. Spence stood in the front addressing the passengers. "Okay, all you new kidnappees, listen up."

It was late afternoon on the East Coast. Senator Check was preparing for a meeting with a man calling himself Randy Greenfeathers. He was the leader of an environmental group based in South Florida. Mr. Greenfeathers, who claimed to be $1/128$ Seminole on his mother's side, wanted the senator's help in opposing an amendment to legislation that threatened to weaken a provision of the Marine Mammal Protection Act, specifically the clause that reduced the number of federally mandated manatee protection areas from 145 to 143.

Senator Check, who wouldn't have known a manatee if one landed on her desk, and who honestly couldn't bring herself to care, was meeting with Mr. Greenfeathers because his group had given her nearly a hundred thousand dollars over the past year on account of her position on the Senate's Agriculture, Nutrition, and

Forestry Committee's Subcommittee on Research, Nutrition, and General Legislation that, believe it or not, dealt with general animal-welfare legislation.

Senator Check looked up from reading the highlights of the act in question. She called out to her assistant, "How long did you give him?" There was no response. "I said, how long did you give—"

Britton appeared in the doorway. "Sorry," she said. "I was getting the new numbers." She waved a sheaf of papers.

"Greenfeathers," the senator said. "How long?"

"Ten minutes. I told him you had an emergency meeting with the House minority whip but that you wanted to talk about the manatees first."

"That's good. Is it true?"

"That you want to talk about the manatees?"

"No, that I have an emergency meeting?"

"No, ma'am." Britton looked at the schedule. "You've got a fund-raiser with the National Crab Cake Manufacturers Association in Baltimore."

"Oh, I love crab cakes."

"Yes, ma'am, they're better than the latest polling numbers."

Peggy's face sagged. "How bad?"

Britton handed the sheaf of papers to her boss. "Webster's up by two points."

Senator Check squinted at the documents, then at her assistant. "How's that even possible? The whole country knows he's in a coma, and his approval ratings go up?"

Britton took the report from Senator Check and flipped to page twenty-three, then handed it back. "According to the pollsters, half the country thinks the coma story is an exaggeration by the liberal press. But that may not be the worst news."

Senator Check dropped the polling data into the trash, then looked up. "Britton, it's late and I'm tired." She poked at the Marine Mammal Protection Act. "I've got this and the crab-cake guys, and I was really hoping that was it. Can this wait?"

"I don't think so, ma'am." Britton reached behind her to close the door. "I heard from my friend with the House Subcommittee on Technical and Tactical Intelligence."

"Congressman Whaley's assistant?"

"Yes, ma'am. She's dating a guy at INFO-SEC. He said they intercepted a communiqué between Secret Service and Martin Brooks's office."

"Why do we care? They talk all the time."

"Not about this," Britton said, lowering her voice. "Apparently they have a contingency organ."

A moment passed before the senator said, "A what?" She propped her elbows on her desk and leaned forward. "You're telling me they have another heart?"

Britton nodded. "Yes, ma'am, and it's still being used."

"Excuse me?" Her eyebrows threatened to pass her hairline.

"Some woman," Britton said with a shrug. "A perfect blood-type match. Secret Service apparently grabbed her."

Senator Check gave it a moment's thought. "And what? They're going to kill her and use her heart?" Even the senator found this shocking.

"The communication wasn't clear on that. But they probably wouldn't kill her unless they had to, right?"

Senator Check opened her bottom drawer and considered the bottle of scotch. *What a day,* she thought. *Two hours ago I was picking my cabinet. And now? Damn it! I thought I was three moves ahead of Brooks.* She looked up at the photo of her mother and the former Speaker of the House. She could hear her mother's voice saying, *You can be the president, but not if you quit.* The senator closed the drawer; it was too soon to start drinking. *I can't just give up. This country needs me.* Senator Check knew it was time for realpolitik.

She figured her best option was to reduce—by at least one—the number of organs available to her political opponent. If Brooks couldn't use Mardell Coleman's heart, he would be forced to kill a civilian, and that was the sort of thing with the potential to come back to haunt an administration. So Mardell's heart had to go. It wasn't the senator's first choice; she had hoped to keep her hands clean on this. *Ah, well,* she thought. *There's no point in playing if you don't play to win.* She looked up at Britton with a wry shake of the head. "Politics is a messy business."

"Yes, ma'am. Should I call the SAS-SOG?"

Senator Check looked at her watch. "In a minute. First tell me all about manatees in thirty seconds or less."

Britton thought about it for a moment, then said, "Well, they're not as tasty as crab cakes."

Matt Christopher leaned toward the camera and said, "So here's an administration inspired by the Hobbesian notion that a strong federal government is necessary to avoid the sort of incrementalism inherent in the bureaucracy with which it's saddled, yet they're spending tremendous political capital to deal—under the aegis of national security, I think it's important to point out, and in an election year, I might add—with an appropriation of de Montesquieuian proportions—is that even a word? I like it even if it's not—so the question is, given their apparent infatuation with the doctrine of divine right—I mean, I actually heard someone from the State Department characterize this as *raison d'etat*—so without resorting to parochialism, Paul, what I'm interested in getting at is your reaction to this revelation on Martin Brooks's medical condition? What are your thoughts?"

Democratic strategist Paul Schultz looked at Matt Christopher and said, "Well, it's what we used to call 'impotence,' right?" He shot a damning glance at the camera.

"Not in polite society," Cynthia Walker said. She was the associate editor of *New Republican* magazine. "Calling Martin Brooks impotent is intentionally demeaning. It's politically motivated, and you know it."

"Oh, please," Paul whined. "And what is it when you call someone who has a substance-abuse problem a stinking drunk?"

"Look, it's very simple," Cynthia said. "Calling Martin Brooks impotent is a cheap and mean-spirited tactic."

"I notice you're not answering my question."

Matt pointed at Paul. "But what about the negative symbolism? Does she have a point?"

"Exactly," Cynthia said. "Paul, what I don't understand is why you liberals always want to run this country down. I love this country, and it hurts me to—"

Paul slapped a hand on the desktop. "And you're accusing me of cheap tactics? Stop it! You're not going to out-flag-wave me on this or any other issue."

"Admit it, it's politically motivated."

"You know, what I find interesting is that if I use the term 'homeless person' for what you call a bum, I'm being politically correct, but—"

"Listen," Cynthia said, "those people can find jobs if they want. Under the current administration joblessness is at a six-month low. But that's not the point. The point is, the phrase 'erectile dysfunction' is medically correct, not politically correct, and that's a critical distinction."

"All I'm saying is, we should call a spade a spade." The moment he said this, Paul looked stricken. He sensed an angry press conference featuring the head of the NAACP, so he continued by saying, "And on the chance that particular idiom is no longer understood, let me just say for the record that I am referring to the garden implement."

"There, that's cleared up," Matt said. "Now, let's be fair—and I think a lot of Americans are with me on this—we don't know yet if Martin Brooks is unable to get hard at all or if he can get stiff for a while and then loses it. Let's give him the benefit of the doubt on this."

"And the larger point I'd like to make is this," Cynthia said. "Just because a man can't get hard enough to penetrate his partner doesn't mean he can't be a good White House chief of staff."

"True." Paul nodded. "Though his title becomes a bit ironic."

"Whoa! We'll be back right after this. You're watching *HardHeads*!"

Agent Hart was facedown on the linoleum, stifling a laugh. "I can't believe you fell for a damn honey trap," he said.

"I wouldn't be throwing the first stone if I were you, Mr. Coffee." Rodgers was struggling to pick the lock on Hart's handcuffs but his vision was blurred due to his detached retina.

Hart twisted his head around to look at his partner. "Hey, she had to sneak up from behind to get me," he said. "From the looks of your nose, at least you saw her coming."

"Yeah, and she seemed sincere, too," Rodgers said. "I really thought she wanted the old 007 tube steak." He popped the lock on the cuffs. "The bitch."

"Ditto on that," Agent Hart said as he sat up, arching his back. "Ooooh, man that hurts." He began to unbutton his shirt. "Help me out of this." Hart noticed that his partner's hands were red, raw, and bleeding in places. "What happened there?"

"She hog-tied me with my belt." He looked at his hands. "Thought I was going to have to chew an arm off to get out. But I finally managed to wiggle free." Rodgers gingerly removed Hart's shirt and looked at his back. "You want me to put some mustard on that?"

Hart pulled away from Rodgers. "The fuck you talking about, mustard?"

Rodgers shrugged. "It's what my mom used to do whenever I got a burn." He gestured toward the kitchen. "They probably have those gallon jugs back there. Wouldn't be any problem."

"You stay away from me with the mustard." Hart shook his head. "I can't believe—" His cell phone began ringing. "Mustard. That's nuts." He found his coat and answered, "SOG Two."

It was Senator Check. "Kill the heart," she said. "Then disappear."

Ten minutes later the two men were walking back toward I-15 with plans to flag down a motorist and commandeer the first car to stop. They came around a bend in the road where the RV was still smoldering on the shoulder. Hart nudged Rodgers, gesturing ahead. "Guess it's our lucky day," he said.

Rodgers looked, trying to see what Hart was talking about. He put a hand over his right eye. "What is it? I can't tell."

"A cop." He pulled Rodgers aside with an idea.

Officer Stew Hunsaker of the Utah Highway Patrol was setting flares on the road when he heard someone yell, "We need help! My friend got burned pretty bad."

Officer Hunsaker looked up to see a shirtless black man being helped along by a white guy in a rumpled suit. The officer went to offer assistance. "What happened?"

"No idea," Rodgers said as they approached. "We were just driving along, and all of a sudden, boom! Big ball of flame. We're lucky to be alive."

When Officer Hunsaker reached out for Agent Hart, they jumped him. They took his .40-caliber Baretta Cougar and his uniform. "Where's your cruiser?"

Officer Hunsaker shook his head. "Motorcycle officer." He pointed to the far side of the Winnebago. "It's over there."

Rodgers and Hart looked at each other and smiled, both of them thinking back to the Loretta Lynn Amateur National Motocross finals. They got to the bike, a Harley FLHTPI Electra Glide. "You better drive," Rodgers said. "My vision's all fucked up."

Hart shook his head. "Shit. Last thing I need is your big ass clinging to my back, peeling off the skin." He gestured at the handlebars. "You drive. I'll be your eyes."

16

Two Hearts Are
Better than One

Rose considered herself lucky. She knew the end was near. Operation or not, she'd be done with the breathless exhaustion, the cold and bloated extremities, the chronic weakness. All that would be over. And thank God. She'd had about all she could take. Rose recently had a nightmare about drowning in her own blood and the fluid that collected in her lungs because her heart was too weak to pump. That's not how she wanted to go. Even if she didn't live to see tomorrow, Rose was happy she hadn't died shuffling down some antiseptic linoleum hallway hooked to an intravenous rigging and a computerized box attached to a pole urging heart contractions by pouring dobutamine into her end-stage organ. That wasn't life, that was just some hideous circumstance made possible by technology.

Rose lay quietly on the seat as the bus rolled north in the waning sunlight. She could see mountains. They were beautiful, and they made her smile. Someone in the back of the bus laughed, and Rose began thinking about her mother, Iris. She was born October 25, 1920, on a farm somewhere in Kansas. Her father was a farmer who managed to scratch a living out of the ground even in the worst years. Like her mother before her, Iris had married a farmer, had two children and a hard life. She labored every day and had virtually no leisure save sleep. Even for her time Iris was stern and stiff, but she wasn't unloving. The result being that when she did show affection, it carried weight.

She rarely smiled, her life not being conducive to such. But every year on her birthday Iris would tell anyone within earshot that she had been born on the same day King Alexander of Greece had died of blood poisoning after being bitten by his pet monkey. She would laugh and tell a story filled with facts she imagined differently every year. It was the only time Iris revealed a sense of humor and Rose looked forward every year to hearing her laughter.

In 1979 Iris was admitted to an intensive-care unit. Her chart said "increased respiratory compromise." Rose returned to Kansas to be with her. She sat with Iris for several days and coaxed her into telling the story about King Alexander and the monkey one last time.

One day, near the end, Iris took her daughter's hand and said, "I signed one of those do-not-resuscitate orders." Iris shook her head. "I don't want to end up like a turnip." She was firm about it. "Life is too precious, and I can't understand people who have such a low opinion of it that being in a coma seems like an acceptable option." Iris died two days later at the age of fifty-nine. Her chart said "chronic obstructive pulmonary disease."

"Mom?" Spence squatted down and put his hand on Rose's arm. "How're you doing?"

Delivered from her memories, Rose looked up at her son. "I'm okay." She took a shallow breath. "Just tired."

"We're almost there." Spence brushed a lock of hair from her forehead. "Is there anything—"

"Be sure to thank them." Rose gestured weakly around the bus. "For helping."

Spence smiled. "Don't worry, I will."

In fact, he already had. What happened was this: About halfway to Provo, Spence converted the Mormons to his cause. He had expected more resistance, quite frankly, but it turned out they weren't big fans of the federal government in the first place. "We had to sue the Census Bureau," the head coach said. "They used a method they call imputation in the last census. They said we were eight hundred fifty-seven residents short of what we needed for a new seat in Congress. Well, since it was ten years before the next count, we decided to look at their numbers, and guess what we found?"

Spence shrugged. "The missing eight hundred fifty-seven people?"

"Even more than that," the man said. "They refused to count our missionaries outside the state, if you can believe it, so we took 'em to court."

Spence figured it would take at least ten years for the matter to work through the court system, but he couldn't think of any good reason to point that out, so instead he just said, "Well, listen, I just want you to know we appreciate what you're doing."

"Glad we could help."

"Could you do me one more favor?"

"Name it."

Spence hesitated the way secular humanists sometimes do before saying, "Pray for us." He then went to check on Rose before going up to where Debbie was working on Officer Bobb, who was missing a strip of flesh from his side and a splinter of rib.

Boyd looked back from the driver's seat. "How is he?"

"He'll be all right," Debbie said. She dressed the wound, then checked her watch and said, "We've got about an hour." She picked up the ECC device and tilted it, listening for ice. "I hope it's still viable. Most hearts don't have to go through so much." She set it down and looked at Spence. "How's your mom?"

Spence glanced toward the back of the bus where Rose was resting. "She says she's tired. But . . ." He shrugged.

"Well, I think she'll make it to the hospital all right,"

Debbie said. "After that, it's anybody's guess. Have you called to see if this Dr. Speyburn is for real?"

"Yeah. They said he'd gone to pre-op for a transplant."

"Good."

Officer Bobb grimaced as he stood up. "Have you called the press?"

Spence shook his head. "Was I supposed to?"

"Well, let's see." Officer Bobb counted on his fingers. "First, the FBI circumvented UNOS transplant protocol when they tried to steal the heart. Second, they created a hostage situation at your brother's house. Then the Mustang and the RV burned up in what I think are safe to characterize as suspicious, not to mention similar, fires, and maybe I'm wrong, but it seems like the CIA just tried to kill some or all of us."

Officer Bobb continued by arguing that the press was their only ally. It didn't matter how bad the coverage was, he said, as long as the media covered it. It didn't matter if one side spun it into a left-wing cartoon while the other side displayed a conservative yet comprehensive ignorance of the facts. None of that was new, nor was it news. It was just market segmentation in the entertainment industry passing as news. "But one thing we know," Officer Bobb said. "People act differently if they know a television camera is trained on them." He offered C-SPAN as an example, suggesting that when you watch senators and congressmen sitting on their committees, they mostly came across as smart, honest people. But put them behind closed doors and policy changes in funny ways. "All I'm saying is, the press might be our best protection in case someone is waiting for us in Salt Lake."

While Spence was calling television and radio stations in Salt Lake, he noticed Jed X and some of the Mormon basketball players talking and laughing in the back of the bus. He wondered if they were talking about skateboarding, theology, basketball, or body piercing.

One of the basketball players leaned over to Jed. "Okay, here's a classic," he said. "A Baptist, a Catholic, and a Mormon were bragging about their families, right? The Baptist said he had four kids—one more and he'd have his own basketball team. The Catholic nodded and said he had eight kids—one more and he'd have his own baseball team. The Mormon waved them both off and said, 'That's nothing. I have seventeen wives—one more and I'll have my own golf course.'"

Five rows up, Rose closed her eyes and listened to Jed's laughter. It reminded her of Iris on her birthday. What a beautiful sound. She thought, *If it's possible to miss things in the hereafter, I'll miss my family, my friends, and laughter. And the smell of lemons.* Rose believed that there was life after death. She didn't know if it was the heaven-and-hell model or something less black-and-white, but she knew there was something. There had to be. She figured her own mother was watching, in some way—looking down, as they say—on everything that had happened since she passed over.

Rose thought about how her mother would have reacted to the way things had changed. How we were able to transplant organs from one body to another like

parts in an engine. How she could have had a lung transplant if she'd been born ten or twenty years later. But Iris
was skeptical about that sort of thing. On hearing about
the first human organ transplants, Iris had said it seemed
like Frankenstein to her. "It's ungodly, and it ought to be
illegal to mess with the natural order of things that way,"
she'd said.

Rose also thought about how her mother would have
reacted to the politics that had put her in the back of
this bus. *Mom would have been appalled.* Iris was a lifelong Republican. She trusted the government, and by
and large she had found her trust well placed. The
Teapot Dome scandal was ancient history by the time
Iris was old enough to understand what a scandal was.
And it was fifty years between that and Watergate. But
had she lived to see the disingenuous smiles and suffer
the spurious rhetoric of all the elected officials impli-
cated, indicted, and impeached since her death; if she
had lived to see the perfidy and mendacity that passed as
democracy at the turn of the twenty-first century . . .
well, she'd have wished she hadn't.

Rose had seen amazing things in her lifetime, in both
science and politics. But with each breath coming
harder, she was beginning to feel she might have seen all
she was going to. She was tired and wanted to rest. She
kept waiting for her life to flash before her eyes, but all
she could do was think back over the events of today,
and, strangely, she smiled. The way she figured it, if this
was the last day of her life, at least she'd be going out
with a bang.

Brigham Memorial Hospital was in downtown Salt
Lake, a ten-story shoe box half a mile from the big taber-
nacle. After the calls from Spence, the press had staked
out camps at opposite corners of the building so they
could see both the main entrance in the front and the
emergency entrance on the west side. As they waited, the
print reporters roamed about trying to capture the milieu
in words. Some of the television camera crews were gathering B-roll footage of the hospital while reporters were
working on their opening sound bites. "I'm standing outside Brigham Memorial Hospital awaiting the arrival of
Tense Spailor and the stolen, goddamn it! Do it again.
Okay, take two. Spence Tailor. Ready? Here we go. I'm
standing outside Brigham Memorial—" The reporter
stopped to listen. "Is that a siren?"

The gathered press reacted like a herd of zebras hearing a twig snap. All heads turned, evaluating the
approaching sound. It was a siren, probably a quarter
mile away. They waited, trying to determine if it was a
passing fire truck or an inbound ambulance. They were
hoping for a police siren, since rumor had it the Mormon school bus would have an escort. As the siren
approached, the camera lights came on and all the reporters began drifting in the direction of the emergency-
room entrance. There was a moment's letdown when an
ambulance rounded the corner a block away. But the disappointment passed quickly. The ambulance took the

corner too fast. The damn thing flipped and skidded across the intersection on its side before crashing into a parked car.

The reporters and cameramen were in a full sprint before the ambulance had come to a stop. There was a great deal of screaming and shoving and even some intentional tripping. One reporter did a sound bite on the run, looking over his shoulder at the camera. "I'm running toward an ambulance that has just overturned about a block from Brigham Memorial Hospital—"

The driver's face was covered in blood. "Get a camera over here!" Someone opened the back of the ambulance and found two paramedics and a semiconscious patient still strapped to a board. A reporter thrust his microphone toward the patient. "Can you tell us how you feel?"

While the press tried to get information from the four Secret Service agents posing as paramedics and a man suffering from appendicitis, two black SUVs approached Brigham Memorial from the opposite direction. They pulled to the service dock in the back of the hospital, out of sight. The doors opened, and the president's cardiologist and his staff got out. Six Secret Service agents deployed to remove the president's stretcher.

Martin Brooks barked at them. "Go! Go! Fourth floor! Get him into OR now!" They got President Webster inside the hospital and on a gurney in fifteen seconds. Martin Brooks was at his side. "Don't worry, sir, we're going to take care of you."

Grant stayed at the loading dock for a moment, yelling at the men who were wrestling with Daisy, "Get her upstairs, too! And move those vehicles out of here now!" A moment later the two SUVs backed out and vanished into the night.

Boyd took the Temple Street Exit and raced toward the hospital. When he pulled into the emergency entrance, there was no media in sight. They were still hovering around the overturned ambulance a block away. Boyd got off the bus first and saw a security guard approaching with his hand held out as if to stop anyone from getting off the bus. "You're not coming in here," the man said. "We don't need any more—"

Boyd tackled the guy, and a fight ensued. A few moments later it was under control. Jed X and a couple of the basketball players ran inside. They came back with a gurney and helped Rose on to it before rolling her into the emergency room.

The moment Debbie stepped into the hospital, her personality changed. This was her world. She was in charge. She led Spence to the emergency check-in. "Looking for Dr. Speyburn," Debbie said.

The admitting nurse spoke without looking up from her paperwork. "Gone to pre-op."

"What floor?" Debbie's muscles tensed, ready to bolt in any direction.

The nurse shook her head and pointed out the building. "Down the street, half a block. Can't miss it."

"What?" Debbie was confused. "Where's the OR?"

The nurse pointed up. "Fourth floor."

It didn't make any sense to Debbie, but there wasn't time to ask about the logistics, so she handed the ECC device to Officer Bobb. "Get this up to four with Rose. We'll be right back."

Although he had been trained to endure all manner of hostile environments, the FBI sniper finally snapped. Thirty-six times back to back was all he could take. If he heard "Baby I'm-a Want You" one . . . more . . . time, someone was going to get hurt. He lined up his shot and fired. The CD player shattered, bringing welcome silence to the neighborhood.

Connie, who was sitting on the sofa, pulled her hands away from her ears, tentatively at first, then with great relief. "Oh, thank God." She checked the monitor to see what they were showing. She was looking at herself with the words TERRORIST'S WIFE below her image. What a strange thing that was. When Connie woke up this morning, the worst thing she had planned was manipulating a few school-board votes, and now she was a "terrorist's wife." For the first time today Connie went from being bewildered and incredulous to being angry. Really angry.

In the hush that followed the sniper's shot, Winston Archer decided to open the airwaves to the vast range of American opinion. "Give us a call right now on our 800 number," he said. "Let us know what you're thinking about America's Heart Held Hostage!"

The calls poured in. Citizens giving full throat to their

contrasting views of the current situation. One caller, who sounded vaguely dull said, "I read somewhere that in China? They execute all the corrupt politicians?"

"Not at the top, my friend," Archer said with a knowing chuckle. "Not at the top."

"But it probably cuts down on it some, don't you think? At least at the bottom?"

"Well, it's worth considering," Archer said. "Let's take another call." He punched another line. "America's Heart Held Hostage, you're on the air."

"Here's what I want to know," the caller said. "You're talking about corrupt leaders? What about old Tricky Dick?"

"Oh, not this again."

"Here's a guy engaged in illegal wiretapping, misuse of the CIA, perjury, bribery, obstruction of justice, and other abuses of executive power, and—"

"Get outta town," Archer said with a dismissive wave at the camera. "Nixon was one of our greatest presidents. Period. Enda story."

"See, that's exactly why I called. Everything we know about Nixon's crimes, and people still talk about him like he was Gandhi. The constant efforts to rehabilitate that man's reputation, the whole Nixon-canonization movement, just serves to downplay his complicity in his crimes."

"Oh, please," Archer said. "The man bent a couple of rules. Get over it. It's not like he was having sex in the Oval Office. Besides, look at his New Federalism policies of revenue sharing and all he did for U.S. relations with China and Russia."

"Excuse me, Mr. Archer," Connie interrupted. "Can I say something?"

Surprised, Winston turned to face her. "Yes, Connie, by all means. Jump on in."

"Wasn't that his job?"

The concept seemed to confuse Archer. "What do you mean?"

"I mean dealing with domestic and foreign-policy issues. Wasn't that just part of his job? Isn't that what we paid him to do? Wasn't that the *very least* we should have expected from him? Why heap praise on a man just for doing what he was supposed to?"

"Well, now"—Archer assumed a condescending tone—"it's more complicated than that."

"Is it?" Connie shook her head. "Is the system that bankrupt?"

"Now, hold on. Let's be fair," Archer said. "Most elected officials work hard and do a lot of good without ever breaking any laws. Think about that."

Connie's head went back a bit, her eyes wide. "That's their goddamn job!"

"Whoa! Connie, we're live here." Winston laughed nervously. "Careful with the language."

"You think we should lower our standards to the point that when a politician merely does his job we should be grateful? That if he doesn't get caught committing a crime he should receive an award?" Connie sighed. "My God, can't we do better than that?"

"Now, let's not get emotional."

"This country makes me emotional," Connie said.

"Because I love it. But . . . look at what's happened! Twenty billion wasted on pork projects last year. You can hire a lot of teachers for twenty billion dollars, but does the 'education administration' do it?" She shook her head. "No. And why?" Connie assumed Archer's condescending tone. "Because it's more complicated than that." She shook her head sadly.

Connie paused to collect her thoughts, which were whirling in a squall. "Here's what I want to know: What happened to the leaders? Hmm? People who inspired with vision and humanity and wisdom? Where are they? I'm not talking about professional politicians, not those hired guns. I'm talking about people whose urge to do the right thing is so strong they're willing to fight without compromise to do the greatest good. Where are those people? That's what I want to know. 'Cause we have a job for them."

Connie paused long enough for the guy on the phone to say, "Yeah, listen, I agree with everything she just said, but if I can just finish my point about Nixon?"

Winston Archer sensed that Connie was on a roll, so he cut the caller off. "You're outta here!"

Connie stood and began pacing her living room. "This country is great *not* because of the government. It's because of us. The people. We the people. This country is great *despite* our government. We don't have leaders anymore, we have politicians, people who say things based on what polls tell them will serve them best in the next election. We have people who don't even say anything when they talk. It's the political equivalent to the dumb-jock preseason interview." She lapsed into a dumb-jock voice. "We'll have to hustle after the loose balls and give a hundred ten percent if we want to improve on last season. And hopefully we'll make it clear that education is our top priority after health care for seniors." Connie turned and looked at the camera. "And let me ask you this. What does it say about us that we've figured out how to do the most extraordinary things like heart transplants but we can't figure out how to guarantee basic medical care for all our children?" Connie pursed her lips before continuing. "You want a great leader? How about my friend Melanie Tatum? She's a court reporter, and she volunteers at our kids' school." Connie punched a finger into the palm of her hand as she said, "I swear to God she could run this country. She's honest. She's educated. And she gets stuff done. She'd be great. And you know what? This country is full of people just like her, people who get stuff done day in and day out. But people keep saying it's more complicated than that. So here's my question: Why is it so goddamn complicated?" She was looking at Archer when she asked.

Winston thought he knew the answer. "Well, uh, it's too many lawyers making laws," he said. "See, if you write something in complex enough language, then the only people qualified to interpret it are other people trained in the language. It's a matter of job security."

"That was a rhetorical question," Connie said to Winston. "But you might be right." She turned back to the camera, pointing. "Look. I understand democracy is difficult. Under a dictatorship you don't have to spend time reading up on the issues. But here? I'm telling you, we're out here doing our best. We try to learn about the people running for office. They tell us they're going to do something, we elect them, and nothing changes—unless it gets worse."

Connie paused, turning away for a moment before looking back at the camera. "My God. Every politician I have ever heard in my entire life has said he or she is going to fix the education system in this country or this state or this city. Know what I heard on the news yesterday? Math scores are down nationally, same with history and science. Have they been lying for forty years, or is it more complicated than that? Well, it's not more complicated than that at my house." She shook her head. "At my house, that's crap. Listen. We're trying to raise our children and do our jobs and volunteer and pay our taxes! And it seems like somebody out there keeps making it more and more complicated! We gotta find these assholes and stop them."

"Well, Connie, that's thought-provoking, all right. Let's take another call—"

"I'm not finished," Connie said. "My God. We are capable of greatness—I've seen it." She looked into the camera as she said, "There was a moment, following that terrible day in September, when we saw how we could unite, when we saw politicians stop acting like petulant schoolchildren, when people recognized the common good was vastly more important than individual self-interest. But it didn't last. And that's a shame. But that's no reason to give up or to lower our standards. See, the good thing is, we know it's possible. We should aspire to greatness, not adequateness. And we should demand greatness from our government. We should have higher standards, not as law—we don't need more laws—but as goals. We shouldn't settle for pretty good when we can be great."

Winston Archer was about to speak when his face spasmed violently as Nancy Mitchell shouted something in his earpiece. Winston slapped himself on both sides of his face trying to remove it. When he recovered enough to speak, Winston held a hand out to silence everyone. He looked into the camera severely. "All right, I have just been told we have some shocking amateur footage taken—" He looked off camera and said, "Taken where? Do we know where? Brigham Memorial? Is that right? In Salt Lake? Yes? Okay. Brigham Memorial in Salt Lake City where the cardioterrorists are at this very point in time." He looked off camera again. "Is it cued up? Where are we? Are we ready? Oh, here we go. This is the tape from the hospital's security camera." He pointed at the monitor.

Onto the screen came a grainy image of the hospital's emergency entrance as the LDS bus pulled to a stop. "Connie," Winston said, "tell us whatever you can."

Someone got off the bus. "Oh, my God, that's Boyd!"

"Okay, your husband. And it looks like, is that a security guard?" It was. He was approaching Boyd with his hand held out to stop them. Boyd took three fast strides and tackled the guard. A fight ensued. Boyd got in a few good punches and took a few as well. A moment later several extremely tall white guys jumped off the bus and waded into the fray.

"Shocking footage indeed!" Archer pointed off camera. "Play that again!" He reached over and touched Connie's arm. "Are those the biggest albinos you've ever seen or what? Who are those people? What kind of a cult is your husband mixed up with? Holy cow! Is it ready to roll again? Let's take another look at this! This is shocking!"

Connie wasn't listening. She was just smiling, thinking about Boyd and how brave he was. How much she loved him. How proud she was.

Spence and Debbie were halfway down the street when he grabbed her arm, jerking her to a stop. "What are you doing?" She tried to pull away. "We don't—" She finally noticed Spence was pointing across the street. Debbie looked. A moment passed as she absorbed the facts. Her face sagged. "No," she said. Her disbelieving eyes took in the alternating green and pink lights of the neon sign. It featured a scalpel continuously cutting a bright green lime. Arching over the fruit, in equally bright pink, the sign flashed: PRE-OP PRE-OP PRE-OP. It was a medically themed restaurant and bar, complete with valets dressed as M.D.'s in white coats. Planet Hospital.

Debbie turned to Spence. "Does your luck always run this bad?"

"No. Even for me this is a record."

They crossed the street and entered the building. The place was packed with off-duty doctors, nurses, and hospital administrators. The waiters wore surgical scrubs, while busboys dressed as orderlies pushed dirty dishes on gurneys. Martini olives were skewered on thermometers. "How are we going to find him?" Debbie asked.

Spence looked up to a wall-mounted television over the hostess stand. It showed the hostage scene at Boyd's house. The crawl underneath read "Unidentified, high-level source claims children at FBI siege have begun hunger strike."

Spence was staring at the television when the hostess returned to the podium. "Hi. Just two?" She looked at the reservation book. "It'll be about twenty minutes. We'll page you." She offered one of those big acrylic pagers that would vibrate and flash when the table was ready.

Debbie deflected it. "We're meeting someone. Dr. Speyburn?"

"Speyburn?" The hostess looked at her seating chart. "His table's not ready yet." She pointed at the bar. "Try the ICU."

Forgetting for a moment they didn't have a clue what Dr. Speyburn looked like, Debbie and Spence waded into the crowded bar, where thirsty patrons were drinking from urine-sample cups and graduated borosilicate glass beakers. Spence noticed a paramedic sucking on a long tube straw that connected to a specialty drink served from an IV bag hanging on a pole. A waitress walked by with a bedpan of fried calamari surrounding a petri dish of aïoli. Spence was savoring the scent of garlic when Debbie cupped her hands around her mouth and yelled, "Paging Dr. Speyburn!" She turned to call to the other side of the room. "Paging Dr. Speyburn!"

A man in scrubs sitting in a booth looked in her direction and raised his hand, waving it slightly. He was sitting with two other doctors. Just as Spence and Debbie reached his table, a waitress arrived carrying a large, anatomically correct plastic heart with several flexible straws poking out of the arch of the aorta. "You guys order the big heart transplant?"

"Indeed we did," Dr. Speyburn said, rubbing his hands together.

After the waitress left, Spence approached and said, "Dr. Speyburn? I'm the guy from the Gates Foundation. We spoke earlier about the heart transplant for Mrs. Gates?"

The doctor took a sip from his drink and smirked. "Yeah, right." He pointed at Spence. "And you almost had me, too. Then I found out Bill Gates's mom is so dead even I can't bring her back to life." The doctor's friends chuckled.

Debbie nudged Spence aside. "Dr. Speyburn, I'm Dr. Robbins. I'm a third-year surgical resident at Mulholland Memorial in Los Angeles and—"

"Hey . . ." Dr. Speyburn's face lit up in sudden recognition. "Wait a minute." He pointed at one of the television sets in the bar, then at Spence. "You're the ones with the heart."

"That's us," Spence said. "And not a lot of time either."

Dr. Speyburn shook his head. "Boy, I'd hate to be in your shoes." He took another sip from his drink. "You guys really terrorists?"

Spence reached down and pinched the doctor's straw. "You shouldn't drink before surgery."

"Listen, my friend, I've been up since four this morning," Dr. Speyburn said. "I started with a heart-lung transplant, followed by a valvuloplasty, two implantable cardiovert defibrillator insertions, and a heart-valve replacement. My feet hurt, and my back is killing me." He tried to pry Spence's fingers from his straw. "I do not drink before surgery, but I sure as hell drink afterward."

Spence kept a firm grip on the straw. "Dr. Speyburn, I don't know how much of the news you've seen or which of the stories you believe, but here's the deal. My mother is dying. That heart is rightfully hers. You can check with UNOS if it'll make you feel better, but I need you to do this operation."

Speyburn looked at Debbie. "He's telling the truth," she said. "I was going to assist with the surgery, and then some hard-on from the FBI showed up trying to take the heart." Debbie glanced up at a clock on the wall. "We've only got about thirty minutes before it's useless. So, Doctor, what are you going to do?"

Dr. Speyburn saw the fire in Debbie's eyes. He remembered when he had that. He wished he still had it, too, but it had been sucked out of him by insurance companies telling him which procedures he could perform on patients they'd never seen. It had been beaten out of him by HMOs forcing him to reduce costs to the point he could no longer ethically practice medicine. It had been ripped out of him by legislators controlled by the trial-lawyer lobby, who failed to bring about adequate tort reform, the result of which was premiums for medical-malpractice insurance that cost nearly seventy-five thousand dollars a year. And it had been bled from him by the IRS, which seemed poised like a vulture to take what little was left after he'd spent a year saving lives. "Ahhhh, shit." Dr. Speyburn stood up. "I'll do it."

President Ronald Reagan was once saved from choking to death by the Heimlich maneuver. According to the Heimlich Institute Web site, the same is true of former New York mayor Ed Koch.

Senator Peggy Check, who was in the process of turning a critical shade of blue, hoped to join this list of notable politicians in the immediate future.

A man set his cocktail on a table and said, "Hang on!" He reared back and hit the senator square between her shoulder blades. The senator's head snapped back and her mouth opened, but nothing came out.

"She's still choking," Britton said. "Somebody do something!"

The party organizer stood on a chair, pleading. "Does anyone know the Heimlich maneuver?"

An eager assistant to a congressman who'd once made a speech in favor of a National Lifesaving Techniques Awareness Week rushed forward to say, "I can do CPR!"

"Stand back!" The eager assistant was shoved aside by the president of the National Crab Cake Manufacturers Association, who had just returned from the can. He wiped his hands on his pants and took a position behind Senator Check, his feet spread to shoulder width. He wrapped his arms around her waist, making a fist and placing the thumb side of his fist against the senator's upper abdomen, just below the rib cage. He grabbed his fist with his other hand and gave a sharp, upward thrust, pressing into the senator's upper abdomen, being careful not to squeeze her rib cage. He repeated this until a wedge of crab cake dislodged and landed on the wingtip of the congressman's eager assistant.

The senator bent over, gasping for breath. "Thank you," she said.

"Here." Britton handed her a glass of water.

The senator pushed it away. "Scotch," she hissed.

As they ran back to the hospital, Debbie recited Rose's vitals to Dr. Speyburn. Nearing the front doors, they saw members of the press drifting back toward the hospital. One of the liberal media recognized Spence and yelled, "Hey, the freedom fighters!" When he started running toward the hospital, the rest of the press followed blindly.

Spence and the two doctors were about ten yards ahead of the media as they approached the hospital doors. Dr. Speyburn held his hospital ID high for the security guards to see. "These two are with me!" he yelled. "Get the doors! Heart transplant!" The guards held the doors for them, then turned to block the entrance from the onslaught of the First Amendment.

A minute later Spence and the two doctors reached the landing on the fourth floor of the hospital stairwell. Spence leaned against the wall gasping for air. "Can't . . . seem to . . . catch . . . my breath."

Speyburn smiled. "We're forty-three hundred feet above sea level. You're not acclimated."

Debbie was bent over, hands on her knees. "Thank God," she huffed. "I thought I was *way* out of shape."

They stepped out of the stairwell at the intersection of two hallways. Spence turned to Speyburn and said, "Got any ideas?"

"OR Four is the second door down there," Speyburn said, pointing. "One, Two, and Three are at the other end of the building."

Spence went to look. "They're here." He gestured for the doctors, then entered the room. Debbie and Dr. Speyburn followed him into OR 4, where they found Boyd, Rose, Officer Bobb, and Jed X waiting. They didn't notice Boyd holding the gauze against the side of his face.

Dr. Speyburn went to the phone automatically. "I need a scrub nurse, a circulating nurse, a perfusionist, and an anesthesiologist," he said. "Stat!" Then, as an afterthought, "And call my attorney."

Debbie went to the sinks to scrub in.

Spence crossed the room to where Rose lay on her gurney. "How are you feeling, Mom?"

Rose didn't open her eyes, but she nodded slightly and whispered, "Tired." Her hands were like ice.

"It's okay," Spence said. "The surgeon's here and—" He looked around the room. A bit of panic crept into his voice when he said, "Where's the heart?"

"They took it," Boyd said.

Spence looked at his brother and noticed the bloody gauze pressed to his face. "What happened?"

"They were waiting for us." Boyd shook his head.

Spence grabbed Boyd's arm. "Who, goddamn it?"

"Secret Service," Officer Bobb said, gesturing. "Boyd tried to stop them." He shook his head. "They're down the hall."

"An' yo," Jed X said, "those dogs was federal. I mean, they was allupinit with they fingers on the trigger, yo. So watch your back."

"They just left you here?" Debbie couldn't believe it. "Without guarding you?" She shook her head. "My tax dollars at work."

"What's to guard?" Boyd pulled free of Spence's grip. "We're not armed. What are we gonna do? Taunt them?"

Dr. Speyburn hung up the phone. "They're in OR Two," he said.

"They've got two agents covering the door," Officer Bobb said. "Probably more inside, I don't know."

"In simple terms," Boyd said, "we're screwed."

"Goddamn it!" Spence was furious.

Debbie glanced up at the wall clock. "Time's running out," she said. "We have to do something pretty quick."

Spence's eyes troubled around the operating room, doing an inventory, checking what he had to work with. A cardiac monitor, an anesthesia machine, a perfusion machine, and a crash cart. "All right. We need a plan," he said, causing Boyd to smile.

Spence started looking in the drawers of the crash cart and the anesthesia apparatus. He saw adenosine, digoxin, epinephrine, indomethacin, prostaglandin, neo-stigmine, midazolam, atropine, pancuronium bromide, and vecuronium. He called Debbie over, gesturing at the drugs. "What do we have here?"

Debbie examined the vials. "Sedatives and paralytics." She pulled some vials from the drawer. "And the beginning of a plan."

17

Open Your Heart

Four stories below the operating rooms, pressed against the front doors, a hundred journalists were trying to put a personal stamp on variations of "I'm standing at the doors of Brigham Memorial Hospital in Salt Lake, where the so-called cardioterrorists—" The reporters were silenced by a sudden blast from the siren of a Utah highway patrol motorcycle. The Harley roared up to the front door, scattering the crowd. There were two men on the motorcycle. The driver was white. He held a hand over his right eye, squinting with the left. The other guy was black and shirtless and blistered. The driver helped his passenger off the bike and headed for the door, yelling, "State Police! Stand back! Where's the burn unit?"

The guards cleared a path and held the doors for the officer and his victim. "Third floor," the guard said as the highway patrolman and the burn victim passed by.

They crossed the lobby. While Rodgers went to call an elevator, Hart paused at the building directory. The elevator arrived, and the two CIA agents boarded it. "OR's on four," Hart said. Rodgers punched the button, and the doors closed. They rode in silence for a moment, both men staring up at the numbers overhead. Then Hart said, "Remind me to get some painkillers while we're here."

Rodgers nodded. The doors opened, and the two men stepped off the elevator. They began a room-to-room search. A few doors down, Rodgers called his partner. "Here! Whaddya see?" Peering through the window, Agent Hart could see Rose on the gurney. Boyd and Officer Bobb standing by the crash cart near the door. Debbie and Spence loading several syringes. Jed X to their right, rooting through some drawers.

"See any guns?"

Hart shook his head. "Don't see the heart either." He wiggled the Baretta at the door and said, "Let's do this." They burst into the OR, the gun sweeping the room. "Hands up!" Debbie dropped a syringe, and they all did as they were told, keeping their eyes on the Baretta. "Where's the heart?" Rodgers asked.

"Your Secret Service buddies have it, down the hall."

"Damn!" Hart turned to Rodgers, trying to figure out a plan.

As the two men schemed, Officer Bobb looked down at

the Serus Z-700 defibrillator system. It was similar to the one he'd trained on in the police-academy course on emergency care. He quietly dialed it up to 360 joules and flipped the power switch. Six seconds later a light indicated that the unit was charged. He measured his target, and, in one fluid motion, he picked up the paddles and pressed them to Rodgers's temples. He hit the button.

Agent Rodgers's muscles seized so hard they caused vertebral compression fractures you could actually hear. His jaws clenched so tight that four of his teeth cracked. He suffered some beastly peripheral nerve palsy, and then he stopped breathing, the skin at his temples charred and smoking like a cartoon coyote.

Agent Hart didn't know what happened. He turned toward his bug-eyed partner and saw him clenched up like a muscle cramp. He tried to take the gun from his partner's hand, but Rodgers's grip was relentless.

As Hart struggled for the gun, Jed X pulled something from a drawer. "Yo, G-man, check it." Hart turned just in time to see Jed coming toward him with a four-inch hypodermic. Jed plunged the needle into Hart's neck, rendering the agent mostly harmless, frozen in a terrified rigor.

Debbie quickly loaded a syringe and gave both agents a shot. "That's midazolam," she said to Hart. "You may experience what we call adverse cardiorespiratory events, including respiratory depression, oxygen desaturation, and/or cardiac arrest, sometimes resulting in permanent neurologic injury or death." She gave Rodgers a pat on the back. "Good luck with it."

After Debbie's disclaimer on the sedative, Rodgers and Hart collapsed in a heap. Officer Bobb took the handcuffs from the highway patrol belt Rodgers was wearing and hooked the two CIA agents together hand to foot. Spence grabbed the gun.

Debbie finished loading syringes. She gave one to Spence, one to Dr. Speyburn, and kept the other. "I assume they know what Spence, Boyd, and I look like." She pointed at Dr. Speyburn. "You're the only one they won't recognize, so leave your mask down so they can see your face. Spence, you get on the gurney and be dead." Debbie pulled her mask up and explained her idea.

They moved Rose to the operating table. Spence got on the gurney and pulled the sheet over his head. Debbie and Dr. Speyburn pushed it out of the room and down the hall toward OR 2. Debbie was at the head of the gurney, pulling as she walked backward. Speyburn was at the feet, face forward, pushing. They shoved through a big pair of swinging doors under a sign that said OPEN HEART STERILE CORE. Down the hall, Speyburn could see the two Secret Service agents guarding OR 2. Dark suits, earpieces, and baby blue surgical masks that didn't match their ties at all. Speyburn started talking, loud enough for the agents to hear. "Worst case of testicular torsion I ever saw!" He paused, then said, "This guy was up in the mountains on a hunting trip when his testicles got all twisted up. Definitely."

"Ay-yi-yi," Debbie said through her mask. "What happened?"

"Where he was, he couldn't get help in time," Spey-
burn said as they slowed to a stop in front of the Secret
Service agents. "Blood was choked off. Gangrene set in.
By the time he got to the hospital, the guy was begging
to be shot. His balls were black." The agents squirmed.
"I've got 'em in a jar back in my office if you want to see."

One of the agents looked at Speyburn and said,
"That's disgusting." A second later he said, "Ouch!" He
felt a stinging in his thigh where Spence had stuck him
with the needle.

When the other agent turned to look, Speyburn stuck
him as well. The two well-trained agents realized it was a
trap. But too late. They tried to reach for their weapons,
but their muscles failed. In a moment they were largely
paralyzed. "Vecuronium bromide," Debbie said. "A nonde-
polarizing muscle relaxant that competitively antagonizes
autonomic cholinergic receptors and causes sympathetic
stimulation. I'll send for respiratory assistance soon as I
can."

Dr. Speyburn nudged Spence. "Nice shot," he said.

Debbie reached into the agents' coats and took their
guns. She gave one to Dr. Speyburn, then turned and
waved back at the window in the swinging doors down
the hall. Officer Bobb, now wearing the Utah highway
patrol uniform, pushed through and joined them. Debbie
handed him the other gun. She tapped Spence on his
foot, then looked at the others. "We ready?"

"Let's do it," Spence said from under the sheet.

Officer Bobb pushed open the doors and blustered

into the OR, all urgent and official. "Got a gunshot victim here." He waved his arms to shoo people out of his way.

The two agents posted inside started for their guns but relaxed when they saw the highway patrol uniform. "This room's in use," one of them said as he positioned himself between Officer Bobb and the operating table. He looked to the hall for the other two agents.

"Sorry," Officer Bobb said. "Isn't this OR Three? They said OR Three was open."

"This is Two," one of the nurses said.

"Oh, my bad." Officer Bobb gestured at the gurney. "Could you help us get this turned around? We need to get this guy to Three."

The Secret Service agent pointed at the gurney. The sheet was pulled over the head of the body. "Looks like you're too late."

"He's an organ donor," Debbie said. "Still fresh, so we're in a hurry. Give us a hand."

When the agents bent over to help, the body under the sheet popped up with a gun in its hand. "Jesus!" The two agents jerked away. Spence leaped off the table, backing one of the agents to the wall at gunpoint, where he disarmed him. At the same time Officer Bobb cracked the other guy's knees with his baton. His legs buckled. Officer Bobb got behind him, put the baton around his neck in a come-along hold, and took his gun.

Debbie pointed at the guy being choked. "Your two playmates in the hallway are about to die," she said. "Get 'em down to ER stat and tell 'em you need some neostigmine and atropine to reverse the effects of Norcuron."

The agents looked to one of the men at the operating table. "Sir?"

"Go ahead." It was Martin Brooks. "The fewer dead, the better." He was at the head of the operating table, next to the anesthesiologist. His attention alternated between the intruders and the surgery.

The two Secret Service agents left for the ER. The transplant surgeon looked up from President Webster's splayed chest. "If you're going to stay in here," he said, nodding to Officer Bobb, "at least put on a mask."

"Yes," Brooks said. "An infection at this point would be regrettable."

From where he stood, Spence could see the tubes running from the inferior and superior vena cavas and the ascending aorta to the heart-lung machine, which hummed and whirred and made everything possible. A monitor beeped steadily but out of sync with the Bill Evans CD that was playing "How My Heart Sings." With everyone wearing a mask, Spence wasn't sure who was who, so he leveled his gun generally at them all. "Where's my mother's heart?"

Brooks looked up from the surgery. "The intrepid Spence Tailor, I presume." Brooks shook his head in admiration. "I'll say this for you, sir, you are persistent." Brooks craned his head to watch as the surgeon deftly sutured the back wall of the president's left atrium to that of Mardell Coleman's. "But I'm afraid you're too late." He nodded toward a rolling lab table Spence hadn't noticed until now. Sitting in a stainless-steel dish on the table were the remaining chambers of the president's old heart, still beating as they starved for blood and oxygen. "You can't change this," Brooks said. He pointed at Webster's chest. "It's already in here."

"That's my mother's."

Brooks shrugged. "What do you think?" he asked gently. "You're going to talk me into giving it back?"

Debbie, Dr. Speyburn, and Officer Bobb knew there was nothing to be done. They figured Spence needed to vent his anger, so they stood by waiting to see what would happen, waiting to see if Spence could control himself.

Spence stared at Brooks, his anger rising. All he could see was a pair of eyes, privileged and unflinching. Spence didn't know what to do. Brooks had seen all his cards. He didn't have a bluff, and everyone knew it.

"What are you going to do?" Brooks made his fingers into a gun and pointed at the operating table. "Shoot the president?" He turned the imaginary gun on himself and the others. "Me? These doctors and nurses? Who would that help?"

The surgeons sutured the back wall of the right atrium to that of the donor heart.

Spence thought about Rose, lying on the operating table down the hall, dying. "It belongs to my mother," he said.

"I understand," Brooks said. "And I know how you must feel, but this is what we have to do. I'm sorry."

Spence leaned his head closer. "You're sorry."

"Yes, in fact, I am. You think I woke up this morning

hoping to kill some perfectly nice old lady? You think I'm some kind of monster?" Brooks was getting irritated. "Christ. Okay, yes, you're right. In a perfect world this wouldn't happen. But I am here to tell you we don't live in a perfect world."

"A perfect world? We're not talking about perfection," Spence said with a wave of the gun. "We're talking about—I don't know—minimum acceptable standards of behavior. Some sort of basic agreement between citizens and government wherein we pay taxes and you don't kill us."

Brooks jerked an angry finger at Spence. "You think you have something to prove? Is that it? You think your comic-book version of justice is in play here?" Brooks pointed at the president. "That man is the leader of the free goddamn world, and his life must be saved, regardless of how. The ends justify the means. Why is that such a hard concept for you?"

Spence looked at the president, then at Martin Brooks. "Because my mother taught me right from wrong."

Brooks snorted dismissively. "Oh, please. It's more complicated than that."

The surgeons connected the president's pulmonary artery and aorta to those of the donor heart. The nerves can't be reconnected. The heart will do what it does without any more communication with a brain. Over in the steel tray, alone and forsaken, the president's old heart slowed its pulse like a fish out of water too long.

Spence's voice cracked as he said, "What if it was your mother?"

"Oh, Christ." Brooks wanted to slap him. "What do you think? You're the only one who loves his mother? I loved mine," Brooks said. "She was a fine woman. And when she died, I shed some tears and then I got over it. You have to grow up, Mr. Tailor. There are greater things."

"All right," the chief surgeon said. "Let's see if she flies." He removed the clamp from the aorta and waited. Everyone inched closer to see what happened. A moment later the heart lapsed into an uncontrolled and rapid fluttering. "Paddles," the surgeon said calmly. Unlike the large external defibrillator paddles, these were long and delicate, like elongated flat spoons for stirring a pitcher of martinis. The surgeon touched the paddles to the heart and gave it a jolt. The heart paused, then found its beat. Rhythmic, heavyweight punches of blood. "Now we're talking." The surgeon removed the remaining clamps to let the heart fill. Then he started removing the tubes to the heart-lung machine.

"There," Brooks said, pointing. "It's done. It's over."

The words refocused Spence. He knew Brooks was right. The heart was in the president's chest and would never beat for Rose. He felt the heft of the .40 caliber in his hand. "That's it?" he asked. "My mom's just collateral damage? The government's done what it's done, and no one's to be held accountable?"

"Well, now, that's the great thing about this country,"

Brooks said, a little too smugly. "Come November, you can vote for somebody else. That's how we hold government officials accountable in a democracy, Mr. Tailor. Just as the Founding Fathers intended."

Spence took a couple of steps toward Brooks. "Except chief of staff isn't on the ballot."

Brooks grinned beneath his mask. "Well, yes, I'll agree. It's an imperfect system."

"Yet you're willing to kill for it?" Spence was within arm's reach of Brooks.

"Yes, obviously."

"But are you willing to die for it?" Spence raised his arm and pressed the gun to the side of Brooks's head.

The chief of staff lost his swagger when he felt the barrel against his skin. "Well, now, hold on," he said. "Let's talk about our options." He sounded afraid.

"I know how you must feel," Spence said. The humanity drained from his eyes.

"Don't do it," Debbie said. "It won't change anything."

"Yeah? Well, there are greater things. I'm sure you understand." Spence pulled the hammer back. "This is what I have to do. I'm sorry."

Debbie reached over to put her hand on his arm. "Spence? Please?"

"If I'm going to jail anyway," Spence said, all affect gone from his voice, "I may as well get my money's worth."

Brooks swallowed hard. "I regret that I have but one—"

The doors to the OR crashed open. Everyone turned to look as a man rushed breathless into the operating room hoisting a picnic cooler. "We got it!"

Rose was up and walking in four days. She was back home in ten. A month later she reported feeling twenty years younger. "It's so nice having warm toes again," she told her doctors. Her body had offered virtually no rejection of the donor heart. Hers was an amazing story and one people wanted to hear, but Rose politely declined all media requests. She never mentioned anything about a federal gag order.

President Webster's recovery was less spectacular, but he was back raising money in a month and wondering why he had ever gone into politics in the first place. Mardell's heart tissue had suffered damage from extended ischemic time. And the rejection was robust. The president was on five separate immunosuppressants, the side effects of which included liver and kidney dysfunction, tremors, nausea, bone loss, fluid retention, and mood swings. He was taking four antibiotics to guard against the increased risk of infection caused by the vast quantity of immunosuppressants in his system. He was also on four different blood-pressure medications, and he was choking down fists full of vitamin supplements and antacids to top it all off. When he stepped into the booth this coming November, he planned to cast his vote for Senator Check.

Vice President Osborne, back from his trade mission, introduced the White House chief of staff to the gathered media and other guests. "I'd like to thank you all for joining us today as we honor some very brave Americans," he said in his introduction. "And it's only appropriate we should meet in this place, given our guest of honor, Rose Tailor." President Webster, sitting near the podium, tilted his head back and faked a laugh. The crowd applauded politely as Rose waved.

It was a late-summer day, and they were in the Rose Garden for a photo op and some PR for the administration. Sitting on the dais next to Rose were Spence and Boyd, along with Debbie, Connie, and the kids. The others were there, too. Officer Bobb in his full-dress LAPD uniform. Jed X, high as a mountain goat, sitting there wondering if there would be food later. He leaned over to show Officer Bobb his newest tat. It was a classic, a heart with the word MOM written through the middle. Dale and Betty Benson were sitting between Polly and the Mormon basketball coach. They had invited Daisy, but she never returned their calls.

For such a momentous occasion one might have expected a bit more verve, but the group was subdued and oddly quiet. They smiled at the appropriate places and applauded where they were supposed to, but that was it. It was as though they were aware of how lucky they were just to be alive, let alone out back of the White House accepting kudos. In fact, it was almost as if someone had said those actual words to them.

Martin Brooks stood at the podium smiling. "By now you know that the story about the Tailors' being domestic terrorists was a ruse. Something we had to do as a matter of national security. Of course there was dissent from some quarters, the sort of traitorous behavior we've come to expect from those kinds of people, but I think most Americans are with me when I say that our need and our ability to deceive the public is, very often, the difference between success and failure in politics."

The audience gave a mild round of applause, as if Brooks had just made an easy putt on the first hole.

Brooks continued by saying, "As you also know by now, the Tailors, along with Officer Randall Bobb, Jebediah Xavier Stuart, and these other brave Americans are here because they worked with us to thwart a group of terrorists who were planning an attempt on the president's life." This proclamation generated a more vigorous round of applause. Brooks held his hands up to quiet the crowd. "We believe that these terrorists, who remain at large, are responsible for the bombing of the CP-1 at Edwards Air Force Base, and this administration vows that, if reelected, we will be the antiterrorist administration."

Martin Brooks concluded his speech by explaining how, as a matter of national security, he couldn't give any details on exactly what the Tailors had done or who the thwarted terrorists might be. "But suffice it to say, America owes a huge debt of gratitude to these brave citizens."

In a small room on the third floor of Brigham Memorial Hospital, Agent Hart stood at the foot of a bed listening to the gentle *beep, beep, beep* of the heart monitor.

A woman tapped on the door as she entered the room respectfully. "Mr. Smith?"

Agent Hart turned and nodded. "Yes."

Beep. . . . . Beep. . . . . Beep.

"All we need is your signature on this." She handed him a clipboard and a pen.

Hart accepted the offer. "Of course." He signed the release forms and handed them back. "And that's it?"

"That's it." The woman looked at the man in the bed, then at Agent Hart. "Forgive me for asking but, you two are . . . related?"

Beep. . . . . Beep. . . . . Beep.

Hart gave a wry smile. "It's a pretty complicated family tree, but yeah. I'm all he had."

The woman nodded understanding. "Well, I'm sorry for your loss."

Hart shrugged. "Thanks."

The woman put her hand on Agent Hart's shoulder. "Would you like me to do it?"

Beep. . . . . Beep. . . . . Beep.

Hart seemed a bit distracted. "What? Oh, no, that's okay. I'll do it." He waited to see if the woman would leave on her own, but she lingered. "Could I have a moment alone?"

"Sure, of course." The woman backed out of the room.

Beep. . . . . Beep. . . . . Beep.

Hart went over and stood respectfully at Rodgers's bedside. He cleared his throat, then said, "Should you die

like this? I'll go see the senator. It won't be in vain." Hart
then stepped over to the respirator and switched it off.

*Beep. . . . . Beep. . . . . Beeee
eeeeeeeeeeeeeeeeeeeeeeeeeeeeeeeeeeeeeeee*

It was the closest election in years. For the most part
the candidates carried the states they were supposed to,
though there were a couple of surprises. Senator Check
won the popular vote, but, due to the quirks of the electoral college and the eventual intervention of the
Supreme Court, President Webster was returned to
office for a second term.

A few months later he was on the mound at Oriole
Park in Camden Yards preparing to throw out the first
pitch of the baseball season. After a turgid windup, President Webster delivered a thirty-mile-an-hour sinker that
died moments before he did. Multiple organ-system failure. Facedown on the mound. Big state funeral. The
whole smash.

Vice President Osborne ascended to the office to
serve his party's benefactors and, to a lesser extent, his
country. As per Section 2 of the Twenty-fifth Amendment
to the Constitution, President Osborne nominated his
own vice president. Following weeks of partisan bickering, both houses of Congress confirmed the nomination
of Martin Brooks.

A year later, with the liberal press nipping at his heels
and calls for reinstatement of the office of special prose-
cutor in the air, President Osborne resigned over some
fund-raising irregularities. A month later both houses of

Congress confirmed President Brooks's nomination of Howard Phillips, the former FBI SAD A-Dic, for vice president. In an effort to help start the nation's political healing process, Martin Brooks issued a presidential pardon for his former boss. Three years later Brooks and Phillips would win their party's nomination and run again.

Senator Check, rumored to be suffering from depression since her defeat, was found in Fort Marcy Park, Virginia. Dead from a gunshot wound to the head. Apparent suicide.

Boyd and Connie renewed their vows in a tender ceremony at the church in Santa Monica where they were first married. Boyd had a new haircut, had dropped twenty pounds, and looked damn good in his tux. Spence was best man. Officer Bobb and Jed X were groomsmen.

Connie had never been so proud and happy. Standing at the altar, she thought about Boyd's heroics at the hospital as he tried to stop the Secret Service and was beaten up for his trouble. The scar on Boyd's cheek would serve as a permanent reminder of how brave her man was.

They invited close friends and family, but Aunt Daisy didn't show. A month later there was still no sign of her. Neither the FBI nor the LAPD had any leads on her disappearance. A witness who said he recalled seeing a black sedan parked in front of Daisy's house died in an automobile accident a week after talking to the press about it. None of Daisy's other neighbors had seen her leave, and no one else would admit to seeing anything that could be characterized as foul play. "Maybe she had Alzheimer's," one person suggested. "Sometimes they just wander off."

But Spence, Debbie, and Boyd had their suspicions. Rose's body had accepted the donor heart as if it were her own, and nothing explained that better than if the heart had belonged to Rose's genetic twin. But there were no clues. It seemed for all the world as if Daisy had walked away from an afternoon of gardening and never looked back. Even with the full cooperation of, and inter-action between, the LAPD, the state of California attor-ney general's investigative office, and several federal agencies, there was no evidence of a crime, let alone gov-ernment involvement.

But Spence kept after it until, four years later, in response to repeated Freedom of Information Act requests and a string of lawsuits, the government sent the following document. The post office delivered it on Tues-day after the first Monday in November. Spence walked into the kitchen, where Debbie was feeding their three-year-old. He held up the envelope. "Look what came." Spence sat at the kitchen table next to Debbie and opened the envelope. He removed a document generated by the FBI and the Security and Intelligence Oversight Subcommittee. At the top of the cover page, in italics, it said, *"This report has been redacted pursuant to the Free-dom of Information Act for public release. Redactions have been made under 5 u.s.c. 522(b)(2), (b)(6)."*

Freedom of Information
and
Privacy Acts

SUBJECT ██████████████████

FILE NUMBER *65-6872*██████

Federal Bureau of Investigation

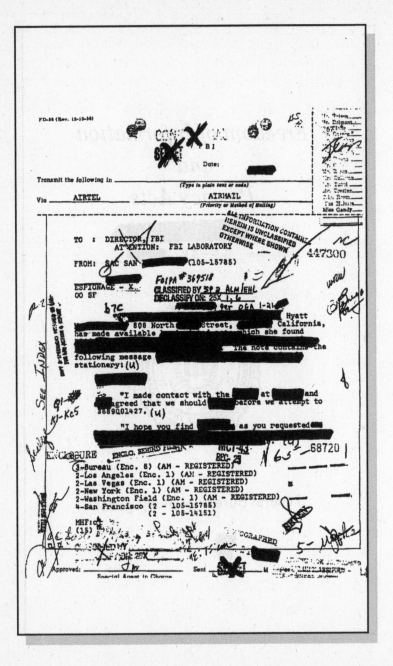

FD-36 (Rev. 12-12-56)

F B I

Date: ████

Transmit the following in _____
(Type in plain text or code)

Via   **AIRTEL** _____   **AIRMAIL**
(Priority or Method of Mailing)

ALL INFORMATION CONTAINED
HEREIN IS UNCLASSIFIED
EXCEPT WHERE SHOWN
OTHERWISE

TO : DIRECTOR, FBI
     ATTENTION: FBI LABORATORY

FROM: SAC SAN ████ (105-15785)

ESPIONAGE - X   FOIPA #369518
00 SF   CLASSIFIED BY ST 2 ALM/EHL
                             DECLASSIFY ON: 25X 1, 6
                                            per OGA 1-31

████ 808 North ████ Street, ████ California,
has made available ████████████ ich she found ████████

following message   ████ The note contains the
stationery: (U)

      "I made contact with the ████ at ████ and
agreed that we should ████ before we attempt to
3589Q01427. (U)

      "I hope you find ████ as you requested" (U)

ENCLOSURE   ENCLO. BEHIND FILE

3-Bureau (Enc. 5) (AM - REGISTERED)
2-Los Angeles (Enc. 1) (AM - REGISTERED)
2-Las Vegas (Enc. 1) (AM - REGISTERED)
2-New York (Enc. 1) (AM - REGISTERED)
2-Washington Field (Enc. 1) (AM - REGISTERED)
4-San Francisco (2 - 105-15785)
               (2 - 105-14151)

MHF:c
(15)

Approved: _____   Sent _____ M
          Special Agent in Charge

MHF:cj
LA 105-15785

It is believed ███████████ that the
refers to ██████████████████ ████████████
general term used ███████ to ████ the ███████ which was
formerly known as the ████████████████ ██████
approximately 20 miles from ███████████████ in
California. It is known that the ████████████
interest in the ███████ have in the past expressed an
interest in the ███████████████

took over operation ████ explained that the █████████████
██████████ in June █████ and the date referred to in
the █████████████ would have to refer to the ████████████
pointed out that the period ███ through ████████ is
their most active ███████████████ also
which is ████ an █████████ every year took place
during that period ███████████████

████████ door with room ████████ This can be ████ at
████████████████████ These particular
██████ located in a section ███████████████████
and located in the building ███████████████████
office. (U)

The ██████████████████████████████████████
██

███
████████████████████████ made available all registration ████████████
for persons who ████████████ follows: (U)

- 2 -

Spence gave the documents a close reading, looking for clues. He made little noises as he read. "Huh. . . . Hmmmm. . . . Tch." Every time he finished a page, he would hand it to Debbie. "Oh. . . . Interesting." After he had read the entire document, he looked up, shaking his head.

Debbie smiled sardonically. "So, I guess that puts your mind at ease, huh?"

"Well, of course that's just part of the story," Spence said, thumping the document with a finger.

Debbie nodded. "Yeah."

"It's more complicated than that."

"Obviously," Debbie said. "It would have to be."

Spence looked at his watch. "What time do the polls close?"

"In about an hour," Debbie said, handing the document to Spence. "You ready?"

"Sure." He tossed the document on the table, and they headed for the door. "You know, sometimes voting seems like buying a lottery ticket. *You* never win, but somebody else always seems to walk away rich."

"Ain't it the truth?" They went into the garage. Debbie strapped Spence Jr. into the child seat, then turned to Spence and said, "So. Decided who you're voting for?"

Spence just looked at her and smiled.